Join Lieutenant

Interlude in Death

Eve is resigned to the fact that she's been ordered to give a seminar at a police conference—and that she'll have to leave Earth to do it. But her dedication to her job only goes so far. And when a legendary commander sets his sights on taking her husband, Roarke, down, Eve will do everything in her power to stop him . . .

Midnight in Death

Eve's name has made a Christmas list, but it's not for being naughty or nice. It's for putting a serial killer behind bars. Now the escaped madman is dogging her steps. With Roarke at her side, Eve must stop the man from exacting his bloody vengeance—or die trying . . .

Haunted in Death

At the scene of a murder, Eve uncovers the remains of a beautiful singer who went missing eighty-five years earlier. Both victims were shot with the same gun, in a building rumored to be haunted by the singer's ghost. But Eve focuses her attention on those in the here-and-now who had a bone to pick with the dead . . .

"Nora Roberts is unmatched in the world of romance, and her series written under the pseudonym 'J. D. Robb' is the best of her best."
—The State

Nora Roberts & J. D. Robb

REMEMBER WHEN

J. D. Robb

NAKED IN DEATH
GLORY IN DEATH
IMMORTAL IN DEATH
RAPTURE IN DEATH
CEREMONY IN DEATH
VENGEANCE IN DEATH
HOLIDAY IN DEATH
CONSPIRACY IN DEATH
LOYALTY IN DEATH
WITNESS IN DEATH
JUDGMENT IN DEATH
BETRAYAL IN DEATH
SEDUCTION IN DEATH
REUNION IN DEATH
PURITY IN DEATH
PORTRAIT IN DEATH
IMITATION IN DEATH
DIVIDED IN DEATH
VISIONS IN DEATH
SURVIVOR IN DEATH
ORIGIN IN DEATH
MEMORY IN DEATH
BORN IN DEATH
INNOCENT IN DEATH
CREATION IN DEATH
STRANGERS IN DEATH
SALVATION IN DEATH
PROMISES IN DEATH

Anthologies

FROM THE HEART
A LITTLE MAGIC
A LITTLE FATE

MOON SHADOWS
(with Jill Gregory, Ruth Ryan Langan, and Marianne Willman)

The Once Upon Series
(with Jill Gregory, Ruth Ryan Langan, and Marianne Willman)
ONCE UPON A CASTLE
ONCE UPON A STAR
ONCE UPON A DREAM
ONCE UPON A ROSE
ONCE UPON A KISS
ONCE UPON A MIDNIGHT

* * *

SILENT NIGHT
(with Susan Plunkett, Dee Holmes, and Claire Cross)

OUT OF THIS WORLD
(with Laurell K. Hamilton, Susan Krinard, and Maggie Shayne)

BUMP IN THE NIGHT
(with Mary Blayney, Ruth Ryan Langan, and Mary Kay McComas)

DEAD OF NIGHT
(with Mary Blayney, Ruth Ryan Langan, and Mary Kay McComas)

THREE IN DEATH

SUITE 606
(with Mary Blayney, Ruth Ryan Langan, and Mary Kay McComas)

Also available . . .

THE OFFICIAL NORA ROBERTS COMPANION
(edited by Denise Little and Laura Hayden)

THREE
IN
DEATH

J. D. Robb

BERKLEY BOOKS, NEW YORK

THE BERKLEY PUBLISHING GROUP
Published by the Penguin Group
Penguin Group (USA) Inc.
375 Hudson Street, New York, New York 10014, USA
Penguin Group (Canada), 90 Eglinton Avenue East, Suite 700, Toronto, Ontario M4P 2Y3, Canada
(a division of Pearson Penguin Canada Inc.)
Penguin Books Ltd., 80 Strand, London WC2R 0RL, England
Penguin Group Ireland, 25 St. Stephen's Green, Dublin 2, Ireland (a division of Penguin Books Ltd.)
Penguin Group (Australia), 250 Camberwell Road, Camberwell, Victoria 3124, Australia
(a division of Pearson Australia Group Pty. Ltd.)
Penguin Books India Pvt. Ltd., 11 Community Centre, Panchsheel Park, New Delhi—110 017, India
Penguin Group (NZ), 67 Apollo Drive, Rosedale, North Shore 0632, New Zealand
(a division of Pearson New Zealand Ltd.)
Penguin Books (South Africa) (Pty.) Ltd., 24 Sturdee Avenue, Rosebank, Johannesburg 2196,
South Africa

Penguin Books Ltd., Registered Offices: 80 Strand, London WC2R 0RL, England

This is a work of fiction. Names, characters, places, and incidents either are the product of the author's imagination or are used fictitiously, and any resemblance to actual persons, living or dead, business establishments, events, or locales is entirely coincidental. The publisher does not have any control over and does not assume any responsibility for author or third-party websites or their content.

THREE IN DEATH

A Berkley Book / published by arrangement with the author

PRINTING HISTORY
Berkley edition / February 2008

ISBN: 978-0-425-21971-3

BERKLEY®
Berkley Books are published by The Berkley Publishing Group,
a division of Penguin Group (USA) Inc.,
375 Hudson Street, New York, New York 10014.
BERKLEY® is a registered trademark of Penguin Group (USA) Inc.
The "B" design is a trademark belonging to Penguin Group (USA) Inc.

PRINTED IN THE UNITED STATES OF AMERICA

10 9 8 7 6

Contents

INTERLUDE
IN
DEATH

Learning is not child's play;
we cannot learn without pain.

—ARISTOTLE

Happy is the child whose father
goes to the devil.

—SIXTEENTH-CENTURY PROVERB

Chapter 1

The faces of murder were varied and complex. Some were as old as time and the furrows scoring them filled with the blood spilled by Cain. One brother's keeper was another's executioner.

Of course, it had been rather elementary to close that particular case. The list of suspects had been, after all, pretty limited.

But time had populated the earth until by the early spring of 2059 it so crawled with people that they spilled out from their native planet to jam man-made worlds and satellites. The skill and ability to create their own worlds, the sheer nerve to consider doing so, hadn't stopped them from killing their brothers.

The method was sometimes more subtle, often more vicious, but people being people could, just as easily, fall back on ramming a sharpened stick through another's heart over a nice patch of lettuce.

The centuries, and man's nature, had developed more

than alternative ways to kill and a variety of victims and motives. They had created the need and the means to punish the guilty.

The punishing of the guilty and the demand for justice for the innocent became—perhaps had been since that first extreme case of sibling rivalry—an art and a science.

These days, murder got you more than a short trip to the Land of Nod. It shut you up in a steel-and-concrete cage where you'd have plenty of time to think about where you went wrong.

But getting the sinner where justice deemed he belonged was the trick. It required a system. And the system demanded its rules, techniques, manpower, organizations, and loopholes.

And the occasional seminar to educate and inform.

As far as Lieutenant Eve Dallas was concerned, she'd rather face a horde of torked-out chemi-heads than conduct a seminar on murder. At least the chemi-heads wouldn't embarrass you to death.

And as if it wasn't bad enough that she'd been drafted to attend the Interplanetary Law Enforcement and Security Conference, as if it wasn't horrifying enough that her own commander had ordered her to give a seminar, the whole ball of goddamn wax had to take shape off-planet.

Couldn't hold the sucker in New York, Eve thought as she lay facedown on the hotel bed. Just couldn't find one spot on the whole fucking planet that could suit up. Nope, just had to send a bunch of cops and techs out into space.

God, she hated space travel.

And of all the places in the known universe, the site-selection committee had to dump them on the Olympus Resort. Not only was she a cop out of her element, but she was a cop out of her element giving a seminar in one of the conference rooms in one of the ridiculously plush hotels owned by her husband.

It was mortifying.

Sneaky son of a bitch, she thought, and wondered if any of the muscles and bones in her body that had dissolved during landing on Olympus had regenerated. He'd planned it, he'd worked it. And now she was paying for it.

She had to socialize, attend meetings. She had to—dear Christ—give a speech. And in less than a week, she would have to get back on that fancy flying death trap of Roarke's and face the journey home.

Since the idea of that made her stomach turn over, she considered the benefits of living out the rest of her life on Olympus.

How bad could it be?

The place had hotels and casinos and homes, bars, shops. Which meant it had people. When you had people, bless their mercenary hearts, you had crime. You had crime, you needed cops. She could trade in her New York Police and Security badge for an Interplanetary Law Enforcement shield.

"I could work for ILE," she muttered into the bedspread.

"Certainly." On the other side of the room, Roarke finished studying a report on one of his other properties. "After a while, you wouldn't think twice about zipping from planet to space station to satellite. And you'd look charming in one of those blue-and-white uniforms and knee-high boots."

Her little fantasy fizzed. Interplanetary meant, after all, interplanetary. "Kiss my ass."

"All right." He walked over, bent down, and laid his lips on her butt. Then began working his way up her back.

Unlike his wife, he was energized by space travel.

"If you think you're getting sex, pal, think again."

"I'm doing a lot of thinking." He indulged himself with the long, lean length of her. When he reached the nape of her neck, he rubbed his lips just below the ends of her short, disordered cap of hair. And feeling her quick shiver, grinned as he flipped her over.

Then he frowned a little, skimming a finger along the shallow dent in her chin. "You're a bit pale yet, aren't you?"

Her deep-golden-brown eyes stared sulkily into his. Her mouth, wide, mobile, twisted into a sneer. "When I'm on my feet again, I'm going to punch you in that pretty face of yours."

"I look forward to it. Meanwhile." He reached down, began unbuttoning her shirt.

"Pervert."

"Thank you, Lieutenant." Because she was his, and it continuously delighted him, he brushed a kiss over her torso, then tugged off her boots, stripped off her trousers. "And I hope we'll get to the perversion part of our program shortly. But for now." He picked her up and carried her out of the bedroom. "I think we'll try a little postflight restorative."

"Why do I have to be naked?"

"I like you naked."

He stepped into a bathroom. No, not a bathroom, Eve mused. That was too ordinary a word for this oasis of sensual indulgence.

The tub was a lake, deep blue and fed by gleaming silver tubes twined together in flower shapes. Rose trees heavy with saucer-size white blooms flanked the marble stairs that led into a shower area where a waterfall already streamed gently down gleaming walls. The tall cylinders of mood and drying tubes were surrounded by spills of flowers and foliage, and she imagined that anyone using one of them would look like a statue in a garden.

A wall of glass offered a view of cloudless sky turned to gold by the tint of the privacy screen.

He set her down on the soft cushions of a sleep chair and walked to one of the curved counters that flowed around the walls. He slid open a panel in the tiles and set a program on the control pad hidden behind it.

Water began to spill into the tub, the lights dimmed, and music, softly sobbing strings, slid into the air.

"I'm taking a bath?" she asked him.

"Eventually. Relax. Close your eyes."

But she didn't close her eyes. It was too tempting just to watch him as he moved around the room, adding something frothy to the bath, pouring some pale gold liquid into a glass.

He was tall and had an innate sort of grace. Like a cat did, she thought. A big, dangerous cat that only pretended to be tame when it suited his mood. His hair was black and thick and longer than her own. It spilled nearly to his shoulders and provided a perfect frame for a face that made her think of dark angels and doomed poets and ruthless warriors all at once.

When he looked at her with those hot and wildly blue eyes, the love inside her could spread so fast and strong, it hurt her heart to hold it.

He was hers, she thought. Ireland's former bad boy who had made his life, his fortune, his place by hook or—well—by crook.

"Drink this."

He liked to tend her, she mused as she took the glass he

offered. She, lost child, hard-ass cop, could never figure out if it irritated or thrilled her. Mostly, she supposed, it just baffled her.

"What is it?"

"Good." He took it back from her, sipped himself to prove it.

When she sampled it, she found that he was right, as usual. He walked behind the chair, the amusement on his face plain when he tipped her back and her gaze narrowed with suspicion. "Close your eyes," he repeated and slipped goggles over her face. "One minute," he added.

Lights bled in front of her closed lids. Deep blues, warm reds in slow, melting patterns. She felt his hands, slicked with something cool and fragrant, knead her shoulders, the knotted muscles of her neck.

Her system, jangled from the flight, began to settle. "Well, this doesn't suck," she murmured, and let herself drift.

He took the glass from her hand as her body slipped into the ten-minute restorative program he'd selected. He'd told her one minute.

He'd lied.

When she was relaxed, he bent to kiss the top of her head, then draped a silk sheet over her. Nerves, he knew, had worn her out. Added to them the stress and fatigue of coming off a difficult case and being shot directly into an off-planet assignment that she detested, and it was no wonder her system was unsettled.

He left her sleeping and went out to see to a few minor details for the evening event. He'd just stepped back in when the timer of the program beeped softly and she stirred.

"Wow." She blinked, scooped at her hair when he set the goggles aside.

"Feel better?"

"Feel great."

"A little travel distress is easy enough to fix. The bath should finish it off."

She glanced over, saw that the tub was full, heaped with bubbles that swayed gently in the current of the jets. "I just bet it will." Smiling, she got up, crossed the room to step down into the sunken pool. And lowering herself neck-deep, she let out a long sigh.

"Can I have that wine or whatever the hell it is?"

"Sure." Obliging, he carried it over, set it on the wide lip behind her head.

"Thanks. I've gotta say, this is some . . ." She trailed off, pressed her fingers to her temple.

"Eve? Headache?" He reached out, concerned, and found himself flipping into the water with her.

When he surfaced, she was grinning, and her hand was cupped possessively between his legs. "Sucker," she said.

"Pervert."

"Oh, yeah. Let me show you how I finish off this little restorative program, ace."

Restored, and smug, she took a quick spin in the drying tube. If she was going to live only a few more days before crashing into a stray meteor and being burned to a cinder by exploding rocket fuel on the flight back home, she might as well make the best of it.

She snagged a robe, wrapped herself in it, and strolled back into the bedroom.

Roarke, already wearing trousers, was scanning what looked like encoded symbols as they scrolled across the screen of the bedroom telelink. Her dress, at least she assumed it was a dress, was laid out on the bed.

She frowned at the sheer flow of bronze, walked over to finger the material. "Did I pack this?"

"No." He didn't bother to glance back; he could see her suspicious scowl clearly enough in his mind. "You packed several days' worth of shirts and trousers. Summerset made some adjustments in your conference wardrobe."

"Summerset." The name hissed like a snake between her lips. Roarke's major domo was a major pain in her ass. "You let him paw through my clothes? Now I have to burn them."

Though he'd made considerable adjustments to her wardrobe in the past year, there were, in his opinion, several items left that deserved burning. "He rarely paws. We're running a little behind," he added. "The cocktail reception started ten minutes ago."

"Just an excuse for a bunch of cops to get shit-faced. Don't see why I have to get dressed up for it."

"Image, darling Eve. You're a featured speaker and one of the event's VIPs."

"I hate that part. It's bad enough when I have to go to your deals."

"You shouldn't be nervous about your seminar."

"Who said I'm nervous?" She snatched up the dress. "Can you see through this thing?"

His lips quirked. "Not quite."

"Not quite" was accurate, she decided. The getup felt thin as a cloud, and that was good for comfort. The flimsy layers of it barely shielded the essentials. Still, as her fashion sense could be etched on a microchip with room to spare, she had to figure Roarke knew what he was doing.

At the sound of the mixed voices rolling out of the ballroom as they approached, Eve shook her head. "I bet half of them are already in the bag. You're serving prime stuff in there, aren't you?"

"Only the best for our hardworking civil servants." Knowing his woman, Roarke took her hand and pulled her through the open doorway.

The ballroom was huge, and packed. They'd come from all over the planet, and its satellites. Police officials, technicians, expert consultants. The brains and the brawn of law enforcement.

"Doesn't it make you nervous to be in the same room with, what, about four thousand cops?" she asked him.

"On the contrary, Lieutenant," he said laughingly. "I feel very safe."

"Some of these guys probably tried to put you away once upon a time."

"So did you." Now he took her hand and, before she could stop him, kissed it. "Look where it got you."

"Dallas!" Officer Delia Peabody, decked out in a short red dress instead of her standard starched uniform, rushed up. Her dark bowl of hair had been fluffed and curled. And, Eve noted, the tall glass in her hand was already half empty.

"Peabody. Looks like you got here."

"The transport was on time, no problem. Roarke, this place is seriously iced. I can't believe I'm here. I really appreciate you getting me in, Dallas."

She hadn't arranged it as a favor, exactly. If she was going to suffer through a seminar, Eve had figured her aide should suffer, too. But from the look of things Peabody seemed to be bearing up.

"I came in with Feeney and his wife," Peabody went on.

"And Dr. Mira and her husband. Morris and Dickhead and Silas from Security, Leward from Anti-Crime—they're all around somewhere. Some of the other guys from Central and the precincts. NYPSD is really well represented."

"Great." She could expect to get ragged on about her speech for weeks.

"We're going to have a little reunion later in the Moonscape Lounge."

"Reunion? We just saw each other yesterday."

"On-planet." Peabody's lips, slicked deep red, threatened to pout. "This is different."

Eve scowled at her aide's fancy party dress. "You're telling me."

"Why don't I get you ladies a drink? Wine, Eve? And Peabody?"

"I'm having an Awesome Orgasm. The drink, I mean, not, you know, personally."

Amused, Roarke brushed a hand over her shoulder. "I'll take care of it."

"Boy, could he ever," Peabody muttered as he walked away.

"Button it." Eve scanned the room, separating cops from spouses, from techs, from consultants. She focused in on a large group gathered in the southeast corner of the ballroom. "What's the deal there?"

"That's the big wheel. Former Commander Douglas R. Skinner." Peabody gestured with her glass, then took a long drink. "You ever meet him?"

"No. Heard about him plenty, though."

"He's a legend. I haven't gotten a look yet because there's been about a hundred people around him since I got here. I've read most of his books. The way he came through the Urban Wars, kept his own turf secure. He was wounded during the Atlanta Siege, but held the line. He's a real hero."

"Cops aren't heroes, Peabody. We just do the job."

Chapter 2

Eve wasn't interested in legends or heroes or retired cops who raked in enormous fees playing the lecture circuit or consulting. She was interested in finishing her one drink, putting in an appearance at the reception—and only because her own commander had ordered her to do so—then making herself scarce.

Tomorrow, she thought, was soon enough to get down to work. From the noise level of the crowd, everyone else thought so, too.

But it appeared the legend was interested in her.

She barely had the wineglass in her hand, was just calculating the least annoying route around the room, when someone tapped on her shoulder.

"Lieutenant Dallas." A thin man with dark hair cut so short it looked like sandpaper glued to his scalp, nodded at her. "Bryson Hayes, Commander Skinner's personal adjutant. The commander would very much like to meet you. If you'd come with me."

"The commander," she returned even as Hayes started to turn away, "looks pretty occupied at the moment. I'll be around all week."

After one slow blink, Hayes simply stared at her. "The commander would like to meet you now, Lieutenant. His schedule through the conference is very demanding."

"Go on." Peabody whispered it as she nudged Eve with her elbow. "Go on, Dallas."

"We'd be delighted to meet with Commander Skinner." Roarke solved the problem by setting his own drink aside, then taking both Eve's and Peabody's arms. It earned him an adoring-puppy look from Peabody and a narrow scowl from his wife.

Before Hayes could object or adjust, Roarke led both women across the ballroom.

"You're just doing this to piss me off," Eve commented.

"Not entirely, but I did enjoy pissing Hayes off. Just a bit of politics, Lieutenant." He gave her arm a friendly squeeze. "It never hurts to play them."

He slipped through the crowd smoothly, and only smiled when Hayes, a muscle working in his jaw, caught up in time to break a path through the last knot of people.

Skinner was short. His reputation was so large, it surprised Eve to note that he barely reached her shoulders. She knew him to be seventy, but he'd kept himself in shape. His face was lined, but it didn't sag. Nor did his body. He'd allowed his hair to gray, but not to thin, and he wore it militarily trim. His eyes, under straight silver brows, were a hard marble blue.

He held a short glass, the amber liquid inside neat. The heavy gold of his fifty-year ring gleamed on his finger.

She took his measure in a matter of seconds as, she noted, he took hers.

"Lieutenant Dallas."

"Commander Skinner." She accepted the hand he held out, found it cool, dry, and more frail than she'd expected. "My aide, Officer Peabody."

His gaze stayed on Eve's face an extra beat, then shifted to Peabody. His lips curved. "Officer, always a pleasure to meet one of our men or women in uniform."

"Thank you, sir. It's an honor to meet you, Commander. You're one of the reasons I joined the force."

"I'm sure the NYPSD is lucky to have you. Lieutenant, I'd—"

"My husband," Eve interrupted. "Roarke."

Skinner's expression didn't waver, but it chilled. "Yes, I recognized Roarke. I spent some of my last decade on the job studying you."

"I'm flattered. I believe this is your wife." Roarke turned his attention to the woman beside Skinner. "It's a pleasure to meet you."

"Thank you." Her voice was the soft cream of the southern United States. "Your Olympus is a spectacular accomplishment. I'm looking forward to seeing more of it while we're here."

"I'd be happy to arrange a tour, transportation."

"You're too kind." She brushed a hand lightly over her husband's arm.

She was a striking woman. She had to be close to her husband in age, Eve thought, as their long marriage was part of Skinner's pristine rep. But either superior DNA or an excellent face-and-body team had kept her beauty youthful. Her hair was richly black, and the gorgeous tone of her skin indicated mixed race. She wore a sleek silver gown and starry diamonds as if she'd been born to such things.

When she looked at Eve it was with polite interest. "My husband admires your work, Lieutenant Dallas, and he's very exacting in his admiration. Roarke, why don't we give these two cops a little time to talk shop?"

"Thank you, Belle. Excuse us, won't you, Officer?" Skinner gestured toward a table guarded by a trio of black-suited men. "Lieutenant? Indulge me." When they sat, the men moved one step back.

"Bodyguards at a cop convention?"

"Habit. I wager you have your weapon and shield in your evening bag."

She acknowledged this with a little nod. She would have preferred to wear them, but the dress didn't allow for her choice of accessories. "What's this about, Commander?"

"Belle was right. I admire your work. I was intrigued to find us on the same program. You don't generally accept speaking engagements."

"No. I like the streets."

"So did I. It's like a virus in the blood." He leaned back, nursed his drink. The faint tremor in his hand surprised her. "But working the streets doesn't mean being on them, necessarily. Someone has to command—from a desk, an office, a war room. A good cop, a smart cop, moves up the ranks. As you have, Lieutenant."

"A good cop, a smart cop, closes cases and locks up the bad guys."

He gave one short laugh. "You think that's enough for captain's bars, for a command star? No, the word 'naive' never came up in any of the reports I've read on you."

"Why should you read reports on me?"

"I may be retired from active duty, but I'm still a consultant. I still have my finger in the pie." He leaned forward again. "You've managed to work and close some very high-profile cases in the murder book, Lieutenant. While I don't always approve of your methods, the results are unarguable. It's rare for me to judge a female officer worthy of command."

"Excuse me. Back up. Female?"

He lifted his hand in a gesture that told her he'd had this discussion before and was vaguely weary of it. "I believe men and women have different primary functions. Man is the warrior, the provider, the defender. Woman is the procreator, the nurturer. There are numerous scientific theories that agree, and certainly social and religious weight to add."

"Is that so?" Eve said softly.

"Frankly, I've never approved of women on the force, or in certain areas of the civilian workplace. They're often a distraction and rarely fully committed to the job. Marriage and family soon—as they should for women—take priority."

"Commander Skinner, under the circumstances, the most courteous thing I can think of to say is you're full of shit."

He laughed, loud and long. "You live up to your reputation, Lieutenant. Your data also indicate that you're smart and that your badge isn't something you just pick up off the dresser every morning. It's what you are. Or were, in any case. We have that in common. For fifty years I made a difference, and my house was clean. I did what had to be done, then I did what came next. I was full commander at the age of forty-four. Would you like to be able to say the same?"

She knew when she was being played, and kept her face and tone neutral. "I haven't thought about it."

"If that's true, you disappoint me. If that's true, start thinking. Do you know, Lieutenant, how much closer you would be right now to a captaincy if you hadn't made some ill-advised personal decisions?"

"Really?" Something began to burn inside her gut. "And how would you know the promotion potential of a homicide cop in New York?"

"I've made it my business to know." His free hand balled into a fist, tapped lightly, rhythmically on the tabletop. "I have one regret, one piece of unfinished business from my active duty. One target I could never keep in my sights long enough to bring down. Between us, we could. I'll get you those captain bars, Lieutenant. You get me Roarke."

She looked down at her wine, slowly ran a fingertip around the rim. "Commander, you gave half a century of your life to the job. You shed blood for it. That's the single reason I'm not going to punch you in the face for that insult."

"Think carefully," he said as Eve got to her feet. "Sentiment over duty is never a smart choice. I intend to bring him down. I won't hesitate to break you to do it."

Riding on fury, she leaned down very close and whispered in his ear. "Try it. You'll find out I'm no fucking nurturer."

She stepped away, only to have one of the bodyguards move into her path. "The commander," he said, "isn't finished speaking with you."

"I'm finished speaking with the commander."

His gaze shifted from her face briefly, and he gave the faintest nod before he edged closer, clamped a hand on her arm. "You'll want to sit down, Lieutenant, and wait until you've been dismissed."

"Move your hand. Move it now, or I'm going to hurt you."

He only tightened his grip. "Take your seat and wait for leave to go. Or you're going to be hurt."

She glanced back at Skinner, then into the guard's face. "Guess again." She used a short-arm jab to break his nose, then a quick snap kick to knock back the guard beside him as he surged forward.

By the time she'd spun around, planted, she had her hand in her bag and on her weapon. "Keep your dogs on a leash," she said to Skinner.

She scanned the faces of cops who'd turned, who'd moved forward, to see if there was trouble coming from another direction. Deciding against it, she turned away and walked through the buzzing crowd.

She was nearly at the door when Roarke fell in step beside her, draped an arm around her shoulders. "You got blood on your dress, darling."

"Yeah?" Still steaming, she glanced down at the small splatter. "It's not mine."

"I noticed."

"I need to talk to you."

"Um-hmm. Why don't we go upstairs, see what the valet can do about that bloodstain? You can talk before we come down to have a drink with your friends from Central."

"Why the hell didn't you tell me you knew Skinner?"

Roarke keyed in the code for the private elevator to the owner's suite. "I don't know him."

"He sure as hell knows you."

"So I gathered." He waited until they were inside the car before he pressed a kiss to her temple. "Eve, over the course of things, I've had a great many cops looking in my direction."

"He's still looking."

"He's welcome to. I'm a legitimate businessman. Practically a pillar. Redeemed by the love of a good woman."

"Don't make me hit you, too." She strode out of the elevator, across the sumptuous living area of the suite, and directly outside onto the terrace so she could finish steaming in fresh air. "The son of a bitch. The son of a bitch wants me to help him bring you down."

"Rather rude," Roarke said mildly. "To broach the subject on such a short acquaintance, and at a cocktail reception. Why did he think you'd agree?"

"He dangled a captaincy in my face. Tells me he can get it for me, otherwise I'm in the back of the line because of my poor personal choices."

"Meaning me." Amusement fled. "Is that true? Are your chances for promotion bogged down because of us?"

"How the hell do I know?" Still flying on the insult, she rounded on him. "Do you think I care about that? You think making rank drives me?"

"No." He walked to her, ran his hands up and down her arms. "I know what drives you. The dead drive you." He leaned forward, rested his lips on her brow. "He miscalculated."

"It was a stupid and senseless thing for him to do. He barely bothered to circle around much before he hit me with it. Bad strategy," she continued. "Poor approach. He wants your ass, Roarke, and bad enough to risk censure for attempted bribery if I report the conversation—and anyone believes it. Why is that?"

"I don't know." And what you didn't know, he thought,

was always dangerous. "I'll look into it. In any case, you certainly livened up the reception."

"Normally I'd've been more subtle, just kneed that jerk in the balls for getting in my way. But Skinner had gone into this tango about how women shouldn't be on the job because they're nurturers. Tagging the balls just seemed too girly at the time."

He laughed, drew her closer. "I love you, Eve."

"Yeah, yeah." But she was smiling again when she wrapped her arms around him.

As a rule, being crowded ass to ass at a table in a club where the entertainment included music that threatened the eardrums wasn't Eve's idea of a good time.

But when she was working off a good mad, it paid to have friends around.

The table was jammed with New York's finest. Her butt was squeezed between Roarke's and Feeney's, the Electronic Detective Division captain. Feeney's usually hangdog face was slack with amazement as he stared up at the stage.

On the other side of Roarke, Dr. Mira, elegant despite the surroundings, sipped a Brandy Alexander and watched the entertainment—a three-piece combo whose costumes were red-white-and-blue body paint doing wild, trash-rock riffs on American folk songs. Rounding out the table were Morris, the medical examiner, and Peabody.

"Wife shouldn't've gone to bed." Feeney shook his head. "You have to see it to believe it."

"Hell of a show," Morris agreed. His long, dark braid was threaded through with silver rope, and the lapels of his calf-length jacket sparkled with the same sheen.

For a dead doctor, Eve thought, he was a very snappy dresser.

"But Dallas here"—Morris winked at her—"was quite some warm-up act."

"Har har," Eve replied.

Morris smiled serenely. "Hotshot lieutenant decks legend of police lore's bodyguards at law enforcement convention on luxury off-planet resort. You've got to play that all the way out."

"Nice left jab," Feeney commented. "Good follow-through on the kick. Skinner's an asshole."

"Why do you say that, Feeney?" Peabody demanded. "He's an icon."

"Who said icons can't be assholes?" he tossed back. "Likes to make out like he put down the Urban Wars single-handed. Goes around talking about them like it was all about duty and romance and patriotism. What it was, was about survival. And it was ugly."

"It's typical for some who've been through combat to romanticize it," Mira put in.

"Nothing romantic about slitting throats or seeing Fifth Avenue littered with body parts."

"Well, that's cheerful." Morris pushed Feeney's fresh glass in front of him. "Have another beer, Captain."

"Cops don't crow about doing the job." Feeney glugged down his beer. "They just do it. I'da been closer, Dallas, I'da helped you take down those spine crackers of his."

Because the wine and his mood made her sentimental, she jabbed him affectionately with her elbow. "You bet your ass. We can go find them and beat them brainless. You know, round out the evening's entertainment."

Roarke laid a hand on her back as one of his security

people came to the table and leaned down to whisper in his ear. Humor vanished from his face as he nodded.

"Someone beat you to it," he announced. "We have what's left of a body on the stairway between the eighteenth and nineteenth floors."

Chapter 3

Eve stood at the top of the stairwell. The once pristine white walls were splattered with blood and gray matter. A nasty trail of both smeared the stairs. The body was sprawled on them, faceup.

There was enough of his face and hair left for her to identify him as the man whose nose she'd broken a few hours before.

"Looks like somebody was a lot more pissed off than I was. Your man got any Seal-It?" she asked Roarke.

When Roarke passed her the small can of sealant, she coated her hands, her shoes. "I could use a recorder. Peabody, help hotel security keep the stairwells blocked off. Morris." She tossed him the can. "With me."

Roarke gave her his security guard's lapel recorder. Stepped forward. Eve simply put a hand on his chest. "No civilians—whether they own the hotel or not. Just wait. Why don't you clear Feeney to confiscate the security disks for this sector of the hotel? It'll save time."

She didn't wait for an answer, but headed down the steps to the body. Crouched. "Didn't do this with fists." She examined his face. One side was nearly caved in, the other largely untouched. "Left arm's crushed. Guy was left-handed. I made that at the reception. They probably went for the left side first. Disabled him."

"Agreed. Dallas?" Morris jerked his head in the direction of the seventeenth floor. A thick metal bat coated with gore rested on a tread farther down the stairs. "That would've done the trick. I can consult with the local ME on the autopsy, but prelim eyeballing tells me that's the weapon. Do you want me to dig up some evidence bags, a couple of field kits?"

She started to speak, then hissed out a breath. The smell of death was in her nostrils, and it was too familiar. "Not our territory. We've got to go through station police. God-damn it."

"There are ways to get around that, with your man own-ing the place."

"Maybe." She poked a sealed finger in a blood pool, nudged something metal and silver. And she recognized the star worn on the epaulets of hotel security.

"Who would be stupid enough to beat a man to death in a hotel full of cops?" Morris wondered.

She shook her head, got to her feet. "Let's get the ball rolling on this." When she reached the top of the steps, she scanned the hallway. If she'd been in New York, she would now give the body a thorough examination, establish time of death, gather data and trace evidence from the scene. She'd call her crime scene unit, the sweepers, and send out a team to do door-to-doors.

But she wasn't in New York.

"Has your security notified station police?" she asked Roarke.

"They're on their way."

"Good. Fine. We'll keep the area secure and offer any and all assistance." Deliberately, she switched off her recorder. "I don't have any authority here. Technically, I shouldn't have entered the crime scene area. I had a previous altercation with the victim, and that makes it stickier."

"I own this hotel, and I hold primary interest in this station. I can request the assistance of any law enforcement agent."

"Yeah, so we've got that clear." She looked at him. "One of your security uniforms is missing a star. It's down there, covered with body fluid."

"If one of my people is responsible, you'll have my full cooperation in identifying and apprehending him."

She nodded again. "So we've got that clear, too. What's your security setup for this sector?"

"Full-range cameras—corridors, elevators, and stairwells. Full soundproofing. Feeney's getting the disks."

"He'll have to hand them to station police. When it's homicide, they have a maximum of seventy-two hours before they're obliged to turn the investigation over to ILE. Since ILE has people on-site, they'd be wise to turn it over now."

"Is that what you want?"

"It's not a matter of what I want. Look, it's not my case."

He took a handkerchief out of his pocket and wiped the blood smear from her hand. "Isn't it?"

Then he turned as the chief of police stepped off the elevator.

Eve hadn't been expecting a statuesque brunette in a tiny black dress with enough hair to stuff a mattress. As she clipped down the hall on towering high heels, Eve heard Morris's reverent opinion.

"Hubba-hubba."

"Jeez, try for dignity," Eve scolded.

The brunette stopped, took a quick scan. "Roarke," she said in a voice that evoked images of hot desert nights.

"Chief. Lieutenant Dallas, NYPSD. Dr. Morris, NYC Medical Examiner."

"Yes. Darcia Angelo. Chief of Olympus Police. Excuse my appearance. I was at one of the welcome events. I'm told we have a possible homicide."

"Verified homicide," Eve told her. "Victim's male, Caucasian, thirty-five to forty. Bludgeoned. The weapon, a metal bat, was left on scene. Preliminary visual exam indicates he's been dead under two hours."

"There's been a prelim exam?" Darcia asked. Coldly.

"Yes."

"Well, we won't quibble about that. I'll verify personally before my team gets here."

"Messy down there." Coolly, Eve handed over the can of Seal-It.

"Thanks." Darcia stepped out of her evening shoes. Eve couldn't fault her for it. She did the same thing herself, when she remembered. When she'd finished, she handed the can back to Eve. Darcia took a small recorder out of her purse, clipped it where the fabric of her dress dipped to hug her breasts.

Morris let out a long sigh as she walked into the stairwell. "Where do you find them?" he asked Roarke. "And how can I get one of my very own?"

Before Eve could snarl at him, Feeney hurried down the hall. "Got a snag with the disks," he announced. "Stairway cams were overridden for a fifty-minute period. You got

nothing but static there, and static for two sixty-second intervals on the twentieth-floor corridor. Somebody knew
what they were doing," he added. "It's a complex system,
with a fail-safe backup plan. It took a pro—with access."

"With that time frame there had to be at least two people involved," Eve stated. "Premeditated, not impulse, not
crime of passion."

"You got an ID on the victim? I can run a background
check."

"Police chief's on scene," Eve said flatly.

For a moment Feeney looked blank. "Oh, right. Forgot
we weren't home, sweet home. The locals going to squeeze
us out?"

"You weren't," Darcia said as she came out of the stairwell, "ever—in an official capacity—in."

"On the contrary," Roarke told her. "I requested the assistance of the lieutenant and her team."

Irritation flickered across Darcia's face, but she controlled it quickly. "As is your privilege. Lieutenant, may I
have a moment of your time?" Without waiting for an answer, Darcia walked down the corridor.

"Arrogant, territorial, pushy." Eve glared at Roarke.
"You sure can pick them."

He only smiled as his wife's retreating back. "Yes, I certainly can."

"Look, Angelo, you want to bust my balls over doing a
visual, you're wasting your time and mine." Eve tugged her
lapel recorder free, held it out. "I verified a homicide, at
the request of the property owner. Then I stepped back. I
don't want your job, and I don't want your case. I get my
fill of walking through blood in New York."

Darcia flipped her mane of glossy black hair. "Four
months ago I was busting illegal dealers in Colombia, risking

my life on a daily basis and still barely able to pay the rent on a stinking little two-room apartment. In the current climate, cops are not appreciated in my country. I like my new job."

She opened her purse, dropped Eve's recorder inside. "Is that job in jeopardy if I refuse to hand over this case to my employer's wife?"

"Roarke doesn't fight my battles, and he doesn't fire people because they might not agree with me."

"Good." Darcia nodded. "I worked illegals, bunko, robbery. Twelve years. I'm a good cop. Homicide, however, is not my specialty. I don't enjoy sharing, but I'd appreciate any help you and your associates are willing to give in this matter."

"Fine. So what was this dance about?"

"Simply? So you and I would both be aware it *is* my case."

"You need to be aware that earlier tonight I punched the dead man in the face."

"Why?" Darcia asked suspiciously.

"He got in my way."

"I see. It'll be interesting to find out if you and I can close this matter without getting in each other's way."

Two hours later, for convenience's sake, the two arms of the investigation gathered in Roarke's on-site office.

"The victim is identified as Reginald Weeks, thirty-eight. Current residence is Atlanta, Georgia, Earth. Married, no children. Current employer, Douglas R. Skinner, Incorporated. Function personal security." Darcia finished, inclined her head at Eve.

"Crime scene examination of body shows massive trauma." Eve picked up the narrative. "Cause of death, most likely, fractured skull. The left side of the head and body were severely traumatized. Victim was left-handed, and this method of attack indicates foreknowledge. Security for the stairwell and the twentieth floor were tampered with prior to and during the act. A metal bat has been taken into evidence and is presumed to be the murder weapon. Also taken into evidence a silver-plated star stud, identified as part of the hotel security team's uniform. Chief Angelo?"

"Background data so far retrieved on Weeks show no criminal activity. He had held his current employment for two years. Prior that, he was employed by Right Arm, a firm that handles personal security and security consults for members of the Conservative Party. Prior to that he was in the military, Border Patrol, for six years."

"This tells us he knows how to follow orders," Eve continued. "He stepped up in my face tonight because Skinner, or one of Skinner's arms, signaled him to do so. He laid hands on me for the same reason. He's trained, and if he was good enough to last six years in the Border Patrol and land a job in Right Arm, he's not the type of guy who would go into a soundproof stairwell with a stranger, even under duress. If he'd been attacked in the corridor, there'd be a sign of it. If they took him on the twentieth floor, what the hell was he doing on the twentieth floor? His room, his security briefing room, and Skinner's suite are all on twenty-six."

"Could've been meeting a woman." Feeney stretched out his legs. "Conventionitis."

"That's a point," Eve allowed. "All evidence points to this being a planned attack, but a woman could have been used as a lure. We need to verify or eliminate that. You want to track it down, Feeney?"

"Captain Feeney may assist my officers in that area of

investigation." Darcia merely lifted her eyebrows when
Eve turned to her. "If he is agreeable. As I hope he will be
to continuing to work with the hotel security team."

"We're a real agreeable group," Eve said with a wide,
wide smile.

"Excellent. Then you have no problem accompanying me
to twenty-six to inform the victim's employer of his death."

"Not a one. Peabody. My aide goes with me," Eve said
before Darcia could speak. "Non-negotiable. Peabody,"
Eve said again, gesturing as she walked out of the room
and left Darcia assigning her officers to different tasks. "I
want your recorder on when we talk to Skinner."

"Yes, sir."

"If I get hung up, I need you to wheedle an update out
of the local ME. If you can't open him up, tag Morris and
have him use the good buddy, same field approach."

"Yes, sir."

"I want to find the uniform that star came from. We
need to check recyclers, the valet, outside cleaning sources.
Get chummy with the home team. I want to know the
minute the sweepers and crime scene units reports are in.
I'm betting there's going to be traces of Seal-It on that bat,
and nobody's blood but the victim's on the scene. Fucking
ambush," she grumbled, and turned as Darcia came out.

Darcia said nothing until she'd called for the elevator
and stepped inside. "Do you have a history with Douglas
Skinner, Lieutenant?"

"No. Not until tonight."

"My information is that he specifically called you to his
table to speak with you privately. You, apparently, had
words of disagreement, and when the victim attempted to
prevent you from leaving the table, you struck him. Would
this be accurate?"

"It would."

"What were those words of disagreement between you and Douglas Skinner?"

"Am I a suspect in this case or a consultant?"

"You're a consultant, and as such I would appreciate any and all data."

"I'll think about it." Eve stepped out on twenty-six.

"If you have nothing to hide."

"I'm a cop," Eve reminded her. "That line doesn't work on me." She rang the bell, waited. She watched the security light blink to green, kept her face blank while she and her companions were scanned. Moments later, Skinner opened the door himself.

"Lieutenant. It's a bit late for paying calls."

"It's never too late for official calls. Chief Angelo, Douglas Skinner."

"Pardon the intrusion, Commander Skinner." Darcia's voice was low and respectful, her face quietly sober. "We have some unfortunate news. May we come in?"

"Of course." He stepped back. He was dressed in the long white robe provided by the hotel, and his face looked pale against it. The large living area was dimly lit and fragrant from the bouquets of roses. He ordered the lights up 10 percent, and gestured toward the sofa.

"Please, ladies, sit. Can I get you anything? Coffee, perhaps?"

"We're not here to chat. Where were you between twenty-two hundred and midnight?"

"I don't like your tone, Lieutenant."

"Please, excuse us." Darcia stepped in smoothly. "It's been a difficult night. If I could ask you to verify your whereabouts, as a formality?"

"My wife and I came up to our suite a bit after ten. We

retired early, as I have a long, busy day scheduled tomorrow. What's happened?"

"Weeks got his brains bashed in," Eve said.

"Weeks? Reggie?" Skinner stared at Eve. Those hard blue eyes widened, darkened, and seemed to draw a cast of gray over his skin as shock shifted into fury. "Dead? The boy is dead? Have you determined Roarke's *whereabouts*? Or would you go so far as to cover up murder to protect him? She attacked Weeks only hours ago." He pointed at Eve. "An unprovoked and vicious assault on one of mine because I questioned her about her alliance with a criminal. You're a disgrace to your badge."

"One of us is," Eve agreed as Skinner sank into a chair.

"Commander." Darcia stepped forward. "I know this is a shock for you. I want to assure you that the Olympus PD is actively pursuing all avenues of investigation."

For a moment he said nothing, and the only sound was his quick, labored breathing. "I don't know you, Chief Angelo, but I know who pays you. I have no confidence in your investigation as long as it's bankrolled by Roarke. Now, excuse me. I have nothing more to say at this time. I need to contact Reggie's wife and tell her she's a widow."

Chapter 4

"Well, that went well." Eve rolled her shoulders as she headed back to the elevator.

"If one doesn't mind being accused of being a fool or a dirty cop."

Eve punched the elevator button. "Ever hear the one about sticks and stones in Colombia?"

"I don't like that one." Obviously stewing, Darcia strode onto the elevator. "And I don't like your Commander Skinner."

"Hey, he's not mine."

"He implies Roarke is my puppet master. Why does he assume that, and why does he believe Roarke is responsible for Weeks's death?"

The quiet, respectful woman was gone, and in her place was a tough-eyed cop with steel in her voice. Eve began to see how Darcia Angelo had risen through twelve years in Colombia.

"One reason is Weeks annoyed me, and since I'm just a

procreating, nurturing female, it would be up to my warrior, defender, penis-owning husband to follow through."

"Ah." Darcia sucked in her cheeks. "This is an attitude I recognize. Still, splattering a man's brains is considerable overcompensation for such a minor infraction. A very large leap of conclusion for the commander to make. There's more."

"Might be. I haven't worked it out yet. Meanwhile, Skinner seemed awfully alert for someone who'd already gone to bed. And while the lights in the living area were on low when we walked in, they were full on in the bedroom off to the right. He didn't close the door all the way when he came out."

"Yes, I noticed that."

"Suite's set up along the same basic floor plan as the one I'm in. Second bedroom off to the left. There was a light on in there, too. His wife had that door open a crack. She was listening."

"I didn't catch that," Darcia mused, then glanced back when Peabody muttered.

"She missed it, too," Eve said. "She hates that. And if Belle Skinner was eavesdropping from the second bedroom, she wasn't snuggled up with the commander in the master, was she? No connubial bliss, which is interesting. And no alibi."

"What motive would Skinner have for killing one of his own bodyguards?"

"Something to think about. I want to check some things out." She stopped the elevator so both Darcia and Peabody could exit. "I'll get back to you."

Being willing to fall into step with Darcia Angelo didn't mean she couldn't make some lateral moves of her own. If she was going to wade into a murder investigation off her own turf, without her usual system and when her badge was little more than a fashion accessory, she was going to make use of whatever tools were available.

There was one particular tool she knew to be very versatile and flexible.

She was married to him.

She found Roarke, as she'd expected to, at work on the bedroom computer. He'd removed his dinner jacket, rolled up his sleeves. There was a pot of coffee beside him.

"What have you got?" She picked up his cup, gulped down half his coffee.

"Nothing that links me or any of my business dealings with Skinner. I have some interests in Atlanta, naturally."

"Naturally."

"Communications, electronics, entertainment. Real estate, of course." He took the cup back from her, idly rubbed her ass with his free hand. "And during one lovely interlude previous to my association with you, a nicely profitable smuggling enterprise. Federal infractions—"

"Infractions," she repeated.

"One could say. Nothing that bumped up against state or local authorities."

"Then you're missing something, because it's personal with him. It doesn't make any sense otherwise. You're not a major bad guy."

"Now you've hurt my feelings."

"Why does he latch on to you?" she demanded, ignoring him. "Fifty years a cop, he'd have seen it all. And he'd have lost plenty. There are stone killers out there, pedophiles, sexual predators, cannibals, for Christ's sake. So why are you stuck in his craw? He's been retired from active, what, six years, and—"

"Seven."

"Seven, then. Seven years. And he approaches me with what could be considered a bribe or blackmail, depending on your point of view, to pressure me into rolling over on you. It was arrogant and ill-conceived."

She thought it through as she paced. "I don't think he expected it to work. I think he expected me to tell him to fuck off. That way he could roll us into a ball together and shoot two for one."

"He can't touch you—or me, for that matter."

"He can make things hot by implicating us in a homicide. And he's laying the groundwork. He pushes my buttons in a public venue, then gets one of his monkeys to get in my face. Altercation ensues. A couple hours later, monkey has his brains splattered all over the stairway of a Roarke Enterprises hotel—and what's this! Why it's a clue, Sherlock, and a dandy one, too. A star stud from one of Roarke Securities uniforms, floating in the victim's blood."

"Not particularly subtle."

"He doesn't have time to be subtle. He's in a hurry," she continued. "I don't know why, but he's rushing things. Shove circumstantial evidence down the throat of the local authorities and they've got to pursue the possibility that the irritated husband and suspected interplanetary hoodlum ordered one of his own monkeys to teach Skinner's a lesson."

"You touched my wife, now I have to kill you?" Roarke's shrug was elegant and careless. "Overdramatic, over-romanticized. Particularly since you punched him in the face before I could ride to the rescue."

"In his narrow little world, men are the hunters, the defenders. It plays when you look at it through his window. It's another miscalculation though, because it's not your style. You want the hell beat out of someone, you do it yourself."

He smiled at her fondly. "I like watching you do it even more, darling."

She spared him a look. "Standard testing on you, any profile would kick the theory out of the park. You're just not hardwired to pay somebody to kill, or to get your dick in a twist because somebody hassles me. We could have Mira run you through a Level One testing just to push that aside."

"No, thank you, darling. More coffee?"

She grunted, paced a bit more while he rose to go to the mini AutoChef for a fresh pot and cups. "It's a sloppy frame. Thing is, Skinner believes you're capable, and that if he dumps enough on the ILE if and when they take over he'll push you into an investigative process that will mess you up—and me by association."

"Lieutenant, the ILE has investigated me in the past. They don't worry me. What does is that if it goes that far, your reputation and career could take some bruises. I won't tolerate that. I think the commander and I should have a chat."

"And what do you think he's counting on?" she demanded.

"Why disappoint him?" Coffee cup in hand, he sat on the arm of his chair. "I've compiled personal and professional data on Skinner. Nothing seems particularly relevant to this, but I haven't studied his case files in depth. Yet."

Eve set down the coffee he'd just poured her with a little snap of china on wood. "Case files? You hacked into his case files? Are you a lunatic? He gets wind of that, you're up on charges and in lockup before your fancy lawyers can knot their fancy ties."

"He won't get wind of it."

"CompuGuard—" She broke off, scowled at the bedroom unit. CompuGuard monitored all e-transmissions and programming on-planet or off. Though she was aware Roarke had unregistered equipment at home, the hotel system was a different matter. "Are you telling me this unit's unregistered?"

"Absolutely not." His expression was innocent as a choirboy's. "It's duly registered and meets all legal requirements. Or did until a couple of hours ago."

"You can't filter out CompuGuard in a few hours."

Roarke sighed heavily, shook his head. "First you hurt my feelings, now you insult me. I don't know why I put up with this abuse."

Then he moved fast, grabbing her up, hauling her against him, and crushing her mouth with a kiss so hot she wondered if her lips were smoking.

"Oh, yes." He released her, picked up his coffee again. "That's why."

"If that was supposed to distract me from the fact that you've illegally blocked CompuGuard and broken into official data, it was a damn good try. But the joke's on you. I was going to ask you to dig up the data."

"Were you really, Lieutenant? You never fail to surprise me."

"They beat him until his bones were dust." Her tone was flat, dull. All cop. "They erased half his face. And left the other half clean so I'd know as soon as I saw him. The minute he stepped in front of me tonight, he was dead. I was the goddamn murder weapon." She looked back at the computer. "So. Let's get to work."

They culled out cases during Skinner's last decade of active duty and cross-referenced with anything relating to them during the seven years of his retirement. It over-lapped the time before Roarke had come to America from Ireland, but it seemed a logical place to start.

As the caseload was enormous, they split it. Eve worked on the bedroom unit, and Roarke set up in the second bedroom.

By three, Eve's temples were throbbing, her stomach raw from caffeine intake. And she'd developed a new and reluctant admiration for Commander Skinner.

"Damn good cop," she acknowledged. Thorough, focused, and up until his retirement, he had apparently dedicated himself, body and soul, to the job.

How had it felt to step away from all that? she wondered. It had been his choice, after all. At sixty-four, retirement was an option, not a requirement. He could have easily put in another ten years on active. He might have risen to commissioner.

Instead, he'd put in his fifty and then used that as a springboard in a run for Congress. And had fallen hard on his face. A half century of public service hadn't been enough to offset views so narrow even the most dug-in of the Conservative Party had balked. Added to that, his platform had swung unevenly from side to side.

He was an unwavering supporter of the Gun Ban, something the Conservatives tried to overturn at every opportunity. Yet he beat the drum to reinstate the death penalty, which alienated the Liberals from mid-road to far left.

He wanted to dissolve legal and regulated prostitution and strike out all legal and tax benefits for cohabiting couples. He preached about the sanctity of marriage, as long as it was heterosexual, but disavowed the government stipend for professional mothers.

Motherhood, the gospel according to Skinner stated, was a God-given duty, and payment in its own right.

His mixed-voice and muddled campaign had gone down in flames. However much he'd rebounded financially via lectures, books, and consults, Eve imagined he still bore the burns of that failure.

Still, she couldn't see how Roarke tied into it.

Rubbing her forehead, she pushed away and got up to work out the kinks. Maybe she was overreacting. Did she want it to be personal for Skinner because he'd made it personal for her? Maybe Roarke was no more than a symbol for Skinner. Someone who had slipped and slid around the system that Skinner himself had dedicated his life to.

She checked her wrist unit. Maybe she'd catch some sleep, go back to it fresh in the morning. She would juggle the data first, though, so that when she looked at it again it would be in a new pattern. Whatever she was missing—and her gut still told her she was missing something—might float to the top.

"Computer, extrapolate any and all references to Roarke . . ." She yawned hugely, shook her head to clear it. "In any and all files, personal and professional, under Skinner, Commander Douglas."

Working . . .

"List references chronologically, first to last, um . . . give me official police records first, followed by personal files."

Understood. Working. . . . No reference to Roarke under Skinner, Commander Douglas police records. Reference under Skinner, Captain Douglas only. . . . Extrapolating personal files . . .

"Yeah, well, you keep saying that, but . . ." Eve whirled around, stared at the monitor. "Computer, stop. List any and all references to Roarke under Skinner, Douglas, any rank."

Working . . . first listed reference in Skinner, Captain Douglas, case file C-439014, to Roarke, Patrick a/k/a O'Hara, Sean, a/k/a MacNeil, Thomas, date stamped March, twelve, twenty-thirty-six. Subject Roarke suspect in illegal weapons running, illegal entry into United States, grand theft auto and conspiracy to murder of police officers. Subject believed to have fled Atlanta area, and subsequently the country. Last known residence, Dublin, Ireland. Case file complete, investigative data available. Do you wish full case file?

"Yes. In hard copy."

Working . . .

Eve sat down again, slowly as the computer hummed. 2036, she thought. Twenty-three years ago. Roarke would have been what, twelve, thirteen?

It wasn't Roarke who was at the root of Skinner's obsession.

It was Roarke's father.

At his own unit, Roarke ran through layers of Skinner's financials. Among the most clear-cut motives for murder were greed, revenge, jealousy, sex, fear of disgrace, and profit. So he'd follow the money first.

There was a possibility, he'd decided, that Skinner had invested in one of his companies—or a competitor's. Perhaps he'd lost a substantial amount of money. Men had hated men for less.

And financially Skinner had taken a beating during his run for Congress. It had left him nearly broke as well as humiliated.

"Roarke."

"Hmm." He held up a finger to hold Eve off as she came into the room. "Communications," he said. "I have an interest in the Atlanta media sources, and they were very unkind to Skinner during his congressional attempt. This would have weighed heavily against his chances of winning. Media Network Link is mine outright, and they were downright vicious. Accurate, but vicious. Added to that, he's invested fairly heavily in Corday Electronics, based in Atlanta. My own company has eroded their profits and customer base steadily for the last four years. I really should finish them off with a takeover," he added as an afterthought.

"Roarke."

"Yes?" He reached around absently to take her hand as he continued to scroll data.

"It goes deeper than politics and stock options. Twenty-three years ago illegal arms dealers set up a base in Atlanta, and Skinner headed up the special unit formed to take them down. They had a weasel on the inside, and solid information. But when they moved in, it was a trap. Weasels turn both ways, and we all know it."

She took a deep breath, hoping she was telling it the way it should be told. Love twisted her up as often, maybe more often, than it smoothed things out for her.

"Thirteen cops were killed," she continued, "six more wounded. They were outgunned, but despite it, Skinner broke the cartel's back. The cartel lost twenty-two men, mostly soldiers. And he bagged two of the top line that night. That led to two more arrests in the next twelve months. But he lost one. He was never able to get his hands on one."

"Darling, I might've been precocious, but at twelve I'd yet to run arms, unless you're counting a few handhelds or homemade boomers sold in alleyways. And I hadn't ventured beyond Dublin City. As for weaseling, that's something I've never stooped to."

"No." She kept staring at his face. "Not you."

And watched his eyes change, darken and chill as it fell into place for him. "Well, then," he said, very softly. "Son of a bitch."

Chapter 5

As a boy, Roarke had been the favored recipient of his father's fists and boots. He'd usually seen them coming, and had avoided them when possible, lived with them when it wasn't.

To his knowledge, this was the first time the old man had sucker punched him from the grave.

Still, he sat calmly enough, reading the hard copy of the reports Eve had brought him. He was a long way from the skinny, battered boy who had run the Dublin alleyways. Though he didn't care much for having to remind himself of it now.

"This double cross went down a couple of months before my father ended up in the gutter with a knife in his throat. Apparently someone beat Skinner to him. He has that particular unsolved murder noted in his file here. Perhaps he arranged it."

"I don't think so." She wasn't quite sure how to approach Roarke on the subject of his father and his boyhood. He tended to walk away from his past, whereas she—well, she tended to walk into the wall of her own past no matter how often, how deliberately, she changed directions.

"Why do you say that? Look, Eve, it isn't the same for me as it is for you. You needn't be careful. He doesn't haunt me. Tell me why if my father slipped through Skinner's fingers in Atlanta, Skinner wouldn't arrange to have his throat slit in Dublin City."

"First, he was a cop, not an assassin. There's no record in the file that he'd located his target in Dublin. There's correspondence with Interpol, with local Irish authorities. He was working on extradition procedures should his target show up on Irish soil, and would likely have gotten the paperwork and the warrant. That's what he'd have wanted," she continued, and rose to prowl the room. "He'd want the bastard back on his own turf, back where it went down and his men were killed. He'd want that face-to-face. He didn't get it."

She turned back. "If he'd gotten it, he could've closed the book, moved on. And he wouldn't be compelled to go after you. You're what's left of the single biggest personal and professional failure of his life. He lost his men, and the person responsible for their loss got away from him."

"Dead wouldn't be enough, without arrest, trial, and sentencing."

"No, it wouldn't. And here you are, rich, successful, famous—and married, for Christ's sake—to a cop. I don't need Mira to draw me a profile on this one. Skinner believes that perpetrators of certain crimes, including any crime that results in the death of a police official, should pay with their life. After due process. Your father skipped out on that one. You're here, you pay."

"Then he's doomed to disappointment. For a number of

reasons. One, I'm a great deal smarter than my father was."
He rose, went to her, skimmed a finger down the dent in her
chin. "And my cop is better than Skinner ever hoped to be."

"I have to take him down. I have to fuck over fifty years
of duty, and take him down."

"I know." And would suffer for it, Roarke thought, as
Skinner never would. As Skinner could never understand.
"We need to sleep," he said and pressed his lips to her brow.

She dreamed of Dallas, and the frigid, filthy room in Texas
where her father had kept her. She dreamed of cold and
hunger and unspeakable fear. The red light from the sex
club across the street flashed into the room, over her face.
And over his face as he struck her.

She dreamed of pain when she dreamed of her father.
The tearing of her young flesh as he forced himself into
her. The snapping of bone, her own high, thin scream when
he broke her arm.

She dreamed of blood.

Like Roarke's, her father had died by a knife. But the
one that had killed him had been gripped in her own eight-
year-old hand.

In the big, soft bed in the plush suite, she whimpered
like a child. Beside her, Roarke gathered her close and held
her until the dream died.

She was up and dressed by six. The snappy jacket that had
ended up in her suitcase fit well over her harness and
weapon. The weight of them made her feel more at home.

She used the bedroom 'link to contact Peabody. At least
she assumed the lump under the heap of covers was
Peabody.

"Whaa?"

"Wake up," Eve ordered. "I want your report in fifteen minutes."

"Who?"

"Jesus, Peabody. Get up, get dressed. Get here."

"Why don't I order up some breakfast?" Roarke suggested when she broke transmission.

"Fine, make it for a crowd. I'm going to spread a little sunshine and wake everybody up." She hesitated. "I trust my people, Roarke, and I know how much I can tell them. I don't know Angelo."

He continued to read the morning stock reports on-screen. "She works for me."

"So, one way or the other, does every third person in the known universe. That tells me nothing."

"What was your impression of her?"

"Sharp, smart, solid. And ambitious."

"So was mine," he said easily. "Or she wouldn't be chief of police on Olympus. Tell her what she needs to know. My father's unfortunate history doesn't trouble me."

"Will you talk to Mira?" She kept her gaze level as he rose, turned toward her. "I want to call her in, I want a consult. Will you talk to her?"

"I don't need a therapist, Eve. I'm not the one with nightmares." He cursed softly, ran a hand through his hair when her face went blank and still. "Sorry. Bloody hell. But my point is we each handle things as we handle them."

"And you can push and nudge and find ways to smooth it over for me. But I can't do that for you."

The temper in her voice alleviated a large slice of his guilt over mentioning her nightmare. "Screen off," he ordered and crossed to her. Took her face in his hands. "Let me tell you what I once told Mira—not in a consult, not in a session. You saved me, Eve." He watched her blink in

absolute shock. "What you are, what I feel for you, what
we are together saved me." He kept his eyes on hers as he
kissed her. "Call your people. I'll contact Darcia."

He was nearly out of the room before she found her
voice. "Roarke?" She never seemed to find the words as he
did, but these came easy. "We saved each other."

There was no way she could make the huge, elegant parlor
feel like one of the conference rooms in Cop Central. Especially when her team was gorging on cream pastries,
strawberries the size of golf balls, and a couple of pigs'
worth of real bacon.

It just served to remind her how much she hated being
off her own turf.

"Peabody, update."

Peabody had to jerk herself out of the image of the good
angel on her shoulder, sitting with her hands properly
folded, and the bad angel, who was stuffing another cream
bun in her greedy mouth. "Ah, sir. Autopsy was completed
last night. They let Morris assist. Cause of death multiple
trauma, most specifically the skull fracture. A lot of the injuries were postmortem. He's booked on a panel this morning, and has some sort of dead doctors' seminar later today,
but Morris will finesse copies of the reports for you. Early
word is the tox screen was clear."

"Sweepers?" Eve demanded.

"Sweepers' reports weren't complete as of oh-six-
hundred. However, what I dug up confirmed your beliefs.
Seal-It traces on the bat, no blood or bodily fluid but the victim's found on scene. No uniform missing an epaulet star
has been found to date. Angelo's team's doing the run on re-
cylers, valets, outside cleaning companies. My information
is the uniforms are coded with the individual's ID number.

When we find the uniform, we'll be able to trace the owner."

"I want that uniform," Eve stated, and when she turned to Feeney, the bad angel won. Peabody took another pastry.

"Had to be an inside job on the security cameras," he said. "Nobody gets access to Control without retina and palm scans and code clearance. The bypass was complicated, and it was done slick. Twelve people were in the control sector during the prime period last night. I'm running them."

"All right. We look for any connection to Skinner, any work-related reprimands, any sudden financial increase. Look twice if any of them were on the job before going into private security." She took a disk off the table, passed it to Feeney. "Run them with the names on here."

"No problem, but I work better when I know why I'm working."

"Those are the names of cops who went down in the line of duty in Atlanta twenty-three years ago. It was Skinner's operation." She took a deep breath. "Roarke's father was his weasel, and he turned a double cross."

When Feeney only nodded, Eve let out a breath. "One of the names on there is Thomas Weeks, father to Reginald Weeks, our victim. My guess is if Skinner had one of his slain officer's kids on his payroll, he's got others."

"Follows if one was used to build a frame around Roarke, another would be," Feeney added.

She checked her wrist unit when the door buzzer sounded. "That'll be Angelo. I want you running those names, Feeney, so I'm not giving them to her. Yet. But I'm going to tell her, and you, the rest of it."

While Eve was opening the door for Darcia, Skinner opened his to Roarke.

"A moment of your time, Commander."

"I have little to spare."

"Then we won't waste it." Roarke stepped inside, lifted a brow at Hayes. The man stood just behind and to the right of Skinner, and had his hand inside his suit jacket. "If you thought I was a threat, you should've had your man answer the door."

"You're no threat to me."

"Then why don't we have that moment in private?"

"Anything you say to me can be said in front of my personal assistant."

"Very well. It would've been tidier, and certainly more efficient, if you'd come after me directly instead of using Lieutenant Dallas and sacrificing one of your own men."

"So you admit you had him killed."

"I don't order death. We're alone, Skinner, and I'm sure you've had these rooms secured against recording devices and surveillance cameras. You want to take me on, then do it. But have the balls to leave my family out of it."

Skinner's lips peeled back over his teeth. "Your father was a dickless coward and a pathetic drunk."

"Duly noted." Roarke walked to a chair, sat. "There, you see. We already have a point of agreement on that particular matter. First let me clarify that by 'family,' I meant my wife. Second, I must tell you you're being too kind regarding Patrick Roarke. He was a vicious, small-minded bully and a petty criminal with delusions of grandeur. I hated him with every breath I took. So you see, I resent, quite strongly resent, being expected to pay for his many sins. I've plenty of my own, so if you want to try to put my head on a platter, just pick one. We'll work from there."

"Do you think because you wear a ten-thousand-dollar suit I can't smell the gutter on you?" Color began to flood Skinner's face, but when Hayes stepped forward, Skinner gestured him back with one sharp cut of the hand. "You're the same as he was. Worse, because he didn't pretend to be anything other than the useless piece of garbage he was. Blood tells."

"It may have once."

"You've made a joke out of the law, and now you hide behind a woman and a badge she's shamed."

Slowly now, Roarke got to his feet. "You know nothing of her. She's a miracle that I can't, and wouldn't, explain to the likes of you. But I can promise you, I hide behind nothing. You stand there, with fresh blood on your hands, behind your shield of blind righteousness and your memories of old glory. Your mistake, Skinner, was in trusting a man like my father to hold a bargain. And mine, it seems, was thinking you'd deal with me. So here's a warning for you."

He broke off as Hayes shifted. Fast as a rattler, Roarke drew a hand laser out of his pocket. "Take your bloody hand out of your coat while you still have one."

"You've no right, no authority to carry and draw a weapon."

Roarke stared at Skinner's furious face, then grinned. "What weapon? On your belly, Hayes, hands behind your head. Do it!" he ordered when Hayes shot Skinner a look. "Even on low these things give a nasty little jolt." He lowered the sight to crotch level. "Especially when they hit certain sensitive areas of the anatomy."

Though his breathing was now labored, Skinner gestured toward Hayes.

"To the warning. You step back from my wife. Step well and cleanly back, or you'll find the taste of me isn't to your liking."

"Will you have me beat to death in a stairwell?"

"You're a tedious man, Skinner," Roarke said with a

sigh as he backed to the door. "Flaming tedious. I'd tell
your men to have a care how they strut around and finger
their weapons. This is my place."

Despite its size, Eve found the living area of the suite as
stifling as a closed box. If she were on a case like this in
New York, she would be on the streets, cursing at traffic as
she fought her way to the lab to harass the techs, letting her
mind shuffle possibilities as she warred with Rapid Cabs
on the way to the morgue or back into Central.

The sweepers would tremble when she called demanding a final report. And the asses she would kick on her way
through the investigation would be familiar.

This time around Darcia Angelo got to have all the fun.

"Peabody, go down and record Skinner's keynote, since
he's playing the show must go on and giving it on schedule."

"Yes, sir."

The morose tone had Eve asking, "What?"

"I know why you're leaning toward him for this, Dallas.
I can see the angles, but I just can't adjust the pattern for
them. He's a legend. Some cops go wrong because the
pressure breaks them inside, or because of the temptations
or just because they were bent that way to begin with. He
never went wrong. It's an awful big leap to see him tossing
aside everything he's stood for and killing one of his own
to frame Roarke for something that happened when Roarke
was a kid."

"Come up with a different theory, I'll listen. If you can't
do the job, Peabody, tell me now. You're on your own time
here."

"I can do the job." Her voice was as stiff as her shoulders as she started for the door. "I haven't been on my own
time since I met you."

Eve set her teeth as the door slammed, and was already formulating the dressing-down as she marched across the room. Mira stopped her with a word.

"Eve. Let her go. You have to appreciate her position. It's difficult being caught between two of her heroes."

"Oh, for Christ's sake."

"Sit, before you wear a rut in this lovely floor. You're in a difficult position as well. The man you love, the job that defines you, and another man who you believe has crossed an indelible line."

"I need you to tell me if he could have crossed that line. I know what my gut tells me, what the pattern of evidence indicates. It's not enough. I have data on him. Most of it's public domain, but not all." She waited a beat while Mira simply continued to study her, calm as a lake. "I'm not going to tell you how I accessed it."

"I'm not going to ask you. I already know quite a bit about Douglas Skinner. He is a man devoted to justice—his own vision of it, one who has dedicated his life to what the badge stands for, one who has risked his life to serve and protect. Very much like you."

"That doesn't feel like much of a compliment right now."

"There is a parting of the ways between you, a very elemental one. He's compelled, has always been compelled, to spread his vision of justice like some are compelled to spread their vision of faith. You, Eve, at your core, stand for the victim. He stands for his vision. Over time, that vision has narrowed. Some can become victims of their own image until they become the image."

"He's lost the cop inside the hype."

"Cleanly said. Peabody's view of him is held by a great many people, a great many in law enforcement. It's not such a leap, psychologically speaking, for me to see him as becoming so obsessed by a mistake—and the mistake was his own—that cost the lives of men in his command that that failure becomes the hungry monkey on his back."

"The man who's dead wasn't street scum. He was a young employee, one with a clean record, with a wife. The son of one of Skinner's dead. That's the leap I'm having trouble with, Dr. Mira. Was the monkey so hungry that Skinner could order the death of an innocent man just to feed it?"

"If he could justify it in his mind, yes. Ends and means. How worried are you about Roarke?"

"He doesn't want me to worry about him," Eve answered.

"I imagine he's much more comfortable when he can worry about you. His father was abusive to him."

"Yeah. He's told me pieces of it. The old man knocked the hell out of him, drunk or sober." Eve dragged a hand through her hair, walked back toward the window. There was barely a hint of sky traffic.

How, she wondered, did people stand the quiet, the stillness?

"He had Roarke running cons, picking pockets, then he'd slap him around if he didn't bring home enough. I take it his father wasn't much good at the rackets because they lived in a slum."

"His mother?"

"I don't know. He says he doesn't know either. It doesn't seem to matter to him." She turned back, sat down across from Mira. "Can that be? Can it really not matter to him what his father did to him, or that his mother left him to that?"

"He knows his father started him on the path of, let's say circumventing the law. That he has a predisposition for violence. He learned how to channel it, as you did. He had a goal—to get out, to have means and power. He accomplished that. Then he found you. He understands where he came from, and I imagine it's part of his pride that he became the kind of man a woman like you would love. And, knowing his . . . profile," Mira said with a smile, "I imagine he's determined to protect you and your career in this matter, every bit as much as you're determined to protect him and his reputation."

"I don't see how . . ." Realization hit, and Eve was just getting to her feet when Roarke walked in the door.

"Goddamn it. Goddamn it, Roarke. You went after Skinner."

Chapter 6

"Good morning, Dr. Mira." Roarke closed the door behind him, then walked over to take Mira's hand. The move was as smooth as his voice, and his voice smooth as cream. "Can I get you some more tea?"

"No." Her lips twitched as she struggled to control a chuckle. "Thanks, but I really have to be going. I'm leading a seminar right after the keynote session."

"Don't think you can use her as a shield. I told you to stay away from Skinner."

"That's the second time someone's accused me of hiding behind a woman today." Though his voice remained mild, Eve knew the edge was there. "It's getting annoying."

"You want annoying?" Eve began.

"You'll have to forgive her," Roarke said to Mira as he walked her to the door. "Eve tends to become overexcited when I disobey."

"She's worried about you," Mira said under her breath.

"Well, she'll have to get over it. Have a good session."

He nudged Mira out the door, closed it. Locked it. Turned. The edge was visible now. "I don't need a fucking shield."

"That was a figure of speech, and don't change the subject. You went at Skinner after I told you to stay clear of him."

"I don't take orders from you, Eve. I'm not a lapdog."

"You're a civilian," she shot back.

"And you're a consultant on someone else's case, and your authority here, in my bloody world, is a courtesy."

She opened her mouth, closed it. Hissed. Then she turned on her heel, strode out through the terrace doors, and kicked the railing several times.

"Feel better now?"

"Yes. Because I imagined it was your stupid, rock-hard head." She didn't look back, but braced her hands on the railing and looked out over what was indeed one of Roarke's worlds.

It was lavish and extravagant. The slick spears of other hotels, the tempting spreads of casinos, theaters, the glitter of restaurants were all perfectly placed. There were fountains, the silver ribbons of people glides, and the lush spread of parks where trees and flowers grew in sumptuous profusion.

She heard the click of his lighter, caught the scent of his obscenely expensive tobacco. He rarely smoked these days, she thought.

"If you'd told me it was important for you to have a face-to-face with Skinner, I'd have gone with you."

"I'm aware of that."

"Oh, Christ. Men. Look, you don't need to hide behind me or anybody. You're a tough, badass son of a bitch with a really big penis and balls of titanium steel. Okay?"

He cocked his head. "One minute. I'm imagining

throwing you off the balcony. Yes." He nodded, took a long drag on the cigarette. "That's indeed better."

"If Skinner took a couple of pops at your ego, it's because he knew it was a good target. That's what cops do. Why don't you just tell me what happened?"

"He made it clear, while Hayes stood there with a hand inside his coat and on his weapon, that my father was garbage and by association so am I. And that it was long past time for my comeuppance, so to speak."

"Did he say anything that led to him ordering Weeks killed?"

"On the contrary, he twice pointed the finger at me. Full of barely restrained fury and seething emotion. You could almost believe he meant it. I don't think he's well," Roarke continued and crushed out his cigarette. "Temper put a very unhealthy color in his face, strained his breathing. I'll have to take a pass through his medical records."

"I want to take a pass at his wife. Angelo agreed, after some minor complaints, to set it up so we can double-team her later this afternoon. Meanwhile, Peabody's on Skinner, between us we'll track down the uniform, and Feeney's running names. Somebody on your security staff worked that bypass. We find out who, we link them back to Skinner and get them into interview, we change the complexion of this. Maybe put it away before ILE comes in."

She glanced back toward the suite as the 'link beeped. "Are we okay now?"

"We seem to be."

"Good. Maybe that's Angelo with the setup for Belle Skinner." She moved past Roarke to the 'link. Rather than Darcia's exotic face, Feeney's droopy one blipped on screen.

"Might have something for you here. Zita Vinter, hotel

security. She was in Control between twenty-one-thirty and twenty-three hundred last night. Crossed her with your list. Popped to Vinter, Detective Carl, Atlanta cop under Skinner. Line of duty during the botched bust. Vinter's wife was pregnant with their second kid—a son, Marshall, born two months after his death. Older kid was five. Daughter, Zita."

"Bull's-eye. What sector is she in now?"

"She didn't come in today. Didn't call in either, according to her supervisor. Got her home address. Want me to ride with you?"

She started to agree, then looked back at Roarke. "No, I got it. See what else you can find on her, okay? Maybe you can tag Peabody when the keynote crap's over. She's good at digging background details. Owe you one, Feeney. Let me have the address."

After she'd ended transmission, Eve hooked her thumbs in her front pockets and looked at Roarke. "You wouldn't know where 22 Athena Boulevard might be, would you?"

"I might be able to find it, yes."

"I bet." She picked up her palm 'link from the desk, stuck it in her pocket. "I'm not riding in a limo to go interview a suspect. It's unprofessional. Bad enough I'm taking some civilian wearing a fancy suit with me."

"Then I'll just have to come up with some alternate transportation."

"While you're at it, dig up your file on Zita Vinter, security sector."

He drew out his palm PC as they started out. "Always a pleasure to work with you, Lieutenant."

"Yeah, yeah." She stepped into the private elevator while he ordered something called a GF2000 brought to a garage slot. "Technically, I should contact Angelo and update her."

"No reason you can't. Once we're on the way."

"No reason. Saves time this way."

"That's your story, darling, and we'll stick to it. Vinter, Zita," he began as she scowled at him. "Twenty-eight. Two years with Atlanta PSD, then into private security. She worked for one of my organizations in Atlanta. Clean work record. Promoted to A Level over two years ago. She put in for the position here six months ago. She's single, lives alone. Lists her mother as next of kin. Her employment jacket's clean."

"When did you contract for this convention deal?"

"Just over six months ago," he said as they stepped off into the garage. "It was one of the incentives to have several of the facilities complete."

"How much do you want to bet Skinner's kept in close contact with his dead detective's daughter over the years? Angelo finesses a warrant for Vinter's 'link records, we're going to find transmissions to and from Atlanta. And not just to her mother."

When he stopped, put his PC away, she stared. "What the hell is this?"

Roarke ran a hand over the sleek chrome tube of the jet-bike. "Alternate transportation."

It looked fast and it looked mean, a powerful silver bullet on two silver wheels. She continued to stare as Roarke offered her a crash helmet.

"Safety first."

"Get a grip on yourself. With all your toys I know damn well you've got something around here with four wheels and doors."

"This is more fun." He dropped the helmet onto her head. "And I'm forced to remind you that part of this little interlude was meant to be a bit of a holiday for us."

He took a second helmet, put it on. Then tidily fastened hers. "This way you can be my biker bitch." When she showed her teeth, he only laughed and swung a leg nimbly over the tube. "And I mean that in the most flattering way possible."

"Why don't I pilot, and you can be my biker bitch?"

"Maybe later."

Swearing, she slid onto the bike behind him. He glanced back at her as she adjusted her seat, cupped her hands loosely at his hips. "Hang on," he told her.

He shot like a rocket out of the garage, and her arms latched like chains around his waist. "Lunatic!" she shouted as he blasted into traffic. Her heart flipped into her throat and stayed there while he swerved, threaded, streaked.

It wasn't that she minded speed. She liked to go fast, when she was manning the controls. There was a blur of color as they careened around an island of exotic wildflowers. A stream of motion when they rushed by a people glide loaded with vacationers. Grimly determined to face her death without blinking, she stared at the snag of vehicular traffic dead ahead.

Felt the boost of thrusters between her legs. "Don't you—"

She could only yip and try not to choke on her own tongue as he took the jet-bike into a sharp climb. Wind screamed by her ears as they punched through the air.

"Shortcut," he shouted back to her, and there was laughter in his voice as he brought the bike down to the road again, smooth as icing on cake.

He braked in front of a blindingly white building, shut off all engines. "Well, then, it doesn't come up to sex, but it's definitely in the top ten in the grand scheme."

He swung off, removed his helmet.

"Do you know how many traffic violations you racked up in the last four minutes?"

"Who's counting?" He pulled off her helmet, then leaned down to bite her bottom lip.

"Eighteen," she informed him, pulling out her palm 'link to contact Darcia Angelo. She scanned the building as she relayed a message to Darcia's voice mail. Clean, almost brutally clean. Well constructed, from the look of it, tasteful and likely expensive.

"What do you pay your security people?"

"A Level?" They crossed the wide sidewalk to the building's front entrance. "About twice what a New York police lieutenant brings in annually, with a full benefit package, of course."

"What a racket." She waited while they were scanned at the door and Roarke coded in his master. The requisite computer voice welcomed him and wished him a safe and healthy day.

The lobby was tidy and quiet, really an extended foyer with straight lines and no fuss. At the visitors' panel, Eve identified herself and requested Zita Vinter.

I'm sorry, Dallas, Lieutenant Eve, Ms. Vinter does not respond. Would you care to leave a message at this time?

"No, I don't care to leave a message at this time. This is police business. Clear me into Apartment Six-B."

I'm sorry, Dallas, Lieutenant Eve, your credentials are not recognized on this station and do not allow this system to bypass standard privacy and security regulations.

"How would you like me to bypass your circuits and stuff your motherboard up your—"

Warning! Verbal threats toward this system may result

in arrest, prosecution, and monetary fines up to five thousand credits.

Before Eve could spit out a response, Roarke clamped a hand on her shoulder. "This is Roarke." He laid his hand on the palm plate. "ID 151, Level A. You're ordered to clear me and Lieutenant Dallas to all areas of this compound."

Identification verified. Roarke and companion, Dallas, Eve, are cleared.

"Lieutenant," Eve said between her teeth as Roarke pulled her toward an elevator.

"Don't take it personally. Level six," he ordered.

"Damn machine treated me like a civilian." The insult of it was almost beyond her comprehension. "A *civilian.*"

"Irritating, isn't it?" He strolled off onto the sixth floor.

"You enjoyed that, didn't you? That 'Roarke and companion' shit."

"I did, yes. Immensely." He gestured. "Six-B." When she said nothing, he rang the buzzer himself.

"She didn't answer before, she's not going to answer now."

"No." He dipped his hands lightly in his pockets. "Technically . . . I suppose you need to ask Chief Angelo to request a warrant for entry."

"Technically," Eve agreed.

"I am, however, the owner of this building, and the woman's employer."

"Doesn't give you any right to enter her apartment without legal authority or permission."

He simply stood, smiled, waited.

"Do it," Eve told him.

"Welcome to my world." Roarke keyed in his master

code, then hummed when the lock light above the door remained red. "Well, well, she appears to have added a few touches of her own, blocked the master code. I'm afraid that's a violation of her lease agreement."

Eve felt the little twist in her gut and slipped her hand under her jacket to her weapon. "Get in."

Neither questioned that whatever methods had been taken, he could get around them. Through them. He took a small case of tools out of his pocket and removed the anti-intruder panel on the scanner and identification plate.

"Clever girl. She's added a number of tricky little paths here. This will take a minute."

Eve took out her 'link and called Peabody. "Track down Angelo," she ordered. "We're at 22 Athena Boulevard. Six-B. She needs to get over here. I want you with her."

"Yes, sir. What should I tell her?"

"To get here." She dropped the 'link back in her pocket, stepped back to Roarke just as the lock lights went green. "Move aside," she ordered and drew her weapon.

"I've been through a door with you before, Lieutenant." He took the hand laser out of his pocket, and ignored her snarl when she spotted it. "You prefer low, as I recall."

Since there wasn't any point in biting her tongue or slapping at him for carrying, she did neither. "On my count." She put a hand on the door, prepared to shove it open.

"Wait!" He caught the faint hum, and the sound sent his heart racing. The panel lights flashed red as he yanked Eve away from the door. They went down in a heap, his body covering hers.

She had that one breathless second to understand before the explosion blasted the door outward. A line of flame shot into the air, roaring across the hall where they'd been standing seconds before. Alarms screamed, and she felt the floor beneath her tremble at a second explosion, felt the blast of vicious heat all over her.

"Jesus! Jesus!" She struggled under him, slapped violently at the smoldering shoulder of his jacket with her bare hands. "You're on fire here."

Water spewed out of the ceiling as he sat up, stripped off the jacket. "Are you hurt?"

"No." She shook her head, shoved the hair soaked with the flood of the safety sprinklers out of her face. "Ears are ringing some. Where are you burned?" Her hands were racing over him as she pushed up to her knees.

"I'm not. The suit's fucked is all. Here, now. We're fine." He glanced back at the scarred and smoldering hole that had been the doorway. "But I'm afraid I'm going to have to evict Six-B."

Though she doubted it was necessary, Eve kept her weapon out as she picked her way over still smoking chunks of wall and door. Smoke and wet clogged the air in the hall, in the apartment, but she could see at one glance that the explosion had been smaller than she'd assumed. And very contained.

"A little paint and you're back in business."

"The explosion was set to blow the door, and whoever was outside it." There were bits of broken crockery on the floor, and a vase of flowers had fallen over, spilling water into the rivers already formed by the sprinkler system.

The furniture was sodden, the walls smeared with streaks from smoke and soot. The hallway walls were a dead loss, but otherwise, the room was relatively undamaged.

Ignoring the shouts and voices from outside the apartment, he moved through it with Eve.

Zita was in bed, her arms crossed serenely across her chest. Holstering her weapon, Eve walked to the bed, used two fingers to check for the pulse in the woman's throat.

"She's dead."

Chapter 7

"Your definition of cooperation and teamwork apparently differs from mine, Lieutenant."

Wet, filthy, and riding on a vicious headache, Eve strained while Darcia completed her examination of the body. "I updated you."

"No, you left a terse message on my voice mail." Darcia straightened. With her sealed hands, she lifted the bottle of pills on the nightstand, bagged them. "When you were, apparently, at the point of illegally entering this unit."

"Property owner or his representative has the right to enter a private home if there is reasonable cause to believe a life or lives may be in danger, or that said property is threatened."

"Don't quote your regulations at me," Darcia snapped. "You cut me out."

Eve opened her mouth, then blew out a long breath. "Okay, I wouldn't say I cut you out, but I did an end run around you. In your place, I'd be just as pissed off. I'm used to being able to pursue a line on an investigation in my own way, on my own time."

"You are not primary on this case. I want this body bagged and removed," Darcia ordered the uniforms flanking the bedroom doors. "Probable cause of death, voluntary self-termination."

"Wait a minute, wait a minute. Wait!" Eve ordered, throwing out a hand to warn the uniforms back. "This isn't self-termination."

"I see an unmarked body, reclining in bed. Hair neatly brushed, cosmetic enhancements unblemished. I see on the bedside table a glass of white wine and a bottle of pills prescribed for use in painless, gentle self-termination. I have here," she continued, holding up another evidence bag containing a single sheet of paper, "a note clearly stating the subject's intention to end her own life due to her guilt about her part in the death of Reginald Weeks. A death she states was ordered by Roarke and for which she was paid fifty thousand, in cash. I see a satchel containing that precise amount of cash on the dresser."

"Roarke didn't order anyone's murder."

"Perhaps not. But I am accustomed to pursuing a line on an investigation in my own way. On my own time." She tossed Eve's words back at her. "Commander Skinner has lodged a complaint claiming that Roarke threatened him this morning, with words and a weapon. Security disks at the hotel verify that Roarke entered the commander's suite and remained there for seven minutes, forty-three seconds. This incident is corroborated by one Bryson Hayes, Skinner's personal assistant, who was present at the time."

There was no point in kicking something again and pretending it was Roarke's head. "Skinner's in this up to his armpits, and if you let him deflect your focus onto Roarke, you're not as smart as I thought. First things first. You're standing over a homicide, Chief Angelo. The second one Skinner's responsible for."

Darcia ordered her men away by pointing her finger. "Explain to me how this is homicide, and why I shouldn't have you taken to the first transport and removed from this station. Why I should not, on the evidence at hand, take Roarke in for interview as a suspect in the murder of Reginald Weeks." Temper pumped into her voice now, hot and sharp. "And let me make this clear: Your husband's money pays my salary. It doesn't buy me."

Eve kept her focus on Darcia. "Peabody!" As she waited for her aide to come to the room, Eve struggled with her own temper.

"Sir?"

"What do you see?"

"Ah. Sir. Female, late twenties, medium build. No sign of struggle or distress." She broke off as Eve took an evidence bag from Darcia, passed it over. "Standard barb, commonly used in self-termination. Prescription calls for four units. All are missing. Date on the bottle is two weeks ago, prescribed and filled in Atlanta, Georgia."

Eve nodded when she saw the flicker in Darcia's eyes, then handed Peabody the note.

"Apparently suicide note, with signature. Computer-generated. The statement therein is contradictory to other evidence."

"Very good, Peabody. Tell Chief Angelo how it contradicts."

"Well, Lieutenant, most people don't have self-termination drugs tucked in their med cabinets. Unless you're suffering from an incurable and painful illness, it takes several tests and legalities to access the drug."

Darcia held up a hand. "All the more reason to have them around."

"No, sir."

"Ma'am," Darcia corrected with a smirk at Eve. "In my country a female superior is addressed as 'ma'am.'"

"Yes, ma'am. It may be different in your country as to the process of accessing this sort of drug. In the States, you have to register. If you haven't—that is, if you're still alive within thirty days of filling the prescription, you're on auto-recall. The drugs are confiscated and you're required to submit to psychiatric testing and evaluation. But besides that, it doesn't play."

"Keep going, Peabody," Eve told her.

"The note claims she decided to off herself because she was guilty over events that took place last night. But she already had the drug in her possession. Why? And how? You established time of death at oh-four-hundred this morning, so she got her payoff and the guilts awful close, then the means to self-terminate just happen to be in her possession. It's way pat, if you follow me."

She paused, and when Darcia nodded a go-ahead, pulled in a breath and kept going. "Added to that, it doesn't follow that she would rig her apartment door to an explosive, or set another in the surveillance area to destroy the security disks of the building. Added to that," Peabody continued, obviously enjoying herself now, "Roarke's profile is directly opposed to hiring out hits, especially since Dallas popped the guy, which is one of the things he admires about her. So when you add that all up, it makes that note bogus, and this unattended death becomes a probable homicide."

"Peabody." Eve dabbed an imaginary tear from her eye. "You do me proud."

Darcia looked from one to the other. Her temper was still on the raw side, which she could admit colored her logic. Or had. "Perhaps, Officer Peabody, you could now explain how person or persons unknown gained access to this unit and persuaded this trained security expert to take termination drugs without her struggling."

"Well . . ."

"I'll take over now." Eve patted her shoulder. "You don't want to blow your streak. Person or persons unknown were admitted to the unit by the victim. Most likely to pay her off or to give her the next stage of instructions. The termination drugs were probably mixed into the wine. Person or persons unknown waited for her to slip into the first stage of the coma, at which time she was carried in here, laid out nice and pretty. The note was generated, the stage set. When it was determined that victim was dead, the explosives were rigged, and person or persons unknown went on their merry way."

"She sort of sees it," Peabody added helpfully. "Not like a psychic or anything. She just walks it through with the killer. Really mag."

"Okay, Peabody. She was a tool," Eve continued. "No more, no less. The same as Weeks was a tool. She probably joined the force to honor her father, and he used that, just as he's using Roarke's father to get to him. They don't mean anything to him as people, as flesh and blood. They're just steps and stages in his twenty-three-year war."

"Maybe not tools, then," Darcia countered, "but soldiers. To some generals they are just as dispensable. Excuse us, Officer Peabody, if you please."

"Yes, ma'am. Sir."

"I want an apology." She saw Eve wince, and smiled.

"Yes, I know it'll hurt, so I want one. Not for pursuing a line of investigation, and so on. For not trusting me."

"I've known you less than twenty-four hours," Eve began, then winced again. "All right, shit. I apologize for not trusting you. And I'll go one better. For not respecting your authority."

"Accepted. I'm going to have the body taken to the ME, as a probable homicide. Your aide is very well trained."

"She's good," Eve agreed, since Peabody wasn't around to hear and get bigheaded about it. "And getting better."

"I missed the date, the significance, and I shouldn't have. I believe I would have seen these things once my annoyance with you had ebbed a bit, but that's beside the point. Now, I need to question Roarke regarding his conversation with the commander this morning, and regarding his association with Zita Vinter. To keep my official records clean, you are not included in this interview. I would appreciate it, however, if you'd remain and lead my team through the examination of the crime scene."

"No problem."

"I'll keep this as brief as I can, as I imagine both you and Roarke would like to go back and get out of those damp, dirty clothes." She tugged the sleeve of Eve's jacket as she passed. "That used to be very attractive."

"She was easier on me than I'd've been on her," Eve admitted as she rolled the stiffness out of her shoulders. She'd hit the floor under Roarke harder than she'd realized and figured she should take a look at the bruises.

After a long, hot shower.

Since Roarke's response to her statement was little more than a grunt as they rode up to their suite, she took his measure. He could use some cleaning up himself, she thought. He'd ditched the ruined jacket, and the shirt beneath it had taken a beating.

She wondered if her face was as dirty as his.

"As soon as we clean up," she began as she stepped out of the elevator and into the parlor. And that was as far as she got before she was pressed up against the elevator doors with his mouth ravaging hers.

Half her brain seemed to slide out through her ears. "Whoa. What?"

"Another few seconds." With his hands gripping her shoulders and his eyes hot he looked down at her. "We wouldn't be here."

"We are here."

"That's right." He jerked the jacket halfway down her arms, savaged her neck. "That's damn right. Now let's prove it." He stripped the jacket away, ripped her shirt at the shoulder. "I want my hands on you. Yours on me."

They already were. She tugged and tore at his ruined shirt, and because her hands were busy, used her teeth on him.

Less than a foot inside the room, they dragged each other to the floor. She rolled with him, fighting with the rest of his clothes, then arching like a bridge when his mouth clamped over her breast.

Need, deep and primal, gushed through her until she moaned his name. It was always his name. She wanted more. More to give, more to take. Her fingers dug into him—hard muscle, damp flesh. The scent of smoke and death smothered under the scent of him so that it filled her with the fevered mix of love and lust that he brought to her.

He couldn't get enough. It seemed he never could, or

would. All of the hungers, the appetites and desires he'd known paled to nothing against the need he had for her— for everything she was. The strength of her, physical and that uniquely tensile morality, enraptured him. Challenged him.

To feel that strength tremble under him, open for him, merge with him, was the wonder of his life.

Her breathing was short, shallow, and he heard it catch, release on a strangled gasp when he drove her over the first peak. His own blood raged as he crushed his mouth to hers again, and plunged inside her.

All heat and speed and desperation. The sound of flesh slapping, sliding against flesh mixed with the sound of ragged breathing.

She heard him murmuring something—the language of his youth, so rarely used, slid exotically around her name. The pressure of pleasure built outrageously inside her, a glorious burn in the blood as he drove her past reason with deep, hard thrusts.

She clung, clung to the edge of it. Then his eyes were locked on hers, wild and blue. Love all but swamped her.

"Come with me." His voice was thick with Ireland. "Come with me now."

She held on, and on, watching those glorious eyes go blind. Held on, and on while his body plunged in hers. Then she let go, and went with him.

Sex, Eve had discovered, could, when it was done right, benefit body, mind, and spirit. She hardly bitched at all about having to dress up to meet with Belle Skinner at a ladies' tea. Her body felt loose and limber, and while the dress Roarke handed her didn't fit her image of cop, the weapon she snugged on under the long, fluid jacket made up for it.

"Are you intending to blast some of the other women over the watercress sandwiches and petit fours?" he asked.

"You never know." She looked at the gold earrings he held out, shrugged, then put them on. "While I'm swilling tea and browbeating Belle Skinner, you can follow up on a hunch for me. Do some digging, see if Hayes was connected to any of the downed cops under Skinner's command during the botched bust. Something there too close for employer/employee relations."

"All right. Shoes."

She stared at the needle-thin heels and flimsy straps. "Is that what you call them? How come guys don't have to wear death traps like those?"

"I ask myself that same question every day." He took a long scan after she'd put them on. "Lieutenant, you look amazing."

"Feel like an idiot. How am I supposed to intimidate anyone dressed in this gear?"

"I'm sure you'll manage."

"Ladies' tea," she grumbled on the way out. "I don't know why Angelo can't just haul the woman in to her cop shop and deal."

"Don't forget your rubber hose and mini-stunner."

She smirked over her shoulder as she stepped onto the elevator. "Bite me."

"Already did."

The tea was already under way when Eve walked in. Women in flowy dresses, and some—Jesus—in hats, milled about and gathered under arbors of pink roses or spilled out onto a terrace where a harpist plucked strings and sang in a quavery voice that instantly irritated Eve's nerves.

Tiny crustless sandwiches and pink frosted cakes were arranged on clear glass platters. Shining silver pots steamed with tea that smelled, to Eve, entirely too much like the roses.

At such times she wondered how women weren't mortified to be women.

She tracked down Peabody first and was more than slightly amazed to see her stalwart aide decked out in a swirly flowered dress and a broad-brimmed straw hat with trailing ribbons.

"Jeez, Peabody, you look like a—what is it—milkmaid or something."

"Thanks, Dallas. Great shoes."

"Shut up. Run down Mira. I want her take on Skinner's wife. The two of you hang close while Angelo and I talk to her."

"Mrs. Skinner's out on the terrace. Angelo just walked in. Wow, she's got some great DNA."

Eve glanced back, nodded to Angelo. The chief had chosen to wear cool white, but rather than flowing, the dress clung to every curve.

"On the terrace," Eve told her. "How do you want to play it?"

"Subtly, Lieutenant. Subtle's my style."

Eve lifted her brows. "I don't think so."

"Interview style," Darcia said and breezed onto the terrace. She stopped, poured tea, then strolled to the table where Belle was holding court. "Lovely party, Mrs. Skinner. I know we all want to thank you for hosting this event. Such a nice break from the seminars and panels."

"It's important to remember that we're women, not just wives, mothers, career professionals."

"Absolutely. I wonder if Lieutenant Dallas and I might have a private word with you? We won't take up much of your time."

She laid a hand on the shoulder of one of the women seated at the table. Subtle, Eve thought. And effective, as the woman rose to give Darcia her chair.

"I must tell you how much I enjoyed the commander's keynote this morning," Darcia began. "So inspiring. It must be very difficult for him, and you, to deal with the convention after your tragic loss."

"Douglas and I both believe strongly in fulfilling our duties and responsibilities, whatever our personal troubles. Poor Reggie." She pressed her lips together. "It's horrible. Even being a cop's wife for half a century . . . you never get used to the shock of violent death."

"How well did you know Weeks?" Eve asked.

"Loss and shock and sorrow aren't connected only to personal knowledge, Lieutenant." Belle's voice went cool. "But I knew him quite well, actually. Douglas and I believe in forming strong and caring relationships with our employees."

Likes Angelo, Eve thought. Hates me. Okay, then. "I guess being full of shock and sorrow is the reason you eavesdropped from your bedroom instead of coming out when we notified Commander Skinner that one of his security team had been murdered."

Belle's face went very blank and still. "I don't know what you're intimating."

"I'm not intimating, I'm saying it straight out. You were in the spare room—not the master with the commander. I know you were awake, because your light was on. You heard us relay the information, but despite this close, personal relationship, you didn't come out to express your shock and loss. Why is that, Mrs. Skinner?"

"Dallas, I'm sure Mrs. Skinner has her reasons." Darcia put a light sting of censure in her voice, then turned a sympathetic smile to Belle. "I'm sorry, Mrs. Skinner. The lieutenant is, quite naturally, on edge just now."

"There's no need for you to apologize, Chief Angelo. I understand, and sympathize—to an extent—Lieutenant Dallas's desire to defend and protect her husband."

"Is that what you're doing?" Eve tossed back. "How far would you go? How many close, personal relationships are you willing to sacrifice? Or didn't you have one with Zita Vinter?"

"Zita?" Belle's shoulders jerked, as if from a blow. "What does Zita have to do with any of this?"

"You knew her?"

"She's our godchild, of course I . . . Knew?" Every ounce of color drained out of the lovely face so that the expertly applied enhancements stood out like paint on a doll. "What's happened?"

"She's dead," Eve said flatly. "Murdered early this morning, a few hours after Weeks."

"Dead? *Dead?*" Belle got shakily to her feet, upending her teacup as she floundered for balance. "I can't—I can't talk to you now."

"Want to go after her?" Darcia asked when Belle rushed from the terrace.

"No. Let's give her time to stew. She's scared now. Over what she knows and what she doesn't know." She looked back at Darcia. "We had a pretty good rhythm going there."

"I thought so. But I imagine playing the insensitive, argumentative cop comes naturally to you."

"Just like breathing. Let's blow this tea party and go get a drink." Eve signaled to Peabody and Mira. "Just us girls."

Chapter 8

In the bar, in a wide, plush booth, Eve brooded over a fizzy water. She'd have preferred the good, hard kick of a Zombie, but she wanted a clear head more than the jolt.

"You've got a smooth, sympathetic style," she said to Darcia. "I think she'll talk to you if you stay in that channel."

"So do I."

"Dr. Mira here, she's got the same deal. You'd be able to double-team her." Eve glanced toward Mira, who was sipping white wine.

"She was shocked and shaken," Mira began. "First, she'll verify the information about the death of her godchild. When she does, grief will tangle with the shock."

"So, she'll be even more vulnerable to the right questions presented in the right style."

"You're a cold one, Dallas," Darcia said. "I like that about you. I'd be very agreeable to interviewing Belle Skinner with Dr. Mira, if that suits the doctor."

"I'm happy to help. I imagine you intend to talk to Skinner again, Eve."

"With the chief's permission."

"Don't start being polite now," Darcia told her. "You'll ruin your image. He won't want to talk to you," she went on. "Whatever his feelings toward you were before, my impression is—after his keynote—he's wrapped you and Roarke together. He hates you both."

"He brought us up at his keynote?"

"Not by name, but by intimation. His inspiring, rather cheerleader-type speech took a turn at the midway point. He went into a tangent on cops who go bad, who forget their primary duties in favor of personal comforts and gains. Gestures, body language . . ." Darcia shrugged. "It was clear he was talking about this place—luxury palaces built on blood and greed, I believe he said—and you. Bedfellows of the wicked. He got very worked up about it, almost evangelical. While there were some who appeared enthusiastic and supportive of that particular line of thought, it seemed to me the bulk of the attendees were uncomfortable—embarrassed or angry."

"He wants to use his keynote to take slaps at me and Roarke, it doesn't worry me." But Eve noticed Peabody staring down into her glass. "Peabody?"

"I think he's sick." She spoke quietly, finally lifted her gaze. "Physically, mentally. I don't think he's real stable. It was hard to watch it happen this morning. He started out sort of, well, eloquent, then it just deteriorated into this rant. I've admired him all my life. It was hard to watch," she repeated. "A lot of the cops who were there stiffened up. You could almost feel layers of respect peeling away. He talked about the murder some, how a young, promising man had become a victim of petty and soulless revenge.

How a killer could hide behind a badge instead of being brought to justice by one."

"Pretty pointed," Eve decided.

"A lot of the terrestrial cops walked out then."

"So he's probably a little shaky now himself. I'll take him," Eve said. "Peabody, you track down Feeney, see what other details you can dig out on the two victims and anyone else on-site who's connected with the bust in Atlanta. That fly with you, Chief Angelo?"

Darcia polished off her wine. "It does."

Eve detoured back to the suite first. She wanted a few more details before questioning Skinner again. She never doubted Roarke had already found them.

He was on the 'link when she got there, talking to his head of hotel security. Restless, Eve wandered out onto the terrace and let her mind shuffle the facts, the evidence, the lines of possibilities.

Two dead. Both victims' fathers martyred cops. And those connected to Roarke's father and to Skinner. Murdered in a world of Roarke's making, on a site filled with police officials. It was so neat, it was almost poetic.

A setup from the beginning? It wasn't a crime of impulse but something craftily, coldly planned. Weeks and Vinter had both been sacrifices, pawns placed and disgarded for the greater game. A chess game, all right, she decided. Black king against white, and her gut told her Skinner wouldn't be satisfied with a checkmate.

He wanted blood.

She turned as Roarke stepped out. "In the end, destroying you won't be enough. He's setting you up, step by step, for execution. A lot of weapons on this site. He keeps the pressure on, piles up the circumstantial so there's enough appearance that you might have ordered these hits. All he needs is one soldier willing to take the fall. I'm betting Hayes for that one. Skinner doesn't have much time to pull it off."

"No, he doesn't," Roarke agreed. "I got into his medical records. A year ago he was diagnosed with a rare disorder. It's complicated, but the best I can interpret, it sort of nibbles away at the brain."

"Treatment?"

"Yes, there are some procedures. He's had two— quietly, at a private facility in Zurich. It slowed the process, but in his case . . . He's had complications. A strain on the heart and lungs. Another attempt at correction would kill him. He was given a year. He has, perhaps, three months of that left. And of that three months, two at the outside where he'll continue to be mobile and lucid. He's made arrangements for self-termination."

"That's rough." Eve slipped her hands into her pockets. There was more—she could see it in Roarke's eyes. Something about the way he watched her now. "It plays into the rest. This one event's been stuck in his gut for decades. He wants to clear his books before he checks out. Whatever's eating at his brain has probably made him more unstable, more fanatic, and less worried about the niceties. He needs to see you go down before he does. What else? What is it?"

"I went down several more layers in his case file on the bust. His follow-ups, his notes. He believed he'd tracked my father before he'd slipped out of the country again. Skinner used some connections. It was believed that my father headed west and spent a few days among some nefarious associates. In Texas. In Dallas, Eve."

Her stomach clenched, and her heart tripped for several beats. "It's a big place. It doesn't mean . . ."

"The timing's right." He walked to her, ran his hands up and down her arms as if to warm them. "Your father and mine, petty criminals searching for the big score. You were found in that Dallas alley only a few days after Skinner lost my father's trail again."

"You're saying they knew each other, your father and mine."

"I'm saying the circle's too tidy to ignore. I nearly didn't tell you," he added, resting his forehead on hers.

"Give me a minute." She stepped away from him, leaned out on the rail, stared out over the resort. But she was seeing that cold, dirty room, and herself huddled in the corner like an animal. Blood on her hands.

"He had a deal going," she said quietly. "Some deal or other, I think. He wasn't drinking as much—and it was worse for me when he wasn't good and drunk when he came back. And he had some money. Well." She took a deep breath. "Well. It plays out. Do you know what I think?"

"Tell me."

"I think sometimes fate cuts you a break. Like it says, okay, you've had enough of that crap, so it's time you fell into something nice. See what you make out of it." She turned back to him then. "We're making something out of it. Whatever they were to us, or to each other, it's what we are now that counts."

"Darling Eve. I adore you."

"Then you'll do me a favor. Keep yourself scarce for the

next couple of hours. I don't want to give Skinner any op-
portunities. I need to talk to him, and he won't talk if
you're with me."

"Agreed, with one condition. You go wired." He took a
small jeweled pin from his pocket, attached it to her lapel.
"I'll monitor from here."

"It's illegal to record without all parties' knowledge and
permission unless you have proper authorization."

"Is it really?" He kissed her. "That's what you get for
bedding down with bad companions."

"Heard about that, did you?"

"Just as I heard that a large portion of your fellow
cops walked out of the speech. Your reputation stands,
Lieutenant. I imagine your seminar tomorrow will be
packed."

"My . . . Shit! I forgot. I'm not thinking about it," she
muttered on the way out. "Not thinking about it."

She slipped into the conference room where Skinner was
leading a seminar on tactics. It was some relief to realize
she'd missed the lecture and had come in during the
question-and-answer period. There were a lot of long looks
in her direction as she walked down the side of the room
and found a seat halfway from the back.

She scoped out the setup. Skinner on stage at the
podium, Hayes standing to his back and his right, at attention. Two other personal security types on his other side.

Excessive, she thought, and obviously so. The message
was that the location, the situation, posed personal jeopardy for Skinner; but he was taking precautions and doing
his job.

Very neat.

She raised her hand, and was ignored. Five questions passed until she simply got to her feet and addressed him. And as she rose, she noted Hayes slide a hand inside his jacket.

She knew every cop in the room caught the gesture. The room went dead quiet.

"Commander Skinner, a position of command regularly requires you to send men into situations where loss of life, civilian and departmental, is a primary risk. In such cases, do you find it more beneficial to the operation to set personal feelings for your men aside, or to use those feelings to select the team?"

"Every man who picks up a badge does so acknowledging he will give his life if need be to serve and protect. Every commander must respect that acknowledgment. Personal feelings must be weighed, in order to select the right man for the right situation. This is a matter of experience and the accumulation, through years and that experience, of recognizing the best dynamic for each given op. But personal feelings—i.e., emotional attachments, private connections, friendships, or animosities—must never color the decision."

"So, as commander, you'd have no problem sacrificing a close personal friend or connection to the success of the op?"

His color came up. And the tremor she had noticed in his hand became more pronounced. "'Sacrificing,' Lieutenant Dallas? A poor choice of words. Cops aren't lambs being sent to slaughter. Not passive sacrifices to the greater good, but active, dedicated soldiers in the fight for justice."

"Soldiers are sacrificed in battle. Acceptable losses."

"No loss is acceptable." His bunched fist pounded the podium. "Necessary, but not acceptable. Every man who has fallen under my command weighs on me. Every child left without a father is my responsibility. Command requires this, and that the commander be strong enough to bear the burdon."

"And does command, in your opinion, require restitution for those losses?"

"It does, Lieutenant. There is no justice without payment."

"For the children of the fallen? And for the children of those who escaped the hand of justice? In your opinion."

"Blood speaks to blood." His voice began to rise, and to tremble. "If you were more concerned with justice than with your own personal choices, you wouldn't need to ask the question."

"Justice is my concern, Commander. It appears we have different definitions of the term. Do you think your god-daughter was the best choice for this operation? Does her death weigh on you now, or does it balance the other losses?"

"You're not fit to speak her name. You've whored your badge. You're a disgrace. Don't think your husband's money or threats will stop me from using all my influence to have that badge taken from you."

"I don't stand behind Roarke any more than he stands behind me." She kept talking as Hayes stepped forward and laid a hand on Skinner's shoulder. "I don't stand on yesterday's business. Two people are dead here and now. That's my priority, Commander. Justice for them is my concern."

Hayes stepped in front of Skinner. "The seminar is over. Commander Skinner thanks you for attending and regrets

Lieutenant Dallas's disruption of the question-and-answer period."

People shuffled, rose. Eve saw Skinner leaving, flanked by the two guards.

"Ask me," someone commented near her, "these seminars could use more fucking disruptions."

She made her way toward the front and came up toe to toe with Hayes.

"I've got two more questions for the commander."

"I said the seminar's over. And so's your little show."

She felt the crowd milling around them, some edging close enough to hear. "You see, that's funny. I thought I came in on the show. Does he run it, Hayes, or do you?"

"Commander Skinner is a great man. Great men often need protection from whores."

A cop moved in, poked Hayes on the shoulder. "You're gonna want to watch the name-calling, man."

"Thanks." Eve acknowledged him with a nod. "I've got it."

"Don't like play cops calling a badge a whore." He stepped back, but he hovered.

"While you're protecting the great man," Eve continued, "you might want to remember that two of his front-line soldiers are in the morgue."

"Is that a threat, Lieutenant?"

"Hell, no. It's a fact, Hayes. Just like it's a fact that both of them had fathers who died under Skinner's command. What about your father?"

Furious color slashed across his cheekbones. "You know nothing of my father, and you have no right to speak of him."

"Just giving you something to think about. For some

reason I get the feeling that I'm more interested in finding out who put those bodies in the morgue than you or your great man. And because I am, I will find out—before this show breaks down and moves on. That one's a promise."

Chapter 9

If she couldn't get to Skinner, Eve thought, she'd get to Skinner's wife. And if Angelo and Peabody hadn't softened and soothed enough, that was too fucking bad. Damned if she was going to tiptoe around weepy women and dying men, then have to turn the case over to the interplanetary boys.

It was her case, and she meant to close it.

She knew that part of her anger and urgency stemmed from the information Roarke had given her. His father, hers, Skinner, and a team of dead cops. Skinner was right about one thing, she thought as she headed for his suite: Blood spoke to blood.

The blood of the dead had always spoken to her.

Her father and Roarke's had both met a violent end. That was all the justice she could offer to the badges lost so many years before. But there were two bodies in cold boxes. For those, whatever they'd done, she would stand.

She knocked, waited impatiently. It was Darcia who

opened the door and sent Eve an apologetic little wince.

"She's a mess," Darcia whispered. "Mira's patting her hand, letting her cry over her goddaughter. It's a good foundation, but we haven't been able to build on it yet."

"Any objections to me giving the foundation a shake?"

Darcia studied her, pursed her lips. "We can try it that way, but I wouldn't shake too hard. She shatters, we're back to square one with her."

With a nod, Eve stepped in. Mira was on the sofa with Belle, and was indeed holding her hand. A teapot, cups, and countless tissues littered the table in front of them. Belle was weeping softly into a fresh one.

"Mrs. Skinner, I'm sorry for your loss." Eve sat in a chair by the sofa, leaned into the intimacy. She kept her voice quiet, sympathetic, and waited until Belle lifted swollen, red-rimmed eyes to hers.

"How can you speak of her? Your husband's responsible."

"My husband and I were nearly blown to bits by an explosive device on Zita Vinter's apartment door. A device set by her killer. Follow the dots."

"Who else had cause to kill Zita?"

"That's what we want to find out. She sabotaged the security cameras the night Weeks was murdered."

"I don't believe that." Belle balled the tissue into her fist. "Zita would never be a party to murder. She was a lovely young woman. Caring and capable."

"And devoted to your husband."

"Why shouldn't she be?" Belle's voice rose as she got to her feet. "He stepped in when her father died. Gave her his time and attention, helped with her education. He'd have done anything for her."

"And she for him?"

Belle's lips quivered, and she sat again, as if her legs quivered as well. "She would never be a party to murder. He would never ask it of her."

"Maybe she didn't know. Maybe she was just asked to deal with the cameras and nothing else. Mrs. Skinner, your husband's dying." Eve saw Belle jerk, shudder. "He doesn't have much time left, and the loss of his men is preying on him as he prepares for death. Can you sit there and tell me his behavior over the last several months has been rational?"

"I won't discuss my husband's condition with you."

"Mrs. Skinner, do you believe Roarke's responsible for something his father did? Something this man did when Roarke was a child, three thousand miles away?"

She watched tears swim into Belle's eyes again, and leaned in. Pressed. "The man used to beat Roarke half to death for sport. Do you know what it feels like to be hit with fists, or a stick, or whatever the hell's handy—and by the person who's supposed to take care of you? By law, by simple morality. Do you know what it's like to be bloody and bruised and helpless to fight back?"

"No." The tears spilled over. "No."

"Does that child have to pay for the viciousness of the man?"

"The sins of the fathers," Belle began, then stopped. "No." Wearily, she wiped her wet cheeks. "No, Lieutenant, I don't believe that. But I know what it has cost my husband, what happened before, what was lost. I know how it's haunted him—this good, good man, this honorable man who has dedicated his life to his badge and everything it stands for."

"He can't exorcise his ghosts by destroying the son of the man who made them. You know that, too."

"He would never harm Zita, or Reggie. He loved them

as if they were his own. But . . ." She turned to Mira again, gripped her hands fiercely. "He's so ill—in body, mind, spirit. I don't know how to help him. I don't know how long I can stand watching him die in stages. I'm prepared to let him go because the pain—sometimes it's so horrible. And he won't let me in. He won't share the bed with me, or his thoughts, his fears. It's as if he's divorcing me, bit by bit. I can't stop it."

"For some, death is a solitary act," Mira said gently. "Intimate and private. It's hard to love someone and stand aside while they take those steps alone."

"He agreed to apply for self-termination for me." Belle sighed. "He doesn't believe in it. He believes a man should stand up to whatever he's handed and see it through. I'm afraid he's not thinking clearly any longer. There are moments . . ."

She steadied her breathing and looked back at Eve. "There are rages, swings of mood. The medication may be partially responsible. He's never shared the job with me to any great extent. But I know that for months now, perhaps longer, Roarke has been a kind of obsession to him. As have you. You chose the devil over duty."

She closed her eyes a moment. "I'm a cop's wife, Lieutenant. I believe in that duty, and I see it all over you. He would see it, too, if he weren't so ill. I swear to you he didn't kill Reggie or Zita. But they may have been killed for him."

"Belle." Mira offered her another tissue. "You want to help your husband, to ease his pain. Tell Lieutenant Dallas and Chief Angelo what you know, what you feel. No one knows your husband's heart and mind the way you do."

"It'll shatter him. If he has to face this, it'll destroy him.

Fathers and sons," she said softly, then buried her face in the tissue. "Oh, dear God."

"Hayes." It clicked for Eve like a link on a chain. "Hayes didn't lose a father during the bust. He's Commander Skinner's son."

"A single indiscretion." Tears choked Belle's voice when she lifted her head again. "During a bump in a young marriage. And so much of it my fault. My fault," she repeated, turning her pleading gaze to Mira. "I was impatient, and angry, that so much of his time, his energies went into his work. I'd married a cop, but I hadn't been willing to accept all that that meant—all it meant to a man like Douglas."

"It isn't easy to share a marriage with duty." Mira poured more tea. "Particularly when duty is what defines the partner. You were young."

"Yes." Gratitude spilled into Belle's voice as she lifted her cup. "Young and selfish, and I've done everything in my power to make up for it since. I loved him terribly, and wanted all of him. I couldn't have that, so I pushed and prodded, then I stepped away from him. All or nothing. Well. He's a proud man, and I was stubborn. We separated for six months, and during that time he turned to someone else. I can't blame him for it."

"And she got pregnant," Eve prompted.

"Yes. He never kept it from me. He never lied or tried to hide it from me. He's an honorable man." Her tone turned fierce when she looked at Eve.

"Does Hayes know?"

"Of course. Of course he knows. Douglas would never shirk his responsibilities. He provided financial support. We worked out an arrangement with the woman, and she agreed to raise the child and keep his paternity private.

There was no point, no point at all in making the matter public and complicating Douglas's career, shadowing his reputation."

"So you paid for his . . . indiscretion."

"You're a hard woman, aren't you, Lieutenant? No mistakes in your life? No regrets?"

"Plenty of them. But a child—a man—might have some problem being considered a mistake. A regret."

"Douglas has been nothing but kind and generous and responsible with Bryson. He's given him everything."

Everything except his name, Eve thought. How much would that matter? "Did he give him orders to kill, Mrs. Skinner? Orders to frame Roarke for murder?"

"Absolutely not. Absolutely not. But Bryson is . . . perhaps he's overly devoted to Douglas. In the past several months, Douglas has turned to him too often, and perhaps, when Bryson was growing up, Douglas set standards that were too high, too harsh for a young boy."

"Hayes would need to prove himself to his father."

"Yes. Bryson's hard, Lieutenant. Hard and cold-blooded. You'd understand that, I think. Douglas—he's ill. And his moods, his obsession with what happened all those years ago is eating at him as viciously as his illness does. I've heard him rage, as if there's something else inside him. And during the rage he said something had to be done, some payment made, whatever the cost. That there were times the law had to make room for blood justice. Death for death. I heard him talking with Bryson, months ago, about this place. That Roarke had built it on the bones of martyred cops. That he would never rest until it, and Roarke, were destroyed. That if he died before he could avenge those who were lost, his legacy to his son was that duty."

"Pick him up." Eve swung to Darcia. "Have your people pick Hayes up."

"Already on it," Darcia answered as she switched on her communicator.

"He doesn't know." Belle got slowly to her feet. "Or he's not allowing himself to know. Douglas is convinced that Roarke's responsible for what's happened here. Convinced himself that you're part of it, Lieutenant. His mind isn't what it was. He's dying by inches. This will finish him. Have pity."

She thought of the dead, and thought of the dying. "Ask yourself what he would have done, Mrs. Skinner, if he were standing in my place now. Dr. Mira will stay with you."

She headed out with Darcia, waited until they were well down the hall. "There should be a way to separate him from Skinner before we bag him. Take him quietly."

Darcia called for the elevator. "You're some ruthless hard-ass, aren't you, Dallas?"

"If Skinner didn't give him a direct order, there's no point in smearing him with Hayes, or making the arrest while he's around. Christ, he's a dead man already," she snapped when Darcia said nothing. "What's the fucking point of dragging him into it and destroying half a century of service?"

"None."

"I can request another interview with Skinner, draw him away far enough for you to make the collar."

"You're giving up the collar?" Darcia asked in a shocked voice as they stepped onto the elevator.

"It was never mine."

"The hell it wasn't. But I'll take it," Darcia added cheerfully. "How'd you click to the relationship between Skinner and Hayes?"

"Fathers. The case is lousy with them. You got one?"

"A father? Doesn't everyone?"

"Depends on your point of view." She stepped off the car on the main lobby level. "I'm going to round up Peabody, give you a chance to coordinate your team." She checked her wrist unit. "Fifteen minutes ought to . . . Well, well. Look who's holding court in the lobby lounge."

Darcia tracked, studied the group crowded at two tables. "Skinner looks to have recovered his composure."

"The man likes an audience. It probably pumps him up more than his meds. We could play it this way. We go over, and I apologize for disrupting the seminar. Distract Skinner, get him talking. You tell Hayes you'd like to have a word with him about Weeks. Don't want to disturb Skinner with routine questions and blah, blah. Can you take him on your own?"

Darcia gave her a bland stare. "Could you?"

"Okay, then. Let's do it. Quick and quiet."

They were halfway across the lobby when Hayes spotted them. Two beats later, he was running.

"Goddamn it, goddamn it. He's got cop instincts. Circle that way," Eve ordered, then charged the crowd. She vaulted the smooth gold rail that separated the lounge from the lobby. People shouted, spilled back. Glassware crashed as a table overturned. She caught a glimpse of Hayes as he swung through a door behind the bar.

She leaped the bar, ignoring the curses of the servers and patrons. Bottles smashed, and there was a sudden, heady scent of top-grade liquor. Her weapon was in her hand when she hit the door with her shoulder.

The bar kitchen was full of noise. A cook droid was sprawled on the floor in the narrow aisle, its head jerking from the damage done by the fall. She stumbled over it, and the blast from Hayes's laser sang over her head.

Rather than right herself, she rolled and came up behind a stainless-steel cabinet.

"Give it up, Hayes. Where are you going to go? There are innocent people in here. Drop your weapon."

"Nobody's innocent." He fired again, and the line of heat scored across the floor and finished off the droid.

"This isn't what your father wants. He doesn't want more dead piling up at his feet."

"There's no price too high for duty." A shelf of dinnerware exploded beside her, showering her with shards.

"Screw this." She sent a line of fire over her head, rolled to the left. She came up weapon first and cursed again as she lost the target around a corner.

Someone was screaming. Someone else was crying. Keeping low, she set off in pursuit. She turned toward the sound of another blast and saw a fire erupt in a pile of linens.

"Somebody take care of that!" she shouted and turned the next corner. Saw the exit door. "Shit!"

He'd blasted the locks, effectively sealing it. In frustration she rammed it, gave it a couple of solid kicks, and didn't budge it an inch.

Holstering her weapon, she made her way back out the mess and smoke. Without much hope, she ran through the lobby, out the main doors to scan the streets. By the time she'd made it to the corner, Darcia was heading back.

"Lost him. Son of a bitch. He had a block and a half on me." Darcia jammed her own weapon home. "I'd never have caught him on foot in these damn shoes. I've got an APB out. We'll net the bastard."

"Fucker smelled the collar." Furious with herself, Eve

spun in a circle. "I didn't give him enough credit. He knocked some people around in the bar kitchen. Offed a droid, started a fire. He's fast and smart and slick. And he's goddamn mean on top of it."

"We'll net him," Darcia repeated.

"Damn right we will."

Chapter 10

"Lieutenant."

Eve winced, turned and watched Roarke walk toward her. "Guess you heard we had a little incident."

"I believe I'll just see to some damage control." Humor cut through the anger on Darcia's face. "Excuse me."

"Are you hurt?" Roarke asked Eve.

"No. But you've got a dead droid in the bar kitchen. I didn't kill it, in case you're wondering. There was a little fire, too. But I didn't start it. The ceiling damage, that's on me. And some of the, you know, breakage and stuff."

"I see." He studied the elegant facade of the hotel. "I'm sure the guests and the staff found it all very exciting. The ones who don't sue me should enjoy telling the story to their friends and relations for quite some time. Since I'll be contacting my attorneys to alert them to a number of civil suits heading our way, perhaps you'd take a moment to fill me in on why I have a dead droid, a number of hysterical guests, screaming staff, and a little fire in the bar kitchen."

"Sure. Why don't we round up Peabody and Feeney, then I can just run through it once?"

"No, I think I'd like to know now. Let's just have a bit of a walk." He took her arm.

"I don't have time to—"

"Make it."

He led her around the hotel, through the side gardens, the patio cafe, wound through one of the pool areas and into a private elevator while he listened to her report.

"So your intentions were to spare Skinner's feelings and reputation."

"Didn't work out, but, yeah, to a point. Hayes made us first glance." The minute she was in the suite, she popped open a bottle of water, glugged. Until that moment she hadn't realized the smoke had turned her throat into a raw desert of thirst. "Should've figured it. Now he's in the wind, and that's on me, too."

"He won't get off the station."

"No, he won't get off. But he might take it in mind to do some damage while he's loose. I'll need to look at the maps and plats for the resort. We'll do a computer analysis, earmark the spots he'd be most likely to go to ground."

"I'll take care of that. I can do it faster," he said before she could object. "You need a shower. You smell of smoke."

She lifted her arm, sniffed it. "Yeah, I guess I do. Since you're being so helpful, tag Peabody and Feeney, will you? I want this manhunt coordinated."

"Too many places for him to hide." An hour later, Eve scowled at the wall screens and the locations the computer had selected. "I'm wondering, too, if he had some sort of backup transpo in case this turned on him, someone he's bribed to smuggle him off-site. If he gets off this station, he could go any fucking where."

"I can work with Angelo on running that angle down," Feeney said. "And some e-maneuvering can bog down anything scheduled to leave the site for a good twenty-four hours."

"Good thinking. Keep in touch, okay?"

"Will do." He headed out, rattling a bag of almonds.

"Roarke knows the site best. He'll take me around to the specified locations. We'll split them up with Angelo's team."

"Do I coordinate from here?" Peabody asked.

"Not exactly. I need you to work with Mira. Make sure Skinner and his wife stay put and report if Hayes contacts them. Then there's this other thing."

"Yes, sir." Peabody looked up from her memo book.

"If we don't bag him tonight, you'll have to cover for me in the morning."

"Cover for you?"

"I've got the notes and whatever in here." Eve tossed her ppc into Peabody's lap.

"Notes?" Peabody stared at the little unit in horror. "Your seminar? Oh, no, sir. Uh-uh. Dallas, I'm not giving your seminar."

"Just think of yourself as backup," Eve suggested. "Roarke?" She walked to the door and through it, leaving Peabody sputtering.

"Just how much don't you want to give that seminar to-morrow?" Roarke wondered.

"I don't have to answer that until I've been given the revised Miranda warning." Eve rolled her shoulders and would have sworn she felt weight spilling off them. "Sometimes things just work out perfect, don't they?"

"Ask Peabody that in the morning."

With a laugh, she stepped into the elevator. "Let's go hunting."

They hit every location, even overlapping into Angelo's portion. It was a long, tedious, and exacting process. Later she would think that the operation had given her a more complete view of the scope of Roarke's pet project. The hotels, casinos, theaters, restaurants, the shops and businesses. The houses and buildings, the beaches and parks. The sheer sweep of the world he'd created was more than she'd imagined.

While impressive, it made the job at hand next to impossible.

It was after three in the morning when she gave it up for the night and stumbled to bed. "We'll find him tomorrow. His face is on every screen on-site. The minute he tries to buy any supplies, we'll tag him. He has to sleep, he has to eat."

"So do you." In bed, Roarke drew her against him. "Turn it off, Lieutenant. Tomorrow's soon enough."

"He won't go far." Her voice thickened with sleep. "He needs to finish it and get his father's praises. Legacies. Bloody legacies. I spent my life running from mine."

"I know." Roarke brushed the top of her head with his lips as she fell into sleep. "So have I."

This time it was he who dreamed, as he rarely did, of the alleyways of Dublin. Of himself, a young boy, too thin, with sharp eyes, nimble fingers, and fast feet. A belly too often empty.

The smell of garbage gone over, and whiskey gone stale, and the cold of the rain that gleefully seeped into bone.

He saw himself in one of those alleyways, staring down at his father, who lay with that garbage gone over, and smelled of that whiskey gone stale. And smelled, too, of death—the blood and the shit that spewed out of a man at his last moments. The knife had still been in his throat, and his eyes—filmed-over blue—were open and staring back at the boy he'd made.

He remembered, quite clearly, speaking.

Well now, you bastard, someone's done for ya. And here I thought it would be me one day who had the pleasure of that.

Without a qualm, he'd crouched and searched through the pockets for any coin or items that might be pawned or traded. There'd been nothing, but then again, there never had been much. He'd considered, briefly, taking the knife. But he'd liked the idea of it where it was too much to bother.

He'd stood then, at the age of twelve, with bruises still fresh and aching from the last beating those dead hands had given him.

And he'd spat. And he'd run.

He was up before she was, as usual. Eve studied him as she grabbed her first cup of coffee. It was barely seven A.M. "You look tired."

He continued to study the stock reports on one screen and the computer analysis of potential locations on another. "Do I? I suppose I could've slept better."

When she crouched in front of him, laid a hand on his thigh, he looked at her. And sighed. She could read him well enough, he thought, his cop.

Just as he could read her, and her worry for him.

"I wonder," he began, "and I don't care to, who did me

the favor of sticking that knife in him. Someone, I think, who was part of the cartel. He'd have been paid, you see, and there was nothing in his pockets. Not a fucking punt or pence on him, nor in the garbage hole we lived in. So they'd have taken it, whatever he hadn't already whored or drank or simply pissed away."

"Does it matter who?"

"Not so very much, no. But it makes me wonder." He nearly didn't say the rest, but simply having her listen soothed him. "He had my face. I forget that most times, remember that I've made myself, myself. But Christ, I have the look of him."

She slid into his lap, brushed her hands through his hair. "I don't think so." And kissed him.

"We've made each other in the end, haven't we, Darling Eve? Two lost souls into one steady unit."

"Guess we have. It's good."

He stroked his cheek against hers, and felt the fatigue wash away. "Very good."

She held on another minute, then drew back. "That's enough sloppy stuff. I've got work to do."

"When it's done, why don't we get really sloppy, you and I?"

"I can get behind that." She rose to contact Darcia and get an update on the manhunt.

"Not a sign of him anywhere," Eve told Roarke, then began to pace. "Feeney took care of transpo. Nothing's left the station. We've got him boxed in, but it's a big box with lots of angles. I need Skinner. Nobody's going to know him as well as Skinner."

"Hayes is his son," Roarke reminded her. "Do you think he'd help you?"

"Depends on how much cop is left in him. Come with

me," she said. "He needs to see us both. He needs to deal with it."

He looked haggard, Eve thought. His skin was gray and pasty. How much was grief, how much illness, she didn't know. The combination of the two, she imagined, would finish him.

But, she noted, he'd put on a suit, and he wore his precinct pin in the lapel.

He brushed aside, with some impatience, his wife's attempt to block Eve.

"Stop fussing, Belle. Lieutenant." His gaze skimmed over Roarke, but he couldn't make himself address the man. "I want you to know I've contacted my attorneys on Hayes's behalf. I believe you and Chief Angelo have made a serious error in judgment."

"No, you don't, Commander. You've been a cop too long. I appreciate the difficulty of your position, but Hayes is the prime suspect in two murders, in sabotage, in a conspiracy to implicate Roarke in those murders. He injured bystanders while fleeing and caused considerable property damage. He also fired his weapon at a police officer. He's currently evading arrest."

"There's an explanation."

"Yes, I believe there is. He's picked up his father's banner, Commander, and he's carrying it where I don't think you intended it to go. You told me yesterday no losses are acceptable. Did you mean it?"

"The pursuit of justice often . . . In the course of duty, we . . ." He looked helplessly at his wife. "Belle, I never meant— Reggie, Zita. Have I killed them?"

"No, no." She went to him quickly, wrapped her arms

around him. And he seemed to shrink into her. "It's not your fault. It's not your doing."

"If you want justice for them, Commander, help me. Where would he go? What would he do next?"

"I don't know. Do you think I haven't agonized over it through the night?"

"He hasn't slept," Belle told her. "He won't take his pain medication. He needs to rest."

"I confided in him," Skinner continued. "I shared my thoughts, my beliefs, my anger. I wanted him to carry on my mission. Not this way." Skinner sank into a chair. "Not this way, but I beat the path. I can't deny that. Your father killed for sport, for money, for the hell of it," he said to Roarke. "He didn't even know the names of the people he murdered. I look at you and see him. You grew out of him."

"I did." Roarke nodded. "And everything I've done since has been in spite of him. You can't hate him as much as I can, Commander. No matter how hard you try, you'll never reach my measure of it. But I can't live on that hate. And I'm damned if I'll die on it. Will you?"

"I've used it to keep me alive these past months." Skinner looked down at his hands. "It's ruined me. My son is a thorough man. He'll have a back door. Someone inside who'll help him gain access to the hotel. He'll need it to finish what he started."

"Assassinate Roarke?"

"No, Lieutenant. Payment would be dearer than that. It's you he'll aim for." He lifted a hand to a face that had gone clammy. "To take away what his target cherishes most."

When he hissed in pain, Eve stepped forward. "You

need medical attention, Commander. You need to be in the hospital."

"No hospitals. No health centers. Try to take him alive, Dallas. I want him to get the help he needs."

"You have to go." Belle stepped in. "He can't take any more of this."

"I'll send Dr. Mira." Even as Eve spoke, Skinner slumped in the chair.

"He's unconscious." Roarke instinctively loosened Skinner's tie. "His breathing's very shallow."

"Don't touch him! Let me—" Belle jerked back as her eyes met Roarke's. She took a long, deep breath. "I'm sorry. Could you help me, please? Take him into his bedroom. If you'd call for Dr. Mira, Lieutenant Dallas, I'd be grateful."

"His body's wearing down," Eve said once Skinner was settled in the bedroom with Mira in attendance. "Maybe it's better all around if he goes before we take Hayes."

"His body was already worn down," Roarke corrected. "But he's let go of his reason to live."

"There's nothing to do but leave him to Mira. The computer didn't think Hayes would come back to the hotel. Skinner does. I'm going with Skinner. Hayes wants me, and he knows Skinner's on borrowed time so he has to move fast." She checked her wrist unit. "Looks like I'm going to give that damn seminar after all."

"And make yourself a target?"

"With plenty of shield. We'll coordinate your security people and Angelo's and pluck him like a goose if he tries for a hit here." She started out, pulling a borrowed communicator out of her pocket.

Then drew her weapon as she saw Hayes step out of the stairway door at the end of the corridor.

"Stop!" She pounded after him when he ducked back into the stairwell. "Get to security!" Eve shouted at Roarke. "Track him!"

Roarke shoved through the door ahead of her. The weapon in his hand was illegal. "No. You track him."

Since cursing was a waste of time, she raced down the stairs with him. "Subject sighted," she called through the communicator as they streaked down the stairs. "Heading down southeast stairwell, now between floors twenty-one and twenty. Moving fast. Consider subject armed and dangerous."

She clicked the communicator off before she spoke to Roarke. "Don't kill him. Don't fire that thing unless there's no choice."

A blast hit the landing seconds before their feet. "Such as now?" Roarke commented.

But it was Eve who fired, leaning over the railing and turning the steps below into rubble. Caught in midstride, Hayes tried to swing back, bolt for the door, but his momentum skewed his balance.

He went down hard on the smoking, broken steps.

And Angelo shoved through the door, weapon gripped in both hands.

"Trying to take my collar, Dallas?"

"All yours." Eve stepped down, onto the weapon that had flown out of Hayes's hand. "Two people dead. For what?" she asked Hayes. "Was it worth it?"

His mouth and his leg were bleeding. He swiped at the blood on his chin while his eyes burned into hers. "No. I should've been more direct. I should've just blown you to hell right away and watched the bastard you fuck bleed over you. That would've been worth everything, knowing he'd live with the kind of pain his father caused. The commander could've died at peace knowing I'd found his justice. I wanted to give him more."

"Did you give Weeks or Vinter a choice?" Eve demanded. "Did you tell them they were going to die for the cause?"

"Command isn't required to explain. They honored their fathers, as I honor mine. There's no other choice."

"You signaled Weeks to move in on me, and he didn't have a clue what it was going to cost him. You had Vinter sabotage the cameras, and when she realized why, you killed her."

"They were necessary losses. Justice requires payment. You were going to be my last gift to him. You in a cage," he said to Roarke. "You in a coffin." He smiled at Eve when he said it. "Why aren't you giving your seminar, Lieutenant? Why the hell aren't you where you're scheduled to be?"

"I had a conflict of . . ." She shot to her feet. "Oh, God. Peabody."

She charged through the door and out into the corridor. "What floor? What floor?"

"This way." Roarke grabbed her hand, pulled her toward the elevator. "Down to four," he said. "We'll head left. Second door on the right takes us behind the stage area."

"Explosives. He likes explosives." She dragged out her communicator again as she willed the elevator to hurry. "She's turned hers off. Son of a bitch! Any officer, any officer, clear Conference Room D immediately. Clear the area of all personnel. Possible explosive device. Alert Explosive Division. Clear that area now!"

She was through the door and streaking to the left.

I sent her there, was all she could think. *And I smirked about it.*

Oh, God, please.

There was a roaring in her ears that was either her own rush of blood, the noise of the audience, or the shouted orders to clear.

But she spotted Peabody standing behind the podium and leaped the three steps on the side of the stage. Leaped again the minute her feet hit the ground and, hitting her aide mid-body, shot them both into the air and into a bruised and tangled heap on the floor.

She sucked in her breath, then lost it again as Roarke landed on top of her.

The explosion rang in her ears, sent the floor under her shaking. She felt the mean heat of it spew over her like a wave that sent the three of them rolling in one ball toward the far edge of the stage.

Debris rained over them, some of it flaming. Dimly she heard running feet, shouts, and the sizzling hiss of a fire.

For the second time in two days, she was drenched with the spray of overhead sprinklers.

"Are you all right?" Roarke said in her ear.

"Yeah, yeah. Peabody." Coughing, eyes stinging with smoke, Eve eased back, saw her aide's pale face, glassy eyes. "You okay?"

"Think so." She blinked. " 'Cept you've got two heads, Dallas, and one of them's Roarke's. It's the prettiest. And I think you've really gained some weight." She smiled vaguely and passed out.

"Got herself a nice concussion," Eve decided, then turned her head so her nose bumped Roarke's. "You are pretty, though. Now get the hell off me. This is seriously undignified."

"Absolutely, Lieutenant."

While the med-techs tended to Peabody, and the

Explosives Division cordoned off the scene, Eve sat outside the conference room and drank the coffee some unnamed and beloved soul had handed her.

She was soaked to the skin, filthy, had a few cuts, a medley of bruises. She figured her ears might stop ringing by Christmas.

But all in all, she felt just fine.

"You're going to have a few repairs on this dump of yours," she told Roarke.

"Just can't take you anywhere, can I?"

She smiled, then got to her feet as Darcia approached. "Hayes is in custody. He's waived his right to attorney. My opinion, he'll end up in a facility for violent offenders, mental defectives. He's not going to serve time in a standard cage. He's warped. If it's any consolation, he was very disappointed to hear you aren't splattered all over what's left of that stage in there."

"Can't always get what you want."

"Hell of a way to skate out of giving a workshop, though. Have to hand it to you."

"Whatever works."

Sobering, Darcia turned. "We beat interplanetary deadline. Thanks."

"I won't say anytime."

"I'll have a full report for your files by the end of the day," she said to Roarke. "I hope your next visit is less . . . complicated," she added.

"It was an experience watching you in action, Chief Angelo. I'm confident Olympus is in good hands."

"Count on it. You know, Dallas, you look like you could use a nice resort vacation." She shot out that brilliant smile. "See you around."

"She's got a smart mouth. I've got to admire that. I'm

going to check on Peabody," she began, then stopped when she saw Mira coming toward her.

"He's gone," Mira said simply. "He had time to say good-bye to his wife, and to ask me to tell you that he was wrong. Blood doesn't always tell. I witnessed the termination. He left life with courage and dignity. He asked me if you would stand in the way of his departmental service and burial."

"What did you tell him?"

"I told him that blood doesn't always tell. Character does. I'm going back to his wife now."

"Tell her I'm sorry for her loss, and that law enforcement has lost one of its great heroes today."

Mira leaned over to kiss Eve's cheek, smiling when Eve squirmed. "You have a good heart."

"And clear vision," Roarke added when Mira walked away.

"Clear vision?"

"To see through the dreck and the shadows to the core of the man."

"Nobody gets through life without fucking up. He gave fifty years to the badge. It wasn't all what it should've been, but it was fifty years. Anyway." She shook off sentiment. "I've got to check on Peabody."

Roarke took her hand, kissed it. "We'll go check on Peabody. Then we'll talk about that nice resort vacation."

In a pig's eye, she thought. She was going home as soon as humanly possible. The streets of New York were resort enough for her.

MIDNIGHT
IN
DEATH

The year is dying in the night.

—TENNYSON

The welfare of the people is the chief law.

—CICERO

Chapter 1

Murder respects no traditions. It ignores sentiment. It takes no holidays.

Because murder was her business, Lieutenant Eve Dallas stood in the predawn freeze of Christmas morning coating the deerskin gloves her husband had given her only hours before with Seal-It.

The call had come in less than an hour before and less than six hours since she'd closed a case that had left her shaky and exhausted. Her first Christmas with Roarke wasn't getting off to a rousing start.

Then again, it had taken a much nastier turn for Judge Harold Wainger.

His body had been dumped dead center in the ice rink at Rockefeller Center. Faceup, so his glazed eyes could stare at the huge celebrational tree that was New York's symbol of goodwill toward men.

His body was naked and already a deep shade of blue. The thick mane of silver hair that had been his trademark had been roughly chopped off. And though his face was severely battered, she had no trouble recognizing him.

She'd sat in his courtroom dozens of times in her ten years on the force. He had been, she thought, a solid and steady man, with as much understanding of the slippery channels of the law as respect for the heart of it.

She crouched down to get a closer look at the words that had been burned deeply into his chest.

JUDGE NOT, LEST YOU BE JUDGED

She hoped the burns had been inflicted postmortem, but she doubted it.

He had been mercilessly beaten, the fingers of both hands broken. Deep wounds around his wrists and ankles indicated that he'd been bound. But it hadn't been the beating or the burns that killed him.

The rope used to hang him was still around his neck, digging deep into flesh. Even that wouldn't have been quick, she decided. It didn't appear that his neck had been broken, and the burst vessels in his eyes and face signaled slow strangulation.

"He wanted you alive as long as possible," she murmured. "He wanted you to feel it all."

Kneeling now, she studied the handwritten note that was flapping gaily in the wind. It had been fixed over the judge's groin like an obscene loincloth. The list of names had been printed in careful square block letters.

JUDGE HAROLD WAINGER
PROSECUTING ATTORNEY STEPHANIE RING
PUBLIC DEFENDER CARL NEISSAN
JUSTINE POLINSKY

DOCTOR CHARLOTTE MIRA
LIEUTENANT EVE DALLAS

"Saving me for last, Dave?"

She recognized the style: gleeful infliction of pain followed by a slow, torturous death. David Palmer enjoyed his
work. His experiments, as he'd called them when Eve had
finally hunted him down three years before.

By the time she'd gotten him into a cage, he had eight
victims to his credit, and with them an extensive file of
discs recording his work. Since then he'd been serving the
eight life-term sentences that Wainger had given him in a
maximum-security ward for mental defectives.

"But you got out, didn't you, Dave? This is your handi-
work. The torture, the humiliations, the burns. Public
dumping spot for the body. No copycat here. Bag him," she
ordered and got wearily to her feet.

It didn't look as though the last days of December 2058
were going to be much of a party.

The minute she was back in her vehicle, Eve ordered the
heat on full blast. She stripped off her gloves and rubbed her
hands over her face. She would have to go in and file her report, but the first order of business couldn't wait for her to
drive to her home office. Damn if she was going to spend
Christmas Day at Cop Central.

She used the in-dash 'link to contact Dispatch and
arrange to have each name on the list notified of possible
jeopardy. Christmas or not, she was ordering uniformed
guards on each one.

As she drove, she engaged her computer. "Computer,
status on David Palmer, mental-defective inmate at Rexal
penal facility."

Working. . . . David Palmer, sentenced to eight consecutive life terms in off-planet facility Rexal reported escaped during transport to prison infirmary, December nineteen. Manhunt ongoing.

"I guess Dave decided to come home for the holidays." She glanced up, scowling, as a blimp cruised over, blasting Christmas tunes as dawn broke over the city. Screw the herald angels, she thought, and called her commander.

"Sir," she said when Whitney's face filled her screen. "I'm sorry to disturb your Christmas."

"I've already been notified about Judge Wainger. He was a good man."

"Yes, sir, he was." She noted that Whitney was wearing a robe—a thick, rich burgundy that she imagined had been a gift from his wife. Roarke was always giving her fancy presents. She wondered if Whitney was as baffled by them as she usually was. "His body's being transferred to the morgue. I have the evidence sealed and am en route to my home office now."

"I would have preferred another primary on this, Lieutenant." He saw her tired eyes flash, the golden brown darkening. Still, her face, with its sharp angles, the firm chin with its shallow dent, the full, unsmiling mouth, stayed cool and controlled.

"Do you intend to remove me from the case?"

"You've just come off a difficult and demanding investigation. Your aide was attacked."

"I'm not calling Peabody in," Eve said quickly. "She's had enough."

"And you haven't?"

She opened her mouth, closed it again. Tricky ground, she acknowledged. "Commander, my name's on the list."

"Exactly. One more reason for you to take a pass here."

Part of her wanted to—the part that wanted, badly, to

put it all aside for the day, to go home and have the kind of normal Christmas she'd never experienced. But she thought of Wainger, stripped of all life and all dignity.

"I tracked David Palmer, and I broke him. He was my collar, and no one knows the inside of his mind the way I do."

"Palmer?" Whitney's wide brow furrowed. "Palmer's in prison."

"Not anymore. He escaped on the nineteenth. And he's back, Commander. You could say I recognized his signature. The names on the list," she continued, pressing her point. "They're all connected to him. Wainger was the judge during his trial. Stephanie Ring was APA. Cicely Towers prosecuted the case, but she's dead. Ring assisted. Carl Neissan was his court-appointed attorney when Palmer refused to hire his own counsel, Justine Polinksy served as jury foreman. Dr. Mira tested him and testified against him at trial. I brought him in."

"The names on the list need to be notified."

"Already done, sir, and bodyguards assigned. I can pull the data from the files into my home unit to refresh my memory, but it's fairly fresh as it is. You don't forget someone like David Palmer. Another primary will have to start at the beginning, taking time that we don't have. I know this man, how he works, how he thinks. What he wants."

"What he wants, Lieutenant?"

"What he always wanted. Acknowledgment for his genius."

"It's your case, Dallas," Whitney said after a long silence. "Close it."

"Yes, sir."

She broke transmission as she drove through the gates of the staggering estate that Roarke had made his home.

Ice from the previous night's storm glinted like silver silk on naked branches. Ornamental shrubs and evergreens glistened with it. Beyond them, the house rose and spread, an elegant fortress, a testament to an earlier century with its beautiful stone, its acres of glass.

In the gloomy half-light of morning, gorgeously decorated trees shimmered in several windows. Roarke, she thought with a little smile, had gotten heavily into the Christmas spirit.

Neither of them had had much in the way of pretty holiday trees with gaily wrapped gifts stacked under them in their lives. Their childhoods had been miseries, and they had compensated for it in different ways. His had been to acquire, to become one of the richest and most powerful men in the world. By whatever means available. Hers had been to take control, to become part of the system that had failed her when she was a child.

Hers was law. His was—or had been—circumventing law.

Now, not quite a year since another murder had put them on the same ground, they were a unit. She wondered if she would ever understand how they'd managed it.

She left her car out front, walked up the steps and through the door into the kind of wealth that fantasies were made of. Old polished wood, sparkling crystal, ancient rugs lovingly preserved, art that museums would have wept for.

She shrugged off her jacket, started to toss it over the newel post. Then, gritting her teeth, she backtracked and hung it up. She and Summerset, Roarke's aide-de-camp, had declared a tacit truce in their sniping war. There would be no potshots on Christmas, she decided.

She could stand it if he could.

Only marginally pleased that he didn't slither into the foyer and hiss at her as he normally did, Eve headed into the main parlor.

Roarke was there, sitting by the fire, reading the first-edition copy of Yeats that she'd given him. It had been the only gift she'd been able to come up with for the man who not only had everything but owned most of the plants where it was manufactured.

He glanced up, smiled at her. Her stomach fluttered, as it so often did. Just a look, just a smile, and her system went jittery. He looked so . . . perfect, she thought. He was dressed casually for the day, in black, his long, lean body relaxing in a chair probably made two hundred years before.

He had the face of a god with slightly wicked intentions, eyes of blazing Irish blue and a mouth created to destroy a woman's control. Power sat attractively on him, as sleek and sexy, Eve thought, as the rich fall of black hair that skimmed nearly to his shoulders.

He closed the book, set it aside, then held out a hand to her.

"I'm sorry I had to leave." She crossed to him, linked her fingers with his. "I'm sorrier that I'm going to have to go up and work, at least for a few hours."

"Got a minute first?"

"Yeah, maybe. Just." And she let him pull her down into his lap. Let herself close her eyes and simply wallow there, in the scent and the feel of him. "Not exactly the kind of day you'd planned."

"That's what I get for marrying a cop." Ireland sang quietly in his voice, the lilt of a sexy poet. "For loving one," he added, and tipped her face up to kiss her.

"It's a pretty lousy deal right now."

"Not from where I'm sitting." He combed his fingers through her short brown hair. "You're what I want, Eve, the woman who leaves her home to stand over the dead. And the one who knew what a copy of Yeats would mean to me."

"I'm better with the dead than with buying presents. Otherwise I'd have come up with more than one."

She looked over at the small mountain of gifts under the tree—gifts it had taken her more than an hour to open. And her wince made him laugh.

"You know, one of the greatest rewards in giving you presents, Lieutenant, is the baffled embarrassment they cause you."

"I hope you got it out of your system for a while."

"Mmm," was his only response. She wasn't used to gifts, he thought, hadn't been given anything as a child but pain. "Have you decided what to do with the last one?"

The final box he'd given her had been empty, and he'd enjoyed seeing her frown in puzzlement. Just as he'd enjoyed seeing her grin at him when he told her it was a day. A day she could fill with whatever she liked. He would take her wherever she wanted to go, and they would do whatever she wanted to do. Off-planet or on. In reality or through the holo-room.

Any time, any place, any world was hers for the asking.

"No, I haven't had much time to think it through. It's a pretty great gift. I don't want to screw it up."

She let herself relax against him another moment with the fire crackling, the tree shimmering, then she pulled back. "I've got to get started. There's a lot of drone work on this one, and I don't want to tag Peabody today."

"Why don't I give you a hand?" He smiled again at the automatic refusal he read in her eyes. "Step into Peabody's sturdy shoes for the day."

"This one's not connected to you in any way. I want to keep it that way."

"All the better." He nudged her up, got to his feet. "I can help you do the runs or whatever, and that way you won't have to spend your entire Christmas chained to your desk."

She started to refuse again, then reconsidered. Most of the data she wanted were public domain in any case. And what wasn't was nothing she wouldn't have shared with him if she'd been thinking it through aloud.

Besides, he was good.

"Okay, consider yourself a drone. But when Peabody's got her balance, you're out."

"Darling." He took her hand, kissed it, watched her scowl. "Since you ask so sweetly."

"And no sloppy stuff," she put in. "I'm on duty."

Chapter 2

The huge cat, Galahad, was draped over the back of Eve's sleep chair like a drunk over a bar at last call. Since he'd spent several hours the night before attacking boxes, fighting with ribbon, and murdering discarded wrapping paper, she left him where he was so he could sleep it off.

Eve set down her bag and went directly to the AutoChef for coffee. "The guy we're after is David Palmer."

"You've already identified the killer."

"Oh, yeah, I know who I'm after. Me and Dave, we're old pals."

Roarke took the mug she brought him, watched her through the steam. "The name's vaguely familiar to me."

"You'd have heard it. It was all over the media three, three and a half years ago. I need all my case files on that investigation, all data on the trial. You can start by—" She broke off when he laid a hand on her arm.

"David Palmer—serial killer. Torture murders." It was

playing back for him, in bits and pieces. "Fairly young. What—mid-twenties?"

"Twenty-two at time of arrest. A real prodigy, our Dave. He considers himself a scientist, a visionary. His mission is to explore and record the human mind's tolerance to extreme duress—pain, fear, starvation, dehydration, sensory deprivation. He could talk a good game, too." She sipped her coffee. "He'd sit there in interview, his pretty face all lit with enthusiasm, and explain that once we knew the mind's breaking point, we'd be able to enhance it, to strengthen it. He figured since I was a cop, I'd be particularly interested in his work. Cops are under a great deal of stress, often finding ourselves in life-and-death situations where the mind is easily distracted by fear or outside stimuli. The results of his work could be applied to members of the police and security forces, the military, even in business situations."

"I didn't realize he was yours."

"Yeah, he was mine." She shrugged her shoulders. "I was a little more low profile in those days."

He might have smiled at that, knowing it was partially her connection to him that had changed that status. But he remembered too much of the Palmer case to find the humor. "I was under the impression that he was safely locked away."

"Not safely enough. He slipped out. The victim this morning was dumped in a public area—another of Dave's trademarks. He likes us to know he's hard at work. The autopsy will have to verify, but the victim was tortured premortem. I'd guess Dave found himself a new hole to work in and had the judge there at least a day before killing him. Death by strangulation occurred on or around midnight. Merry Christmas, Judge Wainger," she murmured.

"And that would be the judge who tried his case."

"Yeah." Absently, she put her mug down, reached into her bag for a copy of the sealed note she'd already sent to the lab. "He left a calling card—another signature. All these names are connected to his case and his sentencing. Part of his work this time around would be, at my guess, letting his intended victims stew about what he has in store for them. They're being contacted and protected. He'll have a tough time getting to any of them."

"And you?" Roarke spoke with studied calm after a glance at the list, and his wife's name. "Where's your protection?"

"I'm a cop. I'm the one who does the protecting."

"He'll want you most, Eve."

She turned. However controlled his voice was, she heard the anger under it. "Maybe, but not as much as I want him."

"You stopped him," Roarke continued. "Whatever was done after—the tests, the trial, the sentence—was all a result of your work. You'll matter most."

"Let's leave those conclusions to the profiler." Though she agreed with them. "I'm going to contact Mira as soon as I look through the case files again. You can access those for me while I start my prelim report. I'll give you the codes for my office unit and the Palmer files."

Now he lifted a brow, smiled smugly. "Please. I can't work if you insult me."

"Sorry." She picked up her coffee again. "I don't know why I pretend you need codes to access any damn thing."

"Neither do I."

He sat down to retrieve the data she wanted, moving smoothly through the task. It was pitifully simple for him, and his mind was left free to consider. To decide.

She'd said he wasn't connected to this, and that she expected him to back away when Peabody was on duty again. But she was wrong. Her name on the list meant he was more involved than he'd ever been before. And no power on earth, not even that of the woman he loved, would cause him to back away.

Close by, Eve worked on the auxiliary unit, recording the stark facts into the report. She wanted the autopsy results, the crime scene team and sweeper data. But she had little hope that she would get anything from the spotty holiday staff before the end of the next day.

Struggling not to let her irritation with Christmas resurface, she answered her beeping 'link. "Dallas."

"Lieutenant, Officer Miller here."

"What is it, Miller?"

"Sir, my partner and I were assigned to contact and guard APA Ring. We arrived at her residence shortly after seven-thirty. There was no response to our knock."

"This is a priority situation, Miller. You're authorized to enter the premises."

"Yes, sir. Understood. We did so. The subject is not in residence. My partner questioned the across-the-hall neighbor. The subject left early yesterday morning to spend the holiday with her family in Philadelphia. Lieutenant, she never arrived. Her father reported her missing this morning."

Eve's stomach tightened. Too late, she thought. Already too late. "What was her method of transpo, Miller?"

"She had her own car. We're en route to the garage where she stored it."

"Keep me posted, Miller." Eve broke transmission, looked over, and met Roarke's eyes. "He's got her. I'd like to think she ran into some road hazard or hired a licensed companion for a quick holiday fling before heading on to her family, but he's got her. I need the 'link codes for the other names on the list."

"You'll have them. One minute."

She didn't need the code for one of the names. With her heart beating painfully, she put the call through to Mira's home. A small boy answered with a grin and a giggle. "Merry Christmas! This is Grandmom's house."

For a moment Eve just blinked, wondering how she'd gotten the wrong code. Then she heard the familiar soft voice in the background, saw Mira come on screen with a smile on her face and strain in her eyes.

"Eve. Good morning. Would you hold for a moment, please? I'd like to take this upstairs. No, sweetie," she said to the boy who tugged on her sleeve. "Run play with your new toys. I'll be back. Just a moment, Eve."

The screen went to a calm, cool blue, and Eve exhaled gratefully. Relief at finding Mira home, alive, well, safe— and the oddity of thinking of the composed psychiatrist as Grandmom played through her mind.

"I'm sorry." Mira came back on. "I didn't want to take this downstairs with my family."

"No problem. Are the uniforms there?"

"Yes." In a rare show of nerves, Mira pushed a hand through her sable-toned hair. "Miserable duty for them, sitting out in a car on Christmas. I haven't figured out how to have them inside and keep my family from knowing. My children are here, Eve, my grandchildren. I need to know if you believe there's any chance they're in danger."

"No." She said it quick and firm. "That's not his style. Dr. Mira, you're not to leave the house without your guards. You're to go nowhere, not the office, not the corner deli, without both of them. Tomorrow you'll be fitted for a tracer bracelet."

"I'll take all the precautions, Eve."

"Good, because one of those precautions is to cancel all patient appointments until Palmer is in custody."

"That's ridiculous."

"You're to be alone with no one, at any time. So unless your patients agree to let you walk around in their heads while a couple of cops are looking on, you're taking a vacation."

Mira eyed Eve steadily. "And are you about to take a vacation?"

"I'm about to do my job. Part of that job is you. Stephanie Ring is missing." She waited, one beat only, for the implication to register. "Do what you're told, Dr. Mira, or you'll be in protective custody within the hour. I'll need a consult tomorrow, nine o'clock. I'll come to you."

She broke transmission, turned to get the 'link codes from Roarke, and found him watching her steadily. "What?"

"She means a great deal to you. If she meant less, you'd have handled that with more finesse."

"I don't have much finesse at the best of times. Let's have the codes." When he hesitated, she sighed and replied, "Okay, okay, fine. She means a lot, and I'll be damned if he'll get within a mile of her. Now give me the goddamn codes."

"Already transferred to your unit, Lieutenant. Logged in, on memory. You've only to state the name of the party for transmission."

"Show-off." She muttered it, knowing it would make him grin, and turned back to contact the rest of the names on Palmer's list.

When she was satisfied that the other targets were where they were supposed to be, and under guard, Eve turned to the case files Roarke had accessed.

She spent an hour going over data and reports, another reviewing her interview discs with Palmer.

Okay, Dave, tell me about Michelle Hammel. What made her special?

David Palmer, a well-built man of twenty-two with the golden good looks of the wealthy New England family he'd sprung from, smiled and leaned forward earnestly. His clear blue eyes were bright with enthusiasm. His caramel-cream complexion glowed with health and vitality.

Somebody's finally listening, Eve remembered thinking as she saw herself as she'd been three years before. He's finally got the chance to share his genius.

Her hair was badly cut—she'd still been hacking at it herself in those days. The boots crossed at her ankles had been new then and almost unscarred. There was no wedding ring on her finger.

Otherwise, she thought, she was the same.

She was young, fit. An athlete, Palmer told her. *Very disciplined, mind and body. A long-distance runner—Olympic hopeful. She knew how to block pain, how to focus on a goal. She'd be at the top end of the scale, you see. Just as Leroy Greene was at the bottom. He'd fogged his mind with illegals for years. No tolerance for disruptive stimuli. He lost all control even before the application of pain. His mind broke as soon as he regained consciousness and found himself strapped to the table. But Michelle . . .*

She fought? She held out?

Palmer nodded cheerfully. *She was magnificent, really. She struggled against the restraints, then stopped when she understood that she wouldn't be able to free herself. There was fear. The monitors registered her rise in pulse rate, blood pressure, all vital physical and emotional signs. I have excellent equipment.*

Yeah, I've seen it. Top of the line.

It's vital work. His eyes had clouded then, unfocused as they did when he spoke of the import of his experiments. *You'll see if you review the data on Michelle that she centered her fear, used it to keep herself alive. She controlled it, initially, tried to reason with me. She made promises, she pretended to understand my research, even to help me. She was clever. When she understood that wouldn't help her, she cursed me, pumping up her adrenaline as I introduced new pain stimuli.*

"He broke her feet," Eve said, knowing Roarke was watching behind her. "Then her arms. He was right about his equipment back then. He had electrodes that when attached to different parts of the body, or placed in various orifices, administered graduating levels of electric shock. He kept Michelle alive for three days until the torture broke her. She was begging for him to kill her toward the end. He used a rope and pulley system to hang her— gradual strangulation. She was nineteen."

Roarke laid his hands on her shoulders. "You stopped him once, Eve, you'll stop him again."

"Damn right I will."

She looked up when she heard someone coming quickly down the corridor. "Save data, and file," she ordered just as Nadine Furst came into the room. Perfect, she thought, a visit from one of Channel 75's top on-air reporters. The fact that they were friends didn't make Eve any less wary.

"Out paying Christmas calls, Nadine?"

"I got a present this morning." Nadine tossed a disc on the desk.

Eve looked at it, then back up at Nadine's face. It was pale, the sharp features drawn. For once, Nadine wasn't perfectly groomed with lip dye, enhancers, and every hair in place. She looked more than frazzled, Eve realized. She looked afraid.

"What's the problem?"

"David Palmer."

Slowly Eve got to her feet. "What about him?"

"Apparently he knows what I do for a living, and that we're friendly. He sent me that." She glanced back down at the disc, struggled to suppress a shudder. "Hoping I'd do a feature story on him—and his work—and share the contents of his disc with you. Can I have a drink? Something strong."

Roarke came around the desk and eased her into a chair. "Sit down. You're cold," he murmured when he took her hands.

"Yeah, I am. I've been cold ever since I ran that disc."

"I'll get you a brandy."

Nadine nodded in agreement, then fisted her hands in her lap and looked at Eve. "There are two other people on the recording. One of them is Judge Wainger. What's left of Judge Wainger. And there's a woman, but I can't recognize her. She's— He's already started on her."

"Here." Roarke brought the snifter, gently wrapped Nadine's hands around the bowl. "Drink this."

"Okay." She lifted the glass, took one long sip, and felt the blast of heat explode in her gut. "Dallas, I've seen a lot of bad things. I've reported them, I've studied them. But I've never seen anything like this. I don't know how you deal with it, day after day."

"One day at a time." Eve picked up the disc. "You don't have to watch this again."

"Yes." Nadine drank again, let out a long breath. "I do."

Eve turned the disc over in her hand. It was a standard-use model. They'd never trace it. She slid it into her unit. "Copy disc and run, display on screen."

David Palmer's youthful and handsome face swam onto the wall screen.

"Ms. Furst, or may I call you Nadine? So much more personal that way, and my work is very personal to me. I've admired your work, by the way. It's one of the reasons I'm trusting you to get my story on air. You believe in what you do, don't you, Nadine?"

His eyes were serious now, professional to professional, his face holding all the youth and innocence of a novitiate at the altar. "Those of us who reach for perfection believe in what we do," he continued. "I'm aware that you have a friendly relationship with Lieutenant Dallas. The lieutenant and I also have a relationship, perhaps not so friendly, but we do connect, and I do admire her stamina. I hope you'll share the contents of this disc with her as soon as possible. By this time she should already be heading the investigation into the death of Judge Wainger."

His smile went bright now, and just a little mad at the edges. "Hello, Lieutenant. You'll excuse me if I just conclude my business with Nadine. I want Dallas to be closely involved. It's important to me. You will tell my story, won't you, Nadine? Let the public themselves judge, not some narrow-minded fool in a black robe."

The next scene slipped seamlessly into place, the audio high so that the woman's screams seemed to rip the air in the room where Eve sat, watching.

Judge Wainger's body was bound hand and foot and suspended several inches from a plain concrete floor. A basic pulley system this time, Eve mused. He'd taken time to set up some of the niceties, but it wasn't yet the complex, and yes, ingenious, system of torture that he'd created before.

Still, he worked very well.

Wainger's face was livid with agony, the muscles

twitching as Palmer burned letters in his chest with a hand laser. He only moaned, his head lolling. Nearby, a system of monitors beeped and buzzed.

"He's failing, you see," Palmer said briskly in a voice-over. "His mind is moving beyond the pain, as it can no longer endure it. His system will attempt to shut down into unconsciousness. That can be reversed, as you'll see here." On screen, he flipped a switch. There was a high whine, then Wainger's body jerked. This time he screamed.

Across the room a woman shrieked and sobbed. The cage she was in swung wildly on its cable and was only big enough to allow her to crouch on hands and knees. A dark fall of hair covered most of her face, but Eve knew her.

Stephanie Ring was Palmer's.

When he turned, engaged another control, the cage sparked and shook. The woman let out a piercing wail, shuddered convulsively, then collapsed.

Palmer turned to the camera, smiled. "She's distracting, but I have only so much time. It's necessary to begin one subject before completing work on another. But her turn will come shortly. Subject Wainger's heart is failing. The data on him are nearly complete."

Using the ropes, he manually lowered Wainger to the floor. Eve noted the flex and bunch of muscles in Palmer's arms. "Dave's been pumping," she murmured. "Getting in shape. He knew he'd have to work harder this round. He likes to prepare."

Palmer slipped a perfectly knotted noose around Wainger's neck and meticulously slid the trailing end through a metal ring in the ceiling. Leading it down, he threaded it through another ring in the floor, then pulled out the slack until Wainger rose to his knees, then his feet, and began gasping for air.

"Stop it, will you?" Nadine leapt to her feet. "I can't watch this again. I thought I could. I can't."

"Stop disc." Eve waited until the screen went blank, then went over to crouch in front of Nadine. "I'm sorry."

"No. I'm sorry. I thought I was tough."

"You are. Nobody's this tough."

Nadine shook her head and, finishing her brandy with one deep gulp, set the snifter aside. "You are. You don't let it get to you."

"It gets to me. But this is for me. I'm going to have a couple of uniforms come and take you home. They're going to hang with you everywhere until Palmer's down."

"You think he'll come after me?"

"No, but why take chances? Go home, Nadine. Put it away."

But after she'd asked Roarke to take Nadine downstairs to wait for the escort, Eve finished watching the disc. And at the end her eyes met Palmer's as he moved toward the camera.

"Subject Wainger died at midnight, December twenty-fourth. You'll last longer, Dallas. We both know that. You'll be my most fascinating subject. I have such wonders planned for you. You'll find me. I know you will. I'm counting on it. Happy holidays."

Chapter 3

Stephanie Ring's car was still in its permit slot in the garage. Her luggage was neatly stowed in the trunk. Eve circled the vehicle, searching for any sign of struggle, any evidence that might have been dropped and gone unnoticed during the snatch.

"He's got two basic MOs," she said, as much to herself as to the uniforms waiting nearby. "One is to gain entrance into the victims' homes by a ruse—delivery, repair, or service con; the other is to come on them in an unpopulated area. He spends time getting to know their routines and habits, the usual routes and schedules. He keeps all that in a log—very organized, scientific, along with bio data on each of them."

They weren't lab rats to him, she mused. It was personal, individualized. That was what excited him.

"In either case," she went on, "he uses a stunner, takes them down quickly, then transports them in his own vehicle. Security cameras operational in here?"

"Yes, sir." One of the uniforms passed her a sealed package of discs. "We confiscated them for the last three days, assuming that the subject may have stalked the victim previous to her abduction."

Eve lifted a brow. "Miller, right?"

"Sir."

"Good thinking. There's nothing more you can do here. Go home and eat some goose."

They didn't exactly race away, but neither did they linger. Eve put the package in her bag and turned to Roarke. "Why don't you do the same, pal? I'll only be a couple of hours."

"We'll only be a couple of hours."

"I don't need an aide to do a pass through Ring's apartment."

Roarke simply took her arm and led her back to the car. "You let the two uniforms go," he began as he started the engine. "Everyone else on Palmer's list is under guard. Why aren't you?"

"We covered that already."

"Partially." He reversed and headed out of the garage. "But I know you, Lieutenant. You're hoping he'll shuffle the order and come after you next. And you don't want some big-shouldered uniforms scaring him off."

For a moment she just drummed her fingers on her knee. In less than a year, the man had learned her inside and out. She wasn't entirely comfortable with that. "And your point would be?"

He nearly smiled at the annoyance in her voice. "I admire my wife's courage, her dedication to duty."

"You tossed in 'my wife' to irritate me, didn't you?"

"Of course." Satisfied, he picked up her hand, kissed the knuckles. "I'm sticking, Eve. Deal with it."

* * *

The pass through Stephanie Ring's apartment was no more than routine, and it turned up nothing but the tidy life of a single career woman who enjoyed surrounding herself with attractive things, spending her city salary on a stylish wardrobe.

Eve thought of the naked woman crouched like an animal in a cage, screaming in terror.

He's killing her now. Eve knew it. And she had no power to stop him.

When she was back in her home office, she reviewed the disc Palmer had sent Nadine. This time she willed herself to ignore what was happening and focus only on the surroundings.

"No windows," she commented. "The floor and walls look like concrete and old brick. The whole area can't be over thirty feet by twenty. It's probably a basement. Computer, pause. Enhance sector eight through fifteen. Magnify."

She paced as the computer went to work, then moved closer to the screen. "There, that's a stair tread. Steps, part of a railing. Behind it is some sort of—what is it—old furnace unit or water tank. He's found himself a hole. It has to be private," she continued, studying the view. "He can't do his work in a building where people might hear. Even if it's soundproofed, he'd risk someone poking around. Maintenance crew, repair team. Anything like that."

"Not an apartment or office building," Roarke agreed. "And with the steps it's not likely a storage facility. From the look of the furnace, it's a good-sized building, but far from new. Nothing built in the last fifteen or twenty years would have had a tank furnace installed. He'd want something in the city, wouldn't he?"

"Yeah, he'd want to be close to all of his marks. He wouldn't go for the 'burbs, and even the boroughs aren't likely. Dave's a true urbanite and New York's his turf. Private home. Has to be. But how did he get his hands on a private residence?"

"Friends?" Roarke suggested. "Family?"

"Palmer didn't have a tight circle of friends. He's a loner. He has parents. They relocated after the trial. Went under the Victim and Survivor's Protection Act."

"Sealed files."

She heard the faintest trace of humor in his voice, turned to scowl at him. For a moment she wrestled with procedure. She could get clearance to access the Palmers' location. And it would take at least two days to hack through the red tape for authorization. Or she could hand the problem to Roarke and have what she needed in minutes.

She could hear Stephanie Ring's screams echoing in her head.

"You'll have to use the unregistered equipment. Compu-Guard will have an automatic block on their file."

"It won't take long."

"I'm going to keep working on this." She gestured toward the screen. "He might have slipped up just enough to have let something identifiable come through."

"All right." But he crossed to her, framed her face in his hands. Lowering his head, he kissed her, long and slow and deep. And felt, as he did, some of the rigid tension in her body ease.

"I can handle this, Roarke."

"Whether you can or not, you will. Would it hurt to hold on to me, just for a minute?"

"Guess not." She slipped her arms around him, felt the familiar lines, the familiar warmth. Her grip tightened.

"Why wasn't it enough to stop him once? Why wasn't it enough to put him away? What good is it if you do your job and it comes back this way?"

He held her and said nothing.

"He wants to show me he can do it all again. He wants to take me through all the steps and stages, the way he did before. Only this time as they're happening. 'Look how clever I am, Dallas.'"

"Knowing that, understanding that, will help you stop him a second time."

"Yeah." She eased back. "Get me the data so I can hammer at his parents."

Roarke skimmed a finger over the dent in her chin. "You'll let me watch, won't you. It's so stimulating to see you browbeat witnesses."

When she laughed, as he'd hoped she would, he went to his private room to circumvent CompuGuard and officially sealed files.

She'd barely had time to review another section of the recording before he came back.

"It couldn't have been that easy."

"Yes." He smiled and passed her a new data disc. "It could. Thomas and Helen Palmer, now known as Thomas and Helen Smith—which shows just how imaginative bureaucrats can be, currently reside in a small town called Leesboro in rural Pennsylvania."

"Pennsylvania." Eve glanced toward her 'link, considered, then looked back at Roarke. "It wouldn't take long to get there if you had access to some slick transpo."

Roarke looked amused. "Which slick transpo would you prefer, Lieutenant?"

"That mini-jet of yours would get us there in under an hour."

"Then why don't we get started?"

If Eve had been more fond of heights, she might have enjoyed the fast, smooth flight south. As it was, she sat, jiggling a foot to relieve a case of nerves while Roarke piloted them over what she imagined some would consider a picturesque range of mountains.

To her they were just rocks, and the fields between them just dirt.

"I'm only going to say this once," she began. "And only because it's Christmas."

"Banking for landing," he warned her as he approached the private airstrip. "What are you only going to say once?"

"That maybe all these toys of yours aren't a complete waste of time. Overindulgent, maybe, but not a complete waste of time."

"Darling, I'm touched."

Once they were on the ground, they transferred from the snazzy little two-person jet to the car that Roarke had waiting. Of course, it couldn't be a normal vehicle, Eve mused as she studied it. It was a sleek black bullet of a car, built for style and speed.

"I'll drive." She held out a hand for the keycode the attendant had given him. "You navigate."

Roarke considered her as he tossed the code in his hand. "Why?"

"Because I'm the one with the badge." She snatched the code on its upward are and smirked at him.

"I'm a better driver."

She snorted as they climbed in. "You like to hotdog. That doesn't make you better. Strap in, ace. I'm in a hurry."

She punched it and sent them flying away from the

terminal and onto a winding rural road that was lined with snow-laced trees and sheer rock.

Roarke programmed their destination and studied the route offered by the onboard computer. "Follow this road for two miles, turn left for another ten point three, then next left for five point eight."

By the time he'd finished, she was already making the first left. She spotted a narrow creek, water fighting its way through ice, over rock. A scatter of houses, trees climbing steeply up hills, a few children playing with new airskates or boards in snow-covered yards.

"Why do people live in places like this? There's nothing here. You see all that sky?" she asked Roarke. "You shouldn't be able to see that much sky from down here. It can't be good for you. And where do they eat? We haven't passed a single restaurant, glide cart, deli, nothing."

"Cozily?" Roarke suggested. "Around the kitchen table."

"All the time? Jesus." She shuddered.

He laughed, smoothed a finger over her hair. "Eve, I adore you."

"Right." She tapped the brakes to make the next turn. "What am I looking for?"

"Third house on the right. There, that two-story prefab, mini-truck in the drive."

She slowed, scanning the house as she turned in behind the truck. There were Christmas lights along the eaves, a wreath on the door, and the outline of a decorated tree behind the front window.

"No point in asking you to wait in the car, I guess."

"None," he agreed and got out.

"They're not going to be happy to see me," Eve warned him as they crossed the shoveled walk to the front door. "If they refuse to talk to me, I'm going to give them some hard shoves. If it comes down to it, you just follow the lead."

She pressed the buzzer, shivered.

"You should have worn the coat I gave you. Cashmere's warm."

"I'm not wearing that on duty." It was gorgeous, she thought. And made her feel soft. It wasn't the sort of thing that worked for a cop.

And when the door opened, Eve was all cop.

Helen Palmer had changed her hair and her eyes. Subtle differences in shades and shapes, but enough to alter her looks. It was still a pretty face, very much like her son's. Her automatic smile of greeting faded as she recognized Eve.

"You remember me, Mrs. Palmer?"

"What are you doing here?" Helen put a hand high on the doorjamb as if to block it. "How did you find us? We're under protection."

"I don't intend to violate that. I have a crisis situation. You'd have been informed that your son has escaped from prison."

Helen pressed her lips together, hunched her shoulders as a defense against the cold that whipped through the open door. "They said they were looking for him, assured us that they'd have him back in custody, back in treatment very soon. He isn't here. He doesn't know where we are."

"Can I come in, Mrs. Palmer?"

"Why do you have to rake this all up again?" Tears swam into her eyes, seeming as much from frustration as grief. "My husband and I are just getting our lives back. We've had no contact with David in nearly three years."

"Honey? Who's at the door? You're letting the cold in." A tall man with a dark sweep of hair came smiling to the door. He wore an old cardigan sweater and ancient jeans with a pair of obviously new slippers. He blinked once, twice, then laid his hand on his wife's shoulder. "Lieutenant. Lieutenant Dallas, isn't it?"

"Yes, Mr. Palmer. I'm sorry to disturb you."

"Let them in, Helen."

"Oh, God, Tom."

"Let them in." His fingers rubbed over her shoulder before he drew her back. "You must be Roarke." Tom worked up what nearly passed for a smile as he offered Roarke his hand. "I recognize you. Please come in and sit down."

"Tom, please—"

"Why don't you make some coffee?" He turned and pressed his lips to his wife's brow. He murmured something to her, and she let out a shuddering breath and nodded.

"I'll make this as quick as I can, Mr. Palmer," Eve told him, as Helen walked quickly down a central hallway.

"You dealt very fairly with us during an unbearable time, Lieutenant." He showed them into a small living area. "I haven't forgotten that. Helen—my wife's been on edge all day. For several days," he corrected himself. "Since we were informed that David escaped. We've worked very hard to keep that out of the center, but . . ."

He gestured helplessly and sat down.

Eve remembered these decent people very well, their shock and grief over what their son was. They had raised him with love, with discipline, with care, and still they had been faced with a monster.

There had been no abuse, no cruelty, no underlying gruel for that monster to feed on. Mira's testing and analysis had corroborated Eve's impression of a normal couple who'd given their only child their affection and the monetary and social advantages that had been at their disposal.

"I don't have good news for you, Mr. Palmer. I don't have easy news."

He folded his hands in his lap. "He's dead."

"No."

Tom closed his eyes. "God help me. I'd hoped—I'd actually hoped he was." He got up quickly when he heard his wife coming back. "Here, I'll take that." He bent to take the tray she carried. "We'll get through this, Helen."

"I know. I know we will." She came in, sat, busied herself pouring the coffee she'd made. "Lieutenant, do you think David's come back to New York?"

"We know he has." She hesitated, then decided they would hear the news soon enough through the media. "Early this morning the body of Judge Wainger was found in Rockefeller Plaza. It's David's work," she continued as Helen moaned. "He's contacted me, with proof. There's no doubt of it."

"He was supposed to be given treatment. Kept away from people so he couldn't hurt them, hurt himself."

"Sometimes the system fails, Mrs. Palmer. Sometimes you can do everything right, and it just fails."

Helen rose, walked to the window, and stood looking out. "You said something like that to me before. To us. That we'd done everything right, everything we could. That it was something in David that had failed. That was kind of you, Lieutenant, but you can't know what it's like, you can't know how it feels to know that a monster has come from you."

No, Eve thought, but she knew what it was to come from a monster, to have been raised by one for the first eight years of her life. And she lived with it.

"I need your help," she said instead. "I need you to tell

me if you have any idea where he might go, who he might go to. He has a place," she continued. "A private place where he can work. A house, a small building somewhere in New York. In the city or very close by."

"He has nowhere." Tom lifted his hands. "We sold everything when we relocated. Our home, my business, Helen's. Even our holiday place in the Hamptons. We cut all ties. The house where David—where he lived that last year—was sold as well. We live quietly here, simply. The money we'd accumulated, the money from the sales is sitting in an account. We haven't had the heart to . . . we don't need it."

"He had money of his own," Eve prompted.

"Yes, inheritance, a trust fund. It was how he financed what he was doing." Tom reached out a hand for his wife's and clasped her fingers tightly. "We donated that money to charity. Lieutenant, all the places where he might have gone are in the hands of others now."

"All right. You may think of something later. However far-fetched, please contact me." She rose. "When David's in custody again, I'll let you know. After that, I'll forget where you are."

Eve said nothing more until she and Roarke were in the car and headed back. "They still love him. After all he did, after what he is, there's a part of them that loves him."

"Yes, and enough, I think, to help you stop him, if they knew how."

"No one ever cared for us that way." She took her eyes off the road briefly, met his. "No one ever felt that bond."

"No." He brushed the hair from her cheek. "Not until we found each other. Don't grieve, Eve."

"He has his mother's eyes," she murmured. "Soft and blue and clear. She's the one who had to change them, I imagine, because she couldn't look in the mirror and face them every morning."

She sighed, shook it off.

"But he can," she said quietly.

Chapter 4

There was nothing else to do, no other data to examine or analyze, no other route to check. Tomorrow, she knew, there would be. Now she could only wait.

Eve walked into the bedroom with some idea of taking a catnap. They needed to salvage some of the day, she thought. To have their Christmas dinner together, to squeeze in some sense of normalcy.

The strong, dreamy scent of pine made her shake her head. The man had gone wild for tradition on this, their first Christmas together. Christ knew what he had paid for the live trees he'd placed throughout the house. And this one, the one that stood by the window in their bedroom, he'd insisted they decorate together.

It mattered to him. And with some surprise she realized it had come to matter to her.

"Tree lights on," she ordered, and smiled a little as she watched them blink and flash.

She stepped toward the seating area, released her weapon

harness, and shrugged it off. She was sitting on the arm of the sofa taking off her boots when Roarke came in.

"Good. I was hoping you'd take a break. I've got some calls to make. Why don't you let me know when you're ready for a meal?"

She angled her head and studied him as he stood just inside the doorway. She let her second boot drop and stood up slowly. "Come here."

Recognizing the glint in her eyes, he felt the light tingle of lust begin to move through his blood. "There?"

"You heard me, slick."

Keeping his eyes on hers he walked across the room. "What can I do for you, Lieutenant?"

Traditions, Eve thought, had to start somewhere. She fisted a hand in the front of his shirt, straining the silk as she pulled him a step closer. "I want you naked, and quick. So unless you want me to get rough, strip."

His smile was as cocky as hers and made her want to sink in with her teeth. "Maybe I like it rough."

"Yeah?" She began to back him up toward the bed. "Well then, you're going to love this."

She moved fast, the only signal was the quick flash of her eyes before she ripped his shirt open and sent buttons flying. He gripped her hips, squeezing hard as she fixed her teeth on his shoulder and bit.

"Christ. Christ! I love your body. Give it to me."

"You want it?" He jerked her up to her toes. "You'll have to take it."

When his mouth would have closed hotly over hers, she pivoted. He countered. She came in low and might have flipped him if he hadn't anticipated her move. They'd gone hand to hand before, with very satisfying results.

They ended face-to-face again, breath quickening. "I'm taking you down," she warned him.

"Try it."

They grappled, both refusing to give way. The momentum took them up the stairs of the platform to the bed. She slipped a hand between his legs, gently squeezed. It was a move she'd used before. Even as the heat shot straight down the center of his body to her palm, he shifted, slid under her guard, and flipped her onto the bed.

She rolled, came up in a crouch. "Come on, tough guy."

She was grinning now, her face flushed with battle, desire going gold in her eyes and the lights of the tree sparkling behind her.

"You look beautiful, Eve."

That had her blinking, straightening from the fighting stance and gaping at him. Even the man who loved her had never accused her of beauty. "Huh?"

It was all she managed before he leapt at her and took her out with a mid-body tackle.

"Bastard." She nearly giggled it even as she scissored up and managed to roll on top of him. But he used the impetus to keep going until he had her pinned again. "Beautiful, my ass."

"Your ass is beautiful." The elbow to his gut knocked some of the breath out of him, but he sucked more in. "And so's the rest of you. I'm going to have your beautiful ass, and the rest of you."

She bucked, twisted, nearly managed to slip out from under him. Then his mouth closed over her breast, sucking, nipping through her shirt. She moaned, arched up against him, and the fist she'd clenched in his hair dragged him closer rather than yanking him away.

When he tore at her shirt, she reared up, hooking strong,

long legs around his waist, finding his mouth with hers again as he pushed back to kneel in the center of the bed.

They went over in a tangle of limbs, hands rough and groping. And flesh began to slide damply over flesh.

He took her up and over the first time, hard and fast, those clever fingers knowing her weaknesses, her strengths, her needs. Quivering, crying out, she let herself fly on the edgy power of the climax.

Then they were rolling again, gasps and moans and murmurs. Heat coming in tidal waves, nerves raw and needy. Her mouth was a fever on his as she straddled him.

"Let me, let me, let me." She chanted it against his mouth as she rose up. Her hands linked tight to his as she took him inside her. He filled her, body, mind, heart.

Fast and full of fury, she drove them both as she'd needed to from the moment he'd come into the room. It flooded into her, swelled inside her, that unspeakable pleasure, the pressure, the frantic war to end, to prolong.

She threw her head back, clung to it, that razor's edge. "Go over." She panted it out, fighting to clear her vision, to focus on that glorious face. "Go over first, and take me with you."

She watched his eyes, that staggering blue go dark as midnight, felt him leap over with one last, hard thrust. With her hands still locked in his, she threw herself over with him.

And when the energy slid away from her like wax from a melting candle, she slipped down, quivering even as she pressed her face into his neck.

"I won," she managed.

"Okay."

Her lips twitched at the smug, and exhausted, satisfaction in his voice. "I did. I got just what I wanted from you, pal."

"Thank Christ." He shifted until he could cradle her against him. "Take a nap, Eve."

"Just an hour." Knowing he would never sleep longer than that himself, she wrapped around him to keep him close.

When she woke at two A.M., Eve decided the brief pre-dinner nap had thrown her system off. Now she was fully awake, her mind engaged and starting to click through the information and evidence she had so far.

David Palmer was here, in New York. Somewhere out in the city, happily going about his work. And her gut told her Stephanie Ring was already dead.

He wouldn't have such an easy time getting to the others on his list, she thought as she turned in bed. Ego would push him to try, and he'd make a mistake. In all likelihood he'd already made one. She just hadn't picked up on it yet.

Closing her eyes, she tried to slip into Palmer's mind, as she had years before when she'd been hunting him.

He loved his work, had loved it even when he'd been a boy and doing his experiments on animals. He'd managed to hide those little deaths, to put on a bright, innocent face. Everyone who'd known him—parents, teachers, neighbors— had spoken of a cheerful, helpful boy, a bright one who studied hard and caused no trouble.

Yet some of the classic elements had been there, even in childhood. He'd been a loner, obsessively neat, compulsively organized. He'd never had a healthy sexual relationship and had been socially awkward with women. They'd found hundreds of journal discs, going back to his tenth year, carefully relating his theories, his goals, and his accomplishments.

And with time, with practice, with study, he'd gotten very, very good at his work.

Where would you set up, Dave? It would have to be somewhere comfortable. You like your creature comforts. You must have hated the lack of them in prison. Pissed you off, didn't it? So now you're coming after the ones who put you there.

That's a mistake, letting us know the marks in advance. But it's ego, too. It's really you against me.

That's another mistake, because no one knows you better.

A house, she thought. *But not just any house. It would have to be in a good neighborhood, close to good restaurants. Those years of prison food must have offended your palate. You'd need furniture, comfortable stuff, with some style. Linens, good ones. And an entertainment complex—got to watch the screen or you won't know what people are saying about you.*

And all that takes money.

When she sat up in bed, Roarke stirred beside her. "Figure it out?"

"He's got a credit line somewhere. I always wondered if he had money stashed, but it didn't seem to matter since he was never getting out to use it. I was wrong. Money's power, and he found a way to use it from prison."

She tossed back the duvet, started to leap out of bed when the 'link beeped. She stared at it a moment, and knew.

Chapter 5

Two teenagers looking for a little adventure snuck out of their homes, met at a prearranged spot, and took their new scoot-bikes for a spin in Central Park.

They'd thought at first that Stephanie Ring was a vagrant, maybe a licensed beggar or a chemi-head sleeping it off, and they started to give her a wide berth.

But vagrants didn't make a habit of stretching out naked on the carousel in Central Park.

Eve had both of them stashed in a black-and-white. One had been violently ill, and the brittle air still carried the smear of vomit. She'd ordered the uniforms to set up a stand of lights so the area was under the glare of a false day.

Stephanie hadn't been beaten, nor had her hair been cut. Palmer believed in variety. There were dozens of long, thin slices over her arms and legs, the flesh around the wounds shriveled and discolored. Something toxic, Eve imagined, something that when placed on a relatively minor open wound would cause agony. The blood had been allowed to drip and dry. Her feet speared out at sharp angles, in a parody of a ballet stance. Dislocated.

Carved into her midriff were the signature block letters.

LET'S KILL ALL THE LAWYERS

He had finally killed this one, Eve thought, with the slow, torturous strangulation he was most fond of. Eve examined the noose, found the rope identical to that used on Judge Wainger.

Another mistake, Dave. Lots of little oversights this time around.

She reached for her field kit and began the routine that followed murder.

She went home to write her report, wanting the quiet she'd find there as opposed to the postholiday confusion at Central. She shot a copy to her commander, then sent messages to both Peabody and Feeney. Once her aide and the top man in the Electronics Detective Division woke and checked their 'links, she was pulling them in.

She fueled on coffee, then set about the tedious task of peeling the layers from Palmer's financial records.

It was barely dawn when the door between her office and Roarke's opened. He came in, fully dressed, and she could hear the hum of equipment already at work in the room behind him.

"You working at home today?" She said it casually, sipping coffee as she studied him.

"Yes." He glanced down at her monitor. "Following the money, Lieutenant?"

"At the moment. You're not my bodyguard, Roarke."

He merely smiled. "And who, I wonder, could be more interested in your body?"

"I'm a cop. I don't need a sitter."

He reached down, cupped her chin. "What nearly happened to Peabody two nights ago?"

"It didn't happen. And I'm not having you hovering around when you should be off doing stuff."

"I can do stuff from here just as easily and efficiently as I can from midtown. You're wasting time arguing. And I doubt you'll find your money trail through Palmer's official records."

"I know it." The admission covered both statements, and frustrated her equally. "I have to start somewhere. Go away and let me work."

"Done with me, are you?" He lowered his head and brushed his lips over hers.

The sound of a throat being loudly and deliberately cleared came from the doorway. "Sorry." Peabody managed most of a smile. She was pale, and more than a little heavy-eyed, but her uniform was stiff and polished, as always.

"You're early." Eve rose, then slid her hands awkwardly into her pockets.

"The message said to report as soon as possible."

"I'll leave you two to work." Alone, Roarke thought, the two of them would slip past the discomfort faster. "It's good to see you, Peabody. Lieutenant," he added before he closed the door between the rooms, "you might want to check the names of deceased relatives. The transfer and disbursement of funds involving accounts with the same last name and blood ties are rarely noticed."

"Yeah, right. Thanks." Eve shifted her feet. The last time she'd seen her aide, Peabody had been wrapped in a blanket, her face blotchy from tears. "You okay?"

"Yeah, mostly."

Mostly, my ass, Eve thought. "Look, I shouldn't have called you in on this. Take a couple of more days to level off."

"Sir. I'd do better if I got back to work, into routine. Sitting home watching videos and eating soy chips isn't the way I want to spend another day. Work clears it out quicker."

Because she believed that herself, Eve moved her shoulders. "Then get some coffee, Peabody, I've got plenty of work here."

"Yes, sir." She stepped forward, pulling a small wrapped box from her pocket, setting it on the desk as she went to the AutoChef. "Your Christmas present. I didn't get a chance to give it to you before."

"I guess we were a little busy." Eve toyed with the ribbon. Gifts always made her feel odd, but she could sense Peabody's eyes on her. She ripped off the red foil, opened the lid. It was a silver star, a little dented, a bit discolored.

"It's an old sheriff's badge," Peabody told her. "I don't guess it's like Wyatt Earp's or anything, but it's official. I thought you'd get a kick out of it. You know, the long tradition of law and order."

Absurdly touched, Eve grinned. "Yeah. It's great." For the fun of it, she took it out and pinned it to her shirt. "Does this make you the deputy?"

"It suits you, Dallas. You'd've stood up wherever, whenever."

Looking up, Eve met her eyes. "You stand, Peabody. I wouldn't have called you in today if I thought different."

"I guess I needed to hear that. Thanks. Well . . ." She hesitated, then lifted her brows in question.

"Problem?"

"No, I just . . ." She pouted, giving her square, sober face a painfully young look. "Hmmm."

"You didn't like your present?" Eve said lightly. "You'll have to take that up with Leonardo."

"What present? What's he got to do with it?"

"He made that wardrobe for your undercover work. If you don't like it . . ."

"The clothes." Like magic, Peabody's face cleared. "I get to keep all those mag clothes? All of them?"

"What the hell am I supposed to do with them? Now are you going to stand around grinning like an idiot or can I get on with things here?"

"I can grin and work at the same time, sir."

"Settle down. Start a run and trace on this rope." She pushed a hard-copy description across the desk. "I want any sales within the last week, bulk sales. He uses a lot of it."

"Who?"

"We'll get to that. Run the rope, then get me a list of private residences—upscale—sold or rented in the metro area within the last week. Also private luxury vehicles—pickup or delivery on those within the last week. He needs transpo and he'd go classy. The cage," she muttered as she began to pace. "Where the hell did he get the cage? Wildlife facility, domestic animal detention? We'll track it. Start the runs, Peabody, I'll brief you when Feeney gets here."

She'd called in Feeney, Peabody thought as she sat down at a computer. It was big. Just what she needed.

"You'll both want to review the investigation discs, profiles, transcripts from the Palmer case of three years ago. Feeney," Eve added, "you'll remember most of it. You tracked and identified the electronic equipment he used in those murders."

"Yeah, I remember the little bastard." Feeney sat,

scowling into his coffee. His habitually weary face was topped by wiry red hair that never seemed to decide which direction it wanted to take.

He was wearing a blue shirt, so painfully pressed and bright that Eve imagined it had come out of its gift box only that morning. And would be comfortably rumpled by afternoon.

"Because we know him, his pattern, his motives, and in this case his victims or intended victims, he's given us an edge. He knows that, enjoys that because he's sure he'll be smarter."

"He hates you, Dallas." Feeney's droopy eyes lifted, met hers. "He hated your ever-fucking guts all along. You stopped him, then you played him until he spilled everything. He'll come hard for you."

"I hope you're right, because I want the pleasure of taking him out again. He got the first two on his list because he had a lead on us," she continued. "The others have been notified, warned, and are under guard. He may or may not make an attempt to continue in order. But once he runs into a snag, he'll skip down."

"And come for you," Peabody put in.

"Everything the others did happened because I busted him. Under the whack is a very logical mind. Everything he does has a reason. It's his reason, so it's bent—but it's there."

She glanced at her wrist unit. "I've got a meeting with Mira at her residence in twenty minutes. I'm going to leave it to Feeney to fill you in on any holes in this briefing, Peabody. Once you have the lists from the runs I ordered, do a probability scan. See if we can narrow the field a bit. Feeney, when you review the disc he sent through Nadine, you might be able to tag some of the equipment. You get a line on it, we can trace the source. We do it in steps, but we do it fast. If he misses on the list, he might settle for someone else, anyone else. He's been out a week and already killed twice."

She broke off as her communicator signaled. She walked to retrieve her jacket as she answered. Two minutes later she jammed it back in her pocket. And her eyes were flat and cold.

"Make that three times. He got to Carl Neissan."

Eve was still steaming when she rang the bell of Mira's dignified brownstone. The fact that the guard on door duty demanded that she show her ID and had it verified before entry mollified her slightly. If the man posted at Neissan's had done the same, Palmer wouldn't have gotten inside.

Mira came down the hall toward her. She was dressed casually in slacks and sweater, with soft matching shoes. But there was nothing casual about her eyes. Before Eve could speak, she lifted a hand.

"I appreciate your coming here. We can talk upstairs in my office." She glanced to the right as a child's laughter bounced through an open doorway. "Under different circumstances I'd introduce you to my family. But I'd rather not put them under any more stress."

"We'll leave them out of it."

"I wish that were possible." Saying nothing more, Mira started upstairs.

The house reflected her, Eve decided. Calming colors, soft edges, perfect style. Her home office was half the size of her official one and must at one time have been a small bedroom. Eve noted that she'd furnished it with deep chairs and what she thought of as a lady's desk, with curved legs and fancy carving.

Mira adjusted the sunscreen on a window and turned to the mini AutoChef recessed into the wall.

"You'll have reviewed my original profile on David Palmer," she began, satisfied that her hands were steady as she programmed for tea. "I would stand by it, with a few additions due to his time in prison."

"I didn't come for a profile. I've got him figured."

"Do you?"

"I walked around inside his head before. We both did."

"Yes." Mira offered Eve a delicate cup filled with the fragrant tea they both knew she didn't want. "In some ways he remains the exception to a great many rules. He had a loving and advantaged childhood. Neither of his parents exhibits any signs of emotional or psychological defects. He did well in school, more of an overachiever than under-, but nothing off the scale. Testing showed no brain deformities, no physical abnormalities. There is no psychological or physiological root for his condition."

"He likes it," Eve said briefly. "Sometimes evil's its own root."

"I want to disagree," Mira murmured. "The reasons, the whys of abnormal behavior are important to me. But I have no reasons, no whys, for David Palmer."

"That's not your problem, Doctor. Mine is to stop him, and to protect the people he's chosen. The first two on his list are dead."

"Stephanie Ring? You're sure."

"Her body was found this morning. Carl Neissan's been taken."

This time Mira's hand shook, rattling her cup in its saucer before she set it aside. "He was under guard."

"Palmer got himself into a cop suit, knocked on the damn door, and posed as the relief. The on-duty didn't question it. He went home to a late Christmas dinner. When the morning duty came on, he found the house empty."

"And the night relief? The real one?"

"Inside the trunk of his unit. Tranq'd and bound but otherwise unharmed. He hasn't come around enough to be questioned yet. Hardly matters. We know it was Palmer. I'm arranging for Justine Polinsky to be moved to a safe house. You'll want to pack some things, Doctor. You're going under."

"You know I can't do that, Eve. This is as much my case as yours."

"You're wrong. You're a consultant, and that's it. I don't need consultation. I'm no longer confident that you can be adequately protected in this location. I'm moving you."

"Eve—"

"Don't fuck with me." It came out sharp, very close to mean, and Mira jerked back in surprise. "I'm taking you into police custody. You can gather up some personal things or you can go as you are. But you're going."

Calling on the control that ran within her like her own bloodstream, Mira folded her hands in her lap. "And you? Will you be going under?"

"I'm not your concern."

"Of course you are, Eve," Mira said quietly, watching the storm of emotions in Eve's eyes. "Just as I'm yours. And my family downstairs is mine. They're not safe."

"I'll see to it. I'll see to them."

Mira nodded, closed her eyes briefly. "It would be a great relief to me to know they were away from here, and protected. It's difficult for me to cope when I'm worried about their welfare."

"He won't touch them. I promise you."

"I'll take your word. Now as to my status—"

"I didn't give you multiple choices, Dr. Mira."

"Just a moment." Composed again, Mira picked up her tea. "I think you'll agree . . . I have every bit as much influence with your superiors as you do. It would hardly serve either of us to play at tugging strings. I'm not being stubborn or courageous," she added. "Those are your traits."

A ghost of a smile curved her mouth when Eve frowned at her. "I admire them. You're also a woman who can see past emotion to the goal. The goal is to stop David Palmer. I can be of use. We both know it. With my family away I'll be less distracted. And I can't be with them, Eve, because if I am I'll worry that he'll harm one of them to get to me."

She paused for a moment, judged that Eve was considering. "I have no argument to having guards here or at my office. In fact, I want them. Very much. I have no intention of taking any unnecessary chances or risks. I'm just asking you to let me do my work."

"You can do your work where I put you."

"Eve." Mira drew a breath. "If you put both me and Justine out of his reach, there's the very real possibility he'll take someone else." She nodded. "You've considered that already. He won't come for you until he's ready. You're the grand prize. If no one else is accessible, he'll strike out. He'll want to keep to his timetable, even if it requires a substitute."

"I've got some lines on him."

"And you'll find him. But if he believes I'm accessible, if I'm at least visible, he'll be satisfied to focus his energies on getting through. I expect you to prevent that." She smiled again, easier now. "And I intend to do everything I can to help you."

"I can make you go. All your influence won't matter if I

toss you in restraints and have you hauled out of here. You'll be pissed off, but you'll be safe."

"I wouldn't put it past you," Mira agreed. "But you know I'm right."

"I'm doubling your guards. You're wearing a bracelet. You work here. You're not to leave the house for any reason." Her eyes flashed when Mira started to protest. "You push me on this, you're going to find out what it feels like to wear cuffs." Eve rose. "Your guards will do hourly check-ins. Your 'link will be monitored."

"That hardly makes me appear accessible."

"He'll know you're here. That's going to have to be enough. I've got work to do." Eve started for the door, hesitated, then spoke without turning around. "Your family, they matter to you."

"Yes, of course."

"You matter to me." She walked away quickly, before Mira could get shakily to her feet.

Chapter 6

Eve headed to the lab from Mira's. From there she planned a stop by the morgue and another at Carl Neissan's before returning to her home office.

Remembering Mira's concern about family, Eve called Roarke on her palm 'link after she parked and started into the building.

"Why are you alone?" was the first thing he said to her.

"Cut it out." She flashed her badge at security, then headed across the lobby and down toward the labs. "I'm in a secured facility, surrounded by rent-a-cops, monitors, and lab dorks. I've got a job to do. Let me do it."

"He's gotten three out of six."

She stopped, rolled her eyes. "Oh, I get it. Shows what kind of faith you have in me. I guess being a cop for ten years makes me as easy a fish as a seventy-year-old judge and a couple of soft lawyers."

"You annoy me, Eve."

"Why? Because I'm right?"

"Yes. And snotty about it." But his smile warmed a little. "Why did you call?"

"So I could be snotty. I'm at the lab, about to tackle Dickhead. I've got a few stops to make after this. I'll check in."

It was a casual way to let him know she understood he worried. And he accepted, in the same tone. "I've several 'link conferences this afternoon. Call in on the private line. Watch your back, Lieutenant. I'm very fond of it."

Satisfied, she swung into the lab. Dickie, the chief tech, was there, looking sleepy-eyed and pale as he stared at the readout on his monitor.

The last time she'd been in the lab, there'd been a hell of a party going on. Now those who'd bothered to come in worked sluggishly and looked worse.

"I need reports, Dickie. Wainger and Ring."

"Jesus, Dallas." He looked up mournfully, hunching his shoulders. "Don't you ever stay home?"

Since he looked ill, she gave him a little leeway. Silently she opened her jacket, tapped the silver star pinned to her shirt. "I'm the law," she said soberly. "The law has no home."

It made him grin a little, then he moaned. "Man, I got the mother of all Christmas hangovers."

"Mix yourself up a potion, Dickie, and get over it. Dave's got number three."

"Dave who?"

"Palmer, David Palmer." She resisted letting out her impatience by cuffing him on the side of the head. But she imagined doing it. "Did you read the damn directive?"

"I've only been here twenty minutes. Jesus." He rolled his shoulders, rubbed his face, drew in three sharp nasal breaths. "Palmer? That freak's caged."

"Not anymore. He skipped and he's back in New York. Wainger and Ring are his."

"Shit. Damn shit." He didn't look any less ill, but his eyes were alert now. "Fucking Christmas week and we get the world's biggest psycho-freak."

"Yeah, and Happy New Year, too. I need the results, on the rope, on the paper. I want to know what he used to carve the letters. You get any hair or fiber from the sweepers?"

"No, wait, just wait a damn minute." He scooted his rolling chair down the counter, barked orders at a computer, muttering as he scanned the data. "Bodies were clean. No hair other than victim's. No fiber."

"He always kept them clean," Eve murmured.

"Yeah, I remember. I remember. Got some dust—like grit between the toes, both victims."

"Concrete dust."

"Yeah. Get you the grade, possible age. Now the rope." He skidded back. "I was just looking at it, just doing the test run. Nothing special or exotic about it. Standard nylon strapping rope. Give me some time, I'll get you the make."

"How much time?"

"Two hours, three tops. Takes longer when it's standard."

"Make it fast." She swung away. "I'm in the field."

She stopped at the morgue next, to harass the chief medical examiner. It was more difficult to intimidate Morse or to rush him.

No sexual assault or molestation, no mutilation or injuries of genitalia.

Typical of Palmer, Eve thought as she ran over Morse's prelim report in her head. He was as highly asexual as anyone she'd come up against. She doubted that he even thought of the gender of his victims other than as a statistic for his experiments.

Subject Wainger's central nervous system had been severely damaged. Subject suffered minor cardiac infarction during abduction and torture period. Anus and interior of mouth showed electrical burns. Both hands crushed with a smooth, heavy instrument. Three ribs cracked.

The list of injuries went on until Morse had confirmed the cause of death as strangulation. And the time of death as midnight, December twenty-fourth.

She spent an hour at Carl Neissan's, another at Wainger's. In both cases, she thought, the door had been opened, Palmer allowed in. He was good at that. Good at putting on a pretty smile and talking his way in.

He looked so damn innocent, Eve thought as she climbed the steps to her own front door. Even the eyes— and the eyes usually told you—were those of a young, harmless man. They hadn't flickered, hadn't glazed or brightened, even when he'd sat in interview across from her and described each and every murder.

They'd taken on the light of madness only when he talked about the scope and importance of his work.

"Lieutenant." Summerset, tall and bony in severe black, slipped out of a doorway. "Do I assume your guests will be remaining for lunch?"

"Guests? I don't have any guests." She stripped off her jacket, tossed it across the newel post. "If you mean my team, we'll deal with it."

He had the jacket off the post even as she started up the stairs. At his low growl of disgust she glanced back. He held in his fingertips the gloves she'd balled into her jacket pocket. "What have you done to these?"

"It's just sealant." Which she'd forgotten to clean off before she shoved them into her pocket.

"These are handmade, Italian leather with mink lining."

"Mink? Shit. What is he, crazy?" Shaking her head, she kept on going. "Mink lining, for Christ's sake. I'll have lost them by next week, then some stupid mink will have died for nothing." She glanced down the hallway at Roarke's office door, shook her head again, and walked into her own.

She was right, Eve noted. Her team could deal with lunch on their own. Feeney was chowing down on some kind of multitiered sandwich while he muttered orders into the computer and scanned. Peabody had a deep bowl of pasta, scooping it up one-handed, sliding printouts into a pile with the other.

Her office smelled like an upscale diner and sounded like cops. Computer and human voices clashed, the printer hummed, and the main 'link was beeping and being ignored.

She strode over and answered it herself. "Dallas."

"Hey, got your rope." When she saw Dickie shove a pickle in his mouth, she wondered if every city official's stomach had gone on alarm at the same time. "Nylon strapping cord, like I said. This particular type is top grade, heavy load. Manufactured by Kytell outta Jersey. You guys run the distributor, that's your end."

"Yeah. Thanks." She broke transmission, thinking Dickie wasn't always a complete dickhead. He'd come through and hadn't required a bribe.

"Lieutenant," Peabody began, but Eve held up a finger and walked to Roarke's door and through it. "Do you own Kytell in New Jersey?"

Then she stopped and winced when she saw that he was in the middle of a holographic conference. Several images turned, studied her out of politely annoyed eyes.

"Sorry."

"It's all right. Gentlemen, ladies, this is my wife." Roarke leaned back in his chair, monumentally amused that Eve had inadvertently made good on her threat to barge in on one of his multimillion-dollar deals just to annoy him. "If you'd excuse me one moment. Caro?"

The holo of his administrative assistant rose, smiled. "Of course. We'll shift to the boardroom momentarily." The image turned, ran her hands over controls that only she could see, and the holos winked away.

"I should have knocked or something."

"It's not a problem. They'll hold. I'm about to make them all very rich. Do I own what?"

"Did you have to say 'my wife' just that way, like I'd just run up from the kitchen?"

"So much more serene an image than telling them you'd just run in from the morgue. And it is a rather conservative company I'm about to buy. Now, do I own what and why do you want to know?"

"Kytell, based in New Jersey. They make rope."

"Do they? Well, I have no idea. Just a minute." He swiveled at the console, asked for the information on the company. Which, Eve thought with some irritation, she could have damn well done herself.

"Yes, they're an arm of Yancy, which is part of Roarke Industries. And which, I assume, made the murder weapon."

"Right the first time."

"Then you'll want the distributor, the stores in the New York area where large quantities were sold to one buyer within the last week."

"Peabody can get it."

"I'll get it faster. Give me thirty minutes to finish up in here, then I'll shoot the data through to your unit."

"Thanks." She started out, turned back. "The third woman on the right? The redhead? She was giving you a leg shot—another inch of skirt lift and it would have been past her crotch."

"I noticed. Very nice legs." He smiled. "But she still won't get more than eighty point three a share. Anything else?"

"She's no natural redhead," Eve said for the hell of it and heard him laugh as she shut the door between them.

"Sir." Peabody got to her feet. "I think I have a line on the vehicle. Three possibles, high-end privates sold to single men in their early to mid-twenties on December twentieth and twenty-first. Two dealerships on the East Side and one in Brooklyn."

"Print hard copies of Palmer's photo."

"Already done."

"Feeney?"

"Whittling it down."

"Keep whittling. Roarke should have some data on the murder weapon inside a half hour. Send what he has to me in the field, will you? Peabody, you're with me."

The first dealership was a wash, and as she pulled up at the second, Eve sincerely hoped she didn't have to head to Brooklyn. The shiny new vehicles on the showroom floor had Peabody's eyes gleaming avariciously. Only Eve's quick elbow jab kept her from stroking the hood of a Booster-6Z, the sport-utility vehicle of the year.

"Maintain some dignity," Eve muttered. She flagged a salesman, who looked none too happy when she flipped out her badge. "I need to talk to the rep who sold a rig like this"—she gestured toward the Booster—"last week. Young guy bought it."

"Lana sold one of the 6Zs a few days before Christmas." Now he looked even unhappier. "She often rounds up the younger men." He pointed to a woman at a desk on the far side of the showroom.

"Thanks." Eve walked over, noting that Lana had an explosion of glossy black curls cascading down her back, a headset over it, and was fast-talking a potential customer on the line while she manually operated a keyboard with fingernails painted a vivid red.

"I can put you in it for eight a month. Eight a month and you're behind the wheel of the sexiest, most powerful land and air unit currently produced. I'm slicing my commission to the bone because I want to see you drive off in what makes you happy."

"Make him happy later, Lana." Eve held her badge in front of Lana's face.

Lana put a hand over the mouthpiece, studied the ID, cursed softly. Then her voice went back to melt. "Jerry, you take one more look at the video, try out the holo run. If you're not smiling by the end of it, the 7000's not the one for you. You call me back and let me know. Remember, I want you happy. Hear?"

She disconnected, glared at Eve. "I paid those damn parking violations. Every one."

"Glad to hear it. Our city needs your support. I need information on a sale you made last week. Booster. You were contacted earlier today and confirmed."

"Yeah, right. Nice guy, pretty face." She smiled. "He knew what he wanted right off."

"Is this the guy?" Eve signaled to Peabody, who took out the photo.

"Yeah. Cute."

"Yeah, he's real cute. I need the data. Name, address, the works."

"Sure, no problem." She turned to her machine, asked for the readout. Then, looking back up at Eve, she narrowed her eyes. "You look familiar. Have I sold you a car?"

Eve thought of her departmental issue, its sad pea-green finish and blocky style. "No."

"You really look— Oh!" Lana lit up like a Christmas tree. "Sure, sure, you're Roarke's wife. Roarke's cop wife. I've seen you on screen. Word is he's got an extensive collection of vehicles. Where does he deal?"

"Wherever he wants," Eve said shortly, and Lana let out a gay laugh.

"Oh, I'm sure he does. I'd absolutely love to show him our brand-new Barbarian. It won't be on the market for another three months, but I can arrange a private showing. If you'd just give him my card, Mrs. Roarke, I'll be—"

"You see this?" Eve took out her badge again, all but pushed it into Lana's pert nose. "It says 'Dallas.' Lieutenant Dallas. I'm not here to liaison your next commission. This is an official investigation. Give me the damn data."

"Certainly. Of course." If her feathers were ruffled, Lana hid it well. "Um, the name is Peter Nolan, 123 East Sixty-eighth, apartment 4-B."

"How'd he pay?"

"That I remember. Straight E-transfer. The whole shot. Didn't want to finance. The transfer was ordered, received, and confirmed, and he drove off a happy man."

"I need all the vehicle information, including temp license and registration number. Full description."

"All right. Gee, what'd he do? Kill somebody?"

"Yeah, he did."

"Wow." Lana busily copied the data disc. "You just can't trust a pretty face," she said and slipped her business card into the disc pack.

Chapter 7

Peter Nolan didn't live at the Sixty-eighth Street address. The Kowaskis, an elderly couple, and their creaky schnauzer had lived there for fifteen years.

A check of the bank showed that the Nolan account had been opened, in person, on December 20 of that year and closed on December 22.

Just long enough to do the deal, Eve thought. But where had he gotten the money?

Taking Roarke's advice, she rounded out a very long day by starting searches on accounts under the name of Palmer. It would, she thought, rubbing her eyes, take a big slice of time.

How much time did Carl have? she wondered. Another day, by her guess. If Palmer was running true to form, he would begin to enjoy his work too much to rush through it. But sometime within the next twenty-four hours, she believed he'd try for Justine Polinsky.

While her machine worked, she leaned back and closed

her eyes. Nearly midnight, she thought. Another day. Feeney was working his end. She was confident they'd have a line on the equipment soon, then there were the houses to check. They had the make, model, and license of his vehicle.

He'd left a trail, she thought. He wanted her to follow it, wanted her close. The son of a bitch.

It's you and me, isn't it, Dave? she thought as her mind started to drift. *How fast can I be, and how clever? You figure it'll make it all the sweeter when you've got me in that cage. It's because you want that so bad that you're making mistakes. Little mistakes.*

I'm going to hang you with them.

She slid into sleep while her computer hummed and woke only when she felt herself being lifted.

"What?" Reflexively she reached for the weapon she'd already unharnessed.

"You need to be in bed." Roarke held her close as he left the office.

"I was just resting my eyes. I've got data coming in. Don't carry me."

"You were dead out, the data will be there in the morning, and I'm already carrying you."

"I'm getting closer, but not close enough."

He'd seen the financial data on her screen. "I'll take a look through the accounts in the morning," he told her as he laid her on the bed.

"I've got it covered."

He unpinned her badge, set it aside. "Yes, Sheriff, but money is my business. Close it down a while."

"He'll be sleeping now." She let Roarke undress her. "In a big, soft bed with clean sheets. Dave likes to be clean and comfortable. He'll have a monitor in the bedroom so he can watch Neissan. He likes to watch before he goes to sleep. He told me."

"Don't think." Roarke slipped into bed beside her, gathered her close.

"He wants me."

"Yes, I know." Roarke pressed his lips to her hair as much to comfort himself as her. "But he can't have you."

Sleep helped. She'd dropped into it like a stone and had lain on the bottom of the dreaming pool for six hours. There'd been no call in the middle of the night to tell her Carl Neissan's body had been found.

Another day, she thought again and strode into her office. Roarke was at her desk, busily screening data.

"What are you doing?" She all but leapt to him. "That's classified."

"Don't pick nits, darling. You were going too broad last night. You'll be days compiling and rejecting all accounts under the name Palmer. You want one that shows considerable activity, large transfers, and connections to other accounts—which is, of course, the trickier part if you're dealing with someone who understands how to hide the coin."

"You can't just sit down and start going through data accumulated in an investigation."

"Of course I can. You need coffee." He looked up briefly. "Then you'll feel more yourself and I'll show you what I have."

"I feel exactly like myself." Which, she admitted, at the moment was annoyed and edgy. She stalked to the AutoChef in the kitchen, went for an oversized mug of hot and black. The rich and real caffeine Roarke could command zipped straight through her system.

"What have you got?" she demanded when she walked back in.

"Palmer was too simple, too obvious," Roarke began, and she narrowed her eyes.

"You didn't think so yesterday."

"I said check for relatives, same names. I should have suggested you try his mother's maiden name. Riley. And here we have the account of one Palmer Riley. It was opened six years ago, standard brokerage account, managed. Since there's been some activity over the last six months, I would assume your man found a way to access a 'link or computer from prison."

"He shouldn't have been near one. How can you be sure?"

"He understands how money works, and just how fluid it can be. You see here that six months ago he had a balance of just over $1.3 million. For the past three years previous, all action was automatic, straight managed with no input from the account holder. But here he begins to make transfers. Here's one to an account under Peter Nolan, which, by the way, is his aunt's husband's name on his father's side. Overseas accounts, off-planet accounts, local New York accounts—different names, different IDs. He's had this money for some time and he waited, sat on it until he found the way to use it."

"When I took him down before, we froze his accounts, accounts under David Palmer. We didn't look deeper. I didn't think of it."

"Why should you have? You stopped him, you put him away. He was meant to stay away."

"If I'd cleared it all, he wouldn't have had the backing to come back here."

"Eve, he'd have found a way." He waited until she looked at him. "You know that."

"Yeah." She let out a long breath. "Yeah, I know that. This tells me he's been planning, he's been shopping, he's been juggling funds, funneling into cover accounts. I need to freeze them. I don't think a judge is going to argue with me, not after what happened to one of their own."

"You'll piss him off."

"That's the plan. I need the names, numbers, locations of all the accounts you can connect to him." She blew out a breath. "Then I guess I owe you."

"Use your present, and we'll call it even."

"My present? Oh, yeah. Where and/or when do I want to go for a day. Let me mull that over a little bit. We get this wrapped, I'll use it for New Year's Eve."

"There's a deal."

A horrible thought snuck into her busy mind. "We don't have like a thing for New Year's, do we? No party or anything."

"No. I didn't want anything but you."

She looked back at him, narrowing her eyes even as the smile spread. "Do you practice saying stuff like that?"

"No." He rose, framed her face and kissed her, hard and deep. "I have all that stuff on disc."

"You're a slick guy, Roarke." She skimmed her fingers through her hair and simply lost herself for a moment in the look of him. Then, giving herself a shake, she stepped back. "I have to work."

"Wait." He grabbed her hand before she could turn away. "What was that?"

"I don't know. It just comes over me sometimes. You, I guess, come over me sometimes. I don't have time for it now."

"Darling Eve." He brushed his thumb over her knuckles. "Be sure to make time later."

"Yeah, I'll do that."

* * *

They worked together for an hour before Peabody arrived. She switched gears, leaving Roarke to do what he did best— manipulate data—while she focused on private residences purchased in the New York area, widening the timing to the six months since Palmer had activated his account.

Feeney called in to let her know he'd identified some of the equipment from the recording and was following up.

Eve gathered her printouts and rose. "We've got more than thirty houses to check. Have to do it door-to-door since I don't trust the names and data. He could have used anything. Peabody—"

"I'm with you, sir."

"Right. Roarke, I'll be in the field."

"I'll let you know when I have this wrapped."

She looked at him, working smoothly, thoroughly, me- thodically. And wondered who the hell was dealing with what she often thought of as his empire. "Look, I can call a man in for this. McNab—"

"McNab." Peabody winced at the name before she could stop herself. She had a temporary truce going with the EDD detective, but that didn't mean she wanted to share her case with him. Again. "Dallas, come on. It's been so nice and quiet around here."

"I've got this." Roarke shot her a glance, winked at Peabody. "I have an investment in it now."

"Whatever. Shoot me, and Feeney, the data when you have it all. I'm going to check out the rope, too. He likely picked up everything himself, but it would only take one delivery to pin down his hole."

After three hours of knocking on doors, questioning pro- fessional parents, housekeepers, or others who chose the work-at-home route, Eve took pity on Peabody and swung by a glide cart.

In this neighborhood the carts were clean, the awnings or umbrellas bright, the operators polite. And the prices obscene.

Peabody winced as she was forced to use a credit card for nothing but coffee, a kabob, and a small scoop of paper-thin oil chips.

"It's my metabolism," she muttered as she climbed back into the car. "I have one that requires fuel at regular intervals."

"Then pump up," Eve advised. "It's going to be a long day. At least half these people aren't going to be home until after the five o'clock shift ends."

She snagged the 'link when it beeped. "Dallas."

"Hello, Lieutenant." Roarke eyed her soberly. "Your data's coming through."

"Thanks. I'll start on the warrant."

"One thing—I didn't find any account with a withdrawal or transfer that seemed large enough for a purchase or down payment on a house. A couple are possible, but if, as you told me, he didn't finance a car, it's likely he didn't want to deal with the credit and CompuGuard checks on his rating and background."

"He's got a damn house, Roarke. I know it."

"I'm sure you're right. I'm not convinced he acquired it recently."

"I've still got twenty-couple to check," she replied. "I have to follow through on that. Maybe he's just renting. He likes to own, but maybe this time he's renting. I'll run it through that way, too."

"There weren't any standard transfers or withdrawals that would indicate rent or mortgage payments."

She hissed out a breath. "It's ridiculous."

"What?"

"How good a cop you'd make."

"I don't think insulting me is appropriate under the circumstances. I have some business of my own to tend to," he said when she grinned at him. "I'll get back to yours shortly."

Palmer had purchased, and personally picked up, 120 yards of nylon rope from a supply warehouse store off Canal. The clerk who had handled the sale ID'd the photo and mentioned what a nice young man Mr. Dickson had been. As Dickson, Palmer had also purchased a dozen heavy-load pulleys, a supply of steel O-rings, cable, and the complete Handy Homemaker set of Steelguard tools, including the accessory laser package.

The entire business had been loaded into the cargo area of his shiny new Booster-6Z—which the clerk had admired—on the morning of December 22.

Eve imagined Palmer had been a busy little bee that day and throughout the next, setting up his private chamber of horrors.

By eight they'd eliminated all the houses on Eve's initial list.

"That's it." Eve climbed back in her vehicle and pressed her fingers to her eyes. "They all check out. I'll drop you at a transpo stop, Peabody."

"Are you going home?"

Eve lowered her hands. "Why?"

"Because I'm not going off duty if you're starting on the list of rentals I ran."

"Excuse me?"

Peabody firmed her chin. Eve could arrow a cold chill up your spine when she took on that superior-officer tone.

"I'm not going off duty, sir, to leave you solo in the field with Palmer on the loose and you as a target. With respect, Lieutenant."

"You don't think I can handle some little pissant, mentally defective?"

"I think you want to handle him too much." Peabody sucked in a breath. "I'm sticking, Dallas."

Eve narrowed her eyes. "Have you been talking to Roarke?" At the quick flicker in Peabody's eyes Eve swore. "Goddamn it."

"He's right and you're wrong. Sir." Peabody braced for the explosion, was determined to weather it, then all but goggled with shock.

"Maybe," was all Eve said as she pulled away from the curb.

Since she was on a roll, Peabody slanted Eve a look. "You haven't eaten all day. You didn't even steal any of my oil chips. You could use a meal."

"Okay, okay. Christ, Roarke's got your number, doesn't he?"

"I wish."

"Zip it, Peabody. We'll fuel the metabolism, then start on the rental units."

"Zipping with pleasure, sir."

Chapter 8

It began to snow near midnight, fat, cold flakes with icy edges. Eve watched it through the windshield and told herself it was time to stop. The night was over. Nothing more could be done.

"He's got all the cards," she murmured.

"You've got a pretty good hand, Dallas." Peabody shifted in her seat, grateful for the heat of the car. Even her bones were chilled.

"Doesn't matter what I've got." Eve drove away from the last rental unit they'd checked. "Not tonight. I know who he is, who he's going to kill. I know how he does it and I know why. And tonight it doesn't mean a damn thing. Odds are, he's done with Carl now."

It was rare to see Eve discouraged. Angry, yes, Peabody thought with some concern. And driven. But she couldn't recall ever hearing that quiet resignation in her lieutenant's voice before. "You covered all the angles. You took all the steps."

"That's not going to mean much to Carl. And if I'd covered all the angles, I'd have the son of a bitch. So I'm missing one. He's slipping through because I can't pin it."

"You've only had the case for three days."

"No. I've had it for three years." As she pulled up at a light, her 'link beeped. "Dallas."

"Lieutenant, this is Detective Dalrymple, assigned to observation on the Polinsky residence. We've got a mixed-race male, mid-twenties, average height and build. Subject is on foot and carrying a small sack. He used what appeared to be a key code to gain access to premises. He's inside now."

"I'm three blocks east of your location and on my way." She'd already whipped around the corner. "Secure all exits, call for backup. Doesn't make sense," she muttered to Peabody as they barreled across Madison. "Right out in the open? Falls right into our laps? Doesn't fucking make sense."

She squealed to a stop a half a block from the address. Her weapon was in her hand before she hit the sidewalk. "Peabody, the Polinsky unit is on four, south side. Go around, take the fire escape. He comes out that way, take him down quick."

Eve charged in at the front of the building and, too impatient for the elevator, raced up the stairs. She found Dalrymple on four, weapon drawn as he waited beside the door.

"Lieutenant." He gave her a brief nod. "My partner's around the back. Subject's been inside less than five minutes. Backup's on the way."

"Good." She studied Dalrymple's face, found his eyes steady. "We won't wait for them. I go in low," she added, taking out her master and bypassing the locks.

"Fine with me." He was ready beside her.

"On three. One, two." They hit the door, went through high and low, back to back, sweeping with their weapons. Music was playing, a primitive backbeat of drums behind screaming guitars. In the tidy living area, the mood screen had been set on deep reds and swimming blues melting into each other.

She signaled Dalrymple to the left, had taken two steps to the right herself when a naked man came out of the kitchen area carrying a bottle of wine and a single red rose.

He screamed and dropped the bottle. Wine glugged out onto the rug. Holding the rose to his balls, he crouched. "Don't shoot! Jesus, don't shoot. Take anything you want. Anything. It's not even mine."

"NYPSD," Eve snapped at him. "On the floor, face-down, hands behind your head. Now!"

"Yes, ma'am, yes, ma'am." He all but dove to the rug. "I didn't do anything." He flinched when Eve dragged his hands down and cuffed them. "I was just going to meet Sunny. She said it would be okay."

"Who the hell are you?"

"Jimmy. Jimmy Ripsky. I go to college with Sunny. We're on winter break. She said her parents were out of town for a few days and we could use the place."

Eve holstered her weapon in disgust. The boy was shaking like a leaf. "Get him a blanket or something, Dalrymple. This isn't our man." She dragged him to his feet and had enough pity in her to uncuff him before gesturing to a chair. "Let's here the whole story, Jimmy."

"That's it. Um"—cringing with embarrassment, he folded his arms over his crotch—"Sunny and I are, like, an item."

"And who's Sunny?"

"Sunny Polinsky. Sheila, I guess. Everybody calls her Sunny. This is her parents' place. Man, her father's going to kill me if he finds out."

"She called you?"

"Yeah. Well, no." He looked up with desperate gratitude when Dalrymple came in with a chenille throw. "I got an e-mail from her this morning and a package. She said her parents were going south for the week and how I should come over tonight. About midnight, let myself in with the key she'd sent me. And I should, um, you know, get comfortable." He tucked the throw more securely around his legs. "She said she'd be here by twelve-thirty and I should, well, ah, be waiting in bed." He moistened his lips. "It was pretty, sort of, explicit for Sunny."

"Do you still have the e-mail? The package the key came in?"

"I dumped the package in the recycler, but I've got the e-mail. I printed it out. It's . . . it's a keeper, you know?"

"Right. Detective, call in your partner and my aide."

"Um, ma'am?" Jimmy began when Dalrymple turned away with his communicator.

"Dallas. Lieutenant."

"Yes, ma'am, Lieutenant. What's going on? Is Sunny okay?"

"She's fine. She's with her parents."

"But—she said she'd be here."

"I think someone else sent you that keeper e-mail. Somebody who wanted me to have a little something extra to do tonight." But she sat, pulled out her palm 'link. "I'm going to check out your story, Jimmy. If it all fits, Detective Dalrymple's going to arrange for a uniform to take you home. You can give him the printout of the e-mail—and your computer."

"My computer? But—"

"It's police business," she said shortly. "You'll get it back."

"Well, that was fun," Peabody said when Eve resecured the door.

"A barrel of laughs."

"Poor kid. He was mortified. Here he was thinking he was going to have the sex of his dreams with his girl, and he gets busted."

"The fact that a rosebud managed to preserve most of his modesty tells me that the sex of his dreams outruns the reality." At Peabody's snort, Eve turned to the elevator. "Sunny backed up his story about them being an item. Not that I doubted it. The kid was too scared to lie. So . . . Dave's been keeping up with the social activities of his marks. He knows the family, the friends, and he knows how to use them."

She stepped out of the elevator, crossed the lobby. "For an MD in a maximum lockup, he managed to get his hands on plenty of data."

She paused at the door and simply stood for a moment looking out at the thin, steady snow. "You got off-planet clearance, Peabody?"

"Sure. It's a job requirement."

"Right. Well, go home and pack a bag. I want you on your way to Rexal on the first transport we can arrange. You and McNab can check out the facilities, find the unit Palmer had access to."

The initial rush from the idea of an off-planet assignment turned to ashes in her mouth. "McNab? I don't need McNab."

"When you find the unit, you'll need a good electronics man." Eve opened the door, and the blast of cold cooled the annoyed flush on Peabody's cheeks.

"He's a pain in the ass."

"Sure he is, but he knows his job. If Feeney can spare him, you're the off-planet team." She reached for her communicator, intending to interrupt Feeney's sleep and get the ball rolling. A scream from the end of the block had her drawing her weapon instead.

She pounded west, boots digging into the slick sidewalk. With one quick gesture, she signaled Dalrymple to stay at his post in the surveillance van.

She saw the woman first, wrapped in sleek black fur, clinging to a man with an overcoat over a tux. He was trying to shield her face and muffle her mouth against his shoulder. The pitch and volume of her screams indicated he wasn't doing a very good job of it.

"Police!" He shouted it as he saw Peabody and Eve running toward them. "Here's the police, honey. My God, my God, what's this city coming to? He threw it out, threw it out right at our feet."

It, Eve saw, was Carl Neissan. His naked and broken body lay faceup against the curb. His head had been shaved, she noted, and the tender skin abraded and burned. His knees were shattered, his protruding tongue blackened. Around his neck, digging deep, was the signature noose. And the message carved into his chest was still red and raw.

WOE UNTO YOU ALSO, YE LAWYERS!

The woman's screaming had turned to wailing now. Eve tuned it out. With her eyes on the body, she pulled out her communicator. "This is Dallas, Lieutenant Eve. I have a homicide."

She gave Dispatch the necessary information, then turned to the male witness. "You live around here?"

"Yes, yes, this building on the corner. We were just coming home from a party when—"

"My aide is going to take your companion inside, away from this. Out of the cold. We'll need her statement. I'd appreciate it if you'd stay out here with me for a few minutes."

"Yes, of course. Yes. Honey." He tried to pry his wife's hands from around his neck. "Honey, you go with the policewoman. Go inside now."

"Peabody," Eve said under her breath, "take honey out of here, get what you can out of her."

"Yes, sir. Ma'am, come with me." With a couple of firm tugs Peabody had the woman.

"It was such a shock," he continued. "She's very delicate, my wife. It's such a shock."

"Yes, sir, I'm sure it is. Can I have your names, please?"

"What? Oh. Fitzgerald. George and Maria."

Eve got the names and the address on record. In a few minutes she would have a crowd to deal with, she knew. Even jaded New Yorkers would gather around a dead, naked body on Madison Avenue.

"Can you—sir, look at me," she added when he continued to stare at the body. He was going faintly green. "Look at me," she repeated, "and try to tell me exactly what happened."

"It was all so fast, so shocking." Reaction began to set in, showing in the way his hand trembled as he pressed it to his face. "We'd just come from the Andersons'. They had a holiday party tonight. It's only a block over, so we walked. We'd just crossed the street when there was a squeal of brakes. I barely paid attention to it—you know how it is."

"Yes, sir. What did you see?"

"I glanced back, just out of reflex, I suppose. I saw a

dark car—black, I think. No, no, not a car—one of those utility vehicles. The sporty ones. It stopped right here. Right here. You can still see the skid marks in the snow. And then the door opened. He pushed—he all but flung this poor man out, right at our feet."

"You saw the driver?"

"Yes, yes, quite clearly. This corner is very well lit. He was a young man, handsome. Light hair. He smiled . . . he smiled at me just as the door opened. Why, I think I smiled back. He had the kind of face that makes you smile. I'm sure I could identify him. I'm sure of it."

"Yeah." Eve let out a breath, watched the wind snatch it away as the first black-and-whites arrived on the scene. *You wanted to be seen, didn't you, Dave?* she thought. *And you wanted me to be close, very close, when you gave me Carl.*

"You can go inside with your wife, Mr. Fitzgerald. I'll be in touch."

"Yes, of course. Thank you. I—it's Christmas week," he said with honest puzzlement in his eyes. "You live in the city, you know terrible things can and do happen. But it's Christmas week."

"Joy to the world," Eve murmured as he walked away. She turned around and ordered the uniforms to secure the scene and prepare for the crime-scene team. Then she crouched beside Carl and got to work.

Chapter 9

Eve spent most of the next thirty hours backtracking, searching for the step she was sure she had missed. With Peabody off-planet, she did the work herself, rerunning searches and scans, compiling data, studying reports.

She did personal drop-bys at both the safe house where Justine and her family were being kept and Mira's home. She ran checks on their security bracelets to confirm that they were in perfect working order.

He couldn't get to them, she assured herself as she paced her office. With them out of reach, he would have no choice but to come for her.

Jesus, she wanted him to come for her.

It was a mistake, she knew it was a mistake, to make it a personal battle. But she could see his face too clearly, hear his soft prep-school voice so perfectly.

But you see, Lieutenant Dallas, the work you do is nothing more than a stopgap. You don't change anything. However many criminals you lock up today, there'll be that

many and more tomorrow. What I'm doing changes every-
thing. The answers to questions every human being asks.
How much is too much, how much will the mind accept,
tolerate, bear, if you will, before it shuts down? And before
it does, what thoughts, what impulses go through the mind
as the body dies?

Death, Lieutenant, is the focus of your work and of
mine. And while we both enjoy the brutality that goes with
it, in the end I'll have my answers. You'll only have more
questions.

She only had one question now, Eve thought. *Where are*
you, Dave?

She turned back to her computer. "Engage, open file
Palmer, H3492-G. Cross-reference all files and data pertaining to David Palmer. Run probability scan. What is the
probability that Palmer, David, is now residing in New
York City?"

Working. . . . Using current data the probability is
ninety-seven point six that subject Palmer now resides in
New York City.

"What is the probability that subject Palmer resides in a
private home?"

Working. . . . probability ninety-five point eight that sub-
ject Palmer is residing in a private home at this time.

"Given the status of the three remaining targets of subject
Palmer, which individual will he attempt to abduct next?"

Working. . . . strongest probability is for target Dallas,
Lieutenant Eve. Attempts on targets Polinsky and Mira are
illogical given current status.

"That's what you're hoping for."

She turned her head. Roarke stood in the doorway between their offices, watching her. "That's what I'm counting on."

"Why aren't you wearing a tracer bracelet?"

"They don't have one that goes with my outfit." She straightened, turned to face him. "I know what I'm doing."

"Do you?" He crossed to her. "Or are you too close to this one? He's gotten to you, Eve. He's upset your sense of balance. It's become almost intimate between you."

"It's always intimate."

"Maybe." He brushed a thumb just above her left cheekbone. Her eyes were shadowed, her face pale. She was, he knew, running on nerves and determination now. He'd seen it before. "In any case, you've interrupted his work. He has no one now."

"He won't wait long. I don't need the computer analysis to tell me that. We've got less than forty hours left in the year. I don't want to start the new one knowing he's out there. He won't want to start it without me."

"Neither do I."

"You won't have to." Because she sensed he needed it, she leaned into him, closed her mouth over his. "We've got a date."

"I'll hold you to it."

When she started to ease back, he slid his arms around her, brought her close. "I'm not quite done here," he murmured, and sent her blood swimming with a hard and hungry kiss.

For a moment that was all there was. The taste of him, the feel of him pressed against her, the need they created in each other time after time erupting inside her.

Giving herself to it, and to him, was as natural as breathing.

"Roarke, remember how on Christmas Eve we got naked and crazy?"

"Mmm." He moved his mouth to her ear, felt her tremble. "I believe I recall something of that."

"Well, prepare yourself for a review on New Year's Eve." She drew his head back, framing his face as she smiled at him. "I've decided it's one of our holiday traditions."

"I feel very warmly toward tradition."

"Yeah, and if I feel much warmer right now, I'm not going to get my job done, so . . ."

She jumped away from him when her 'link beeped and all but pounced on it. "Dallas."

"Lieutenant." Peabody's face swam on, swam off again, then came shakily back.

"Peabody, either your transmission's poor or you've grown a second nose."

"The equipment here's worse than what we deal with at Central." The audio came through with a snake hiss of static. "And I don't even want to talk about the food. When you're planning your next holiday vacation, steer clear of Rexal."

"And it was top of my list. What have you got for me?"

"I think we just caught a break. We've tracked down at least one unit Palmer had access to. It's in the chapel. He convinced the padre he'd found God and wanted to read Scripture and write an inspirational book on salvation."

"Glory hallelujah. Can McNab access his files?"

"He says he can. Shut up, McNab." Peabody turned her head. The fact that her face became a vivid orange could have been temper or space interference. "I'm giving this report. And I'm reporting, sir, that Detective McNab is still one big butt ache."

"So noted. What does he have so far?"

"He found the files on the book Palmer used to hose the

preacher. And he *claims* he's working down the levels. Hey!"

The buzzing increased and the screen blurred with color, lines, figures. Eve pressed her fingers to her eyes and prayed for patience.

McNab's cheerful, attractive face came on. Eve noted that he wore six tiny silver hoops in one ear. So he hadn't decided to tone down his look for a visit to a rehabilitation center.

"Dallas. This guy knows his electronics, so he took basic precautions with his personal data, but—take a hike, She-Body, this is my area. Anyway, Lieutenant, I'm scraping off the excess now. He's got stuff tucked under his praise-the-Lord hype. It won't take me long to start picking it out. The trouble, other than your aide's constant griping, is transmitting to you. We've got crap equipment here and a meteor storm or some such happy shit happening. It's going to cause some problems."

"Can you work on the unit on a transport?"

"Ah . . . sure. Why not?"

"Confiscate the unit, catch the first transpo back. Report en route."

"Wow, that's iced. Confiscate. You hear that, She-Body? We're confiscating this little bastard."

"Get started," Eve ordered. "If they give you any grief, have the warden contact me. Dallas out."

Eve drove into Cop Central, making three unnecessary stops on the way. If Palmer was going to make a move on her, he'd do it on the street. He'd know he would never be able to break through the defenses of Roarke's fortress. But she spotted no tail, no shadow.

More, she didn't feel him.

Would he go for her in the station? she wondered as she

took the glide up to the EDD sector to consult with Feeney. He'd used a cop's disguise to get to Carl. He could put it to use again, slip into the warrenlike building, blend with the uniforms.

It would be a risk, but a risk like that would increase the excitement, the satisfaction.

She studied faces as she went. Up glides, through breezeways, down corridors, past cubes and offices.

Once she'd updated Feeney and arranged for him to consult with McNab on the unit en route, she elbowed her way onto a packed elevator to make the trip to Commander Whitney's office.

She spent the morning moving through the building, inviting a confrontation, then she took to the streets for the afternoon.

She recanvassed the houses she and Peabody had already hit. Left herself in the open. She bought bad coffee from a glide cart, loitered in the cold and the smoke of grilling soy-dogs.

What the hell was he waiting for? she thought in disgust, tossing the coffee cup into a recycling bin. The sound of a revving engine had her glancing over her shoulder. And she looked directly into Palmer's eyes.

He sat in his vehicle, grinned at her, blew her an exaggerated kiss. Even as she leaped forward, he hit vertical lift, shot up, and streaked south.

She jumped into her car, going air as she squealed away from the curb. "Dispatch, Dallas, Lieutenant Eve. All units, all units in the vicinity of Park and Eighty respond. I'm in ground-to-air chase with murder suspect. Vehicle is a black new-issue Booster-6Z, New York license number Delta Able Zero-4821, temporary. Heading south on Park."

"Dispatch, Dallas. Received and confirmed. Units dispatched. Is subject vehicle in visual range?"

"No. Subject vehicle went air at Park and Eighty, headed south at high speed. Subject should be considered armed and dangerous."

"Acknowledged."

"Where'd you go, where'd you go, you little son of a bitch?" Eve rapped the wheel with her fist as she zipped down Park, shot down cross streets, circled back. "Too fast," she muttered. "You went under too fast. Your hole's got to be close."

She set down, did her best to bank her temper, to use her head and not her emotions. She'd let the search run another thirty minutes, though she'd already decided it was useless. He'd had the vehicle tucked away in a garage or lot minutes after she'd spotted him. After he'd made certain she'd spotted him.

That meant canvasses of every parking facility in three sectors. Public and private. And with the budget, it would take days. The department wouldn't spare the manpower necessary to handle the job any quicker.

She stayed parked where she was, on the off chance that Palmer would try another taunt. After aborting the search, she did slow sweeps through the sectors herself, working off frustration before she drove home through the dark and the snarling traffic.

She didn't bother to snipe at Summerset, though he gave her ample opportunity. Instead, scooping up the cat, which circled her legs, she climbed the stairs. Her intent was to take a blistering-hot shower, drink a gallon of coffee, and go back to work.

Her reality was to fall facedown on the bed. Galahad climbed onto her butt, kneaded his way to comfort, curled up, and went on guard with his eyes slitted on the door.

That's how Roarke found them an hour later.

"I'll take over from here," he murmured, giving the cat a quick scratch between the ears. But when he started to drape a blanket over his wife, Eve stirred.

"I'm awake. I'm just—"

"Resting your eyes. Yes, I know." To keep her prone, Roarke stretched out beside her, stroked the hair away from her cheek. "Rest them a bit longer."

"I saw him today. The son of a bitch was ten feet away, and I lost him." She closed her eyes again. "He wants to piss me off so I stop thinking. Maybe I did, but I'm thinking now."

"And what are you thinking, Lieutenant?"

"That I've been counting too much on the fact that I know him, that I've been inside his head. I've been tracking him without factoring in one vital element."

"Which is?"

She opened her eyes again. "He's fucking crazy." She rolled over, stared at the sky window and the dark beyond it. "You can't predict insanity. Whatever the head shrinkers call it, it comes down to crazy. There's no physical, no psychological reason for it. It just is. He just is. I've been trying to predict the unpredictable. So I keep missing. It's not his work this time. It's payback. The other names on the list are incidental. It's me. He needed them to get to me."

"You'd already concluded that."

"Yeah, but what I didn't conclude, and what I'm concluding now, is he's willing to die, as long as he takes me out. He doesn't intend to go back to prison. I saw his eyes today. They were already dead."

"Which only makes him more dangerous."

"He has to find a way to get to me, so he'll take risks.

But he won't risk going down before he's finished with me.
He needs bait. Good bait. He must know about you."

She sat up now, raking her hair back. "I want you to
wear a bracelet."

He lifted a brow. "I will if you will."

A muscle in her cheek jumped as she set her teeth. "I
phrased that incorrectly. You're *going* to wear a bracelet."

"I believe such things are voluntary unless the subject
has committed a crime." He sat up himself, caught her chin
in his hand. "He won't get to you through me. That I can
promise. But if you expect me to wear NYPSD accessories, you'll have to wear a matching one. Since you
won't, I don't believe this conversation has a point."

"Goddamn it, Roarke. I can slap you into protective
custody. I can order taps on all your communcations, have
you shadowed—"

"No," he interrupted, and infuriated her by kissing her
lightly. "You can't. My lawyers will tap-dance all over your
warrants. Stop." He tightened his grip on her chin before she
could curse him again. And this time there was no light kiss,
no flicker of amusement in his eyes. "You leave here every
day to do a job that puts you in constant physical jeopardy. I
don't ask you to change that. It's one of the reasons I fell
in love with you. Who you are, what you do, why you do it.
I don't ask you to change," he repeated. "Don't you ask me."

"It's just a precaution."

"No, it's a capitulation. If it was less, you'd be wearing
one yourself."

She opened her mouth, shut it again, then shoved away
and rose. "I hate when you're right. I really hate it. I'm going to take a shower. And don't even think about joining
me and trying anything because I'm not too happy with
you right now."

He merely reached out, snagged her hand, and yanked her back onto the bed. "I dare you to say that again in five minutes," he challenged and rolled on top of her.

She didn't say anything in five minutes, could barely speak in thirty. And when she did finally make it to the shower, her blood was still buzzing. She decided it was wiser not to comment when he joined her there. It would only appeal to his competitive streak.

She kept her silence and stepped out of the shower and into the drying tube. It gave her a very nice view. She let herself relax enough to enjoy it, watching the jets of water pulse and pound over Roarke as the hot air swirled around her.

She was back in the bedroom, just tugging on an ancient NYPSD sweatshirt and thinking about coffee and a long evening of work when her palm 'link rang. Vaguely irritated with a call on her personal, she plucked it up from where she'd dumped it on the bedside table.

"Dallas."

"It was nice to see you today. In person. Face-to-face."

"Hello, Dave." With her free hand, she reached in her pocket, switched her communicator on, and plugged in Feeney's code. "Nice vehicle."

"Yes, I like it very much. Fast, efficient, spacious. You're looking a bit tired, Lieutenant. A bit pale. Overworked, as usual? Too bad you haven't been able to enjoy the holidays."

"They've had their moments."

"Mine have been very rewarding." His handsome face glowed with a smile. "It's so good to be back at work. Though I did manage to keep my hand in while I was away. But you and I—I'm sure we'll agree—know there's nothing like New York. Nothing like being home and doing what we love best."

"Too bad you won't be able to stay long."

"Oh, I intend to be here long enough to see the celebration in Times Square tomorrow night. To ring in the new year. In fact, I'm hoping we'll watch it together."

"Sorry, Dave. I have plans." From the corner of her eye, she watched Roarke come out of the bath. Watched him keep out of range, move directly to the bedroom computer, and begin to work manually.

"I think you'll change them. When you know who else I've invited to the party. I picked her up just a little while ago. You should be getting a call shortly from the guards you'd posted. The police haven't gotten any smarter since I've been gone." He let out a charming laugh. "I took a little video for you, Dallas. Take a look. I'll be in touch later to tell you what you need to do to keep her alive."

The image shifted. Eve's blood iced as she saw the woman in the cage. Unconscious, pale, one slim hand dangling through the bars.

"Transmitted from a public 'link," Roarke said from behind her. "Grand Central."

Dimly she heard Feeney giving her the same information through her communicator. Units were already on their way to the location.

He'd be gone. Of course they knew he'd already be gone.

"He has Mira." It was all she could say. "He has Mira."

Chapter 10

Panic wanted to win. It crawled in her belly, snaked up her throat. It made her hands shake until she balled them into fists.

It wanted to swallow her when she moved through Mira's house, when she found the broken security bracelet on the floor of the office.

"He used laser tools." Her voice was steady and cool as she bagged the bracelet. "He anticipated that she'd be wearing one and brought what was necessary to remove it."

"The MTs are taking the guards in. The two from outside were just stunned. But one of the inside team's in bad shape." Feeney crouched down next to her. "Looks like Palmer got in the back, bypassed the security system like a pro. He hit the one guard in the kitchen, used a stunner to take him out quick and quiet. From the looks of the living area, the second one gave him more trouble. They went a round in there. Mira must have been up here. If she had the door closed and was working, she wouldn't have heard anything. Room's fully soundproofed."

"So he takes out the security, four experienced cops, waltzes right in, dismantles her bracelet, and waltzes out with her. We underestimated him, Feeney." And for that she would forever blame herself. "He's not what he was when I took him down before. He's studied up, he's learned, he's gotten himself into condition. He made good use of three years in a cage."

"She knows how his mind works." Feeney laid his hand on her shoulder. "Mira knows how to handle this kind of guy. She'll use that. She'll keep her cool and use it."

"No one knows how his mind works this time around. Thinking I did was part of the problem all along. I fucked up here, Feeney, and Mira's going to pay for it."

"You're wrong. The only fucking up you're doing is thinking that way now."

"I thought he might use Roarke as bait. Because if he's been studying me he knows that's where he could hit me the hardest." She made herself breathe slow as she got to her feet. "But he knows me better than I figured. He knows she matters to me."

"And he'll count on that messing you up. You gonna let it?"

"No." She breathed in again, exhaled. "No. I need Mc-Nab to shake something loose. What's their ETA?"

"Midday tomorrow. They had some transpo delays. The transmissions are full of blips, but I got that he's dug into some financials."

"Shoot whatever you've got to my home unit. I'll be working from there."

"We'll want to tap your palm 'link."

"Yeah, he'll have figured that, but we'll do it anyway." She met Feeney's eyes. "We take the steps."

"We'll get her back, Dallas."

"Yeah, we will." She turned the sealed bracelet over in her hand. "If he hurts her, I'm taking him out." She lifted her gaze again. "Whatever line I have to cross, I take him out."

When she walked outside, Roarke was waiting. She hadn't argued when he'd come with her and could only be grateful that he was there to drive home so her mind could be free to think.

"Feeney's going to be sending me data," she began as she climbed into the car. "Financials. You'll be able to extrapolate faster. The sweepers will go through Mira's house, but he won't have left much, if anything. Anyway, it's not a question of IDing him. Peabody and McNab won't be back until midday tomorrow, so we'll be working with whatever they can send us while they're en route."

"I took a look at the alarms and security. It's a very good system. He used a sophisticated bypass unit to take it out without triggering the auto. It's not something your average citizen can access easily. I can help you trace the source."

"Doesn't matter at this point. Later we can deal with it. It's just another thread he left dangling, figuring I'd waste time pulling it and getting nowhere."

She rubbed at the headache behind her eyes. "I've got uniforms canvassing. One of the neighbors might have seen or heard something. It's useless, but it's routine and we might get lucky."

She closed her eyes, forced herself to think past the fear. "She's got until tomorrow, midnight. Dave wants some tradition and symbolism. He wants to welcome in the new year with me, and he needs her to get me there."

Her voice was too cool, Roarke thought. Too controlled. He'd seen the hint of panic in her eyes, and the grief. He let her hold in both as they arrived home, as she walked directly up to her office and called up all necessary files.

She added hard-copy data to the investigator's board she'd set up. And when she shifted Mira's photo from one area to the other, her fingers shook.

"Eve." He took her shoulders, turned her around. "Let it out."

"Can't. Don't talk to me."

"You can't work around it." He only tightened his grip when she tried to jerk away. "Let it out. Let it out," he said in a gentler tone. "I know what she means to you."

"God." She wrapped her arms around him, curling her hands up over his shoulders as she pressed her face into his neck. "Oh, God. Hold on. Just for a minute, hold on."

Her body shook, one hard wave of shudders after another. She didn't weep, but her breath hitched as he held her close. "I can't think about what he might do to her. If I think about it, I'll lose it."

"Then remember she's strong, and she's smart. She'll know what she has to do."

"Yeah." Her 'link signaled incoming data. "That'll be the financials."

"I'll start on them." He eased her back. "He won't win this round."

"Damn right."

She worked until her eyes and mind went blurry, then fueled up with coffee and worked some more. At just after two A.M. Feeney shot her more data. It told her that he, Peabody, and McNab were all still on the job.

"Basically," Roarke said, "this is just confirming what we already have. The accounts, the transfers. You need to find more. You need to look from a different angle." He glanced up to see Eve all but swaying on her feet. "And you need to sleep."

She would have argued, but it would have wasted time. "We both do. Just a little while. We can share the sleep chair. I want to stay close to this unit."

The caffeine in her system couldn't fight off exhaustion. Moments after closing her eyes, she fell into sleep. Where nightmares chased her.

Images of Mira trapped in a cage mixed and melded with memories of herself as a child, locked in a room. Horror, pain, fear lived in both places. He would come—Palmer, her father—he would come and he would hurt her because he could. Because he enjoyed it. Because she couldn't stop him.

Until she killed him.

But even then he came back and did it all again in her dreams.

She moaned in sleep, curled into Roarke.

It was the smell of coffee and food that woke her. She sat up with a jerk, blinked blindly in the dark, and found herself alone in the chair. She stumbled into the kitchen and saw Roarke already taking food from the AutoChef.

"You need to eat."

"Yeah, okay." But she went for the coffee first. "I was thinking about what you said, looking at a different angle." She sat, because he nudged her into a chair, and shoveled in food because it was in front of her. "What if he bought or rented this place he's got before he got to New York? A year ago, two years ago?"

"It's possible. I still haven't found any payments."

"Has to be there. Somewhere." She heard the ring of her palm 'link from the other room and was on her feet. "Stay in here, do what you can to trace."

Deliberately she moved behind her desk, sat, composed her face. "Dallas."

"Good morning, Lieutenant. I hope you slept well."

"Like a top, Dave." She curled a hand under the desk.

"Good. I want you rested up for our date tonight. You've got, oh, let's see, just over sixteen and a half hours to get here. I have every confidence in you."

"You could tell me where you are, we can start our date early."

He laughed, obviously delighted with her. "And spoil the fun? I don't think so. We're puzzle solvers, Dallas. You find me by midnight and Dr. Mira will remain perfectly safe. That's providing you come to see me alone. I'll know if you bring uninvited guests, as I have full security. Any gate-crashers, and the good doctor dies immediately and in great physical distress. I want to dance with you, Dallas. Just you. Understood?"

"It's always been you and me, Dave."

"Exactly. Come alone, by midnight, and we'll finish what we started three years ago."

"I don't know that she's still alive."

He only smiled. "You don't know that she's not." And broke transmission.

"Another public 'link," Roarke told her. "Port Authority."

"I need the location. If I'm not there by midnight, he'll kill her." She rose, paced. "He's got a place, one with full security. He's not bullshitting there. He'll have cameras, in and out. Sensors. He didn't have time to set all that up in a week, so either the place came equipped with them or he ordered them from prison courtesy of the chaplain."

"We can access tax records, blueprints, specs. It'll take time."

"Time's running out. Let's get started."

At two she received word that Peabody and McNab had landed, and she ordered them to bring the unit to her home office. He was close, she thought again, and none of them should waste time working downtown.

The minute they walked in, she began outlining her plan of attack. "McNab, set up over there. Start checking out any financials, transfers, transmissions, using the chaplain's name. Or a combo of his and Palmer's. Peabody, contact Whitney, request a canvass of all private garages in the suspect area. I want uniforms, every warm body we can find, hitting the public parking facilities with orders to confiscate and review all security tapes for the past week."

"All, Lieutenant?"

"Every last one."

She swung around and into Roarke's office. Using his auxiliary unit, she called up data, shot it to screen. "I've got the residences of Palmer's targets in blue," she told Roarke. "We run from mid to upper Manhattan, heaviest population on the East Side. We need to concentrate on private homes in this ten-block radius. Unless something jumps out at you, disregard anything that doesn't fit this profile."

She rolled her shoulders to relieve the tension, closed her eyes to clear her mind. "It'll have a basement. Probably two stories in addition to it. Fully soundproofed and most likely with its own vehicle storage area. I've got them looking at public storage, but I'm betting he has his own. He wants me to find him, goddamn it, so it can't be that hard. He wants me to work for it but not to fail. It's just personal for him, and without me . . ."

She trailed off, whirled around. "He needs me. Jesus. Check my name. Check deeds, mortgages, leases using my name."

"There's your new angle, Lieutenant," Roarke murmured as he set to work. "Very good."

"Toss it on screen," she asked even as she moved to stand behind him and watch. As her name popped up with a list of liber and folio numbers she swore again. "How the hell did he get all that property?"

"That's not his, it's yours."

"What do you mean mine? I don't own anything."

"Properties I've transferred into your name." Roarke spoke absently as he continued the scan.

"Transferred? What the hell for?"

He skimmed a finger lightly over her wedding ring and earned a punch in the shoulder. "You're welcome."

"Take it back. All of it."

"It's complicated. Taxes. Really, you're doing me a favor. No, there's nothing here that isn't yours. We'll try a combination of names."

She wanted, badly, to seethe, but she didn't have time.

They found three listings for the name David Dallas in Manhattan.

"Get the property descriptions."

"I'm working on it. It takes a moment to hack into City Hall."

Barely more than that for Roarke, Eve noted as the data flashed on screen. "No, that's downtown. Sex club. Try the next." She gripped the back of his chair, straining with impatience. "That's just out of the target area, but possible. Hold that and run the last. I'll be damned." She almost whispered it. "He reverted to type after all. That's his parents' house. He bought their place."

"Two and a half years ago," Roarke confirmed. "Using the name David Dallas. Your man was thinking ahead. Very far ahead. We'll find accounts in that name, or an account that he had and closed."

"Five blocks from here. The son of a bitch is five blocks from here." She leaned down, kissed the top of Roarke's head, and strode back into her office. "I've found it," she announced, then looked at her wrist unit. "We've got seven hours to figure out how to take him down."

She would go in alone. She insisted on it. She agreed to go in wired. Agreed to surveillance and backup at half-block intervals surrounding the house. For luck she pinned on the badge Peabody had given her, then waited with growing impatience as Feeney checked the transmitter.

"You're on," he told her. "Nothing I found on the video disc had equipment that can tag this pretty little bug. We've got a decoy so he'll think he's found one and deactivated it."

"Good thinking."

"You got to do it this way." He nodded at her. "I'd do the same. But you better understand I hear anything I don't like, I'm coming in. Roarke." He stepped back as Roarke came into the room. "I'll give you a minute here."

Roarke crossed to her, tapped a finger on her badge. "Funny, you don't look like Gary Cooper."

"Who?"

He smiled. "*High Noon*, darling Eve, though the clock's turned around on this one. We have a date in a couple of hours."

"I remember. I've got a present coming. I can do this."

"Yes." He kissed her, softly. "I know. Give my best to Mira."

"You bet. The team's moving into place now. I have to go."

"I'll see you soon."

He waited until she was gone, then walked outside himself and climbed casually into Feeney's unit. "I'll be riding with you."

Feeney scratched his chin. "Dallas won't like it."

"That's a pity. I spent the last few hours studying the schematics for the security on the Palmer house. I can bypass it, by remote."

"Can you, now?" Feeney said mildly.

Roarke turned his head, gave Feeney a level look. "I shouldn't need more than twenty minutes clear to manage it."

Feeney pursed his lips and started down the drive. "I'll see what we can do about that."

She went in at ten. It was best, she'd decided, not to cut it too close to the deadline. The old brownstone was lovely, in perfect repair. The security cameras and sensors were discreetly worked into the trim so as not to detract from its dignity.

As she walked to the door she was certain Palmer was watching. And that he was pleased. She gave the overhead camera a brief glance, then bypassed the locks with her master.

She closed the door at her back, heard the locks snick automatically back into place. As they did, the foyer lights flashed on.

"Good evening, Dallas." Palmer's voice flowed out of

the intercom. "I'm so pleased you could make it. I was just assuring Doctor Mira that you'd be here soon so we could begin our end-of-year celebration. She's fine, by the way. Now, if you'd just remove your weapon—"

"No." She said it casually as she moved forward. "I'm not stripping down for you, Dave, so you can take me out as I come down the stairs. Let's not insult each other."

He laughed. "Well, I suppose you're right. Keep it. Take it out. Engage it. It's fine. Just remember, Doctor Mira's fate is in your hands. Come join us, Lieutenant. Let's party."

She'd been in the house before, when she interviewed his parents. Even if the basic setup hadn't come back to her, she'd taken time to study the blueprints. Still, she didn't move too quickly, but scanned cautiously for booby traps on the way through the house.

She turned at the kitchen, opened the basement door. The sound of cheering blasted up at her. The lights were on bright. She could see streamers, balloons, festive decorations.

She took her weapon out and started down.

He had champagne chilling in a bucket, pretty canapés spread on silver trays on a table draped with a colorful cloth.

And he had Mira in a cage.

"Lieutenant Dallas." Mira said it calmly, though her mind was screaming. She'd been careful to call Eve by her title, to keep their relationship professional, distant.

"Doctor." Palmer clucked his tongue. "I told you I'd do the talking. Lieutenant, you see this control I'm holding. Just so we understand each other right away, if I press this button, a very strong current will pass through the metal of the doctor's temporary home. She'll be dead in seconds.

Even with your weapon on full, I'll have time to engage it. Actually, my nervous system will react in such a way to the shock that my finger will twitch involuntarily, and the doctor, shall we say, is toasted."

"Okay, Dave, but I intend to verify that Doctor Mira is unharmed. Are you hurt, Doctor?"

"No." And she'd managed so far to hold back hysteria. "He hasn't hurt me. And I don't think he will. You won't hurt me, will you, David? You know I want to help you. I understand how difficult all this has been for you, not having anyone who appreciates what you've been working to achieve."

"She's really good, isn't she?" he said to Eve. "So soothing. Since I don't want to show her any disrespect— you'll note I didn't remove her clothing for our little experiment—maybe you should tell her to shut the fuck up. Would you mind, Dallas?"

"Dave and I need to handle this, Dr. Mira." Eve moved closer. "Don't we, Dave? It's you and me."

"I've waited for this for so long. You can see I've gone to quite a bit of trouble." He gestured with his free hand. "Maybe you'd like a drink, an hors d'oeuvre. We have a celebration going on. The end of the old, the birth of the new. Oh, and before I jam that wire you're wearing, tell the backup team that if anyone attempts entry, you both die."

"I'm sure they heard you. And they already have orders to hold back. You said to come alone," she reminded him. "So I did. I always played it straight with you."

"That's right. We learned to trust each other."

"Why stop now? I've got a deal for you, Dave. A trade. Me for Mira. You let her out of there, you let her go, and I'll get in. You'll have what you want."

"Eve, don't—" Mira's composure started to slip.

"This is between me and Dave." She kept her eye on him, level and cool. "That's what you want, isn't it? To put me in a cage, the way I put you in one. You've been thinking about it for three years. You've been planning it, working for it, arranging it step by step. And you did a damn good job this time around. Let her go, Dave. She was just bait, you got me here by using her. Let her go and I'll put down my weapon. I'll get in, and you'll have the kind of subject you've always wanted."

She took another step toward him, watching his eyes now, watching them consider. Desire. "She's a shrink, and she's not in the kind of condition I'm in—mental or physical. She sits at a desk and pokes into other people's minds. You start on her, she'll go down fast, give you no satisfaction. Think how long I'll last. Not just hours, days. Maybe weeks if you can hold the outside team off that long. You know it's going to end here, for both of us."

"Yes, I'm prepared for that."

"But this way, you can get your payback and finish your work. Two for one. But you have to let her out."

Music crashed out of the entertainment unit. On screen the revelers in Times Square swarmed like feverish ants.

"Put down the weapon now."

"Tell me it's a deal." She held her breath, lifted her weapon, aimed it at the center of his body. "Tell me it's a deal or I take you down. She goes, but I live. And you lose all around. Take the deal, Dave. You'll never get a better one."

"I'll take the deal." All but quivering with excitement, he rubbed a hand over his mouth. "Put the weapon down. Put it down and move away from it."

"Bring the cage down first. Bring it down to the floor so I know you mean it."

"I can still kill her." But he reached out to the console, touched a switch. The cage began to sway and lower.

"I know it. You've got the power here. I've just got a job. I'm sworn to protect her. Unlock the cage."

"Put the weapon down!" He shouted it out now, raising his voice over the music and cheers. "You said you'd put it down, now do it!"

"Okay. We've got a deal." Sweat slid down her back as she bent to lay the weapon on the floor. "You don't kill for the hell of it. It's for science. Unlock the cage and let her go." Eve lifted her hands, palms out.

On a bright laugh, he grabbed up a stunner, jabbed the air with it. "Just in case. You stay where you are, Dallas."

Her heart began to beat again when he put the control down, hit the button to release the locks. "Sorry you have to leave the party, Doctor Mira. But I promised this dance to the lieutenant."

"I need to help her out." Eve crouched to take Mira's hand. "Her muscles are stiff. She wouldn't have lasted for you, Dave." She gave Mira's hand one hard squeeze.

"Get in, get in now."

"As soon as she's clear." Eve remained crouched, pushed Mira aside. As she used her body as a shield, she had time to register a movement on the stairs, then her clinch piece was in her hand.

"I lied, Dave." She watched his eyes go round with shock, saw him grab for the control, lower the stunner. The crowd cheered wildly as her blast took him full in the chest.

His body jerked, a quick and obscene dance. He was right, she noted, about the finger twitch. It depressed convulsively on the control even as he fell onto the cage.

Sparks showered from it, from his quaking body as she dragged Mira clear and curled herself over her.

"Your jacket's caught fire, Lieutenant." With admirable calm, Roarke bent over and patted out the spark that burned the leather at her shoulder.

"What the hell are you doing here?"

"Just picking up my wife for our date." He reached down gently and helped Mira to her feet. "He's gone," Roarke murmured, and brushed tears from her checks.

"I couldn't reach him. I tried, for hours after I woke up in that . . . in that thing. But I couldn't reach him." Mira turned to Eve. "You could, in the only way that was left. I was afraid you'd—" She broke off, shook her head. "I was afraid you'd come, and afraid you wouldn't. I should have trusted you to do what had to be done."

When she caught Eve in a hard embrace, pressed her cheek against hers, Eve held on, just held on, then eased away, awkwardly patting Mira's back. "It was a team effort—including this civilian this time around. Go spend New Year's with your family. We'll worry about the routine later."

"Thank you for my life." She kissed Eve's cheek, then turned and kissed Roarke's. And didn't begin to weep again until she was upstairs.

"Well, Lieutenant, it's a very fitting end."

She followed Roarke's gaze, studied Palmer, and felt nothing but quiet relief. "To the man or the year?"

"To both." He stepped to the champagne, sniffing it as he drew it from the bucket. "Your team's on the way in. But I think we could take time for a toast."

"Not here. Not with that." She took the bottle, dumped it back into the bucket. On impulse, she took the badge off her shirt, pinned it on his. "Routine can wait. I want to collect on my present."

"Where do you want to go?"

"Just home." She slid an arm around his waist, moving toward the stairs as cops started down. "Just home, with you." She heard the crowd erupt with another cheer. "Happy New Year."

"Not quite yet. But it will be."

HAUNTED
IN
DEATH

There nearly always is method in madness.

—CHESTERTON

There needs no ghost, my lord, come from
the grave to tell us this.

—SHAKESPEARE

Chapter 1

Winter could be murderous. The slick streets and icy sidewalks broke bones and cracked skulls with gleeful regularity. Plummeting temperatures froze the blood and stopped the hearts of a select few every night in the frigid misery of Sidewalk City.

Even those lucky enough to have warm, cozy homes were trapped inside by the bitter winds and icy rains. In the first two weeks of January 2060—post-holiday—bitch winter was a contributing factor to the sharp rise in domestic disturbance calls to the New York City Police and Security Department.

Even reasonably happy couples got twitchy when they were bound together long enough by the cold ropes of winter.

For Lieutenant Eve Dallas, double d's weren't on her plate. Unless some stir-crazy couple killed each other out of sheer boredom.

She was Homicide.

On this miserable, bone-chilling morning, she stood over the dead. It wasn't the cold or the ice that had killed Radcliff C. Hopkins III. She couldn't say, as yet, if the blue-tipped fingers of winter had been a contributing factor. But it was clear someone had put numerous nasty holes in Radcliff C.'s chest. And another, neatly centered on his wide forehead.

Beside her, Eve's partner, Detective Delia Peabody, crouched for a closer look. "I've never seen these kinds of wounds before, outside of training vids."

"I have. Once."

It had been winter then, too, Eve remembered, when she'd stood over the first victim in a series of rape/murders. The gun ban had all but eliminated death by firearm, so gunshot wounds were rare. Not that people didn't continue to kill each other habitually. But the remote violence and simplicity of a bullet into flesh and bone wasn't often the method of choice these days.

Radcliff C. might have been done in by an antiquated method, but it didn't make him any less dead.

"Lab boys will rub their hands together over this one," Eve murmured. "They don't get much call to play with ballistics."

She was a tall woman, with a lean build inside a long black leather coat. Her face was sharp with angles, her eyes long and brown and observant. As a rare concession to the cold, she'd yanked a black watch cap over her short, usually untidy brown hair. But she'd lost her gloves again.

She continued to stand, let her partner run the gauge for time of death.

"Six wounds visible," Eve said. "Four in the body, one in the right leg, one to the head. From the blood spatter, blood trail, it looks like he was hit first there." She gestured a few feet away. "Force knocks him back, down, so he tries to crawl. Big guy, fleshy, with a strong look to him. He maybe had enough in him to crawl some, maybe to try to get up again."

"Time of death, oh-two-twenty." Peabody, her dark hair in a short, sassy flip at the base of her neck, looked up. Her square, sturdy face was cop solemn, but there was a gleam in her eye, dark as her hair. "ID confirmed. You know who he is, right?"

"Hopkins, Radcliff C. With the fussy Roman numerals after."

"Your lack of interest in culture trivia's showing again. His grandfather was Hop Hopkins, and made a couple of fortunes in the swinging Sixties. Nineteen-sixties. Sex, drugs, and rock 'n' roll. Night clubs, music venues. L.A.-based, mostly, before the big one hit California, but he had a hot spot here in New York."

Peabody shifted her weight. "Ran hot for a couple of decades, then hit a serious patch of bad luck. The even more legendary Bobbie Bray—she was—"

"I know who Bobbie Bray was." Eve hooked her thumbs in her pockets, rocking back on her heels as she continued to study the body, the scene. "I'm not completely oblivious to popular culture. Rock star, junkie, and a cult figure now. Vanished without a trace."

"Yeah, well, she was his wife—third or fourth—when she poofed. Rumor and gossip figured maybe he offed her or had her done, but the cops couldn't find enough evidence to indict. He went spooky, did the hermit thing, lost big fat piles of dough, and ended up OD'ing on his drug of choice—can't remember what it was—right here in New York."

Peabody pushed to her feet. "From there it's urban legend time. Place where he OD'd was upstairs from the club, that's where he'd holed himself up. In the luxury apartment he'd put in on the top floor. Building passed from hand to hand, but nobody could ever make a go of it. Because . . ."

Peabody paused now, for effect. "It's haunted. And cursed. Anyone who's ever tried to live there, or put a business in, suffers personal and/or physical misfortunes."

"Number Twelve. Yeah, I've heard of it. Interesting." Hands still in her pockets, Eve scanned the large, dilapidated room. "Haunted and cursed. Seems redundant. Guess maybe Radcliff C. figured on bucking that."

"What do you mean?" Then Peabody's jaw dropped. "This is the place? *This?* Oh boy. Jeez."

"Anonymous tip does the nine-one-one. Gonna want to review that transmission, because it's likely it was the killer. What I've got is the vic owned the building, was having it rehabbed, redesigned. Maybe looking for some of his grandfather's glory days. But what's our boy doing hanging around in a cursed, haunted building at two in the morning?"

"This is the place," Peabody repeated, reverently now. "Number Twelve."

"Since the addy's Twelve East Twelfth, I'm going to go out on a limb and say, yeah. Let's turn him."

"Oh, right."

When they rolled the body, Eve pursed her lips. "Somebody really wanted this guy dead. Three more entry

wounds on the back. Lab will confirm, but I'm thinking . . ."

She crossed the room toward a set of old circular iron
stairs. "Standing about here, facing the attacker. Pow, pow.
Takes it in the chest." She slapped a hand on her own.
"Stumbles back, goes down. The smeared blood trail tells
me the vic tried crawling away, probably toward the
doors."

"Doors were locked from the inside. First on scene
said," Peabody added.

"Yeah. So he's crawling, and the killer moves in. Pow,
pow, into the back." The sound of the shots must have
blasted the air in here, Eve thought. Must have set the ears
ringing. "But it's not enough. No, we're not finished yet.
Body falls, has to be dead or dying, but it's not enough.
Turns the body over, puts the barrel of the gun to the forehead. See the burn marks around the forehead wound?
Contact. I did a lot of studying up on firearms during the
DeBlass case a couple years ago. Puts the barrel right
against the head and pow. Coup de grace."

Eve saw it in her head. Heard it, smelled it. "You put a
gun like this." She pressed her fingertip to her own brow.
"You put it right against the skin and fire, it's personal. You
put that many steel missiles in somebody, you're seriously
pissed off."

"Vic's got his bright, shiny wristwatch—looks
antique—his wallet—cash and credit inside—key codes,
ppc, pocket 'link. Killer didn't bother making it look like
robbery."

"We'll run the electronics. Let's have a look at the
'link."

Eve took the 'link in her sealed hands, called up the last

transmission. There was a whispering, windy sound, which Eve had to admit tingled her spine just a bit. The husky female voice wove through it.

Number Twelve. Two A.M. Bring it. Bring it, and we'll party.

"Maybe robbery plays in after all."

"Did you hear that voice?" Peabody sent a cautious look over her shoulder. "It sounded, you know, unearthly."

"Funny, sounded computer-generated to me. But maybe that's because I know ghosts don't make 'link transmissions, or shoot guns. Because—and this may be news to you, Peabody—ghosts don't exist."

Peabody only shook her head, sagely. "Oh yeah? Tell that to my great-aunt Josie who died eight years ago and came back half a dozen times to nag my great-uncle Phil about fixing the leaky toilet in the powder room. She left him alone after he called the plumber."

"And how much does your great-uncle Phil drink?"

"Oh, come on. People see ghosts all the time."

"That's because people, by and large, are whacked. Let's work the case, Peabody. It wasn't a ghostly finger that pulled the trigger here. Or lured the vic to an empty building in the middle of the night. Let's do a run. Spouse, family, beneficiaries, business partners, friends, enemies. And let's keep it to the corporeal."

Eve reexamined the body, wondering if he'd brought whatever *it* was. "They can bag and tag. Start checking doors and windows. Let's find out how the killer got out of the building. I'll have another talk with the first on scene."

"You want me to stay in here? To wander around in here. Alone?"

"Are you kidding?" One look at Peabody's face told Eve her partner was absolutely serious. "Well, for God's sake. You take the first on scene. I'll take the building."

"Better plan. You want crime scene in now, and the body transported?"

"Get it done."

Eve took a visual sweep on the main floor. Maybe it had been a hot spot in the last century, but now it was derelict. She could see where some of the work had begun. Portions of the grimy walls had been stripped away to their bones to reveal the old, and certainly out-of-code, electrical wiring. Portable lights and heating units were set up, as well as stacks of materials in what seemed to be tidy and organized piles.

But the drop cloths, the material, the lights all had a coat of dust. Maybe Hopkins had started his rehab, but it looked as if there'd been a long lag since the last nail gun popped.

The remains of an old bar hulked in the center of the room. As it was draped with more dusty protective cloth, she assumed Hopkins had intended to restore it to whatever its former glory might have been.

She checked the rear exit door, found it, too, secured from inside. Through another door she found what might have been a storeroom at one time, and was now a junk heap. The two windows were about big enough for a cat to squeeze through, and were riot barred.

The toilet facilities on the main level were currently pits, with no outside access.

"Okay, unless you're still here, waiting for me to cuff you and read you your rights, you found a way up and out."

She glanced at the ancient elevator; opted for the spindly iron stairs.

The sweepers were going to have a hell of a time finding usable prints or physical evidence, she thought. There were decades of dust, grime, considerable water damage, what seemed to be old scorching from a fire.

She recorded and marked some blurry footprints smudged on the dirty floor.

Cold, she thought. *Freaking cold in here.*

She moved along the second-floor landing, imagined it packed with tables and people during its heyday. Music pumping out to shatter ear drums, the fashionable drugs of the time passed around like party favors. The chrome safety railings would have been polished to a gleam, flashing with the wild colors of the lights.

She stood as she was a moment, looking down as the ME drones bagged the body. Good view from there, she mused. See whatever you want to see. People ass to elbow below, sweating and grinding on the dance floor and hoping somebody was watching.

Did you come up here tonight, Hopkins? Did you have enough brains before they got blown out to come early, scope the place out? Or did you just walk in?

She found the exit at a second-story window, unlocked and partially open, with the emergency stairs deployed.

"So much for that mystery. Suspect most likely exited the building," she stated for the record, "from this point. Sweepers will process the window, stairs, and surrounding areas for prints and other evidence. And lookie, lookie." She crouched, shined her light on the edge of the window-sill. "Got a little blood, probably vic's. Suspect may have had some spatter, or transferred some blood to his clothing when he moved in for the head shot."

Frowning, she shined the light farther down, onto the floor where something sparkled. "Looks like jewelry. Or . . . hmm. Some sort of hair decoration," she amended when she lifted it with tweezers. "Damn if it doesn't look like diamonds to me, on some kind of clip. About a half-inch wide, maybe two inches long. No dust on it—stones are clean and bright in what I'd guess to be a platinum setting. Antique looking."

She bagged it.

She started to head back down, then thought she heard the floor creak overhead. Old buildings, she reminded herself, but drew her weapon. She moved to the back wall, which was partially caved in, and the old metal stairs behind it.

The sound came again, just a stealthy little creak. For a moment she thought she heard a woman's voice, raw and throaty, singing about a bleeding heart.

At the top of the stairs the floors had been scrubbed clean. They were scarred and scorched, but no dust lay on them. There was old smoke and fire damage on some of the interior walls, but she could see the area had been set up into a large apartment, and what might have been an office.

She swept, light and weapon, but saw nothing but rubble. The only sound now was the steady inhale, exhale of her own breath, which came out in veritable plumes.

If heat was supposed to rise, why the hell was it so much colder up here? She moved through the doorless opening to the left to do a thorough search.

Floors are too clean, she thought. And there was no debris here as there was in the other smaller unit, no faded graffiti decorating the walls. Eve cocked her head at the large hole in the wall on the far right. It looked as though it had been measured and cut, neatly, as a doorway.

She crossed the room to shine her light into the dark.

The skeleton lay as if in repose. In the center of the skull's forehead was a small, almost tidy hole.

Cupped in the yellowed fingers was the glittery mate to the diamond clip. And near the other was the chrome gleam of a semi-automatic.

"Well son of a bitch," Eve murmured, and pulled out her communicator to hail Peabody.

Chapter 2

"It's her. It's got to be her."

"Her being the current vic's ancestor's dead wife." Eve drove through spitting ice from the crime scene to the victim's home.

"Or lover. I'm not sure they were actually married now that I think about it. Gonna check on that," Peabody added, making a note in her memo book. "But here's what must've gone down: Hopkins, the first one, kills Bobbie, then bricks the body up in the wall of the apartment he used over the club."

"And the cops at the time didn't notice there was a spanking new brick wall in the apartment?"

"Maybe they didn't look very hard. Hopkins had a lot of money, and a river of illegal substances. A lot of connections, and probably a lot of information certain high connections wouldn't want made public."

"He bought off the investigation." Whether it happened eighty-five years ago or yesterday, the smell of bad cops

offended Eve's senses. But . . . "Not impossible," she had
to admit. "If it is the missing wife/girlfriend, it could be
she wasn't reported missing until he had everything fairly
tidied up. Then you got your payoff, or classic blackmail
regarding the investigators, and he walks clean."

"He did sort of go crazy. Jeez, Dallas, he basically
locked himself up there in that place for over ten years,
with a body behind the wall."

"Maybe. Let's get the bones dated and identified before
we jump there. The crime scene guys were all but weeping
with joy over those bones. While they're having their fun,
we've got an active case, from this century."

"But you're curious, right? You gotta wonder if we just
found Bobbie Bray. And the hair clips. Is that spooky or
what?"

"Nothing spooky about a killer planting them. Wanted
us to find the bones, that's a given. So connecting the dots,
the skeleton and our vic are linked, at least in the killer's
mind. What do we have on Hopkins so far?"

"Vic was sixty-two at TOD. Three marriages, three di-
vorces. Only offspring—son from second marriage."
Peabody scanned her memo book. "Bounced back and
forth between New York and New L.A., with a couple of
stints in Europe. Entertainment field, mostly fringe. Didn't
seem to have his grandfather's flair. Parents died in a private plane crash twenty-five years back. No sibs."

Peabody glanced over. "The Hopkins line doesn't go toward longevity and propagation. Part of the curse."

"Part of birth control practices and lousy luck," Eve
corrected. "What else—salient—do we have?"

"You gotta wonder," Peabody went on. "I mean, Hopkins
number two was married four times. Four. One surviving
son—or surviving until now. He had a daughter from an-

other marriage who drowned when she was a teenager, and another son—still another marriage—who hanged himself when he was twenty-three. That's the kind of consistent bad luck that says curse to me."

"It says pretty irrelevant background data to me. Give me something on our vic."

"Okay, okay. Rad Hopkins went through a lot of the money his father managed to recoup, and most of what he'd inherited from his mother, who was a socialite with some traces of blue blood. He had a few minor smudges for illegals, solicitation, gray-area business practices. No time served. Oh, no collector's license for firearms."

"Where are the ex-wives?"

"Number one's based in New L.A. B-movie actress. Well, B-minus, really. Number three's in Europe, married to some minor English aristocrat. But number two's here in New York. Fanny Gill—dance instructor. The son's Cliff Gill Hopkins—though he dropped the Hopkins legally at age twenty-one. They run a dance studio."

"New York's an easy place to get to and get out of. We'll run them all. Business partners?"

"None currently. He's had a mess of them, off and on. But he was the sole owner and proprietor of Number Twelve Productions, which has the same address as his residence. He bought the building he died in at auction about six months ago."

"Not much work done in there in six months."

"I tagged the construction company from the name on the building permit. Owner tells me they got called off after three weeks. Their scuttlebutt is Hopkins ran out of money and scrambled around for some backers. But he said he had a call from the vic a few days ago, wanting to schedule work to start up again."

"So maybe he got some money, or wheeled some sort of deal."

She found the miracle of a street-level spot a half block from Hopkins's building.

"Decent digs," Eve noted. "Fancy antique wrist unit, designer wallet, pricey shoes. Doesn't give the appearance of hurting financially."

She flashed her badge at the doorman. "Hopkins," she said. "Radcliff C."

"I'll ring up and let him know you'd like to speak with him."

"Don't bother. He's in the morgue. When's the last time you saw him?"

"Dead?" The doorman, a short, stocky mixed-race man of about forty, stared at Eve as his jaw dropped. "Mr. Hopkins is dead? An accident?"

"Yes, he's dead. No, it wasn't an accident. When did you last see him?"

"Yesterday. He went out about twelve-thirty in the afternoon, came back around two. I went off duty at four. My replacement would have gone off at midnight. No doorman from midnight to eight."

"Anybody come to see him?"

"No one that checked in with me. The building's secured. Passcodes are required for the elevators. Mr. Hopkins's apartment is on the sixth floor." The doorman shook his head, rubbed a gloved hand over the back of his neck. "Dead. I just can't believe it."

"He live alone?"

"He did, yes."

"Entertain much?"

"Occasionally."

"Overnight entertaining? Come on, Cleeve," Eve

prompted, scanning his brass name tag. "Guy's dead."

"Occasionally," he repeated and puffed out his cheeks. "He, ah, liked variety, so I couldn't say there was any particular lady. He also liked them young."

"How young?"

"Mid-twenties, primarily, by my gauge. I haven't noticed anyone visiting the last couple of weeks. He's been in and out nearly every day. Meetings, I assume, for the club he's opening. Was opening."

"Okay, good enough. We're going up."

"I'll clear the code for you." Cleeve held the door for them, then walked to the first of two elevators. He skimmed his passcode through the slot, then keyed in his code. "I'm sorry to hear about Mr. Hopkins," he said as the doors opened. "He never gave me any trouble."

"Not a bad epitaph," Eve decided as the elevator headed up to six.

The apartment was single-level, but spacious. Particularly since it was nearly empty of furnishings. There was a sleep chair in the living room, facing a wall screen. There were a multitude of high-end electronics and carton after carton of entertainment discs. It was all open space with a colored-glass wall separating the sleeping area.

"There was art on the walls," Eve noted. "You can see the squares and rectangles of darker paint where they must've hung. Probably sold them to get some capital for his project."

A second bedroom was set up as an office, and from the state of it, Eve didn't judge Hopkins had been a tidy or organized businessman. The desk was heaped with scribbled notes, sketches, memo cubes, coffee cups, and plates from working meals.

A playback of the desk 'link was loaded with oily conversations with the recently deceased pitching his project to potential backers or arranging meetings where she supposed he'd have been doing the same.

"Let's have EDD go through all the data and communication." The Electronic Detective Division could comb through the transmissions and data faster and more efficiently than she. "Doesn't look like he's entertained here recently, which jibes with our doorman's statement. Nothing personal in the last little while on his home 'link. It's all about money."

She walked through the apartment. The guy wasn't living there so much as surviving. Selling off his stuff, scrambling for capital. "The motive's not all about money, though. He couldn't have had enough for that. The motive's emotional. It's personal. Kill him where the yellowing bones of a previous victim are hidden. Purposeful. Building was auctioned off six months ago? Private or public?"

"I can check," Peabody began.

"I got a quicker source."

It seemed to her the guy she'd married was always in, on his way to, or coming back from some meeting. Then again, he seemed to like them. It took all kinds.

And she had to admit when that face of his filled her screen, it put a little boost in her step to think: *mine*.

"Quick question," she began. "Number Twelve. Any details on its auction?"

His dark brows raised over those intense blue eyes. "Bought for a song, which will likely turn out to be a dirge. Or has it already?" Roarke asked her.

"You're quick, too. Yeah, current owner's in the morgue. He got it on the cheap?"

"Previous owners had it on the market for several years, and put it up for public auction a few months ago after the last fire."

"Fire?"

"There've been several. Unexplained," he added with that Irish lilt cruising through his voice. "Hopkins, wasn't it? Descendent of infamy. How was he killed?"

"Nine-millimeter Smith and Wesson."

Surprise moved over that extraordinary face. "Well now. Isn't that interesting? You recovered the weapon, I take it."

"Yeah, I got it. Fill you in on that later. The auction, you knew about it, right?"

"I did. It was well-publicized for several weeks. A building with that history generates considerable media attention as well."

"Yeah, that's what I figured. If it was a bargain, why didn't you snap it up to add it to your mega-Monopoly board?"

"Haunted. Cursed."

"Yeah, right." She snorted out a laugh, but he only continued to look out from the screen. "Okay, thanks. See you later."

"You certainly will."

"Couldn't you just listen to him?" Peabody let out a sigh. "I mean couldn't you just close your eyes and listen?"

"Snap out of it, Peabody. Hopkins's killer had to know the building was up for sale. Maybe he bid on it, maybe he didn't. He doesn't move on the previous owners, but waits for Hopkins. Goes back to personal. Lures him, kills him, leaves the weapon and the hair clips with the skeleton behind the brick. Making a statement."

Peabody huffed out a breath. "This place doesn't make much of a statement, personal or otherwise."

"Let's toss it anyway. Then we're going dancing."

The Gill School of Dance was on the third floor of a stubby post–Urban War building on the West Side. It boasted a large, echoing room with a mirrored wall, a barre, a huddle of chairs, and a decorative screen that sectioned off a minute desk.

The space smelled of sweat heavily covered with floral air freshener.

Fanny Gill herself was skinny as an eel, with a hard, suspicious face and a lot of bright blonde hair tied up with a red scarf. Her pinched face went even tighter as she set her tiny ass on the desk.

"So somebody killed the rat bastard. When's the funeral? I got a red dress I've been saving for a special occasion."

"No love lost, Ms. Gill?"

"Oh, all of it lost, honey. My boy out there?" She jerked a chin toward the screen. On the other side, a man in a sleeveless skinsuit was calling out time and steps to a group of grubby-looking ballerinas. "He's the only decent thing I ever got from Rad the Bad. I was twenty-two years old, fresh and green as a head of iceberg."

She didn't sigh so much as snort, as if to signal those salad days were long over.

"I sure did fall for him. He had a line, that bastard, he had a way. Got married, got pregnant. Had a little money, about twenty thou? He took it, *invested* it." Her lips flattened into one thin, red line. "Blew it, every dollar. Always going to wheel the deal, strike the big time. Like hell. Cheated on me, too. But I stuck, nearly ten years, because I wanted my boy to have a father. Finally figured out no father's better than a lousy one. Divorced him—hired a fucking shark lawyer—excuse the language."

"No problem. Cops hear words like *lawyer* all the time."

Fanny barked out a laugh, then seemed to relax. "Wasn't much to get, but I got my share. Enough to start this place up. And you know, that son of a bitch tried to hit me up for a loan? Called it a business investment, of course. Just a couple months ago. Never changes."

"Was this business investment regarding Number Twelve?"

"Yeah, that's it. Like I'd have anything to do with that place—or Rad."

"Could you tell us where you were last night, Ms. Gill? From say midnight to three?"

"In bed, asleep. I teach my first class at seven in the morning." She sniffed, looking more amused than offended to be considered a suspect in a homicide. "Hey, if I'd wanted to kill Rad, I'd've done it twenty years ago. You're going to ask my boy, too, aren't you?"

"It's routine."

Fanny nodded. "I sleep alone, but he doesn't."

"Dead? Murdered?" Cliff lowered the towel he'd used to dry his damp face. "How? When?"

"Early this morning. The how is classified for the moment. Can you give us your whereabouts between midnight and three?"

"We got home about one. We'd been out with friends. Um . . . give me a second." He picked up a bottle of water, stared at it, then drank. He was a well-built thirty, with streaked blond hair curling in a tail worn halfway down his back. "Lars Gavin, my cohab. We met some friends at Achilles. A club uptown. We went to bed right after we got home, and I got up about seven, seven-thirty. Sorry, I think I want to sit down."

"We're going to need names and contact information on the people you were with, and a number where we can reach your cohab."

"Yeah, sure. Okay. How? How did it happen?" He lifted dazed eyes to Eve's. "Was he mugged?"

"No. I'm not able to give you many details at this time. When's the last time you had contact with your father?"

"A couple months ago. He came by to try to hit my mother up for some money. Like that would work." Cliff managed a half smile, but it wobbled. "Then he put the line on me. I gave him five hundred."

He glanced over to where Fanny was running another group through barre exercises. "Mom'll skin me if she finds out, but I gave him the five."

"That's not the first time you gave him money," Eve deduced.

"No. I'd give him a few hundred now and then. It kept him off my mother's back, and we do okay here. The school, I mean. We do okay. And Lars, he understands."

"But this time he went to your mother first."

"Got to her before I could steer him off. Upsets her, you know? He figured he could sweet talk her out of a good chunk for this investment. Get rich deal—always a deal." Now Cliff scrubbed his hands over his face.

"They fight about it?" Eve asked him.

"No. My mother's done fighting with him. Been done a long time ago. And my father, he doesn't argue. He . . . he cajoles. Basically, she told him to come by again when Hell froze over. So he settled for me, on the sly, and the five hundred. He said he'd be in touch when the ball got rolling, but that was just another line. Didn't matter. It was only five. I don't know how to feel. I don't know how I'm supposed to feel."

"I can't tell you, Mr. Gill. Why did you remove Hopkins from your legal name?"

"This place—Gill School of Dance. My mother." He lifted his shoulder, looked a little abashed. "And well, it's got a rep. Hopkins. It's just bad luck."

Chapter 3

Eve wasn't surprised ME Morris had snagged Hopkins. Multiple gunshot wounds had to be a happy song and dance for a medical examiner. An interesting change of pace from the stabbings, the bludgeonings, strangulations, and overdoses.

Morris, resplendent in a bronze-toned suit under his clear protective cape, his long dark hair in a shining tail, stood over the body with a sunny smile for Eve.

"You send me the most interesting things."

"We do what we can," Eve said. "What can you tell me I don't already know?"

"Members of one family of the fruit fly are called peacocks because they strut on the fruit."

"Huh. I'll file that one. Let's be more specific. What can you tell me about our dead guy?"

"The first four wounds—chest—and the leg wound—fifth—could have been repaired with timely medical intervention. The next severed the spine, the seventh damaged the kidney. Number eight was a slight wound, meaty part of the shoulder. But he was dead by then. The final, close contact, entered the brain, which had already closed down shop."

He gestured to his wall screen, and called up a program. "The first bullets entered at a near level angle," Morris continued as the graphics played out on-screen. "You see, the computer suggested, and I concur, that the assailant fired four times, rapidly, hitting body mass. The victim fell after the fourth shot."

Eve studied the reenactment as Morris did, noting the graphic of the victim took the first two shots standing, the second two slightly hunched forward in the beginning of a fall.

"Big guy," Peabody commented. "Stumbles back a little, but keeps his feet for the first couple shots. I've only seen training and entertainment vids with gun death," she added. "I'd have thought the first shot would slap him down."

"His size, the shock of the impact," Morris said, "and the rapidity of fire would have contributed to the delay in his fall. Again, from the angles by which the bullets entered the body, it's likely he stumbled back, then lurched forward slightly, then went down—knee, heels of the hand taking the brunt of the fall."

He turned to Eve. "Your report indicated that the blood pattern showed the victim tried to crawl or pull himself away across the floor."

"That'd be right."

"As he did, the assailant followed, firing over and down, according to the angle of the wounds in the back, leg, shoulder."

Eyes narrowed now, Eve studied the computer-generated

replay. "Stalking him, firing while he's down. Bleeding, crawling. You ever shoot a gun, Morris?"

"Actually, no."

"I have," she continued. "Feels interesting in your hand. Gives this little kick when it fires. Makes you part of it, that little jolt. Runs through you. I'm betting the killer was juiced on that. The jolt, the *bang*! Gotta be juiced to put more missiles into a guy who's crawling away, leaving his blood smeared on the floor."

"People always find creative and ugly ways to kill. I'd have said using a gun makes the kill less personal. But it doesn't feel that way in this case."

She nodded. "Yeah, this was personal, almost intimate. The ninth shot in particular."

"For the head shot, the victim—who as you say had considerable girth—had to be shoved or rolled over. At that time, the gun was pressed to the forehead. There's not only burning and residue, but a circular bruising pattern. When I'm able to compare it, I'm betting my share that it matches the dimensions of the gun barrel. The killer pressed the gun down into the forehead before he fired."

"See how you like *that*, you bastard," Eve murmured.

"Yes, indeed. Other than being riddled with bullets, your vic was in reasonably good health, despite being about twenty pounds overweight. He dyed his hair, had an eye and chin tuck within the last five years. He'd last eaten about two hours prior to death. Soy chips, sour pickles, processed cheese, washed down with domestic beer."

"The bullets?"

"On their way to the lab. I ran them through my system first. Nine-millimeter." Morris switched programs so that images of the spent bullets he'd recovered came on screen.

"Man, it messes them up, doesn't it?"

"It doesn't do tidy work on flesh, bone, and organ either. The vic had no gunpowder residue on his hands, no defensive wounds. Bruising on the left knee, which would have been inflicted when he fell. As well as some scraping on the heels of both hands, consistent with the fall on the floor surface."

"So he didn't fight back, or have the chance to. Didn't turn away." She angled her own body as if preparing for flight. "No indication he tried to run when and if he saw the gun."

"That's not what his body tells me."

Nor was it what it had told her on scene.

"A guy doesn't usually snack on chips and pickles if he's nervous or worried," Peabody put in. "Run of his entertainment unit showed he last viewed a soft porn vid about the time he'd have had the nibbles. This meet didn't have him sweating."

"Somebody he knew and figured he could handle," Eve agreed. She looked at the body again. "Guess he was dead wrong about that one."

"Number Twelve," Morris said as Eve turned to go.

"That's right."

"So the legend of Bobbie Bray comes to a close."

"That would be the missing woman, presumed dead."

"It would. Gorgeous creature, Bobbie, with the voice of a tormented angel."

"If you remember Bobbie Bray, you're looking damn good for your age, Morris."

He flashed that smile again. "There are thousands of websites devoted to her, and a substantial cult following. Beautiful woman with her star just starting to rise vanishes. Poof! Of course, sightings of her continued for decades after. And talk of her ghost haunting Number Twelve continues even today. Cold spots, apparitions, music coming from thin air. You get any of that?"

Eve thought of the snatch of song, the deep chill. "What I've got, potentially, are her bones. They're real enough."

"I'll be working on them with the forensic anthropologist at the lab." Morris's smile stayed sunny. "Can't wait to get my hands on her."

Back at Central, Eve sat in her office to reconstruct Hopkins's last day. She'd verified his lunch meeting with a couple of local movers and shakers who were both alibied tight for the time in question. A deeper check of his financials showed a sporadic income over the past year from a shop called Bygones, with the last deposit mid-December.

"Still skimming it close, Rad. How the hell were you going to pay for the rehab? Expecting a windfall, maybe? What were you supposed to bring to Number Twelve last night?"

Gets the call on his pocket 'link, she mused. *Deliberately spooky. But he doesn't panic. Sits around, has a snack, watches some light porn.*

She sat back at her desk, closed her eyes. The security disc from Hopkins's building showed him leaving at 1:35. Alone. Looked like he was whistling a tune, Eve recalled. Not a care in the world. Not carrying anything. No briefcase, no package, no bag.

"Yo."

Eve opened her eyes and looked at Feeney. The EDD captain was comfortably rumpled, his wiry ginger hair exploding around his hangdog face. "Whatcha got?"

"More what you've got," he said and stepped into the office. "Number Twelve."

"Jeez, why does everybody keep saying that? Like it was its own country."

"Practically is. Hop Hopkins, Bobbie Bray, Andy Warhol, Mick Jagger." For a moment, Feeney looked like a devotee at a sacred altar. "Christ, Dallas, what a place it must've been when it was still rocking."

"It's a dump now."

"Cursed," he said, so casually she blinked.

"Get out. You serious?"

"As a steak dinner. Found bricked-up bones, didn't you? And a body, antique gun, diamonds. Stuff legends are made of. And it gets better."

"Oh yeah?"

He held up a disc. "Ran your vic's last incoming transmission and the nine-one-one, and for the hell of it, did a voice-print on both. Same voice on both. Guess whose it is?"

"Bobbie Bray's."

"Hey." He actually pouted.

"Has to figure. The killer did the computer-generated deal, used Bray's voice, probably pieced together from old media interviews and such. Unless you're going to sit there and tell me you think it was a voice from, you know, beyond the grave."

He pokered up. "I'm keeping an open mind."

"You do that. Were you able to dig up any old transmissions?"

He held up a second disc. "Dug them out, last two weeks. You're going to find lots of grease. Guy was working it, trying to pump up some financing. Same on the home unit. Some calls out for food, a couple to a licensed companion service. Couple more back and forth to some place called Bygones."

"Yeah, I'm going to check that out. Looks like he was selling off his stuff."

"You know, he probably had some original art from his grandfather's era. Music posters, photographs, memorabilia."

Considering, Eve cocked her head. "Enough to buy Number Twelve, then finance the rehab?"

"You never know what people'll pay. Got your finger pointed at anyone?"

"Talked to one of his exes, and a son. They don't pop for me, but I'm keeping an open mind. Going through some business associates, potential backers, other exes. No current lady friend, or recently dumped, that I can find. Fact is, the guy comes off as a little sleazy, a little slippery, but mostly harmless. A fuck-up who talked big. Got no motive at this point, except a mysterious something he may or may not have taken with him to Number Twelve."

She eased back. "Big guy. He was a big guy. Easy for a woman to take him down if she's got access to a gun, reasonable knowledge of how it works. Second ex-wife is the kind who holds a grudge, hence my open mind. I've got Peabody trying to run the weapon."

"The thing is," Peabody told her, "it's really old. A hundred years back, a handgun didn't have to be registered on purchase, not in every state, and depending on how it was bought. This one's definitely from the Hop Hopkins/Bobbie Bray era. They discontinued this model in the Nineteen-eighties. I've got the list of owners with collector's licenses in the state of New York who own that make and model, but . . ."

"It's not going to be there. Not when it was deliberately planted on the scene. The killer wanted it found, identified. Lab comes through, we should know tomorrow if the same gun was used to kill Hopkins and our surprise guest."

She considered for a moment, then pushed away from her desk. "Okay, I'm going to go by the lab, give them a little kick in the ass."

"Always entertaining."

"Yeah, I make my own fun. After, I'm going by this collectibles place, scope it out. It's uptown, so I'll work from home after. I've got Feeney's list of transmissions. You want to take that? Check out the calls, the callers?"

"I'm your girl."

Dick Berenski, the chief lab tech, was known as Dickhead for good reason. But besides being one, he was also a genius in his field. Generally, Eve handled him with bribes, insults, or outright threats. But with her current case, none were necessary.

"Dallas!" He all but sang her name.

"Don't grin at me like that." She gave a little shudder. "It's scary."

"You've brought me not one but two beauties. I'm going to be writing these up for the trade journals and be the fair-haired boy for the next ten freaking years."

"Just tell me what you've got."

He scooted on his stool, and tapped his long, skinny fingers over a comp screen. He continued to grin out of his strangely egg-shaped head.

"Got my bone guy working with Morris with me running the show. You got yourself a female, between the age of twenty and twenty-five. Bobbie Bray was twenty, twenty-three when she poofed. Caucasian, five-foot-five, about a hundred and fifteen pounds, same height and weight on Bobbie's ID at the time of her disappearance. Broken tibia, about the age of twelve. Healed well. Gonna wanna see if we can access any medical records on Bobbie to match the bone break. Got my forensic sculptor working on the face. Bobbie Bray, son of a bitch."

"Another fan."

"Shit yeah. That skirt was *hot*. Got your cause of death, single gunshot wound to the forehead. Spent bullet retrieved from inside the skull matches the caliber used on your other vic. Ballistics confirms both were fired from the weapon recovered from the scene. Same gun used, about eighty-five years apart. It's beautiful."

"I bet the killer thinks so, too."

Sarcasm flew over Dickhead like a puffy white cloud in a sunny blue sky. "Weapon was cleaned and oiled. Really shined it up. But . . ."

He grinned again, tapped again. "What you're looking at here is dust. Brick dust, drywall dust. Samples the sweepers took from the secondary crime scene. And here? Traces of dust found inside the weapon. Perfect match."

"Indicating that the gun was bricked up with the body."

"Guess Bobbie got tired of haunting the place and decided to take a more active role."

And that, Eve determined, didn't warrant even sarcasm as a response. "Shoot the reports to my home and office units, copy to Peabody's. Your sculptor gets an image, I want to see it."

She headed out again, pulling out her 'link as it beeped. "Dallas."

"Arrest any ghosts lately?"

"No. And I'm not planning on it. Why aren't you in a meeting about world domination?"

"Just stepped out," Roarke told her. "My curiosity's been nipping at me all day. Any leads?"

"Leads might be a strong word. I have avenues. I'm heading to one now. The vic was selling off his stuff—

HAUNTED IN DEATH 261

antique popular culture stuff, I gather—to some place up-town. I'm going to check it out."

"What's the address?"

"Why?"

"I'll meet you. I'll be your expert consultant on antiques and popular culture. You can pay my fee with food and sex."

"It's going to be pizza, and I think I've got a long line to credit on the sex."

But she gave him the address.

After ending the transmission, she called the collectibles shop to tell the proprietor to stay open and available. On a hunch, she asked if they carried any Bobbie Bray memorabilia.

And was assured they had the most extensive collection in the city.

Interesting.

Chapter 4

He beat her there, and was being served coffee and fawning attention by a young, elegant redhead in a slick black suit.

Eve couldn't blame the woman. Roarke was ridiculously handsome, and could, if it served him, ooze charm like pheromones. It seemed to suit him now as he had the redhead flushed and fluttering as she offered cookies with the coffee.

Eve figured she'd benefit from Roarke's charisma herself. She hardly ever got cookies on the job.

"Ah, here's the lieutenant now. Lieutenant Dallas, this is Maeve Buchanan, our hostess, and the daughter of the proprietor."

"Is the proprietor here?"

"My wife. Straight to business. Coffee, darling?"

"Sure. This is some place."

"We're very happy with it," Maeve agreed.

It was pretty, bright—like their hostess—and charmingly organized. Nothing at all like the cluttered junk heap Eve had expected. Art and posters lined the walls, but in a way she supposed someone might arrange them in their home if they were crazy enough to want things everywhere.

Still, tables, display cabinets, shining shelves held memorabilia in a way that escaped the jumbled, crowded stocking style many shops of its kind were victim to. Music was playing unobtrusively—something full of instruments and certainly not of the current era. It added an easy appeal.

"Please, have a seat," Maeve invited. "Or browse if you like. My father's just in the back office. He's on the 'link with London."

"Late for business over there," Eve commented.

"Yes. Private collector. Most of our business is from or to private collections." Maeve swept a wave of that pretty red hair back from her face. "Is there anything I can do for you in the meantime?"

"You've bought a number of pieces over the last several months from Radcliff C. Hopkins."

"Mr. Hopkins, of course. Nineteen-sixties through Eighties primarily. We acquired a number of pieces from him. Is there a problem?"

"For Hopkins there is. He was killed last night."

"Oh!" Her cheery, personal-service smile flashed into shock. "Killed? Oh my God."

"Media's run reports on it through the day."

"I . . . I hadn't heard." Maeve's hands were pressed to her cheeks, and her round blue eyes were wide. "We've been open since ten. We don't keep any current screen shows or radio on in the shop. Spoils the . . . the timeless ambiance. My father's going to be so upset."

"They were friends?"

"Friendly, certainly. I don't know what to say. He was in only a few weeks ago. How did he die?"

"The details are confidential." *For the moment*, Eve thought. There were always leaks and the media couldn't wait to soak them up, wring them dry. "I can tell you he was murdered."

Maeve had a redhead's complexion, and her already pale skin went bone white. "Murdered? This is horrible. It's—" She turned as a door in the back opened.

The man who came out was tall and thin, with the red hair he'd passed to his daughter dusted with a little silver. He had eyes of quiet green, and a smile of greeting ready. It faded when he saw his daughter's face.

"Maeve? What's the matter? Is there a problem?"

"Daddy. Mr. Hopkins, he's been murdered."

He gripped his daughter's arm, and those quiet eyes skimmed from Roarke to Eve and back again. "Rad Hopkins?"

"That's right." Eve held out her badge. "I'm Lieutenant Dallas. You and Mr. Hopkins had business?"

"Yes. Yes. My God, this is such a shock. Was it a burglary?"

"Why would you ask?"

"His collection. He had a very extensive collection of antique art."

"You bought a good chunk of that collection."

"Bits and pieces. Excellent bits and pieces." He rubbed his daughter's shoulder and drew her down to the arm of the chair as he sat. The gesture seemed to help both of them compose themselves.

"I was hoping to eventually do a complete appraisal and give him a bid on the whole of it. But he was . . ." He pushed at his hair and smiled. "He was canny. Held me off, and whet my appetite with those bits."

"What do you know about Number Twelve?"

"Number Twelve?" He looked blank for a moment, then shook his head. "Sorry, I'm feeling muddled by all this. Urban legend. Haunted. Some say by Hop Hopkins's ghost, others by Bobbie Bray's. Others still say both, or any number of celebrities from that era. Bad luck building, though I admit I'm always on the lookout for something from its heyday that can be authenticated. Rad managed to acquire the building a few months ago, bring it back into his family."

"Do you know how it got out of his family?"

"Ah, I think Rad told me it was sold off when he was a boy. His father inherited it when his grandfather died. Tragically, a drug overdose. And it was Rad's plan to bring it back to its former glory, such as it was."

"He talked about it all the time," Maeve added. "Whenever he came in. Now he'll never . . . It's so sad."

"To be frank," Buchanan continued, "I think he might have overreached a bit. A huge undertaking, which is why he found it necessary—in my opinion—to sell some of his artwork and memorabilia. And because I have a number of contacts in the business who might have been helpful when and if he was ready to outfit the club, it was a good, symbiotic relationship. I'm sorry this happened."

"When was the last time you had contact with him?"

"Just last week. I joined him for a drink, at his invitation. That would be . . ." He closed his eyes a moment, held up a finger. "Wednesday. Wednesday evening of last week. I knew he was going to try to persuade me, again, to invest in this club of his. It's just not the sort of thing I do, but he's a good client, and we were friendly."

When he sighed, Maeve covered his hand with hers. "So I met with him. He was so excited. He told me he was ready to begin the rehab again, seriously this time. He projected opening next summer."

"But you turned him down, investmentwise."

"I did, but he took it well. To be frank again, I did a bit of research when he first approached me months ago. Nothing thrives in that building. Owners and backers go bankrupt or worse. I couldn't see this being any different."

"True enough," Roarke confirmed. "The owners before Hopkins had plans for a small, exclusive spa with restaurant and retail. The buyer fell, broke both his legs while doing a run-through with the architect. His brother and cobuyer were brutally mugged just outside the building. Then his accountant ran off with his wife, taking the bulk of his portfolio."

"Bad luck happens," Eve said flatly. "Could you tell me where you were last night, between midnight and three?"

"Are we suspects?" Maeve's eyes rounded. "Oh my God."

"It's just information. The more I have, the more I have."

"I was out—a date—until about eleven."

"Eleven-fifteen," Buchanan said. "I heard you come in."

"Daddy . . ." Maeve rolled her eyes. "He waits up. I'm twenty-four and he still waits up."

"I was reading in bed." But her father smiled, a little sheepishly. "Maeve came in, and I . . . well . . ." He sent another look toward his daughter. "I went down about midnight and checked security. I know, I know," he said before Maeve could speak. "You always set it if you come in after I'm in bed, but I feel better doing that last round. I went to bed after that. Maeve was already in her room. We had breakfast together about eight this morning, then we were here at nine-thirty. We open at ten."

"Thanks. Is it all right if we take a look around?"

"Absolutely. Please. If you have any questions—if

there's anything we can do . . ." Buchanan lifted his hands. "I've never dealt with anything like this, so I'm not sure what we can or should do."

"Just stay available," Eve told him. "And contact me at Central if anything comes to mind. For now, maybe you can point me toward what you've got on Bobbie Bray."

"Oh, we have quite a collection. Actually, one of my favorites is a portrait we bought from Rad a few months ago. This way." Buchanan turned to lead them through the main showroom. "It was done from the photograph taken for her first album cover. Hop—the first Hopkins—had it painted, and it hung in the apartment he kept over Number Twelve. Rumor is he held long conversations with it after she disappeared. Of course, he ingested all manner of hallucinogens. Here she is. Stunning, isn't it?"

The portrait was perhaps eighteen by twenty inches, in a horizontal pose. Bobbie reclined over a bed spread with vivid pink and mounded with white pillows.

Eve saw a woman with wild yards of curling blonde hair. There were two sparkling diamond clips glinting in the masses of it. Her eyes were the green of new spring leaves, and a single tear—bright as the diamonds, spilled down her cheek. It was the face of a doomed angel—lovely rather than beautiful, full of tragedy and pathos.

She wore thin, filmy white, and between the breasts was deep red stain in the blurred shape of a heart.

"The album was *Bleeding Heart*, for the title track. She won three Grammys for it."

"She was twenty-two," Maeve put in. "Two years younger than me. Less than two years later, she vanished without a trace."

There was a trace, Eve thought. There always was, even if it was nearly a century coming to light.

Outside, Eve dug her hands into her pockets. The sky had stopped spitting out nasty stuff, but the wind had picked up. She was pretty sure she'd left her watch cap in her office.

"Everybody's got an alibi, nobody's got a motive. Yet. I think I'm going to go back to the scene, take another look around."

"Then you can fill me in with what must be a multitude of missing details on the way. I had my car taken home," Roarke continued when she frowned at him. "So I could get a lift with my lovely wife."

"You were just hoping to get a look at Number Twelve."

"And hope springs. Want me to drive?"

When she slid behind the wheel, she tapped her fingers on it. "What's something like that painting going to go for on the open market?"

"To the right collector? Sky would be the limit. But I'd say a million wouldn't be out of the park."

"A million? For a painting of a dead woman. What's wrong with people? Top transaction in the vic's account from Bygones was a quarter of that. Why'd Hopkins sell so cheap?"

"Scrambling for capital. Bird in the hand's worth a great deal more than a painting on the wall."

"Yeah, there's that. Buchanan had to know he was getting bargain basement there."

"So why kill the golden goose?"

"Exactly. But it's weird to me neither of them had heard by this time that Hopkins bought it at Number Twelve. They eat breakfast at eight? No media reports while you're scoping out the pickings on the AutoChef or pulling on your pants?"

"Not everyone turns on the news."

"Maybe not. And nobody pops in today, mentions it? Nobody say, 'Hey! Did you hear about that Hopkins guy? Number Twelve got another one.' Just doesn't sit level for me." Then she shrugged, pulled away from the curb.

"Hit the lab before this. The same gun that killed Hopkins killed the as-yet-unidentified female whose remains were found behind the wall at Number Twelve."

"Fascinating."

"Weapon was bricked up with her. Killer must have found her, and it. Cleaned the weapon. You see those, the hair jewelry, she had on in the picture? Recovered at the scene, also clean and shiny. One by the window, which the killer likely used to escape, one left with the bones."

"Someone wants to make sure the remains are identified. Do you doubt it's her?"

"No, I don't doubt it's her. I don't doubt Hop Hopkins put a bullet in her brain, then got handy with brick and mortar. I don't know why. I don't know why someone used that same gun on Hop's grandson eighty-five years later."

"But you think there's a connection. A personal one."

"Had to reload to put the bullet in the brain. That's extremely cold. Guy's dead, or next to it. But you reload, roll the body over, press the barrel down hard enough to scorch the skin and leave an imprint of the barrel, and give him one last hit. Fucking cold."

Chapter 5

Eve gave him details on the drive. She could, with Roarke, run them through like a checklist, and it always lined them up in her mind. In addition, he always seemed to know something or someone that might fill in a few of the gaps.

"So, did you ever do business with Hopkins?"

"No. He had a reputation for being generous with the bullshit, and often short on results."

"Big plans, small action," Eve concluded.

"That would be it. Harmless, by all accounts. Not the sort to con the widow and orphans out of the rent money, but not above talking them out of a portion of it with a view to getting rich quick."

"He cheated on his wives, and recently squeezed five hundred out of the son he abandoned."

"Harmless doesn't always mean moral or admirable. I made a few calls—curiosity," he explained. "To people who like to buy and sell real estate."

"Which includes yourself."

"Most definitely. From what I'm told the bottom dropped out of Twelve for Hopkins only a couple of weeks after he'd signed the papers on it. He was in fairly deep—purchase price, legal fees, architects and designers, construction crew, and so on. He'd done a lot of tap dancing to get as far as he did, and was running out of steam. He'd done some probing around—more legal fees—to see if he could wrangle having the property condemned, and get back some of his investment. Tried to wrangle some money from various federal agencies, historic societies. He played all the angles and had some success. A couple of small grants. Not nearly enough, not for his rather ambitious vision."

"What kind of money we talking, for the building and the vision?"

"Oh, easily a hundred and fifty million. He'd barely scratched the surface when he must have realized he couldn't make it without more capital. Then, word is, a few days ago, he pushed the green light again. Claimed Number Twelve was moving forward."

"I'm waiting on the lab to see if they can pinpoint when that wall was taken down. Could be talking days." Her fingers tapped out a rhythm on the wheel as she considered. "Hopkins finds the body. You get a wealth of publicity out of something like that. Maybe a vid deal, book deals. A guy with an entrepreneurial mind-set, he could think of all kinds of ways to rake it in over those bones."

"He could," Roarke agreed. "But wouldn't the first question be how he knew where to look?"

"Or how his killer knew."

"Hop killed her," she began as she hunted for parking. "Argument, drug-induced, whatever. Bricks up the body, which takes some doing. Guy liked cocaine. That'll keep you revved for a few hours. Has to cover up the brick, put things back into reasonable shape. I'm trying to access the police reports from back then. It hasn't been easy so far. But anyway, no possible way the cops just missed a brand-new section of wall, so he paid them off or blackmailed them."

"Corrupt cops? I'm stunned. I'm shocked."

"Shut up. Hop goes over the edge—guilt, drugs, fear of discovery. Goes hermit. Guy locks himself up with a body on the other side of the wall, he's going to go pretty buggy. Wouldn't surprise me if he wrote something down, told someone about it. If cops were involved, *they* knew or suspected something. The killer, or Hopkins does some homework, pokes around. Gets lucky, or unlucky as the case may be."

"It takes eight and a half decades to get lucky?"

"Place gets a rep," Eve said as they walked from the car toward Number Twelve. "Bray gets legend status. People report seeing her, talking to her. A lot of those people, and others, figure she just took off 'cause she couldn't handle the pressure of her own success. Hop has enough juice to keep people out of the apartment during his lifetime. By then, there're murmurs of curses and hauntings, and that just grows as time passes. A couple of people have some bad luck, and nobody much wants to play in Number Twelve anymore."

"More than a couple." Roarke frowned at the door as Eve uncoded the police seal. "The building just squats here, and everyone who's tried to disturb it, for whatever reason, ends up paying a price."

"It's brick and wood and glass."

"Brick and wood and glass form structure, not spirit."

She raised her brows at him. "Want to wait in the car, Sally?"

"Now you shut up." He nudged her aside to walk in first.

She turned on the lights, took out her flashlight for good measure. "Hopkins was between those iron stairs and the bar." She moved across the room, positioned herself by the stairs. "From the angles, the killer was here. I'm seeing he got here first, comes down when Hopkins walks in. Hopkins still had his coat on, his gloves, a muffler. Cold in here, sure, but a man's going to probably pull off his gloves, unwrap his scarf, maybe unbutton his coat when he's inside. You just do."

Understanding his wife, Roarke moved into what he thought had been Hopkins's standing position. "Unless you don't have the chance."

"Killer comes down. He'd told Hopkins to bring something, and Hopkins walks in empty-handed. Could have been small—pocket-sized—but why would the killer shoot him so quickly, and with such rage, if he'd cooperated?"

"The man liked to spin the wheels. If he came empty, he may have thought he could work a deal."

"So when he starts the whole 'Let's talk about this,' the killer snaps. Shoots him. Chest, leg. Four shots from the front. Vic goes down, tries to crawl, killer keeps firing, moving toward the target. Leg, back, shoulder. Eight shots. Full clip for that model. Reloads, shoves the body over, leans down. Looks Hopkins right in the eyes. Eyes are dead, but he looks into them when he pulls the trigger the last time. He wants to see his face—as much as he needs to echo the head shot on Bray, he needs to see the face, the eyes, when he puts that last bullet in."

She crossed over, following what she thought was the killer's route as she'd spoken. "Could have gone out the front. But he chooses to go back upstairs."

Now she turned, started up. "Could have taken the

weapon, thrown it in the river. We'd never have found it. Wants us to find it. Wants us to know. Cops didn't put Hop in the system. Why should we do anything about his grandson? Took care of that himself. Payment made. But he wants us to know, everyone to know, that Bobbie's been avenged at last."

She stopped in front of the open section of wall. " 'Look what he did to her. Put a bullet in that young, tragic face, silenced that voice. Ended her life when it was just getting started. Then he put a wall up, locked her away from the world. She's free now. I set her free.' "

"She'll be more famous, more infamous, than ever. Her fans will make a shrine out of this place. Heap flowers and tokens outside, stand in the cold with candles for vigils. And, to add a cynical note, there'll be Bobbie Bray merchandising through the roof. Fortunes will be made out of this."

Eve turned back to Roarke. "Damn right, they will. Hopkins would have known that. He'd have had visions of money falling on him from the sky. Number Twelve wouldn't just be a club, it would be a freaking cathedral. And he's got the main attraction. Fame and fortune off her bones. You bet your ass. Killer's not going to tolerate that. 'You think you can use her? You think I'd let you?' "

"Most who'd have known her personally, had a relationship with her, would be dead now. Or elderly."

"Don't have to be young to pull a trigger." But she frowned at the cut in the wall. "But you'd have to be pretty spry to handle the tools to do this. I just don't think this part was Hopkins's doing. Nothing in his financials to indicate he'd bought or rented the tools that could handle this. And he doesn't strike me as the type who'd be able to do this tidy a job with them. Not on his own. And the killer had the gun, the hair clips. The killer opened this grave."

The cold was sudden and intense, as if a door had been flung open to an ice floe, and through that frigid air drifted a raw and haunting voice.

In my dark there is no dawn, there is no light in my world since you've been gone. I thought my love would stand the test, but now my heart bleeds from my breast.

Even as Eve drew her weapon, the voice rose, with a hard, throbbing pump of bass and drums behind it. She rushed out to the level overlooking the main club.

The voice continued to rise, seemed to fill the building. Under it, over it, were voices, cheers, and whistles. For an instant, she thought she could smell a heavy mix of perfume, sweat, smoke.

"Somebody's messing with us," she murmured.

Before she could swing toward the stairs to investigate, there was a shout from the nearly gutted apartment above. A woman's voice called out:

"No. Jesus, Hop. Don't!"

There was the explosion of a shot and a distinct thud.

Keeping her weapon out, she vaulted up the stairs again with Roarke. At the doorway, his hand clamped over her shoulder.

"Holy Mother of God. Do you see?"

She told herself it was a shadow—a trick of the poor light, the dust. But for an instant there seemed to be a woman, her mass of curling blonde hair falling over her shoulders, standing in front of the open section of wall. And for an instant, it seemed her eyes looked straight into Eve's.

Then there was nothing but a cold, empty room.

"You saw her," Roarke insisted as Eve crawled around behind the wall.

"I saw shadows. Maybe an image. If I saw an image, it

was because someone put it there. Just like someone flipped some switch to put on that music. Got some electronics set up somewhere. Triggered by remote, most likely."

He crouched down. Eve's hair, face, hands were all coated with dust and debris. "You felt that cold."

"So, he dropped the temp in here. He's putting on a show, that's what he's doing. Circus time. So the cop goes back and reports spooky happenings, apparitions. Bull-*shit*!"

She swiped at her filthy face as she crawled out. "Hopkins left debts. His son is beneficiary of basically nada. Building's no-man's-land until it goes up to public auction. Keep the curse crap going, keep the price down. Snap it up cheaper than dirt."

"With what's happened here, discovering the body here, that could go exactly the opposite way. It could drive the price up."

"That happens, you bet your ass someone's going to have some document claiming they were partners with Hopkins. Maybe I was wrong about it being personal. Maybe it's been profit all along."

"You weren't wrong. You know you weren't. But you're sitting there, in a fairly disgusting state, I might add, trying to turn it around so you don't have to admit you've seen a ghost."

"I saw what some mope wants me to believe is a ghost and he apparently pulled one over on you, ace."

"I know electronic imagery when I see it." The faintest edge of irritation flickered into his eyes at her tone. "I know what I saw, what I heard, what I felt. Murder was done here, then adding to it, the insult, the callousness of what was done after."

He glanced back into the narrow opening, toward the former location of the long-imprisoned bones. And now there was a hint of pity in his eyes as well. "All while claiming to be so concerned, so upset, offering rewards for her safe return, or for substantiated proof she was alive and well. All that while she was moldering behind the wall he'd built to hide her.

"If her body never left here, why should her spirit?"

"Because—" With a shake of her head, Eve scattered dust. "Her body's not here now. So shouldn't she be haunting the morgue?"

"This place has been home to her for a long time, hasn't it?" *Pragmatism,* he thought, *thy name is Eve.* Then he took out a handkerchief, used it to rub the worst of the dust and grime from her face.

"Homemade crypts aren't what I'd call home, sweet home," she retorted. "And you know what? Ghosts don't clean guns or shoot them. I've got a DB in the morgue. And I'm ordering the sweepers, with a contingent from EDD in here tomorrow. They're going to take this place apart."

She brushed some of the dirt from her shirt and pants before picking up her coat. "I want a shower."

"I want you to have a shower, too."

As they went downstairs, she called in the order for two units to search Number Twelve for electronic devices. If she thought she heard a woman's husky laugh just before she closed and secured the door, Eve ignored it.

Chapter 6

When she'd showered and pulled on warm, comfortable sweats, Eve gave another thought to pizza. She figured she could down a slice or two at her desk while she worked.

She was headed toward the office she kept at home when she heard Bobbie Bray's voice, gritting out her signature song.

> *Broken, battered, bleeding, and still I'm begging,*
>   *pleading*
> *Come back. Come back and heal my heart*
> *Come back. Come back and heal my heart*

With her own heart thudding, Eve covered the rest of the distance at a dash. Except for the fat cat, Galahad, snoring in her sleep chair, her office was empty.

Then she narrowed her eyes at the open door that joined her office to Roarke's. She found him at his desk, with the title track beginning its play again through the speakers of his entertainment unit.

"You trying to wig me out?"

"No." He smiled a little. "Did I?" When she gave him a stony stare, he shrugged. "I wanted to get better acquainted with our ghost. She was born in Louisville, Kentucky, and according to this biography, left home at sixteen to migrate to Haight-Ashbury, as many of her generation did. She sang in some clubs, primarily for food or a place to sleep, drifted around, joined a band called Luv—that's L-U-V— where she stood out like a rose among weeds, apparently. Did some backup singing for one or two important artists of the time, then met Hopkins in Los Angeles."

"Bad luck for her. Can you turn that off?"

"Music off," he ordered, and Bobbie's voice stopped. "She bothers you," Roarke realized. "Why is that?"

"She doesn't bother me." *The correct term,* Eve thought, *would be she creeps me.* But damned if she was going to fall into the accepted pattern on Number Twelve, or Bobbie Bray.

"She's part of my investigation—and a secondary vic, even though she was killed a half century before I was born. She's mine now, like Hopkins is mine. But she's always part of the motive."

"And as such, I'd think you'd want to know all you could about her."

"I do, and I will. But I don't have to hear her singing." It was too sad, Eve admitted to herself. And too spooky. "I'm going to order up some pizza. You want in on that?"

"All right." Roarke rose to follow her into the kitchen attached to her office. "She was twenty when Hop scooped her up. He was forty-three. Still, it was two years before her album came out—which he produced, allegedly handpicking every song. She did perform during that period, exclusively in Hopkins's venues."

"So he ran her."

"All but owned her, from the sound of it. Young, naive girl—at least from a business standpoint, and from a generation and culture that prided itself on not being bound by property and possessions. Older, canny, experienced man, who discovered her, romanced her, and most certainly fed any appetite she might have had for illegal substances."

"She'd been on her own for five years." Eve debated for about five seconds on pepperoni and went for it. "Naive doesn't wash for me."

"But then you're not a sentimental fan or biographer. Still, I'd lean toward the naivete when it came to contracts, royalties, business, and finance. And Hopkins was a pro. He stood as her agent, her manager, her producer."

"But she's the talent," Eve reasoned and snagged some napkins. "She's got the youth, the looks. Maybe her culture or whatever said pooh-pooh to big piles of money, but if she's bringing it in, getting the shine from it, she's going to start to want more."

"Agreed. She left him for a few months in 1972, just dropped off the radar. Which is one of the reasons, I'd assume, he got away with her murder three years later. She'd taken off once, why not again?"

He stepped out to choose a wine from the rack behind a wall panel. "When she came back, it was full-court press professionally, with a continual round of parties, clubs, drugs, sex. Her album hit, and big, with her touring internationally for six months. More sex, more drugs, and three Grammys. Her next album was in the works when she disappeared."

"Hop must've gotten a percentage of her earnings." Eve brought the pizza in, dumped it and plates on her desk.

"As her manager and producer, he'd have gotten a hefty one."

"Stupid to kill the goose."

"Passion plus drugs can equal extreme stupidity."

"Smart enough to cover it up, and keep it covered for eighty-five years. So his grandson ends up paying for it. Why? My vic wasn't even born when this went down. If it's revenge . . ."

"Served very cold," Roarke said as he poured wine.

"The killer has a connection with the older crime, the older players. Financial, emotional, physical. Maybe all three."

She lifted up a slice, tugged at the strings of cheese, expertly looping them up and over the triangle.

"If it's financial," she continued, "who stands to gain? The son inherits, but he's alibied and there isn't a hell of a lot to scoop once the debts are offset. So maybe something of value, something the killer wanted Hopkins to bring to Number Twelve. But if it's a straight give-me-what-I-want/deserve, why set the scene? Why put on that show for us tonight?"

When Roarke said nothing, Eve chewed contemplatively on her slice. "You don't seriously believe that was some ghostly visitation? Grab a little corner of reality."

"Do you seriously believe your killer has been dogging that building, its owners, for eight and a half decades? What makes that more logical than a restless, angry spirit?"

"Because dead people don't get angry. They're dead." She picked up her wine. "It's my job to get pissed for them."

Roarke studied her over his own glass, his gaze thoughtful, seeking. "Then there's nothing after? As close as you've been to the dead, you don't see something after?"

"I don't know what I see." This sort of conversation always made her uncomfortable, somehow sticky along the skin. "Because you don't see it—if it's there to see—until you're dead. But I don't believe the dead go all *whoooo*, or start singing. The original Hopkins paid an investigation off, this killer wants to weird one off. It's not going to work."

"Consider the possibility," he suggested. "Bobbie Bray's spirit wants her revenge as much as you want justice. It's a powerful desire, on both parts."

"That's not a possible possibility."

"Closed-minded."

"Rational," she corrected, with some heat now. "Jesus, Roarke, she's bones. Why now then? Why here and now? How'd she manage to get someone—flesh and blood—to do the descendent of her killer? If Hop Hopkins *was* her killer—which hasn't yet been proven."

"Maybe she was waiting for you to prove it."

"Oh yeah, *that's* rational. She's been hanging around, waiting for the right murder cop to come along. Listen, I've got the reality of a dead body, an antique and banned weapon used in a previous crime. I've got no discernible motive and a media circus waiting to happen. I can't take the time to wonder and worry about the disposition of a woman who's been dead eighty-five years. You want to waste your time playing with ghosts, be my guest. But I've got serious work on my plate."

"Fine then, since it pisses you off, I'll just leave you to your serious work while I go waste my time."

She scowled at him when he got up and carried his glass

of wine with him to his office. And she cursed under her breath when he closed the door behind him.

"Great, fine, fabulous. Now I've got a ghost causing marital discord. Just makes it all perfect."

She shoved away from her desk to set up the case board she used at home. Logic was what was needed here, she told herself. Logic, cop sense, facts, and evidence.

Must be that Irish in Roarke's blood that tugged him into the fanciful. Who knew he'd head that way?

But her way was straight, narrow, and rational.

Two murders, one weapon. Connection. Two murders, one location, second connection. Second vic, blood descendent of suspected killer in first murder. Connect those dots, too, she thought as she worked.

So, okay, she couldn't set the first murder aside. She'd use it.

Logic and evidence dictated that both victims knew their killer. The first appeared to be a crime of passion, likely enhanced by illegal substances. Maybe Bray cheated on Hop. Or wanted to break things off professionally and/or personally. She could have had something on him, threatened exposure.

Had to be an act of passion, heat of the moment. Hop had the money, the means. If he'd planned to kill Bray, why would he have done it in his own apartment?

But the second murder was a deliberate act. The killer lured the victim to the scene, had the weapon. Had, in all likelihood discovered the previous body. The killing had been an act of rage as well as deliberation.

"Always meant to kill him, didn't you?" she murmured as she studied the crime scene photos on her board. "Wanted whatever you wanted first—but whether or not you got it, he was a dead man. What did she mean to you?"

She studied the photos of Bobbie Bray.

Obsessed fan? Not out of the realm, she thought, but low on her list.

"Computer, run probability with evidence currently on active file. What is probability that the killers of Bray, Bobbie, and Hopkins, Radcliff C. are linked?"

Working . . .

Absently, Eve picked up her wine, sipping as she worked various scenarios through her head.

Task complete. Probability is eighty-two-point-three . . .

Reasonably strong, Eve mused, and decided to take it one step further. "What is the probability that the killer of Hopkins, Radcliff C. is linked with the first victim, Bray, Bobbie?"

Working . . .

Family member, Eve thought. *Close friend, lover. Bray would be, what . . . Damn math*, she cursed as she calculated. *Bray would be around about one-oh-nine if she'd lived. People lived longer now than they did in the mid-twentieth. So a lover or tight friend isn't out of the realm either.*

But she couldn't see a centenarian, even a spry one, cutting through that brick.

Task complete. Probability is ninety-four-point-one that there is a connection between the first victim and the second killer . . .

"Yeah, that's what I think. And you know what else? Blood's the closest connection. So who did Bobbie leave behind? Computer, list all family members of first victim. Display on wall screen one."

Working . . . Display complete.

Parents and older brother deceased, Eve noted. A younger sister, age eighty-eight, living in Scottsdale Care

Center, Arizona. Young for a care center, Eve mused, and made a note to find out what the sister's medical condition was.

Bobbie would have had a niece and nephew had she lived, and a couple of grandnieces and nephews.

Worth checking into, Eve decided, and began a standard run on all living relations.

While the computer worked, she set up a secondary task and took a closer look at Hopkins.

"Big starter," she said aloud. "Little finisher."

There were dozens of projects begun, abandoned. Failed. Now and then he'd hit, at least enough to keep the wolves from the door, set up the next project.

Failed marriages, ignored offspring. No criminal on any former spouse or offspring.

But you had to start somewhere, she figured.

She went back to the board. Diamond hair clips. Bray had worn them for her first album cover—possibly a gift from Hop. Most likely. The scene told Eve it was likely Bray had been wearing them when she'd been killed, or at least when she'd been bricked up.

But the killer hadn't taken them as a souvenir. Not a fan, just didn't play. The killer had shined them up and left them behind.

"She was a diamond," Eve murmured. "She shined. Is that what you're telling me? Here's the gun he used to kill her, and here's where I found it. He never paid and payment needed to be made. Is that the message?"

She circled the boards, studied the runs when the computer displayed them. There were a couple of decent possibilities among Bobbie's descendents.

They'd all have to be interviewed, she decided.

One of them contacts Hopkins, she speculated. *Maybe*

even tries to buy the building but can't come up with the scratch. Has to get access though, to uncover the body. How was access gained?

Money. Hopkins needed backers. Maybe charged his murderer a fee to tour Number Twelve. Get in once, you can get in again.

How'd you find the body? How did you know?

What did she have here? she asked herself. Younger sister in a care facility. Niece a data drone. Nephew deceased—Urban War fatality. Grandniece middle-management in sales, grandnephew an insurance salesman. Rank and file, no big successes, no big failures.

Ordinary.

Nothing flashy. Nobody managed to cash in on Bobbie's fame and fortune, or her untimely death.

Nobody, she mused, except Hopkins. That would be a pisser, wouldn't it? Your daughter, sister, aunt is a dead cult figure, but you've got to do the thirty-five hours a week to get by. And the grandson of the bastard who killed her is trying to rake it in. You're scraping by, getting old and . . .

"Wait a minute, wait a minute. Serenity Bray, age eighty-eight. Twenty-two years younger than Bobbie. Not a sister. A daughter."

She swung to the adjoining door, shoved it open. "Bobbie had a kid. Not a sister. The timing's right. She had a kid."

Roarke merely lifted an eyebrow. "Yes. Serenity Bray Massey, currently in Scottsdale in a full-care nursing facility. I've got that."

"Showoff. She had a kid, and the timing makes it most likely Hop's. There's no record of a child. No reports from that time of her pregnancy. But she separated from him for several months, which would coincide with the last few months of her pregnancy and the birth."

"After which, it would seem, she gave the child to her own mother. Who then moved her family to a ranch outside Scottsdale, and Bobbie went back to Hop, and her previous lifestyle. I've found some speculation that during her period of estrangement from Hop she went into rehab and seclusion. Interviews and articles from the time have her clean and sober when she returned to the scene, then backsliding, I suppose you could say, within weeks."

He angled his head. "I thought you were leaving Bobbie to me."

"The ghost part's yours. The dead part's mine."

Chapter 7

They were into their second year of marriage, and being a trained observer, Eve knew when he was irritated with her. It seemed stupid, just *stupid* to have a fight or the undercurrent of one over something as ridiculous as ghosts.

Still, she brooded over it another moment, on the verge of stupidity. Then she huffed out a breath.

"Look," she began.

After a pause, he sat back. "I'm looking."

"What I'm getting at is . . . shit. Shit." She paced to his window, to the doorway, turned around again.

Rules of marriage—and hell, one of the benefits of it, she admitted—were that she could say to him what she might even find hard to say to herself.

"I have to live with so many of them." There was anger in her over it, and a kind of grief she could never fully explain. "They don't always go away when you close the case, never go away if you leave a crack in it. I got a freaking army of dead in my head."

"Whom you've defended," he reminded her. "Stood over, stood for."

"Yeah, well, that doesn't mean they're going to say 'Thanks, pal,' then shuffle off the mortal whatever."

"That would be coil—and they've already done the shuffle before you get there."

"Exactly. Dead. But they still have faces and voices and pain, at least in my head. I don't need to think about one wifting around sending me messages from beyond. It's too much, that's all. It's too much if I have to start wondering if there's some spirit hovering over my shoulder to make sure I do the job."

"All right."

"That's it?"

"Darling Eve," he said with the easy patience he could pull out and baffle her with at the oddest times. "Haven't we already proven that you and I don't have to stand on exactly the same spot on every issue? And wouldn't it be boring if we did?"

"Maybe." Tension oozed back out of her. "I guess. I just never expected you'd take something like this and run with it."

"Then perhaps I shouldn't tell you that if I die first, I'm planning to come back to see you naked as often as possible."

Her lips twitched, as he'd intended them to. "I'll be old, with my tits hanging to my waist."

"You don't have enough tit to hang that low."

She pursed her lips, looked down as if to check. "Gotta point. So are we good now?"

"We may be, if you come over here and kiss me. In payment for the insult."

She rolled her eyes. "Nothing's free around here." But she skirted the desk, leaned down to touch her lips to his.

The moment she did, he yanked her down into his lap. She'd seen it coming—she knew him too well not to—but was in the mood to indulge him.

"If you think I'm playing bimbo secretary and horny exec—"

"There were actually a few insults," he interrupted. "And you've reminded me that you're going to get old eventually. I should take advantage of your youth and vitality, and see you naked now."

"I'm not getting naked. Hey! Hey!"

"*Feel* you naked then," he amended, as his hands were already under her sweatshirt and on her breasts. "Good things, small packages."

"Oh yeah? Is that what I should say about your equipment?"

"Insult upon insult." Laughing, he slid his hand around to her back to hold her more firmly in place. "You have a lot of apologizing to do."

"Then I guess I'd better get started."

She put some punch into the kiss, swinging around to straddle him. It would take some agility as well as vitality to pull off a serious apology in his desk chair, but she thought she was up to the job.

He made her feel so many things, all of them vital and immediate. The hunger, the humor, the love, the lust. She could taste his heat for her, his greed for her as his mouth ravished hers. Her own body filled with that same heat and hunger as he tugged at her clothes.

Here was his life—in this complicated woman. Not just the long, alluring length of her, but the mind and spirit inside the form. She could excite and frustrate, charm and annoy—and all there was of her somehow managed to fit against him, and make him complete.

Now she surrounded him, shifting that body, using those quick hands, then taking him inside her with a long, low purr of satisfaction. They took each other, finished each other, and then the purr was a laughing groan.

"I think that squares us," she managed.

"You may even have some credit."

For a moment, she curled in, rested her head on his shoulder. "Ghosts probably can't screw around in a desk chair."

"Unlikely."

"It's tough being dead."

At eight-fifteen in the morning, Eve was in her office at Central scowling at the latest sweeper and EDD reports.

"Nothing. They can't find anything. No sign of electronic surveillance, holographic paraphernalia, audio, video. Zilch."

"Could be it's telling you that you had a paranormal experience last night."

Eve spared one bland look for Peabody. "Paranormal my ass."

"Cases have been documented, Dallas."

"Fruitcakes have been documented, too. It's going to be a family member. That's where we push. That and whatever Hopkins may or may not have had in his possession that his killer wanted. Start with the family members. Let's eliminate any with solid alibis. We'll fan out from there."

She glanced at her desk as her 'link beeped—again— and, scanning the readout, sneered. "Another reporter. We're not feeding the hounds on this one until so ordered. Screen all your incomings. If you get cornered, straight no comment, investigation is active and ongoing. Period."

"Got that. Dallas, what was it like last night? Skin-crawly or wow?"

Eve started to snap, then blew out a breath. "Skin-crawly, then annoying that some jerk had played with me and made my skin crawl for a minute."

"But kind of frigid, too, right? Ghost of Bobbie Bray serenading you."

"If I believed it was the ghost of anyone, I'd say it was feeling more pissy than entertaining. What someone wants us to think is we're not welcome at Number Twelve. Trying to scare us off. I've got Feeney's notes on the report from EDD. He says a couple of his boys heard singing. Another swears he felt something pat his ass. Same sort of deal from the sweepers. Mass hysteria."

"Digging in, I found out two of the previous owners tried exorcisms. Hired priests, psychics, parapsychologists, that kind of deal. Nothing worked."

"Gee, mumbo didn't get rid of the jumbo? Why doesn't that surprise me? Get on the 'link, start checking alibis."

Eve took her share, eliminated two, and ended up tagging Serenity Massey's daughter in the woman's Scotts-dale home.

"It's not even seven in the morning."

"I'm sorry, Ms. Sawyer."

"Not even seven," the woman said testily, "and I've already had three calls from reporters, and another from the head nurse at my mother's care center. Do you know a reporter tried to get to her? She has severe dementia—can barely remember me when I go see her—and some idiot reporter tries to get through to interview her over Bobbie Bray. My mother didn't even *know* her."

"Does your mother know she was Bobbie Bray's daughter?"

The woman's thin, tired face went blank. But it was there in her eyes, clear as glass. "What did you say?"

"She knows, then—certainly you do."

"I'm not going to have my mother harassed, not by reporters, not by the police."

"I don't intend to harass your mother. Why don't you tell me when and how she found out she was Bobbie's daughter, not her sister."

"I don't know." Ms. Sawyer rubbed her hands over her face. "She hasn't been well for a long time, a very long time. Even when I was a child . . ." She dropped her hands now and looked more than tired. She looked ill. "Lieutenant, is this necessary?"

"I've got two murders. Both of them relatives of yours. You tell me."

"I don't think of the Hopkins family as relatives. Why would I? I'm sorry that man was killed because it's dredged all this up. I've been careful to separate myself and my own family from the Bobbie phenomenon. Check, why don't you? I've never given an interview, never agreed to one or sought one out."

"Why? It's a rich pool, from what I can tell."

"Because I wanted *normal*. I'm entitled to it, and so are my kids. My mother was always frail. Delicate, mind and body. I'm not, and I've made damn sure to keep me and mine out of that whirlpool. If it leaks out that I'm Bobbie's granddaughter instead of a grandniece, they'll hound me."

"I can't promise to keep it quiet, I can only promise you that I won't be giving interviews on that area of the investigation. I won't give out your name or the names of your family members."

"Good for you," Sawyer said dully. "They're already out."

"Then it won't hurt you to answer some questions. How did your mother find out about her parentage?"

"She told me—my brother and me—that she found letters Bobbie had written. Bobbie's mother kept them. She wrote asking how her baby was doing, called my mother by name. Her Serenity she called her, as if she was a state of mind instead of a child who needed her mother."

The bitterness in the words told Eve she wasn't talking to one of Bobbie Bray's fans.

"Said she was sorry she'd messed up again. My mother claimed Bobbie said she was going back into rehab, that she was leaving Hop, the whole scene. She was going to get clean and come back for her daughter. Of course, she never came back. My mother was convinced Hop had killed her, or had her killed."

"What do you think?"

"Sure, maybe." The words were the equivalent of a shrug. "Or maybe she took off to Bimini to sell seashells by the seashore. Maybe she went back to San Francisco and jumped off the Golden Gate Bridge. I don't know, and frankly don't much care."

Sawyer let out a long sigh, pressed her fingers to her eyes. "She wasn't, and isn't, part of my world. But she all but became my mother's world. Mom swore Bobbie's ghost used to visit her, talk to her. I think it's part of the reason, this obsession, that she's been plagued by emotional and mental problems as long as I can remember. When my brother was killed in the Urbans, it just snapped her. He was her favorite."

"Do you have the letters?"

"No. That Hopkins man, he tracked my mother down.

I was in college, my brother was overseas, so that was, God, more than thirty years ago. He talked her out of nearly everything she had that was Bobbie's or pertained to her. Original recordings, letters, diaries, photographs. He said he was going to open some sort of museum in California. Nothing ever came of it. My brother came home and found out. He was furious. He and my mother had a horrible fight, one they never had a chance to reconcile. Now he's gone and she might as well be. I don't want to be Bobbie Bray's legacy. I just want to live my life."

Eve ended the transmission, tipped back in her chair. She was betting the letters were what the killer had been after.

With Peabody she went back to Hopkins's apartment for another thorough search.

"Letters Bobbie wrote that confirm a child she had with Hop. Letters or some sort of document or recording from Hop that eventually led his grandson to Serenity Massey. Something that explosive and therefore valuable," she said to her partner. "I bet he had a secure hidey-hole. Security box, vault. We'll start a search of bank boxes under his name or likely aliases."

"Maybe he took them with him and the killer already has them."

"I don't think so. The doorman said he walked out emptyhanded. Something like that, figuring the value, he's going to want a briefcase, a portfolio. Guy liked accessories— good suit, shoes, antique watch—why miss a trick with something that earns one? But . . . he was hunting up money. Maybe he sold them, or at least dangled them."

"Bygones?"

"Worth a trip."

At the door, Eve paused, turned to study the apartment again. There'd be no ghosts here, she thought. Nothing here but stale air, stale dreams.

Legacies, she thought as she closed the door. Hopkins left one of unfulfilled ambitions, which to her mind carried on the one left by his father.

Bobbie Bray's granddaughter had worked hard to shut her own heritage out, to live simply. Didn't want to be Bobbie Bray's legacy, Eve recalled.

Who could blame her? Or anyone else for that matter.

"If you're handed crap and disappointment—*inherited* it," Eve amended, "what do you do?"

"Depends, I guess." Peabody frowned as they headed down. "You could wallow in it and curse your ancestors, or shovel yourself out of it."

"Yeah. You could try to shine it up into gold and live the high life—like Hopkins. Obsess over it like Bray's daughter. Or you could shut the door on it and walk away. Like Bray's granddaughter."

"Okay. And?"

"There's more than one way to shut a door. You drive," Eve said when they were outside.

"Drive? Me? It's not even my birthday!"

"Drive, Peabody." In the passenger seat, Eve took out her ppc and brought up John Massey's military ID data. She cocked her head as she studied the photo.

He'd been young, fresh-faced. A little soft around the mouth, she mused, a little guileless in the eyes. She didn't see either of his grandparents in him, but she saw something else.

Inherited traits, she thought. Legacies.

Using the dash 'link, she contacted police artist Detective Yancy.

"Got a quick one for you," she told him. "I'm going to shoot you an ID photo. I need you to age it for me."

Chapter 8

Eve had Peabody stop at the bank Hopkins had used for his loan on Number Twelve. But there was no safety-deposit box listed under his name, or Bray's, or any combination.

To Peabody's disappointment, Eve took the wheel when they left the bank.

She couldn't justify asking Roarke to do the search for a safety-deposit box, though it passed through her mind. He could no doubt pinpoint one, if one was there to be pinpointed, faster than she could. Even faster than EDD. But she couldn't term it a matter of life and death.

Just a matter of irritation.

She put in a request to Feeney to assign the task to EDD ace, and Peabody's heartthrob, Ian McNab, while she and Peabody headed back to Bygones.

"McNab will be so completely jazzed about this." Smiling—as if even saying his name put a dopey look on her face—Peabody wiggled in the passenger seat. "Looking for a ghost and all that."

"He's looking for a bank box."

"Well yeah, but in a roundabout way, it's about Bobbie Bray and the ghost thereof. Number Twelve."

"Stop saying that." Eve wanted to grip her own hair and yank, but her hands were currently busy on the wheel. She used those hands to whip around a farting maxibus with a few layers of paint to spare. "I'm going to write an order forbidding anyone within ten feet of me from saying *Number Twelve* in that—what is it—awed whisper."

"But you just gotta. Did you know there are all these books, and there are vids, based on Number Twelve, and Bobbie and the whole deal from back then? I did some research. McNab and I downloaded one of the vids last night. It was kind of hokey, but still. And we're working the case. Maybe they'll make a vid of *that*—you know, like they're going to do one of the Icove case. Completely uptown. We'll be famous, and—"

Eve stopped at a light, turned her body slowly so she faced her partner. "You even breathe that thought, I'll choke you until your eyes pop right out of their sockets, then plop into your open gasping mouth where you'll swallow them whole. And choke to death on your own eyeballs."

"Well, jeez."

"Think about it, think carefully, before you breathe again."

Peabody hunched in her seat and kept her breathing to a minimum.

When they found the shop closed and locked, they detoured to the home address on record.

Maeve opened the door of the three-level brownstone. "Lieutenant, Detective."

"Closed down shop, Ms. Buchanan?"

"For a day or two." She pushed at her hair. Eve watched the movement, the play of light on the striking red. "We were overrun yesterday, only about an hour after you left. Oh, come in, please. I'm a little flustered this morning."

"Overrun?" Eve repeated as she stepped into a long, narrow hallway brightened by stained-glass windows that let in the winter sun.

"Customers, and most of them looking for bargains. Or wanting to gawk over the Bobbie Bray collection." Maeve, dressed in loose white pants, a soft white sweater and white half boots led the way through a wide doorway into a spacious parlor.

Tidy, Eve thought, but not fussy. Antiques—she knew how to recognize the real thing, as Roarke had a penchant for them. Deep cushions in rich colors, old rugs, what looked to be old black-and-white photographs in pewter frames adorning the walls.

No gel cushions, no mood screen, no entertainment unit in sight. Old-world stuff, Eve decided, very much like their place of business.

"Please, have a seat. I've got tea or coffee."

"Don't worry about it," Eve told her. "Your father's here?"

"Yes, up in the office. We're working from here, at least for today. We're buried in inquiries for our Bray collection, and we can handle those from home."

She moved around the room, turning on lamps with colored shades. "Normally, we'd love the walk-in traffic at the shop, but not when it's a circus parade. With only the two of us, we just couldn't handle it. We have a lot of easily lifted merchandise."

"How about letters?"

"Letters?"

"You carry that sort of thing? Letters, diaries, journals?"

"We absolutely do. On Bobbie again?" Maeve walked back to sit on the edge of a chair, crossed her legs. "We have what's been authenticated as a letter she wrote to a friend she'd made in San Francisco—ah . . . 1968. Two notebooks containing original lyrics for songs she'd written. There may be more, but those spring to mind."

"How about letters to family, from her New York years?"

"I don't think so, but I can check the inventory. Or just ask my father," she added with a quick smile. "He's got the entire inventory in his head, I swear. I don't know how he does it."

"Maybe you could ask him if he could spare us a few minutes."

"Absolutely."

When she hesitated, Eve primed her. "Is there something else, something you remember?"

"Actually, I've been sort of wrestling with this. I don't think it makes any difference. I didn't want to say anything in front of my father." She glanced toward the doorway, then tugged lightly—nervously, Eve thought—on one of the sparkling silver hoops she wore in her ears. "But . . . well, Mr. Hopkins—Rad—he sort of hit on me. Flirted, you know. Asked me out to dinner, or drinks. He said I could be a model, and he could set me up with a photographer who'd do my portfolio at a discount."

She flushed, the color rising pink into her cheeks, and cleared her throat. "That kind of thing."

"And did you? Have drinks, dinner, a photo session?"

"No." She flushed a little deeper. "I know when I'm getting a line. He was old enough to be my father, and well, not really my type. I won't say there wasn't something appealing about him. Really, he could be charming. And it wasn't nasty, if you know what I mean. I don't want you to think . . ."

She waved a hand in the air. "It was all sort of friendly and foolish. I might have even been tempted, just for the fun. But I've been seeing someone, and it's turning into a thing. I didn't want to mess that up. And frankly, my father wouldn't have liked it."

"Because?"

"The age difference for one, and the type of man Rad was. Opportunistic, multiple marriages. Plus, he was a client and that can get sticky. Anyway." Maeve let out a long, relieved breath. "It was bothering me that I didn't mention it to you, and that you might hear about it and think I was hiding something."

"Appreciate that."

"I'll go get my father," she said as she rose. "You're sure you won't have coffee? Tea? It's bitter out there today."

"I wouldn't mind either," Peabody put in. "Dealer's choice. The lieutenant's coffee—always black."

"Fine. I'll be back in a few. Make yourselves comfortable."

"She was a little embarrassed about the Hopkins thing. She wanted to serve us something," Peabody said when Maeve left the room. "Makes it easier for her."

"Whatever floats." Eve got to her feet, wandered the room. It had a settled, family feel about it, with a thin sheen of class. The photos were arty black-and-whites of cities— old-timey stuff. She was frowning over one when Buchanan came in. Like his daughter, he was wearing at-home clothes. And still managed to look dignified in a blue sweater and gray pants.

"Ladies. What can I do for you?"

"You have a beautiful home, Mr. Buchanan," Peabody began. "Some wonderful old pieces. Lieutenant, it makes me wonder if Roarke's ever bought anything from Mr. Buchanan."

"Roarke?" Buchanan gave Peabody a puzzled look. "He has acquired a few pieces from us. You're not saying he's a suspect in this."

"No. He's Lieutenant Dallas's husband."

"Of course, I forgot for a moment." He shifted his gaze to Eve with a smile. "My business keeps me so much in the past, current events sometimes pass me by."

"I bet. And speaking of the past," Eve continued, "we're interested in any letters, journals, diaries you might have that pertain to Bobbie Bray."

"That's a name I've heard countless times today. Maeve might have told you that's why we decided to work from home. And here she is now."

Maeve wheeled in a cart holding china pots and cups.

"Just what we need. I've put the 'links on auto," her father told her. "We can take a short break. Letters." He took a seat while Maeve poured coffee and tea. "We do have a few she wrote to friends in San Francisco in 1968 and 1969. And one of our prizes is a workbook containing drafts of some of her song lyrics. It could, in a way, be considered a kind of diary as well. She wrote down some of her thoughts in it, or notes to herself. Little reminders. I've fielded countless inquiries about just that this morning. Including one from a Cliff Gill."

"Hopkins's son?"

"So he said. He was very upset, nearly incoherent really." Buchanan patted Maeve's hand when she passed him a cup. "Understandable under the circumstances."

"And he was looking specifically for letters?" Eve asked.

"He said his father had mentioned letters, a bombshell as he put it. Mr. Gill understood his father and I had done business and hoped I might know what it was about. I think he hopes to clear his family name."

"You going to help him with that?"

"I don't see how." Buchanan spread his hands. "Nothing I have pertains."

"If there was something that pertained, or correspondence written near the time of her disappearance, would you know about it?"

He pursed his lips in thought. "I can certainly put out feelers. There are always rumors, of course. Several years ago someone tried to auction off what they claimed was a letter written by Bobbie two years after her disappearance. It was a forgery, and there was quite a scandal."

"There have been photos, too," Maeve added. "Purportedly taken of Bobbie after she went missing. None have ever been authenticated."

"Exactly." Buchanan nodded. "So substantiating the rumors and the claims, well, that's a different matter. Do you know of correspondence from that time, Lieutenant?"

"I've got a source claiming there was some."

"Really." His eyes brightened. "If they're authentic, acquiring them would be quite a coup."

"Were you name-dropping, Peabody?" Eve gave her partner a mild look as she slid behind the wheel.

"Roarke's done business there before, and you guys went there together. But he doesn't mention Roarke at all. And being in business, I figured Buchanan would keep track of his more well-heeled clients, you know, and should've made an immediate connection."

"Yeah, you'd think. Plausible reason he didn't."

"You'd wondered, too."

"I wonder all kinds of things. Let's wonder our way over to talk to Cliff Gill."

Like Bygones, the dance school was locked up tight. But as Fanny Gill lived in the apartment overhead, it was a short trip.

Cliff answered looking flushed and harassed. "Thank God! I was about to contact you."

"About?"

"We had to close the school." He took a quick look up and down the narrow hallway then gestured them inside. "I had to give my mother a soother."

"Because?"

"Oh, this is a horrible mess. I'm having a Bloody Mary."

Unlike the Buchanan brownstone, Fanny's apartment was full of bright, clashing colors, a lot of filmy fabrics and chrome. Artistic funk, Eve supposed. It was seriously lived in to the point of messy.

Cliff was looking pretty lived-in himself, Eve noted. He hadn't shaved, and it looked like he'd slept in the sweats he was wearing. Shadows dogged his eyes.

"I stayed the night here," he began as he stood in the adjoining kitchen pouring vodka. "People came into the studio yesterday afternoon, some of them saying horrible things. Or they'd just call, leaving horrible, nasty transmissions. I've turned her 'links off. She just can't take any more."

He added enough tomato juice and Tabasco to turn the vodka muddy red, then took a quick gulp. "Apparently we're being painted with the same brush as my grandfather.

Spawn of Satan." He took another long drink, then blushed. "I'm sorry. I'm sorry, what can I get you?"

"We're fine," Eve told him. "Mr. Gill, have you been threatened?"

"With everything from eternal damnation to public flogging. My mother doesn't deserve this, Lieutenant. She's done nothing but choose poorly in the husband department, which she rectified. At least I carry the same blood as Hopkins." His mouth went grim. "If you think along those lines."

"Do you?"

"I don't know what I think any more." He came back into the living area, dropped onto a candy-pink sofa heaped with fluffy pillows. "At least I know what to feel now. Rage, and a little terror."

"Did you report any of the threats?"

"She asked me not to." He closed his eyes, seemed to gather some tattered rags of composure. "She's embarrassed and angry. Or she started out that way. She didn't want to make a big deal about it. But it just kept up. She handles things, my mother, she doesn't fall apart. But this has just knocked her flat. She's afraid we'll lose the school, with all the publicity, the scandal. She's worked so hard, and now this."

"I want you to make a copy of any of the transmissions regarding this. We'll take care of it."

"Okay. Okay." He scooped his fingers through his disordered hair. "That's the right thing to do, isn't it? I'm just not thinking straight. I can't see what I should do."

"You contacted the owner of a shop called Bygones. Care to tell me why?"

"Bygones? Oh, oh, right. Mr. Buchanan. My father sold

him some memorabilia. I think maybe Buchanan was one of the backers on Number Twelve. My father mentioned him when I gave him the five hundred. Said something like Bygones may be Bygones, but he wouldn't be nickel-and-diming it anymore. How he'd pay me back the five ten times over because he was about to hit the jackpot."

"Any specific jackpot?"

"He talked a lot, my father. Bragged, actually, and a lot of the bragging was just hot air. But he said he'd been holding onto an ace in the hole, waiting for the right time. It was coming up."

"What was his hole card?"

"Can't say he actually had one." Cliff heaved out a breath. "Honestly, I didn't really listen because it was the same old, same old to me. And I wanted to get him moving before my mother got wind of the loan. But he said something about letters Bobbie Bray had written. A bombshell, he said, that was going to give Number Twelve just the push he needed. I didn't pay much attention at the time because he was mostly full of crap."

He winced now, drank again. "Hell of a thing to say about your dead father, huh?"

"His being dead doesn't make him more of a father to you, Mr. Gill," Peabody said gently.

Cliff's eyes went damp for a moment. "Guess not. Well, when all this started happening. I remembered how he talked about these letters, and I thought maybe he'd sold them to Bygones. Maybe there was something in them that would clear my grandfather. Something, I don't know. Maybe she committed suicide and he panicked."

He lowered his head, rubbed the heel of his hand in the center of his brow as if to push away some pain. "I don't even care, or wouldn't, except for what's falling down from it on my mother. I don't know what I expected Mr. Buchanan to do. I was desperate."

"Did your father give you any indication of the contents of the letters?" Eve asked. "The timing of them?"

"Not really, no. At the time I thought it was just saving face because I was giving him money. Probably all it was. Buchanan said he hadn't bought any letters from my father, but I could come in and look at what he had. Waste of time, I guess. But he was nice about it—Buchanan, I mean. Sympathetic."

"Have you discussed this with your mother at all?" Peabody asked him.

"No, and I won't." Any grief seemed to burn away as anger covered his face. "It's a terrible thing to say, but by dying my father's given her more trouble than he has since she divorced him. I'm not going to add to it. Chasing a wild goose anyway." He frowned into his glass. "I have to make some arrangements for—for the body. Cremation, I guess. I know it's cold, but I'm not going to have any sort of service or memorial. I'm not going to drag this out. We just have to get through this."

"Mr Gill—"

"Cliff," he said to Eve with a weak smile. "You should call me Cliff since I'm dumping all my problems on you."

"Cliff. Do you know if your father kept a safety-deposit box?"

"He wouldn't have told me. We didn't see each other much. I don't know what he'd have kept in one. I got a call from some lawyer this morning. Said my father'd made a will, and I'd inherit. I asked him to ballpark it, and the gist was when it all shakes out, I'll be lucky to have enough credits to buy a soy dog at a corner cart."

"I guess you were hoping for better," Peabody commented.

Cliff let out a short, humorless laugh. "Hoping for better with Rad Hopkins would be another waste of time."

Chapter 9

"You have to feel for the guy." Peabody bundled her scarf around her neck as they walked back outside.

"We'll pass off the copy of his 'link calls to a couple of burly uniforms, have them knock on some doors and issue some stern warnings. About all we can do there for now. We're going back to Central. I want a quick consult with Mira, and you can update the Commander."

"Me?" Peabody's voice hit squeak. "Alone? Myself?"

"I expect Commander Whitney would be present as you're updating him."

"But you do the updates."

"Today you're doing it. He's going to want to set up a media conference," Eve added as she got into their vehicle. "Hold him off."

"Oh my God."

"Twenty-four hours. Make it stick," Eve added and pulled out into traffic as Peabody sat pale and speechless beside her.

Mira was the top profiler attached to the NYPSD for good reason. Her status kept her in high demand and made Eve's request for a consult without appointment similar to trying to squeeze her head through the eye of a needle that was already threaded.

She had a headache when she'd finished battling Mira's admin, but she got her ten minutes.

"You ought to give her a whip and a chain," Eve commented when she stepped into Mira's office. "Not that she needs one."

"You always manage to get past her. Have a seat."

"No thanks, I'll make it fast."

Mira settled behind her desk. She was a sleek, lovely woman who favored pretty suits. Today's was power red and worn with pearls.

"This would be pertaining to Number Twelve," Mira began. "Two murders, nearly a hundred years apart. Your consults are rarely routine. Bobbie Bray."

"You, too? People say that name like she's a deity."

"Do they?" Mira eased back in her chair, her blue eyes amused. "Apparently my grandmother actually heard her perform at Number Twelve in the early Nineteen-seventies. She claimed she exchanged an intimate sexual favor with the bouncer for the price of admission. My grandmother was a wild woman."

"Huh."

"And my parents are huge fans, so I grew up hearing that voice, that music. It's confirmed then? They were her remains?"

"Lab's forensic sculptor's putting her money on it as of this morning. I've got the facial image she reconstructed from the skull, and it looks like Bray."

"May I see?"

"I've got it in the file." Eve gave Mira the computer codes, then shifted so she, too, could watch the image come on-screen.

The lovely, tragic face, the deep-set eyes, the full, pouty lips somehow radiated both youth and trouble.

"Yes," Mira murmured. "It certainly looks like her. Something so sad and worn about her, despite her age."

"Living on drugs, booze, and sex tends to make you sad and worn."

"I suppose it does. You don't feel for her?"

Eve realized she should have expected the question from Mira. Feelings were the order of the day in that office. "I feel for anyone who gets a bullet in the brain—then has their body closed up in a wall. She deserves justice for that—deserves it for the cops who looked the other way. But she chose the life she led to that point. So looking sad and worn at twenty-couple? No, I can't say I feel for that."

"A different age," Mira said, studying Eve as she'd studied the image on screen. "My grandmother always said you had to be there. I doubt Bobbie would have understood you and the choices you've made any more than you do her and hers."

Mira flicked the screen off. "Is there more to substantiate identity?"

"The bones we recovered had a broken left tibia, which corresponds with a documented childhood injury on Bray. We extracted DNA, and I've got a sample of a relative's on its way to the lab. It's going to confirm."

"A tragic waste. All that talent snuffed out."

"She didn't live what you could call a careful life."

"The most interesting people rarely do." Mira angled her head. "You certainly don't."

"Mine's about the job. Hers was about getting stoned and screwing around, best I can tell."

Now Mira raised a brow. "Not only don't you feel for her, you don't think you'd have liked her."

"Can't imagine we'd have had much in common, but that's not the issue. She had a kid."

"What? I've never heard that."

"She kept it locked. Likelihood is it was Hop Hopkins's offspring, though it's possible she got knocked up on the side. Either way, she went off, had the kid, dumped it on her mother. Sent money so the family could relocate—up the scale some. Mother passed the kid off as her own."

"And you find that deplorable, on all counts."

Irritation shadowed Eve's face, very briefly. "That's not the issue either. Female child eventually discovered her heritage through letters Bray allegedly wrote home. The ones shortly before her death, again allegedly, claimed that she was planning to clean up her act—again—and come back for the kid. This is hearsay. The daughter relayed it to her two children. Purportedly the letters and other items were sold, years ago, to Radcliff C. Hopkins—the last."

"Connections within connections. And this, you believe goes to motive."

"You know how Hopkins was killed?"

"The walls are buzzing with it. Violent, specific, personal—and somehow tidy."

"Yeah." It was always satisfying to have your instincts confirmed. "The last shot. Here's what he did to her. There's control there, an agenda fulfilled, even through the rage."

"Let me see if I understand. You suspect that a descendent of Bobbie Bray killed a descendent of Hopkins to avenge her murder."

"That's a chunk of it, buttonholed. According to Bray's granddaughter, the murder, the abandonment, the obsession ruined her mother's health. Series of breakdowns."

"You suspect the granddaughter?"

"No, she's covered. She's got two offspring herself, but I can't place them in New York during the time in question."

"Who does that leave you?"

"There was a grandson, reported killed in action during the Urbans."

"He had children?"

"None on record. He was pretty young, only seventeen. Lied about his age when he joined up—a lot of people did back then. Oddly enough, he was reported killed here in New York."

Pursing her lips, Mira considered. "As you're one of the most pragmatic women I know, I find it hard to believe you're theorizing that a ghost killed your victim to avenge yet another ghost."

"Flesh and blood pulled the trigger. I've got Yancy aging the military ID. The Urban Wars were a chaotic time, and the last months of them here in New York were confusing from a military standpoint. Wouldn't be hard, would it, for a young man, one who'd already lied about his age to enlist in the Home Force, to put his official ID on a mangled body and vanish? War's never what you think it's going to be. It's not heroic and adventurous. He could've deserted."

"The history of mental illness in the family—on both sides—the horrors of war, the guilt of abandoning his duty. It would make quite a powder keg. Your killer is purposeful, specific to his goal, would have some knowledge of firearms. Rumor is the victim was shot nine times—the weapon itself is a symbol—and there were no stray bullets found on scene."

"He hit nine out of nine, so he had some knowledge of handguns, or some really good luck. In addition, he had to reload for the ninth shot."

"Ah. The others were the rage, that slippery hold on control. The last, a signature. He's accomplished what he meant to do. There may be more, of course, but he has his eye for an eye, and he has the object of his obsession back in the light."

"Yeah." Eve nodded. "I'm thinking that matters here."

"With Bobbie's remains found, identified, and her killer identified—at least in the media—he's fulfilled his obligation. If the killer is the grandson—or connected to the grandson, as even if he did die in the Urbans, it's certainly possible to have produced an offspring at seventeen—he or she knows how to blend."

"Likely to just keep blending," Eve added.

"Most likely. I don't believe your killer will seek the spotlight. He doesn't need acknowledgment. He'll slide back into his routine, and essentially vanish again."

"I think I know where to find him."

"Yancy does good work." Eve held the photos of John Massey—youth and maturity—side-by-side.

"He does," Roarke agreed. "As do you, Lieutenant. I doubt I'd have looked at the boy and seen the man."

"It's about legacies. Redheads ran in Bray's family. Her father, her daughter. Her grandson."

"And Yancy's work indicates he's alive and living in New York."

"Yeah. But even with this I've got nothing but instinct and theories. There's no evidence linking the suspect to the crime."

"You've closed a case on a murder that happened decades before you were born," Roarke reminded her. "Now you're greedy."

"My current suspect did most of the work there. Discovered the body, unearthed it, led me to it. The rest was basically lab and leg work. Since the perpetrator of that crime is long dead, there's nothing to do but mark the file and do the media announcement."

"Not very satisfying for you."

"Not when somebody kills a surrogate figuring that evens things up. And plays games with me. So it's our turn to play." Eve shifted in the limo. She felt ridiculous riding around in the big black boat.

But no one would expect Roarke to ride the subway, or even use a common Rapid Cab. Perception was part of the game.

"I can't send you in wired," she added. "Never get a warrant for eyes or ears with what I've got. You know what to say, right? How to play it?"

"Lieutenant, have a little faith."

"I got all there is. Okay," she added, ducking down a little to check out the window when the limo glided to the curb. "Showtime. I'll be cruising around in this thing, making sure the rest of this little play is on schedule."

"One question: Can you be sure your suspect will hit his cue in this play of yours?"

"Nothing's a given, but I'm going with the odds on this. Obsession's a powerful motivator. The killer is obsessed with Bray, with Number Twelve—and there's a sense of theatrics there. Another legacy, I'd say. We dangle the bait, he's going to bite."

"I'll do my best to dangle it provocatively."

"Good luck."

"Give us a kiss then."

"That's what you said last night, and look what happened." But she gave him a quick one. When he slipped out of the limo, she pulled out her 'link to check on the rest of the game.

Roarke walked into Bygones looking like a man with plenty of money and an eye to spend it as he liked. He gave Maeve an easy smile and a warm handshake. "Ms. Buchanan? I appreciate you opening for me this afternoon. Well, it's nearly evening, isn't it?"

"We're happy to oblige. My father will be right out. Would you like a glass of wine? I have a very nice cabernet breathing."

"I'd love one. I've met your father, though it's been three or four years, I suppose, since we've done business."

"I'd have been in college. He mentioned you'd bought a particularly fine Georgian sideboard and a set of china, among other things."

"He has an excellent memory."

"He never forgets a thing." She offered the wine she'd poured, then gestured to a silver tray of fruit and cheese. "Would you like to sit? If you'd rather browse, I can point you in a direction, or show you whatever you'd like. My father has the piece you inquired about. He wanted to make sure it was properly cleaned before he showed it to you."

"I'll just wait then, if you'll join me." As he sat, he glanced toward the portrait of Bobbie on the far wall. "It's actually Bobbie Bray who put me in mind to come here."

"Oh? There's always interest in her and her memorabilia, but in the last day it's piqued."

"I imagine." He shifted as he spoke so he could scan the black-and-white photographs Eve had told him about. And two, as she'd mentioned, were desert landscapes. "Just as I imagine it won't ebb anytime soon," he continued. "Certainly not with the publicity that will be generated from the case finally being solved."

Maeve's hands went very still for a moment. "It's certain then?"

"I have an inside source, as you might suspect. Yes, it's certain. She's been found, after all these years. And the evidence proves it was Hopkins who hid her body."

"Horrible. I—Daddy." She got to her feet as Buchanan came into the shop. He carried a velvet case. "You remember Roarke."

"I certainly do. It's good to see you again." They shook hands, sat. "Difficult circumstances when you were here recently with your wife."

"Yes. Terrible. I was just telling your daughter that they've confirmed the identity of the remains found at Number Twelve, and found Hopkins's—the first's—fingerprints on the inside of the wall, on several of the bricks."

"There's no doubt any longer then."

"Hardly a wonder he went mad, locking himself up in that building, knowing what he'd done, and that she was behind that wall, where he'd put her. A bit of 'The Telltale Heart,' really."

Keeping it conversational, Roarke settled back with his drink. "Still, it's fascinating, isn't it? Time and distance tend to give that sort of brutality an allure. No one can speak of anything else. And here I am, just as bad. Is that the necklace?"

"Oh, yes. Yes." Buchanan unsnapped the case, folded back the velvet leaves. "Charming, isn't it? All those little beads are hand-strung. I can't substantiate that Bobbie made it herself, though that's the story. But it was worn by her to the Grammy Awards, then given by her to one of her entourage. I was able to acquire it just last year."

"Very pretty." Roarke held up the multistrand necklace. The beads were of various sizes, shapes, colors, but strung in a way that showed the craftsman had a clever eye. "I think Eve might like this. A memento of Bobbie, since she's the one who's finally bringing her some sense of justice."

"Can there be, really?" Eyes downcast, Maeve murmured it. "After all this time?"

"For my cop, justice walks hand-in-hand with truth. She won't let the truth stay buried, as Bobbie was." He held up the beads again. "I'm hoping to take her away for a quick tropical holiday, and this sort of thing would suit the tropics, wouldn't it?"

"After this New York weather?" Maeve said with a laugh as she lifted her gaze once more. "The tropics would suit anything."

"With our schedules it's difficult to get away. I'm hoping we can find that window. Though with what they've found today, it may take a bit longer."

"They found something else?" Buchanan asked.

"Mmm. Something about a bank box, letters, and so on. And apparently something the former Hopkins recorded during his hermitage. My wife said he spoke of a small vault in Number Twelve, also walled in. Hopkins must have been very busy. They're looking for it, but it's a good-sized building. It may take days."

"A vault." Maeve breathed the words. "I wonder what's in it."

"More truth?" But Buchanan's voice was strained now. "Or the ramblings of a madman, one who'd already killed?"

"Perhaps both," Roarke suggested. "I know my wife's hoping for something that will lead her to Rad Hopkins's killer. The truth, and justice for him as well."

He laid the necklace on the velvet. "I'm very interested in this piece." Roarke sipped his wine. "Shall we negotiate?"

Chapter 10

In Number Twelve, Eve stood in the area that had once held a stage. Where there had been sound and light and motion, there was silence, dark, and stillness. She could smell dust and a faint whiff of the chemicals the sweepers used on-scene. And could feel nothing but the pervading chill that burned through the brick and mortar of an old building.

Still, the stage was set, she thought. If her hunch was off, she'd have wasted a lot of departmental time, manpower, and money. Better that, she decided, than to play into the current media hype that the curse of Number Twelve was still vital, still lethal.

"You've got to admit, it's creepy." Beside Eve, Peabody scanned the club room. There was a lot of white showing in her eyes. "This place gives me the jeebies."

"Keep your jeebies to yourself. We're set. I'm going up to my post."

"You don't have to go up right this minute." Peabody's

hand clamped like a bundle of live wires on Eve's wrist. "Seriously. We've got plenty of room on the timetable."

"If you're afraid of the dark, Detective, maybe you should've brought a nice little teddy bear to hold onto."

"Couldn't hurt," Peabody mumbled when Eve pulled free. "You'll stay in contact, right? I mean, communications open? It's practically like you're standing beside me."

Eve only shook her head as she crossed to the stairs. She'd gone through doors with Peabody when death or certainly pain was poised on the other side. She'd crawled through blood with her. And here her usually stalwart partner was squeaking over ghosts.

Her bootsteps echoed against the metal steps—and okay, maybe it was a little creepy. But it wasn't creaking doors and disembodied moans they had to worry about tonight. It was a stone killer who could come for letters from the dead.

There were no letters, of course. None that she knew of, no vault to hide them in. But she had no doubt the prospect of them would lure Rad Hopkins's killer into Number Twelve.

No doubt that killer was descended from Bray and Hopkins. If her hunch didn't pay off tonight, she was going to face a media storm tomorrow—face it either way, she admitted. But she'd rather deal with it with the case closed.

Funny how Bygones had old-timey photos of the desert. Maybe they were Arizona, maybe not, but she was laying her money that they were. There'd been old photos of San Francisco, too, before the quake had given it a good, hard shake. Others of New York during that time period, and of L.A. All of Bobbie's haunts.

Coincidence, maybe. But she agreed with one of the detectives in her squad on a case recently closed—a case that also included switched identities.

Coincidences were hooey.

She crossed the second tier, and started up to the old apartments.

Eve didn't doubt Roarke had played his part, and played it well. With the bait he'd dangled, she was gambling that Radcliff C. Hopkins's killer, and Bobbie Bray's murderous descendent, would bite quickly. Would bite tonight.

She took her position where she could keep the windows in view, put her back to the wall. Eve flipped her communications channel to Peabody's unit, and said, "Boo."

"Oh yeah, that's funny. I'm rib-cracking down here."

"When you're finished with your hilarity, we'll do a check. Feeney, you copy?"

"Got your eyes, your ears, and the body-heat sensors. No movement."

"You eating a doughnut?"

"What do you need electronic eyes and ears for, you can tell I'm eating a cruller from in there?" There was a slurping sound as Feeney washed down the cruller with coffee. "Roarke bought the team a little something to keep us alert."

"Yeah, he's always buying something." She wished she had a damn cruller. Better, the coffee.

"You should have worn the beads, Lieutenant," Roarke's voice cruised on. "I think they might have appealed to Bobbie."

"Yeah, that's what I need. Baubles and beads. I could use them to—"

"Picking up something," Feeney interrupted.

"I hear it." Eve went silent, and as she focused, the sound—a humming—took on the pattern of a tune, and a female flavor. She drew her weapon.

"Exits and egresses," she murmured to Feeney.

"Undisturbed," he said in her ear. "I've got no motion,

no visual, no heat-sensor reading on anything but you and Peabody."

So it was on a timer, Eve decided. An electronic loop EDD had missed.

"Dallas?" Peabody's voice was a frantic hiss. "You read? I see—"

The earpiece went to a waspy buzz. And the air went to ice.

She couldn't stop the chill from streaking up her spine, but no one had to know about it. She might have cursed the glitch in communications and surveillance, but she was too busy watching the amorphous figure drift toward her.

Bobbie Bray wore jeans widely belled from the knees down, slung low at the hips and decorated with flowers that twined up the side of each leg. The filmy white top seemed to float in a breeze. Her hair was a riotous tangle of curls with the glitter of diamond clips. As she walked, as she hummed, she lifted a cigarette to her lips and drew deeply.

For an instant, the sharp scent of tobacco stung the air.

From the way the image moved, Eve decided tobacco wasn't the only thing she'd been smoking. As ghosts went, this one was stoned to the eyeballs.

"You think I'm buying this?" Eve pushed off the wall. But when she started to move forward something struck out at her. Later, she would think it was like being punched with an ice floe.

She shoved herself forward, following the figure into what had been the bedroom area of the apartment.

The figure stopped, as if startled.

I didn't know you were up here. What's it about? I told you, I'm bookin'. So I packed. Don't give me any more shit, Hop.

The figure moved as it spoke, mimed pouring something

into a glass, drinking. There was weariness in the voice, and the blurriness of drugs.

Because I'm tired and I'm sick. I'm so fucking messed up. This whole scene is fucked up, and I can't do it anymore. I don't give a shit about my career. That was all you. It's always been all you.

She turned, stood hipshot and blearily defiant.

Yeah? Well, maybe I have lapped it up, and now I'm just puking it out. For Christ's sake look at us, Hop. Look at yourself. We're either stoned or strung out. We got a kid. Don't tell me to shut up. I'm sick of myself and I'm sick of you. I will *stay straight this time.*

The image flung an arm out as if heaving a glass against the wall.

I'm not humping some other guy. I'm not signing with another label. I'm done. Don't you get it? I'm done with this, and I'm done with you. You're fucking crazy, Hop. You need help more than I do. Put that down.

The image threw up its hands now, stumbling back.

You gotta calm down. You gotta come down. We'll talk about it, okay? I don't have to leave. I'm not lying. I'm not. Oh God. Don't. No. Jesus, Hop. Don't!

There was a sharp crack as the figure jerked back, then fell. The hole in the center of the forehead leaked blood.

"Hell of a show," Eve said, and her voice sounded hoarse to her own ears. "Hell of a performance."

Eve heard the faint creak behind her, pivoted. Maeve stepped into the room, tears pouring down her cheeks. And a knife gleaming dully in her hand.

"He shot me dead. Dead was better than gone—that's what he said."

Not John Massey, Eve realized. The Bray/Hopkins legacy had gone down another generation.

"You look alive to me, Maeve."

"Bobbie," she corrected. "She's in me. She speaks through me. She is me."

Eve let out a sigh, kept her weapon down at her side. "Oh step back. Ghosts aren't ridiculous enough, now we have to go into possession?"

"And he killed me." Maeve crooned it. "Took my life. He said I was nothing without him, just a junky whore with a lucky set of pipes."

"Harsh," Eve agreed. "I grant you. But it all happened before you were born. And both players are long dead. Why kill Hopkins?"

"He walled me up." Her eyes gleamed, tears and rage and madness. "He paid off the cops, and they did *nothing*."

"No, he didn't. His grandfather did."

"There's no difference." She turned a slow circle as she spoke, arms out. "He was, I was. He is, I am." Then spun, pointed at Eve with the tip of the knife. "And you, you're no different than the cops who let me rot in there. You're just another pig."

"Nobody pays me off. I finish what I start, and let me tell you something: This stops here."

"It never stops. I can't get out, don't you get it?" Maeve slapped a hand over her lips as if to hold back the gurgle of laughter that ended on a muffled sob. "Every day, every night, it's the same thing. I can't get away from it, and I go round and round and round, just like he wanted."

"Well, I'm going to help you get out of here. And you can spend every day, every night of the rest of your natural life in a cage. Might be a nice padded one, in your case."

Maeve smiled now. "You can't stop it. You can't stop me, you can't stop it. 'You're never leaving me.' That's what he said when he was walling me up in there. He made me, that's what he said, and I wasn't going anywhere. Ever. Fucking bastard killed me, cursed me, trapped me. What the hell are you going to do about it?"

"End it. Maeve Buchanan, you're under arrest for the murder of Radcliff Hopkins. You have the right to remain silent—"

"You'll pay for leaving me in there!" Maeve hacked out with the knife she held and missed by a foot.

"Jesus, you fight like a girl." Eve circled with her, watching Maeve's eyes. "I'm not an overweight dumbass, and you don't have a gun this time. So pay attention. Stunner, knife. Stunner always wins. You want a jolt, Maeve?"

"You can't hurt me. Not in this place. I can't be harmed here."

"Wanna bet?" Eve said, and hit Maeve with a low stun when the redhead charged again.

The knife skittered out of Maeve's hand as she fell back, hit hard on her ass. There was another swipe of cold, this time like ice-tipped nails raking Eve's cheek. But she pushed by it, yanking out her restraints as she dragged Maeve's arms behind her back.

Maeve struggled, her body bucking as she gasped out curses. And the cold, whipped by a vicious wind, went straight down to the bone.

"This stops here," Eve repeated, breathless as what felt like frigid fists pounded at her back. "Radcliff C. Hopkins will be charged with murder one in the unlawful death of Bobbie Bray, posthumously. That's my word. Period. Now leave me the hell alone so I can do my job."

Eve hauled Maeve to her feet as the wind began to die. "We're going to toss in breaking and entering and assault on an officer just for fun."

"My name is Bobbie Bray, and you can't touch me. I'm Bobbie Bray, do you hear me? I'm Bobbie Bray."

"Yeah, I hear you." Just as she heard the sudden frantic squawking of voices in her ear and the thunder of footsteps on the stairs.

"I couldn't get to the stairs," Peabody told her. "All of a sudden the place is full of people and music. Talk about jeebies. My communication's down, and I'm trying to push through this wall of bodies. Live bodies—well, not live. I don't know. It's all jumbled."

"We went to the doors soon as communications went down," Feeney added. "Couldn't get through them. Not even your man there with his magic fingers. Then all of a sudden, poof, com's back, locks open, and we're in. Damned place." Feeney stared at Number Twelve as they stood on the sidewalk. "Ought to be leveled, you ask me. Level the bastard and salt the ground."

"Maeve Buchanan rigged it, that's all. We'll figure out how." That was her story, Eve told herself, and she was sticking with it. "I'm heading in, taking her into interview. She's just whacked enough she may not lawyer up straight off."

"Can I get a lift?"

Eve turned to Roarke. "Yeah, I'll haul you in. Uniforms are transporting the suspect to Central. Peabody, you want to supervise that?"

"On it. Glad to get the hell away from this place."

When he settled in the car beside Eve, Roarke said simply, "Tell me."

"Maeve was probably already inside. We just missed her in the sweep. She had a jammer and a program hidden somewhere."

"Eve."

She huffed out a breath, cursed a little. "If you want to be fanciful or whatever, I had a conversation with a dead woman."

She told him, working hard to be matter-of-fact.

"So it wasn't Maeve who bruised and scratched your face."

"I don't know what it was, but I know this is going to be wrapped, and wrapped tight tonight. Buchanan's being picked up now. We'll see if he was in this, or if Maeve worked alone. But I'm damn sure she's the one who fired the gun. She's the one who lured Hopkins there. He had a weakness for young women. He'd never have felt threatened by her. Walked right in, alone, unarmed."

"If she sticks with this story about being Bobbie Bray, she could end up in a psychiatric facility instead of prison."

"A cage is a cage—the shape of it isn't my call."

At Central, Eve let Maeve stew a little while as she waited for Mira to be brought in and take a post in observation. So she took Buchanan first.

He was shaking when she went into interview room B, his face pale, his eyes glossy with distress.

"They said—they said you arrested my daughter. I don't understand. She'll need a lawyer. I want to get her a lawyer."

"She's an adult, Mr. Buchanan. She'll request her own representation if she wants it."

"She won't be thinking straight. She'll be upset."

"Hasn't been thinking straight for a while, has she?"

"She's . . . she's delicate."

"Here." Peabody set a cup of water on the table for him. "Have a drink. Then you can help us help your daughter."

"She needs help," Eve added. "Do you know she claims to be Bobbie Bray?"

"Oh God. Oh God." He put his face in his hands. "It's my fault. It's all my fault."

"You are John Massey, grandson of Bobbie Bray and Radcliff Hopkins?"

"I got away from all that. I had to get away from it. It destroyed my mother. There was nothing I could do."

"So during the Urbans, you saw your chance. Planted your ID after an explosion. Mostly body parts. All that confusion. You walked away."

"I couldn't take all the killing. I couldn't go back home. I wanted peace. I just wanted some peace. I built a good life. Got married, had a child. When my wife died, I devoted myself to Maeve. She was the sweetest thing."

"Then you told her where she'd come from, who she'd come from."

He shook his head. "No. She told me. I don't know how she came to suspect, but she tracked down Rad Hopkins. She said it was business, and I wanted to believe her. But I was afraid it was more. Then one day she told me she'd been to Number Twelve, and she understood. She was going to take care of everything, but I never thought she meant . . . Is this ruining her life now, too? Is this ruining her life?"

"You knew she went back out the night Hopkins was killed," Eve said. "You knew what she'd done. She'd have told you. You covered for her. That makes you an accessory."

"No." Desperation was bright in his eyes as they darted around the room. "She was home all night. This is all a terrible mistake. She's upset and she's confused. That's all."

They let him sit, stepped out into the hall. "Impressions, Peabody?"

"I don't think he had an active part in the murder. But he knew—maybe put his head in the sand about it, but he knew. We can get him on accessory after the fact. He'll break once she has."

"Agreed. So let's go break her."

Maeve sat quietly. Her hair was smoothed again, her face was placid. "Lieutenant, Detective."

"Record on." Eve read the data into the recorder, recited the revised Miranda. "Do you understand your rights and obligations, Ms. Buchanan?"

"Of course."

"So Maeve." Eve sat at the table across from her. "How long did you know Hopkins?"

A smirky little smile curved her lips. "Which one?"

"The one you shot nine times in Number Twelve."

"Oh, that Hopkins. I met him right after he bought the building. I read about it, and thought it was time we resolved some matters."

"What matters?"

"Him killing me."

"You don't look dead."

"He shot me so I couldn't leave him, so I wouldn't be someone else's money train. Then he covered it up. He covered me up. I've waited a long time to make him pay for it."

"So you sent him the message so he'd come to Number Twelve. Then you killed him."

"Yes, but we'd had a number of liaisons there before. We had to uncover my remains from that life."

"Bobbie Bray's remains."

"Yes. She's in me. I am Bobbie." She spoke calmly, as if they were once again sitting in the classy parlor in her brownstone. "I came back for justice. No one gave me any before."

"How did you know where the remains were?"

"Who'd know better? Do you know what he wanted to

do? He wanted to bring in the media, to make another fortune off me. He had it all worked out. He'd bring the media in, let them put my poor bones on-screen, give interviews—at a hefty fee, of course. Using me again, like he always did. Not this time."

"You believed Rad Hopkins was Hop Hopkins reincarnated?" Peabody asked.

"Of course. It's obvious. Only this time I played him. Told him my father would pay and pay and pay for the letters I'd written. I told him where we had to open the wall. He didn't believe that part, but he wanted under my skirt."

She wrinkled her nose to show her mild distaste. "I could make him do what I wanted. We worked for hours cutting that brick. Then he believed."

"You took the hair clips and the gun."

"Later. We left them while he worked on his plan. While, basically, he dug his own grave. I cleaned them up. I really loved those hair clips. Oh, there were ammunition clips, too. I took them. I was there."

Her face changed, hardened, and her voice went raw, went throaty. "In me, in the building. So sad, so cold, so lost. Singing, singing every night. Why should I sing for him? Murdering bastard. I gave him a child, and he didn't want it."

"Did you?" Eve asked her.

"I was messed up. He got me hooked—the drugs, the life, the buzz, you know? Prime shit, always the prime shit for Hop. But I was going to get straight, give it up, go back for my kid. I was gonna—had my stuff packed up. I wrote and told my old lady, and I was walking on Hop. But he didn't want that. Big ticket, that's what I was. He never wanted the kid. Only me, only what I could bring in. Singing and singing."

"You sent Rad a message, to get him to Number Twelve."

"Sure. Public 'link, easy and quick. I told him to come, and when to come. He liked when I used Bobbie's voice—spliced from old recordings—in the messages I sent him. He thought it was sexy. Asshole. He stood there, grinning at me. I brought it, he said."

"What was it?"

"His watch. The watch he had on the night he shot me. The one I bought him when my album hit number one. He had it on his wrist and was grinning at me. I shot him, and I kept shooting him until the clip was empty. Then I pushed the murdering bastard over, and I put the gun right against his head, right against it, and I shot him again. Like he did to me."

She sat back a little, smiled a little. "Now he can wander around in that damn place night after night after night. Let's see how he likes it."

Epilogue

When Eve stepped out, rubbed her hands over her face, Mira slipped out of observation.

"Don't tell me," Eve began. "Crazy as a shithouse rat."

"That might not be my precise diagnosis, but I believe we'll find with testing that Maeve Buchanan is legally insane and in desperate need of treatment."

"As long as she gets it in a cage. Not a bit of remorse. Not a bit of fear. No hedging."

"She believes everything she did was justified, even necessary. My impression, at least from observing this initial interview, is she's telling you the truth exactly as she knows it. There's the history of mental illness on both sides of her family. This may very well be genetic. Then discovering who her great-grandmother was helped push her over some edge she may very well have been teetering on."

"How did she discover it?" Eve added. "There's a question. Father must have let something slip."

"Possibly. Haven't you ever simply *known* something?

Or felt it? Of course, you have. And from what I'm told happened tonight, you had an encounter."

Frowning, Eve ran her fingers over her sore cheek. "I'm not going to stand here and say I was clocked by a ghost. I'm sure as hell not putting that in my report."

"Regardless, you may at the end of this discover the only reasonable way Maeve learned of her heritage was from Bobbie Bray herself. That she also learned of the location of the remains from the same source."

"That tips out of the reasonable."

"But not the plausible. And that learning these things snapped something inside her. Her way of coping was to make herself Bobbie. To believe she's the reincarnation of a woman who was killed before her full potential was realized. And who, if she'd lived—if she'd come back to claim her child—would have changed everything."

"Putting a lot of faith in a junkie," Eve commented. "And using, if you ask me, a woman who was used, exploited, and murdered, to make your life a little more important."

Now she rubbed her eyes. "I'm going to get some coffee, then hit the father again. Thanks for coming down."

"It's been fascinating. I'd like to do the testing on her personally. If you've no objection."

"When I'm done, she's all yours."

Because her own AutoChef had the only real coffee in all of Cop Central, Eve detoured there first.

There he was, sitting at her desk, fiddling with his ppc.

"You should go home," Eve told Roarke. "I'm going to have an all-nighter on this."

"I will, but I wanted to see you first." He rose, touched his hand to her cheek. "Put something on that, will you?" Until she did, he put his lips there. "Do you have a confession?"

"She's singing—ha-ha. Chapter and verse. Mira says she's nuts, but that won't keep her out of lockup."

"Sad, really, that an obsession with one woman could cause so much grief, and for so long."

"Some of it ends tonight."

This time he laid his lips on hers. "Come back to me when you can."

"You can count on that one."

Alone, she sat. And alone she wrote up a report, and the paperwork that charged Radcliff C. Hopkins I with murder in the first degree in the unlawful death of Bobbie Bray. She filed it, then after a moment's thought, put in another form.

She requested the release of Bobbie Bray's remains to herself—if they weren't claimed by next of kin—so that she could arrange for their burial. Quietly.

"Somebody should do it," she stated aloud.

She got her coffee, rolled her aching shoulders. Then headed back to work.

In Number Twelve, there was silence in the dark. No one sang, or wept, or laughed. No one walked there.

For the first time in eighty-five years, Number Twelve sat empty.

Turn the page for
an excerpt from J. D. Robb's exciting novel

Strangers in Death

Available from The Berkley Publishing Group

Murder harbored no bigotry, no bias. It subscribed to no class system. In its gleeful, deadly, and terminally judicious way, murder turned a blind eye on race, creed, gender, and social strata. As Lieutenant Eve Dallas stood in the sumptuous bedroom of the recently departed Thomas A. Anders, she considered that.

Only the night before she'd caught—and closed—a case dealing with the homicide of a twenty-year-old woman who'd been throttled, beaten, then chucked out the window of her nine-story flop.

The rent-by-the week flop, Eve mused, where the victim's boyfriend claimed to have slept through her demise, smelled of stale sex, stale Zoner, and really bad Chinese. Anders? His Park Avenue bedroom smelled of candy-colored tulips, cool, clean wealth, and dead body. Death had come to him on the luxurious sheets of his massive silk canopied bed. And to Tisha Brown it had come on the stained mattress tossed on the floor of a junkie's flop. The header to the sidewalk had just been the flourish.

The point was, Eve supposed, no matter who you were—sex, race, tax bracket—death leveled it all out. As a murder cop for the NYPSD going on a dozen years, she'd seen it all before.

It was barely seven in the morning, and she was alone with the dead. She had the first officers on scene downstairs with the housekeeper who'd called in the 911. With her hands and boots sealed, she walked around the edges of the room while her recorder documented.

"Victim is identified as Anders, Thomas Aurelious, of this address. Male, caucasian, age sixty-one. Vic is married—spouse is reported to be out of town, and has been notified by Horowitz, Greta, domestic, who discovered the body at approximately oh-six-hundred and placed the nine-one-one at oh-six-twelve."

Eve cocked her head. Her hair was a short, somewhat shaggy brown around a face of angles and planes. Her eyes, a few shades lighter than her hair, were all cop-sharp, cynical, and cool as they studied the dead man in the big, fancy bed.

"Anders was reputed to be alone in the house. There are two domestic droids, both of which were shut down. On cursory exam, there are no signs of forced entry, no signs of burglary, no signs of struggle."

On long legs, she crossed to the bed. Over her lean body she wore rough trousers, a plain cotton shirt, and a long coat of black leather. Behind her, over a gas fireplace where flames simmered gold and red, the view screen popped on.

Good morning, Mr. Anders!

Narrow-eyed, Eve turned to stare at the screen. The

computerized female voice struck her as annoying perky, and the sunrise colors bleeding onto the screen wouldn't have been her choice of wake-up call.

It's now seven-fifteen on Tuesday, March eighteenth, twenty-sixty. You have a ten o'clock tee time at the club, with Edmond Luce.

As the computer chirpily reminded Anders what he'd ordered for breakfast, Eve thought: *No egg-white omelette for you this morning, Tom.*

Across the room in an ornate sitting area, a mini AutoChef with bright brass fittings beeped twice.

Your coffee's ready! Enjoy your day!

"Not so much," Eve murmured.

The screen flipped to the morning's headline news, anchored by a woman only slightly less perky than the computer. Eve tuned her out.

The headboard gleamed brass, too, all of its sleek, shiny rungs. Black velvet ropes tied Anders's wrists to two of them, while two more bound his ankles by a length to the footboard. The four matching ropes were joined by the fifth, which wrapped around Anders's throat, pulling his head off the pillows. His eyes were wide, and his mouth hung open as if he was very surprised to find himself in his current position.

Several sex toys sat on the table beside the bed. Anal probe, vibrator, colorful cock rings, gliding/warming lotions and lubricants. The usual suspects, Eve thought. Leaning down, Eve studied, sniffed, Anders's thin, bare chest. Kiwi, she thought, and angled her head to read labels on the lotions.

Definitely the kiwi. It took all kinds.

As she'd noticed something else, she lifted the duvet from where it pooled at Anders's waist. Under it, three neon (possibly glow-in-the-dark) cock rings rode on an impressive erection.

"Not bad for a dead man."

Eve eased open the drawer in the nightstand. Inside, as she'd suspected, was an economy pack of the top-selling erection enhancer, Stay Up. "Hell of a product endorsement."

She started to open her field kit, then stopped when she heard approaching footsteps. Or the clomp of boots she recognized as her partner's shit-kickers. Whatever the calendar said about the approach of spring, in New York that was a big, fat lie. As if to prove the point, Detective Delia Peabody stepped through the door in an enormous, and puffy, purple coat, a long, striped scarf that appeared to be wrapped around her neck three times. Between that and the cap pulled over her ears, only her eyes and the bridge of her nose were visible.

"It's freaking five degrees," somebody who might have been Peabody said against the muffle of scarf.

"I know."

"With the windchill, they said it's like freaking minus ten."

"I heard that."

"It's freaking March, three days before spring. It's not right."

"Take it up with them."

"Who?"

"The *they* who have to go mouthing off about it being freaking minus ten. You're colder and pissier because they have to blabber about it. Take some of that shit off. You look ridiculous."

"Even my teeth are frozen."

But Peabody began to peel off the multiple layers covering her sturdy body. Scarf, coat, gloves, insulated zippy.

Eve wondered how the hell she managed to walk with all of them weighing her down. With the hat discarded Peabody's dark hair with its sassy little flip at the nape appeared to frame her square face. She still sported a pink-from-cold tipped nose.

"Cop on the door said it looked like sex games gone bad."

"Could be. Wife's out of town."

"Bad boy." Down to her street clothes, sealed up, Peabody carted her field kit to the bed. Scanned the nightstand. "Very bad boy."

"Let's verify ID, get TOD." Eve examined one of the limp hands. "Looks like he had a nice manicure recently. Nails are short, clean, and buffed." She angled her head. "No scratches, no bruises, no apparent trauma other than the throat. And . . ." She lifted the duvet again.

Peabody dark brown eyes popped. "Wowzer!"

"Yeah, fully loaded. Place like this has to have good security, so we'll check that. Two domestic droids—we'll check their replay. Take a look at his house 'links, pocket 'links, memo, date, address books. Tom had company. He didn't hoist himself up like this."

"*Cherchez le femme.* It's French for—"

"I know it's French. We could also be cherching the . . . whatever guy is in French."

"Oh. Yeah."

"Finish with the body," Eve ordered. "I'll take the room."

It was a hell of a room—if you went for a lot of gold accent, shiny bits, curlicues. Besides the big bed Anders had apparently died in, a sofa, a couple of oversized scoop chairs, and a full-service sleep chair offered other places to stretch out. In addition to the AutoChef, the bedroom boasted a brass friggie, wet bar, and an entertainment unit. The his and hers bathrooms both held jet tubs, showers, drying tubes, entertainment and communication centers within their impressive acreage. The space continued with two tri-level closets with attached dressing areas.

Eve wondered why they needed the rest of the house.

She should talk, she admitted. Living with Roarke meant living in enough space to house a small city—with all the bells and whistles big, fat fists of money could buy. He had better taste—thank God—than the Anderses. She wasn't entirely sure she could've fallen for him, much less married him, if he'd surrounded himself with gold and glitter and tassels, and Christ knew.

But as much *stuff* as there was jammed into the space, it all looked . . . in place, she decided. No sign or sense anything had been riffled through. She found a safe in each closet—concealed so a child of ten with dirt in both eyes could have found them. She'd check with the wife on those, but she wasn't smelling theft or burglary.

Walking out into the main bedroom again, she took another, hard look around.

"Prints verify ID as Anders, Thomas A., of this address," Peabody began. "Gauge give me three-thirty-two as time of death. That's really late or really early to be playing tie-me-up, tie-me-down games."

"If killer and vic came up here together, where are his clothes?"

Peabody turned toward her lieutenant, pursed her lips. "Considering you're married to the hottest guy on- or off-planet, I shouldn't have to tell you that the point in the tie-me-wherever game is to be naked while you're doing it."

"One of the other points is to get each other naked. If they came in here together," Eve considered, "if they came up here for games, is he going to strip down, *then* hang up his clothes or dump his shorts in the hamper? You got that on the menu—" She gestured to the sex toys. "You're not thinking about tidy. Clothes get pulled, tugged, torn, yanked off—fall on the floor. Even if this is an old game with a usual playmate, wouldn't you just toss your shirt over the chair?"

"I hang up my clothes. Sometimes." Peabody shrugged now. She angled her head to study the scene again, absently flicked back the hair that fell over her cheek. "But yeah, that's going to be when I'm not thinking about jumping McNab, or he's not already jumping me. Everything looks pretty tidy in here and in the rest of the house I got a look at on the way up. Vic could've been a neat freak."

"Could. The killer could've come in when he was already in bed. Three in the morning, surprise, surprise. Then things got out of hand—accidentally or on purpose. Killer comes in—the probability's high the vic or another household member knew the killer. No sign of break-in, and there's a high-end security system. Maybe this is another part of the game. You come in after I'm asleep. Surprise me. Wake me up. Trusses him up, works him up. Toys and games."

"And went too far."

Eve shook her head. "It went as far as he or she meant it to go. The erotic asphyxiation oops doesn't play."

"But . . ." Peabody studied the body again, the scene, and wished she could see whatever Eve could. "Why?"

"If it was all in fun, and went wrong, why did the killer leave the noose around Anders's neck? An accident, but you don't loosen it, try to revive when he starts choking, convulsing?"

"Maybe in the throes . . . Okay, that's a stretch, but if it happened fast, and she—or he—panicked."

"Either way, we've got a corpse, we've got a case. We'll see what the ME thinks about accidental. We'll go interview the housekeeper, let the sweepers in here."

Greta Horowitz was a sturdy-looking woman with a long rectangle of a face and a no-nonsense 'tude Eve appreciated. She offered coffee in the big silver-and-black kitchen, then served it with steady hands and dry eyes. With her strong, German-accented voice, direct blue eyes, and Valkyrie build, Eve assumed Greta handled what came her way,

"How long have you been here, Ms. Horowitz?"

"I am nine years in this employment, and in this country."

"You came to the U.S. from . . ."

"Berlin."

"How did you come to be employed by the Anderses?"

"Through an employment agency. You want to know how I came here and why. This is simple, and then we can speak of what is important. My husband was in the military. He was killed twelve years ago. We had no children. I am accomplished in running households, and to work I signed with an agency in Germany. I came to wish to come here. A soldier's wife sees much of the world, but I had never seen New York. I applied for this position, and after several interviews via 'link and holo, was hired."

"Thank you. Before we get to what's important, do you know why the Anderses wanted a German housekeeper, particularly?"

"I am house manager."

"House manager."

"Mr. Anders's grandmother was from Germany, and as a boy he had a German nanny."

"Okay. What time did you arrive this morning?"

"Six. Precisely. I arrive at six precisely every morning but Sunday, which is my full day off. I leave at four, precisely, but for Tuesdays and Thursdays when I leave at one. My schedule can be adjusted as needed, and with sufficient prior notice."

"When you arrived at precisely six this morning, what did you do? Precisely?"

Greta's lips twitched, very slightly. It might have been humor. "Precisely, I removed my coat, hat, scarf, gloves and stored them in the closet. Then I engaged the in-house security cameras. Mr. Anders disengages them every night prior to retiring. He dislikes the sensation of being watched, even if no one is in the house. My first duty in the morning is to turn them on again. After doing so, I came in here. I turned on the news, as is my habit, then checked the communication system. My employers most usually leave their breakfast orders the night before. They prefer I prepare them, rather than using the AutoChef. Mr. Anders ordered sliced melon, an egg-white omelette with dill, and two slices of wheat toast with butter and orange marmalade. Coffee—he takes his with cream and one sugar—and a glass of tomato juice."

"Do you know what time he put the order in?"

"Yes. At twenty-two-seventeen."

"So you started breakfast?"

"I did not. Mr. Anders would have breakfasted today at eight-fifteen. My next morning duty would have been to re-engage the two domestic droids, as these are shut down every evening before Mr. and Mrs. Anders retire, and to give them the day's work schedule. The droids are kept in the security room, there." She gestured. "I went in to deal with them, but I noticed the security screens—the in-house. I saw Mr. Anders's bedroom door was open. Mr. Anders *never* leaves his door open. If he's inside the room, or has left the room, the door is closed. If I'm required to be in the room, I'm to leave the door open while I'm inside, then close it again when I leave. It's the same for the domestics."

"Why?"

"It's not my place to ask."

It's my place, Eve thought. "You saw the door was open, but you didn't notice the dead man in bed?"

"The bedroom camera screens only the sitting area. Mr. Anders programmed it that way."

"A little phobic, maybe?"

"Perhaps. I will say he's a very private man."

"So his door was open."

"Nine years," Greta continued. "The door has never been open when I arrive in the morning, unless my employers are not in residence. I was concerned, so I went upstairs without booting up the droids. When I got to the bedroom, I saw the fire in the hearth. Mr. Anders will not allow the fire when he sleeps—or when he is out of the room. I was more concerned, so I went into the room. I saw him immediately. I went to the bedside, and I saw that I couldn't help him. I went downstairs again, very quickly, and called nine-one-one."

"Why downstairs?"

Greta looked puzzled. "I thought, from books and plays and vids, that I was not to touch anything in the room. Is that wrong?"

"No, it's exactly right. You did exactly the right thing."

"Good." Greta gave a brisk, self-congratulatory nod. "Then I contacted Mrs. Anders, and waited for the police to come. They came in perhaps five or six minutes. I took the two officers upstairs, then one brought me back down to the kitchen and waited here with me until you stepped in."

"I appreciate the details. Can you tell me who has the security codes to the house?"

"Mr. and Mrs. Anders and myself. The codes are changed every ten days."

"No one else has the codes? A good friend, another employee, a relative?"

Greta shook her head, decisively. "No one else has the codes."

"Mrs. Anders is away."

"Yes. She left on Friday for a week on St. Lucia with some female friends. This is an annual trip—though they don't go to the same place necessarily."

"You contacted her."

"Yes." Greta shifted slightly. "I realize, after thinking more clearly, I should have waited, and the police would have notified Mrs. Anders. But . . . they're my employers."

"How did you contact her?"

"Through the resort. When she goes on holiday, she often shuts off her pocket 'link."

"And her reaction?"

"I told her there had been an accident, that Mr. Anders was dead. I don't think she believed me, or understood me initially. I had to repeat it, twice—and I felt, under the circumstances, I couldn't tell her when she asked what kind of accident. She said she would come home immediately."

"Okay, Greta. You have a good relationship with the Anderses?"

"They are very good employers. Very fair, very correct."

"How about their relationship, with each other? It's not gossip," Eve said, reading Greta perfectly. "It's very fair, and it's very correct for you to tell me any and everything you can that may help me find out what happened to Mr. Anders."

"They seemed very content to me, very well suited. It would be my impression that they enjoyed each other, and their life together."

Enjoying each other wasn't what the crime scene transmitted, Eve thought. "Did either, or both of them, have relationships outside the marriage?"

"You mean sexual. I couldn't say. I manage the house. When I'm in the house, I've never seen anything that would lead me to believe either, or both, engaged in adulterous affairs."

"Can you think of anyone who'd want him dead?"

"No." Greta eased back slowly. "I thought—I assumed—that someone had broken in to steal, and that Mr. Anders was killed by the thief."

"Have you noticed anything missing or out of place?"

"No. No. But I haven't looked."

"I'm going to have you do that now. One of the officers will take you around." She glanced over as Peabody came in. "Peabody, get one of the uniforms. I want Mrs. Horowitz escorted while she looks around the house. You're free to go afterward," Eve told Greta. "If you'd give my partner or me the contact information where you'll be."

"I prefer to stay, until Mrs. Anders arrives, if this is allowed. She may need me."

"All right then." Eve rose, signalling the end to the initial interview. "Thanks for your cooperation."

As Greta went out, Eve walked to the room off the kitchen. Inside two droids, disengaged, stood. One male, one female, both uniformed and dignified in appearance. The security screens Greta has spoken of ranged over a wall—and as she'd stated, the master bedroom camera showed only the sitting area.

"Dallas?"

"Huh?"

"House security was disengaged at two-twenty-eight, reengaged at three twenty-six."

Eve turned to frown at Peabody. "Reengaged before TOD?"

"Yeah. All security discs for the twenty-four-hour period before the security was reset are gone."

"Why I'm shocked. We'll get EDD in here to see if they can dig something out. So Anders's night visitor left him hanging, and still alive. That doesn't sound like sex games gone wrong."

"No," Peabody agreed. "Sounds like murder."

Eve pulled out her communicator when it signaled. "Dallas."

"Sir, Mrs. Anders just got here. Should I bring her in?"

"Bring her straight back to the kitchen." Eve switched off. "Okay, let's see what the widow has to say."

Turning back to the screens, she watched Ava Anders sweep through the front door, her sable coat swinging back from a slim body dressed in deep blue. Her hair, a delicate blonde was pulled severely back from a face of high planes. Fat pearl drops swung at her ears, shaded glasses masked her eyes as she crossed the wide, marble foyer, through ornate archways, in skinny-heeled boots with the uniform at her side.

Eve stepped back into the kitchen, took her seat at the sunny breakfast nook seconds before Ava strode in. "You're in charge?" She pointed a finger at Eve. "You're the one in charge? I demand to know what's going on. Who the hell *are* you?"

"Lieutenant Dallas, NYPSD. Homicide."

"Homicide? What do you mean Homicide?" She pulled off her sunglasses, revealing eyes as blue and deep as her suit, tossed them onto the counter. "Greta said there'd been an accident. Tommy was in an accident. Where's my husband? Where's Greta?"

Eve got to her feet. "Mrs. Anders, I'm sorry to tell you your husband was killed this morning."

Ava stood where she was, her eyebrows drawing together, her breath coming in short little bursts. "Killed. Greta said . . . but I thought." She braced a hand on the counter, then slowly walked over to sit. "How? Did he . . . did he fall? Did he get sick, or . . ."

Always best to stab quick and clean, Eve thought. "He was strangled in his bed."

Ava lifted a hand, pressed it to her mouth. Lifted the other to cross it over the first. Those deep blue eyes filled, and the tears spilled as she shook her head.

"I'm sorry, but I need to ask you some questions."

"Where's Tommy?"

"We're taking care of him now, Mrs. Anders." Peabody stepped over, offered a glass of water.

She took the water, and when her hand shook, gripped the glass with both. "Someone broke in? I don't see how that can be. We're secure, we're very secure here. Fifteen years—we've been here for fifteen years. We've never had a break-in."

"There weren't any signs of a break-in."

"I don't understand."

"Whoever killed your husband either knew the security code, or was given access to the house."

"That can't be." Ava waved a hand in quick dismissal. "No one other than Tommy and myself and Greta has the code. Surely you're not suggesting Greta—"

"I'm not, no." Though she'd be doing a thorough check on the house manager. "There wasn't a break-in, Mrs. Anders. Thus far there's no sign anything in the house was taken, or disturbed."

Ava laid a hand between her breast where a rope of luminous pearls rested. "You're saying Tommy let someone in, and they killed him. But that doesn't make sense."

"Mrs. Anders, was your husband involved with someone, sexually or romantically?"

She turned away immediately, first her face, then her body. "I don't want to talk about this now. I'm not going to talk about this now. My husband is dead."

"If you know anyone who could gain access to the house, to his bedroom—while you were out of the country—it could tell us who killed your husband, and why."

"I don't know. I don't. And I can't *think* about something like that." The anger slapped out at Eve. "I want you to leave me alone. I want you out of my house."

"That's not going to happen. Until we clear it, this house is part of a homicide investigation. Your husband's bedroom is a crime scene. I suggest you make arrangements to stay elsewhere for the time being, and to stay available. If you don't want to finish this now, we'll finish it later."

"I want to see my husband. I want to see Tommy."

"We'll arrange that as soon as possible. Do you want us to contact anyone for you?"

"No." Ava looked out the sunny window. "I don't want anyone. I don't want anyone now."

Outside, Eve climbed behind the wheel while Peabody sat shotgun in their vehicle. "Rough," Peabody commented. "You're soaking up tropical drinks and rays one minute, and the next, your husband's dead."

"She knows he was screwing around. She knows something about it."

"I guess they probably always do. The spouse, I mean, of the screwing-arounder. And I think a lot of times they can just block it out, pretend it's not happening hard enough so they believe it."

"Would you be shedding tears for McNab's dead body if he'd been screwing around on you?"

Peabody pursed her lips. "Well, since I'd've been the one who killed him, I'd probably be shedding tears for me because you'd be arresting me. And that would really make me sad. Easy enough to verify Ava Anders was out of the country when Anders died."

"Yeah, do that. And we'll check her financials. They've got plenty of dough to roll. Maybe she cut off some to hire somebody to kill him. Paid his playmate to do it."

"Man, how cold would *that* be?"

"We'll run friends, business associates, golf partners—"

"Golf?"

"He had a golf game scheduled this morning with an Edmond Luce. Maybe we'll shake loose something on who he played other games with when the wife was off with the girls."

"Wouldn't you like to do that? Have a girl trip?"

"No."

"Ah, come on, Dallas." The very idea brightened Peabody's voice. "Go somewhere with girlfriends, hang, drink lots of wine or fussy drinks, get facials and spa treatments, or lie on the beach, and talk about stuff half the night."

Eve glanced over. "I'd rather be dragged naked over jagged glass."

"Well, I think we should do it some time. You, me, Mavis, maybe Nadine and Louise. And Trina—she could do our hair and—"

"If Trina comes on this mythical nightmare, I get to drag *her* naked over jagged glass. That's my bottom line."

"You'd have fun," Peabody muttered.

"I would, I would probably would. I'd feel bad about dragging her over jagged glass ten or twenty years later, but at the time, I'd have fun."

Giving up, Peabody huffed out a breath, took out her ppc, and began to do the checks and runs.

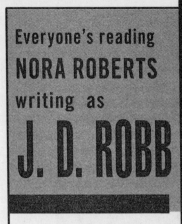

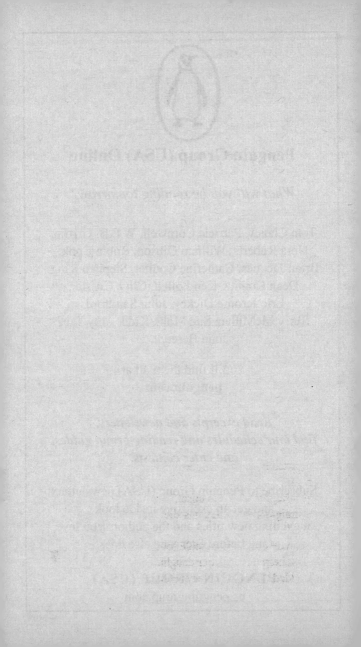